Praise for

IT'S CLASSIFIED

"The cast of characters from *Eighteen Acres* returns to keep the pot boiling in this fast-paced behind-the-scenes political drama."

—*Booklist*

"Essential reading for all political fiction junkies but especially for those who enjoyed Wallace's first novel."

—*Library Journal*

"Reads like a lighthearted novel for people interested in politics, but it's also a pretty big indictment of how the political process works."

—TIME.com

. . . and for Nicolle Wallace's page-turning debut,

EIGHTEEN ACRES

"May be the best novel ever written about life in the White House."

—*The Washington Post*

"If you're the least bit interested in how Washington works behind the scenes—the backstabbing, the deception, the doubts—take a stroll across these eighteen acres."

—*USA Today*

"Intrigue, love, betrayal, politics, family, and an international crisis—this insider novel about life in the White House really delivers. I couldn't put it down!"

—Lauren Weisberger, #1 *New York Times* bestselling author

ALSO BY NICOLLE WALLACE

Eighteen Acres

IT'S
CLASSIFIED

A Novel

Nicolle Wallace

EMILY BESTLER BOOKS
—
WASHINGTON SQUARE PRESS

New York   London   Toronto   Sydney   New Delhi

WASHINGTON SQUARE PRESS
A Division of Simon & Schuster, Inc.
1230 Avenue of the Americas
New York, NY 10020

First Emily Bestler Books / Washington Square Press trade paperback edition June 2012

EMILY BESTLER BOOKS / WASHINGTON SQUARE PRESS and colophons are
trademarks of Simon & Schuster, Inc.

For information about special discounts for bulk purchases,
please contact Simon & Schuster Special Sales at 1-866-506-1949 or
business@simonandschuster.com.

The Simon & Schuster Speakers Bureau can bring authors to your
live event. For more information or to book an event, contact the
Simon & Schuster Speakers Bureau at 1-866-248-3049 or
visit our website at www.simonspeakers.com.

Designed by Kyoko Watanabe

Manufactured in the United States of America

10   9   8   7   6   5   4   3   2   1

The Library of Congress has cataloged the hardcover edition as follows:

Wallace, Nicolle.
    It's classified : a novel / by Nicolle Wallace.
       p. cm.
    Sequel to: Eighteen acres.
 1. Women presidents—United States—Fiction. 2. Political fiction.
 I. Title.
    PS3623.A4437I75 2011
    813'.6—dc22   2011018395

ISBN 978-1-4516-1096-3
ISBN 978-1-4516-1097-0 (pbk)
ISBN 978-1-4516-1098-7 (ebook)

For Mark

Tara

"Tara?" Marcus yelled, for the fourth time in as many minutes.

She held perfectly still and said nothing.

"Isn't it your job to watch her?" he snapped at one of the Secret Service agents assigned to protect his wife.

"Not anymore, sir," the agent said.

Tara almost smiled. She leaned back in her chair on the top floor of the Naval Observatory and watched the movers as they taped and then lifted the refrigerator-sized boxes onto the moving van. The movers had arrived two hours earlier, and everything in the house they'd inhabited for the past year had been packed in bubble wrap and carefully placed inside the boxes.

The agents had asked Tara if there was anything she wanted put aside for the trip before the movers started their packing. She had shaken her head and wandered up to the attic, where she sat watching the activity below. Marcus had run around like a madman, grabbing plates, bowls, and utensils so he could feed their eight-year-old daughter before the entire contents of their home was packed in boxes and all traces of Tara's tenure as vice president were expunged.

Tara stared at the stack of official stationery she'd been holding in her lap and started again. "Dear Madam President," she wrote. It was as far as she ever got. Every time she wrote anything else, the letter ended up crumpled on the floor beneath her.

"There you are," Marcus barked, causing Tara to jump. She hadn't heard him climb the stairs.

"What the hell are you doing up here?" he asked.

"I'm, um, trying to write a note to Charlotte," she said.

"Do you have any idea how fucking traumatic this is for our daughter?" he demanded.

"I know, I know, I'm sorry. I'll be right down."

"Now," he ordered.

She wanted to finish the letter to Charlotte before they left Washington.

"Can I have five more minutes?"

He stared at her. She stared back.

"Fine," he said. Marcus stormed back down the stairs and slammed the door behind him.

Tara turned to her letter with renewed focus. She had wanted to leave a note for Dale as well, but the movers were working faster than she'd anticipated. They'd probably be miles from Washington, D.C., before Dale emerged from her grand jury testimony. She pressed her pen onto the cream-colored notecard. "Dear Madam President, I am so very sorry for everything," she wrote. She chewed on the pen for a few seconds and then continued. "I would do anything to take it all back—to have never agreed to serve as your running mate or to have refused to assume the oath of office—anything to take away the suffering and embarrassment I have caused you. For the rest of my days, I will seek your forgiveness. With deep regret and sincere apologies, Tara."

Dale

"Miss Smith, do you understand the rules regarding contact with your attorney?" the judge asked.

"Yes sir," she said.

"You may stop the questioning at any time to speak with your attorney, but he will not be allowed in the room during your grand jury testimony," he said.

"Yes sir, I understand."

"Very well, then. We will proceed. Special Prosecutor Kirkpatrick will begin the questioning."

Dale shifted in her seat and looked over at the members of the grand jury. The reporter in her wondered what their lives were like before they were summoned to jury duty. She watched one woman turn off her cell phone and imagined that her final text was to a babysitter or a nanny who was watching her children while she weighed whether White House officials had committed a crime by hiding the vice president's condition from the public.

Dale would have loved to have done that story for the network where she'd worked before joining the White House staff. She leaned back and tried to listen to the special prosecutor's question.

"Are you having trouble hearing me, Miss Smith?" he asked.

"No, I'm sorry, would you mind repeating the question?"

"Not a problem. Miss Smith, I'd like for you to tell us at what point—give me a week or a day or a month, if you are able to be that specific—at what point did it first cross your mind that perhaps the vice president wasn't doing well, and who did you reach out to when, or if, you had those concerns?" he asked.

"What week?" Dale asked.

"If it's easier for you to describe a situation or a period, that's fine, too. We understand from your e-mail records that you were, quote, worried, about the vice president. In an e-mail to the White House chief of staff seeking guidance on press questions about the vice president's frequent absences, you sought counsel. Is that an accurate description of those e-mails, Miss Smith?" he asked.

"Yes sir," she said.

"And what were you told in response to e-mails seeking guidance about how to handle questions concerning the vice president?" the prosecutor asked.

"I was instructed to manage the situation. I mean, I was expected to manage the situation. It was my job."

"And did you ever wonder why you were given this job? I mean, had you ever worked for a politician before you came to serve as one of the most senior advisors on the vice president's staff?" the prosecutor asked.

"No," she said.

"And it didn't strike you as odd that you'd been given such a huge responsibility?" the prosecutor asked.

She looked him in the eye.

"No."

"I want to move on to the precise statements you gave to the press as you watched the vice president deteriorate. You described the vice president as tough and resilient in an article dated June 30. Is that accurate?" the prosecutor asked.

"Yes, it sounds like something I would say," Dale said.

"Here it is, Miss Smith. I brought a copy of the article. The headline is 'Vice President Increasingly out of Sight,' and it goes on to quote unnamed White House sources who say she was struggling with the pressures of the office. And you, Miss Smith, are in the article saying that those quotes were uninformed and that she was tough and resilient," the prosecutor said, reading from the *Washington Post* article.

"Yes, I remember that now," Dale said.

"Were you telling the truth?" he asked.

"I mean, there were days in which she did seem tough and resilient," Dale said.

"And there were days when she did not, is that accurate?" he asked.

Dale nodded.

"Is that a yes?"

"Yes," she said.

"And was it your job to tell the whole truth or just parts of it?" he asked.

Dale turned to the judge.

"May I be excused to consult with my attorney?" she asked him.

"Of course," the judge replied.

The prosecutor turned to the grand jury and shrugged his shoulders.

"Didn't seem like a tough question to me," he said to one of his colleagues. He spoke loud enough for members of the grand jury to hear him, and a few of them snickered.

Dale rushed from the room and into the hallway where her attorney was waiting.

"How's it going?" he asked.

"Not good," she said. "Kirkpatrick wants to know if it was my job to lie," she said.

Her attorney smiled.

"That's his specialty. He indicts the ugliness of politics, and then he gets the individual," he said.

"What am I supposed to do?" she asked.

"Tell the truth, Dale. It's your only shot," he said, putting his arm around her shoulders. "Tell these guys everything, and maybe they'll see you as an innocent bystander, someone who kept quiet for the good of Kramer's presidency," he said. "They're not after you, Dale. They want Kramer."

Charlotte

"Madam President, are you ready?" the lawyer asked.

Am I ready? Charlotte thought. She nearly laughed out loud.

"Give me one minute, please."

"Of course, Madam President," he said, fading into the line of a dozen similarly dressed lawyers with briefcases who'd been assembled from Washington's top law firms to defend the president of the United States in her impeachment proceedings before the U.S. Congress.

Charlotte walked over to the window in the House Minority Leader's office. A group of schoolchildren stood huddled together watching a news crew from Philadelphia lug heavy equipment from its truck to the live-shot location. Another group of tourists stood behind the network anchors, waving. Charlotte watched a couple smile at each other as they carried twin boys up the steps of the Capitol in a double stroller. Instinctively, Charlotte glanced at her BlackBerry to reread the messages her twins had sent the night before.

"Give them hell, Mom," Penelope had written.

"Don't let the jerks get you down," her son, Harry, had written.

She sighed and watched the activity outside the window. News trucks surrounded the Capitol, and reporters from across the country and around the world stood shoulder to shoulder in heavy winter coats and hats to shield them from the cold weather that had blown in for the occasion. From the television that was on in the Minority Leader's office, Charlotte could hear one of the network anchors speaking in hushed, authoritative tones.

"All eyes are on the committee room as we await President Kramer's testimony. If she does, in fact, testify, as we are told by White House aides she plans to do, she would become the first U.S. president in history to testify in her own impeachment proceeding. We can only assume that she is engaged in frantic last-minute preparations for this, the most important day of her career and quite, possibly, of her life." Charlotte looked over at the lawyers. She'd hardly spoken to them since they'd wrapped up their practice session the previous afternoon. Before any of the attorneys interpreted her glance as an invitation to speak, she returned her gaze to the window.

Her first inauguration felt like it had occurred in another lifetime, but her second inauguration was still fresh in her mind. A year earlier, Charlotte had stood on the steps of the Capitol with her twins next to her and her parents and best friends, Brooke and Mark Pfeiffer, behind her. She had placed her hand on her grandmother's Bible and sworn to uphold the Constitution—an oath she took as seriously as she took her responsibility as a mother and citizen. It was a cold January morning, but the sun was so bright, it had warmed the podium. She smiled at the memory of standing there after such a hard-fought reelection effort. Charlotte had believed that all of the struggles of her first term as president were part of the price she'd paid for what she'd hoped would be a less-trying second term. Now, she shook her head gently and wrapped her arms around her body. Someone had turned the volume up on one of the televisions.

"Stay with us. Coming up in minutes, President Charlotte Kramer will go before the House Judiciary Committee, which last week won a key vote in the House of Representatives to proceed with impeachment proceedings against the president of the United States of America. The impeachment resolution alleges that President Kramer behaved in a manner grossly incompatible with the purpose of the office she holds."

Charlotte turned to face her army of lawyers. She caught a glimpse of herself in the mirror and cringed. Her normally thick, blond hair looked thin and flat. It was pulled into a low bun at the nape of her neck. A few small pieces of hair had broken free and hung in front of her eyes. She pushed them behind her ears and noticed her pale blue eyes had turned gray, as they often did when she was sleep-deprived. She was wearing a light gray Armani skirt and matching jacket that she had purchased the year before. Both hung loosely on her now. She took a deep breath, pushed her shoulders back, and uncrossed her arms.

"I suppose it's time to get this over with," she said. She pushed the corners of her mouth into a closed-lip smile and tried to feign enthusiasm as the lawyers turned off their BlackBerrys and phones and nodded. They formed a huddle behind her.

Her Secret Service agent, Rich, walked alongside her and spoke more quietly than usual into the microphone in his sleeve as Charlotte walked out the door.

"Wayfarer departing hold room en route to committee room. Repeat: Wayfarer departing hold room en route to committee room," he said.

"Rich, please don't," Charlotte said, placing her hand on his arm as they walked.

"Madam President?" he asked.

"Don't whisper around me like I'm already dead," she said.

Rich smiled sheepishly. They'd been around the world together several times over, including a dozen trips to the war zones.

"Sorry about that, Madam President," he said.

As they walked down the long marble hallway, the only sound was the clicking of Charlotte's high heels and the shuffling of a dozen pairs of men's loafers. The gaggle slowed as it neared the door to the chamber. In a normal voice, Rich spoke into his sleeve again: "Wayfarer has arrived at committee room; Wayfarer has arrived."

Charlotte turned and looked back at the lawyers one last time before nodding at Rich. "I'm ready," she said.

CHAPTER ONE

Tara

One Year Earlier

"W here are we going?" Tara whispered to her personal aide, Karen.

"To the hold room, Madam Vice President."

Tara nodded and followed her Secret Service agents. They'd entered the hotel through the loading area and were winding their way through the kitchen toward a service elevator. Three hotel workers waved excitedly at her. She still wasn't sure what the protocol was when that happened, so she stopped to shake their hands. One of the workers pulled out a cell phone and asked the nearest agent to take his picture with the vice president. Tara knew that wasn't the agent's job. Before she could nudge Karen, her aide had the cell phone in her hand and was asking everyone to say cheese. Tara couldn't tell if the agents were annoyed or indifferent.

"Thank you for your hospitality," Tara said.

"Thank you, Mrs. Vice President," they replied. "We love you."

Tara waved good-bye and followed her agents into the elevator. She walked to the back of the large space and watched as more than a dozen of her new staff members crammed into the elevator with them. She wondered if any of her predecessors had been claustrophobic. One of the agents held up his hand and ordered the staff that arrived after the doors began to close to take the next one. Tara smiled sympathetically at one of her new advisors who didn't make it and shrugged at the agents as if to say "oh well." They didn't break a smile. No one spoke during the slow ride up to the twenty-first floor. The service elevator stopped with a thud. Tara felt her stomach do a small flip. She watched the agents whisper into their sleeves and then file purposefully into the hallway.

"Right this way, ma'am," Walter, her lead agent, said. He was the only one who ever looked her in the eye. Since being sworn in as vice president two weeks earlier, she'd been given a new team of Secret Service agents. They were more serious than those who'd traveled with her during the campaign, and she was more than a little intimidated by their formality.

She followed Walter into a room marked "Presidential Suite" and tried to mask her pleasure. A note that read "Welcome to the Ritz" was taped to a bottle of champagne. A fruit tray overflowing with kiwi, mango, strawberries, pineapple, and three different kinds of grapes was placed next to a veggie display piled high with red, yellow, and green bell peppers; asparagus; cherry tomatoes; and carrots. Dozens of perfect cubes of cheese were stacked on a board next to a basket full of crackers. Tara's eyes moved from the appetizer buffet to a smaller table covered with desserts. An oversized platter was stacked four deep with brownies, cookies, and petit fours. All Tara could think about was digging in.

"Madam Vice President, would you like to do the prebrief now, or would you like to rest a little bit?" Karen asked. Karen was her personal aide, known in most White Houses as "the body person." She was responsible for making sure Tara got from point A to point B with a smile on her face. It would also fall to Karen to attend to the most intimate details of Tara's life.

"I don't know, Karen, what do you think?"

"We have about an hour and a half before we have to leave for the stadium."

They were in Atlanta for the Super Bowl. The network had requested a live interview with Tara for its pregame show. The audience would be huge.

"Why don't you give me ten minutes to change and check in

with Marcus and Kendall and then we'll bring everyone in for the prebrief."

"Yes ma'am."

"Karen, were *all* those people in the elevator here for the prebrief?"

"I'm not sure about all of them, but a good number, ma'am."

"I see." Suddenly, Tara was nervous. How in-depth was the interview going to be fifteen minutes before kickoff? She felt her stomach start to churn, and she looked around the suite for her purse. A large bottle of Tums was quickly becoming her best friend.

"Ma'am, I'll let everyone know you'll be ready in fifteen minutes."

"Thank you, Karen."

Tara wandered around the suite. She felt, as she often did lately, like someone was watching her. She approached the buffet with caution and eyed the fruits and vegetables. She leaned in closer to get a look at the brownies and picked one up to examine it. No nuts. She ate the brownie in two bites and picked up another. She moved the cookies around so it wouldn't look like she'd eaten anything. She was still rearranging the desserts when she heard someone knocking on her door.

"Who is it?"

"Madam Vice President, it's Dale. I wanted to make sure you had the event briefing for the interview. I can come back in fifteen minutes with the others, or I can just slip it under your door."

Dale was her new communications advisor. Tara had selected a reporter as her top press aide to help ingratiate herself with the national press. Dale was also the girlfriend of the president's estranged husband. The decision had generated a lot of buzz. Tara had been assured by the president's advisors that her marital problems predated any involvement on Dale's part and that the president didn't have any objections to her hiring Dale.

"I'll be right there," Tara called out.

When she opened the door, Dale was standing there with a small folder in her hands. She was wearing black pants and a black sweater and had on black heels. She looked stylish in the effortless way that women who have lived and worked in New York City always look stylish. Tara was admiring Dale's long, dark hair and tiny frame when she realized that Dale was still standing in the doorway.

"I'm sorry to disturb you, Madam Vice President. I just didn't want to hand this to you in front of everyone. It has all of the instructions about where to sit and what they plan to ask and all of that. I should have given it to you on the plane, but I didn't know if you were working or resting. I'm sorry. I'm still new at all this." Dale was fidgeting nervously.

"Don't worry about it. We're all new." Tara smiled. "Do you want to come inside and have something to eat while I change?"

"Uh, no, no, I should leave you alone."

"Good god, there's enough food in here to feed an army. Please come in," Tara insisted.

Dale smiled. "Okay, thank you."

"What sorts of questions do you think I'll get?"

"Oh, I did a call with the network this morning. I put the list of the questions that the producer had written for Bob in the briefing paper."

"Great. I'll take a look at it." Tara put the file under her arm.

"Let me know if you have any questions and I'll get answers to them while you're in the policy briefing."

"Dale, do you have any idea who all those people are who traveled with me today for the briefing?"

Dale laughed. "Not really. I'm still getting to know everyone."

"I guess I better get used to large crowds."

"Yes ma'am. It looks like your days of traveling light are over," Dale said.

"So much for sneaking out for a trip to Krispy Kreme."

"I'm sure there are a dozen aides standing by for requests along those exact lines."

Tara laughed. "You're probably right about that. It's strange."

"I'm finding the transition from White House correspondent to White House staffer to be far more significant than I'd expected. I can't begin to imagine what it's like for you and your family."

"It's a bit of a whirlwind," Tara admitted. She liked Dale. For all of her sophistication, she was surprisingly sweet and down to earth. And she seemed devoted.

"I'm going to check in with my husband and daughter before everyone gets here. Do you mind entertaining the troops if they arrive before I get off the phone?"

"No problem."

"And Dale, I'm really glad you're here."

"Me too, Madam Vice President. Thank you for the opportunity."

Tara heard the rest of her staff shuffling outside the door and rushed into the bedroom to change. She stared at the assorted separates she'd packed for the interview and wished she'd brought something sleek like the outfit Dale was wearing. She settled on a pair of gray slacks and a powder blue sweater set. Tara frowned at her reflection in the bathroom mirror. Her face was too round; her hair a mousy, dull shade of brown; and her body too pudgy. When she turned to the side to examine herself from another angle, things got worse. Her back fat was visible around her bra straps and she could barely find her waist. She resolved to stick to her diet starting immediately. When she returned to the sitting area, a dozen men in suits were assembled around her suite with small plates of food in front of them.

"Good afternoon, Madam Vice President. We thought we'd start with foreign policy and then move to the economy and finish with domestic policy. Is that acceptable to you?"

She looked at the white-haired gentleman who was addressing her and strained to remember his name.

"That sounds great, Chester. Thanks so much for making the trip on a Sunday."

Chester beamed and started in with an overview of the situation in North Korea.

"Madam Vice President, the question usually comes in the form of an invitation to weigh in on the success or failure of the six-party talks. Do you have a good grasp on the pros and cons of the six-party talks as a structure for dealing with North Korea?"

"I think so, but why don't you give me your best formulation and I'll try to internalize it."

He launched into a wonky four-part answer that Tara could never imagine reciting, especially on Super Bowl Sunday. As if on cue, Dale piped in from where she was standing near the back of the room.

"Chester, with all due respect to the importance of the topic, I think we can all rest assured that Bob Costas is not going ask the vice president about North Korea today."

Tara watched as the power in the room shifted from the front to the back. All heads turned to watch Dale.

"Madam Vice President, we can expect a couple of general questions about the big issues facing the administration—like the weak economy, the ongoing deployments in Iraq and Afghanistan, and the upheaval in Libya and Syria. But more than anything, Bob wants to get a sense of who you are and where you came from."

Tara nodded.

"Understood." She looked around at the crestfallen faces of the policy team members. She didn't want any of them to feel unneeded, but she also didn't want to crowd her head with details of policies that would never come up.

"I've got an idea. Why don't each of you tell me how you'd answer a question about the most significant policy challenge—domestic or foreign—facing the administration," she suggested.

The policy boys were beaming again. Throughout the briefing, they seemed intent on outdoing each other. Tara was surprised by how competitive the entire exercise felt. It didn't dawn on her until they were almost done that they were trying to impress her. Dale followed the pack toward the door and smiled at Tara when the last policy advisor had left the room.

"Nice job, Madam Vice President."

"Why don't you ride over to the stadium with me, Dale?"

"Yes ma'am. That sounds great."

As soon as the hallway outside the suite was quiet, Tara turned and looked at Dale with an amused look on her face. "I thought Chester was going to cry when you said that Bob Costas wouldn't ask about the six-party talks."

"I thought he was going to throw something at me. I felt terrible."

"It was great. I had to fight the impulse to laugh. Last year, Marcus and I were at a neighbor's Super Bowl party while Kendall played outside in the snow with her friends. This year, I'm in the presidential suite at a Ritz-Carlton getting briefed on North Korea before my nationally televised interview with Bob Costas."

"Quite a shock to the system, I'm sure." Dale smiled.

Tara took a deep breath and smiled back. "That it is." The Secret Service knocked and they gathered their things. Tara and Dale followed Karen and the agents to the service elevators. They traveled down twenty-one floors and retraced their tracks from earlier until they arrived at the motorcade parked in the hotel's loading zone.

CHAPTER TWO

Dale

Dale watched the vice president take her seat on the elaborate set that had been built for the half-time show. Normally, a president is interviewed by the anchor from the network broadcasting the Super Bowl. NBC broke tradition first by inviting the vice president instead of the president, and then, despite the fact that it caused rancor, Dale requested that Bob Costas conduct the interview. As Dale watched her new boss schmooze with the beloved sports anchor, she was glad she'd suggested him.

"Good evening, ladies and gentlemen. As the sun begins to set on this Super Bowl Sunday, we have a special guest with us tonight. Joining me for her first *ever* live national interview as vice president is Tara Meyers. How are you doing, and more importantly, who are you rooting for?"

"Good evening, Bob. I promise you that I'm going to answer that like a fan, not a politician, before I leave here tonight, but first I have to say hello to my husband and our daughter, Kendall. They are at our new home in Washington, D.C., tonight. Hi honey, hi Kendall, sweetheart. Don't stay up too late!"

"Madam Vice President, if you don't mind, I'd like to ask you how it is that an ordinary, working mom who seems to juggle a lot of the same things that all women juggle ended up as the second most powerful person in the country?"

"Oh, gosh, Bob, I wonder the same thing. I guess I'd say that I was in the right place at the right time. But I don't want to minimize the importance of President Kramer's willingness to show the American people that Democrats and Republicans can govern as one team. It doesn't have to be the way it's always been with the two parties haggling over everything. We plan to govern as two different leaders with distinct principles who put the best ideas from both sides of the aisle to work for America. I think that's what she had in mind when she asked me to join her on the ticket, and I know that's what she was talking about in her Inaugural address just a couple weeks ago, when she promised an end to the era of low expectations for our national leaders and the beginning of a time of universally recognized and realized exceptionalism."

The vice president looked away from Costas while she was thinking through her answer. When she looked back at him, he was smiling at her warmly. Tara had a natural ability to connect, and she'd tapped into it with her request to say hello to her husband and daughter. It was the same thing that had drawn Dale to her the first time they'd met on the campaign trail.

Dale leaned against the wall and relaxed for the first time since they'd landed in Atlanta three hours earlier. The only policy advisor who'd proven useful during the prebrief was the deputy national security advisor, who'd brought a laptop into the room. The vice president wanted statistics about the teams playing that day, and without knowing that he was an accomplished expert on counterinsurgencies, she'd asked him to Google the teams' records.

Now, Dale turned up the volume on the monitor to listen to the interview. Costas was sticking to the script. Everything he'd asked the vice president so far was written on the briefing paper Dale had handed her. Dale felt as if she might be cut out for work on the other side, after all.

"Madam Vice President, *Oprah Magazine* just named you the most admired woman in America. What does that feel like?"

As Tara launched into the answer they'd practiced on the ride over, about how humbling it was to have an opportunity to serve, Dale reflected on the strange turn that her life had taken. Less than a year earlier, she'd been a television reporter for one of the networks where she'd covered President Kramer during the week and anchored the evening newscast from New York on the weekends. Most people described her as having a bright future in broadcasting.

She was also in a passionate and loving relationship with a man she adored. She'd never felt more satisfied personally or professionally. But her contentment was a delusion. Her lover was the president's husband, and her job was to cover the president she was deceiving.

Ironically, it was the president who had brought her relationship with Peter into the open and made it possible for them to be together publicly. A near-fatal helicopter accident had cast the affair in a strange new light. In hindsight, Dale realized that Charlotte had grown weary of carrying around the secret that her marriage had been over for years. Charlotte had revealed the affair and separated from Peter immediately following the crash so he could be at Dale's bedside while she recovered from her injuries. It had sounded like a superhuman gesture to most, and Dale had wondered herself how Charlotte could be so generous. In the short time that she'd served on the White House staff, she'd observed a little-known side of Charlotte. She treated her staff with a decency and tenderness that no one on the outside would have ever suspected, and that everyone on the inside guarded as though it were a highly classified piece of top secret information.

After the accident, Dale had walked away from Washington, D.C., and from her career in television to live with Peter in San Francisco. Giving up the daily thrill of chasing a story and delivering the news left a hole in her that she could not fill with Peter. She'd been miserable. Dale had left San Francisco to cover the final month of Charlotte's reelection bid for a local television station. That's where she'd met Tara. As Charlotte's surprise pick as a running mate, Tara was an overnight sensation. She'd sat for an interview with Dale five days before the election.

Now, the sound of the crowd cheering snapped Dale's attention back to the set where Tara was still sitting with Bob Costas. "What happened?" she asked one of the crew members.

"She said she was rooting for the Chicago Bears and that she expected them to win in a blowout."

"Really?"

"Yep. She seems pretty ballsy."

Dale smiled. She was so relieved that the interview was going well. Some of her new colleagues criticized the decision to place the newly minted vice president in such a high-stakes setting for her first interview. Dale had argued that the vice president was more than capable of rising to the occasion, and luckily for her, she'd been correct. She was so proud of her new boss. She felt elated in a way that she couldn't recall ever feeling in the newsroom.

She smiled back at the crew member.

"She is."

CHAPTER THREE

Charlotte

W here is everyone going?" Melanie asked.

"Oh, it's time for Tara's weekly 'Big Think' meeting," Charlotte replied.

"Her what?"

"She brings people from different areas of expertise together every Friday to brainstorm on ways to make the federal government more responsive to the public."

"You're kidding, right?"

"No, and I think it's a lovely idea. You should consider something similar at the Pentagon. It makes stakeholders feel more invested in our agenda."

"Madam President, that's Washington-speak for talking to the has-beens." Melanie scowled in the direction of the hallway. She and Charlotte were standing in the reception area of the Oval Office looking at photos of the Parrot Cay resort in Turks and Caicos on the president's assistant's computer. Melanie was thinking about taking her boyfriend, Brian Watson, a network correspondent she met while serving as Charlotte's chief of staff, away for his birthday.

"Do you like this? Does it scream 'marry me'? Or is it a simple, elegant retreat?"

"I wouldn't call it simple, but it's perfect. Who cares if he feels a little added pressure?"

"If it feels like a destination wedding venue he'll freak out."

"About what? You guys have been together for almost a year. Besides, Brian doesn't seem like the type to freak out."

"I've always wanted to go."

"It's amazing. Trust me."

"I do. And you should trust me. Watch out for Tara and all of her big thinking. People are overthrowing their leaders all over the Mideast. You could be next."

Charlotte laughed. They walked through the Oval Office and into her private dining room, where they were having lunch. Charlotte sat down, crossed her arms, and eyed Melanie smugly.

"What?" Melanie asked.

"Say it."

"Say what?"

"Oh, come on, Mel. Can't you admit that maybe you were a little too hard on Tara?"

"I'm glad that she is working out," Melanie conceded, primly.

Charlotte raised an eyebrow. "That's it?"

"It's been a month. The jury is still out," Melanie insisted.

"Well, the jury may still be out, but the public loves her. She has an eighty-four percent approval rating," Charlotte boasted.

"She hasn't done anything yet except attend the Inauguration and the Super Bowl."

"She did a live interview."

"With *Bob Costas*."

"She did great."

"She did better than I thought she'd do. In my opinion, she's simply basking in the afterglow of that brilliant Inaugural address I wrote for you."

"That's one hell of an afterglow," Charlotte taunted.

She saw Melanie suppress a laugh and stuff a large bite of her chicken Casear salad into her mouth.

"You are such a bitch," Charlotte said.

"That's why you like me so much."

"It's why I need you here." Charlotte stabbed at her Cobb salad.

"You seem to be doing just fine without me. You have Tara and Ralph to keep you company."

"We're managing. I think you're going to regret leaving us."

Melanie had served as Charlotte's chief of staff for the entire first term, as White House press secretary for Charlotte's predecessor, and as a press aide to the president who preceded him.

Charlotte would have liked for Melanie to have stayed on as chief of staff, but after fifteen years at the White House, she'd resigned on the night of Charlotte's reelection. She'd said that it was time to move on. Charlotte wooed Melanie back to her administration with an offer she couldn't refuse, and one that many in Washington thought was motivated by cronyism, pure and simple. But Charlotte was confident that Melanie had seen enough as a confidante to three presidents during a time of several wars to be plenty seasoned as the nation's secretary of defense.

"I'm in charge of the goddamned Pentagon. Isn't that enough of a contribution for any human being to make to her country?"

"Melanie, we both know you aren't human."

"It's nice to know you miss me, Madam President."

"Of course I miss you. But you're enjoying it, right?"

"It's weird. I know every corner of this place, and I can hardly find my own office over there."

"I could ask the new chief of staff if I could make a trip over there for a briefing next week?" Charlotte offered.

"I knew it wouldn't take long before you couldn't say his name out loud, either."

Now it was Charlotte who pretended not to laugh.

"Ralph has been on his best behavior," Charlotte insisted.

"Yes, and he's looking great, too." Ralph had gained about fifteen pounds since the campaign ended and was bursting out of his pants. He refused to buy new suits.

Charlotte threw her napkin at Melanie and steered the conversation away from Tara. Melanie had gone out on a limb during the campaign to knock down a story about Tara serving time in rehab. Melanie had defended Tara as skillfully as she did everything else, but Charlotte knew she'd been uncomfortable with Tara and Marcus's inability to provide anything concrete for Melanie to push back with. Charlotte suspected that Melanie would never completely forgive her for putting her in a position where her own credibility was on the line for someone she hardly knew, but in many regards, their friendship had started to deepen now that Melanie was serving as her defense secretary.

Melanie was thriving at DOD and had taken a methodical approach to winning over her detractors. Still, Charlotte had a hunch that Melanie experienced moments of angst about being away from the mother ship. In many ways, after fifteen years, the White House defined Melanie more than it did Charlotte. She was known around Washington as Charlotte's alter ego, a reputation that served both women well. Charlotte would not have survived her first term without Melanie. They had endured every brutal moment together. Only now that Melanie was no longer her chief of staff did Charlotte appreciate just how much Melanie had had on her plate during the first term.

After they both devoured large bowls of fat-free vanilla soft serve smothered in chocolate sauce, Melanie returned to the Pentagon, and Charlotte settled in to read a stack of memos. She thought about how different things were since her reelection.

During her first years in office, Charlotte often felt deeply wounded by the constant stream of criticism directed at her from Washington's permanent ruling class—the lobbyists, pundits, journalists, and lawmakers who served up play-by-play analysis of her every move. Charlotte had arrived in D.C. completely unprepared for the personal nature of the attacks aimed at her administration. In the early days, every morning started with a thorough review of the major newspapers, which were filled with nit-picking of her policies and performance. Despite Melanie's warnings, she'd watch the cable news shows each night after she retreated to the White House residence. Charlotte had also relied heavily on pollsters and consultants to guide her actions by analyzing the pros and cons of any move. Ultimately, turning to everyone else had paralyzed her. She'd reached a point where she couldn't make a single decision without sitting through a dozen meetings and hearing from cabinet secretaries, deputies, and policy experts. Her confidence in her own instincts— the instincts that had served her well as governor of California and as a candidate for president—had been buried. After teetering at the brink of defeat and disgrace, she'd traveled an unlikely path of political redemption. She had won reelection with fifty-four percent of the vote—a landslide in modern presidential politics.

Charlotte looked up from her paperwork to greet the dogs. Her longtime personal assistant, Samantha, brought her three vizslas over for a visit each afternoon. The youngest dog, Emma, jumped onto the sofa and looked as though she might pee on it.

"Get off of the couch, monkey," Charlotte ordered.

Mika and Cammie had their paws in her lap and were licking her face. Charlotte nuzzled them both and laughed when Cammie, the oldest of the three, climbed onto her and curled up with a soft moan.

"You are so silly," she murmured. Charlotte returned her attention to the memo in front of her while the dogs chewed on bones and napped away the afternoon in the Oval Office.

CHAPTER FOUR

Tara

Tara could hear what sounded like a mob of staffers shuffling around and speaking in low tones on the other side of her door. They'd been waiting for more than twenty minutes to brief her on the president's alternative energy initiative, which she'd been asked to promote in a roundtable discussion with energy experts and local entrepreneurs on a trip to Michigan the following week. She opened the top drawer of her desk and looked for something to take the edge off her headache. She'd felt it coming on before she got out of bed that morning. It started on the tops of her shoulders, and as the morning dragged on, the pain made its way up her neck. Now it felt as if her head was in a vise. She was nauseous and hungry at the same time. She'd called in sick the day before, and twice the week before that. Tara was sure that she'd missed more work in less than two months on the job than Charlotte had missed during her entire first term. She couldn't go home early again.

She stared at the white paper in front of her and tried to focus. She couldn't bear the thought of another endless meeting. All she'd done for the past eight weeks was get on and off Air Force Two, enter and exit motorcades, shake hands on rope lines, and endure endless briefings about topics she never thought she'd have to master. She glanced up at the television and saw CNN tease another story about her. The media's obsession with her unlikely rise to the vice presidency was beginning to alarm her. The press painted a picture of her idyllic home life that bore little resemblance to reality. A columnist at the *New York*

Times had pronounced her the new standard-bearer for having it all.

She clicked off the television and tried one more time to read through the briefing.

Tara had never been the smartest girl in class, but she'd always worked the hardest. In college, she snuck out of parties in her dorm to return to the library. In law school, she lived on Red Bull and chocolate-covered espresso beans to power herself through all-night study sessions; and as a young attorney, she scored points with her superiors for her work ethic.

As New York's first female attorney general with a child in diapers, she'd been given ample latitude with the voters of New York to pass on the social aspects of elected office. What the public didn't know was that she didn't spend her time away from the office raising her child. She left that to her husband. Tara spent all her time working. As A.G., she pulled all-nighters several times a week to make sure she was always prepared for her official responsibilities. The strategy had paid off.

It hadn't been a total shock to everyone that she'd been tapped to run as vice president the year before. Tara's husband, Marcus, was an FBI agent she'd met while working as an assistant U.S. attorney in Manhattan. He carefully cultivated Tara's image as an independent-minded Democrat who wasn't hostage to party or ideology. His effort, which began as endearing spousal cheerleading, became a full-time endeavor. He'd taken a leave of absence from the FBI during the campaign and had extended his leave to help them get settled in Washington.

In law enforcement, Tara mused, it wasn't too difficult to cast one-self as above the fray. In her case, she simply hadn't had the time or the energy for politics. Her superiors misinterpreted the limits of her bandwidth for high-mindedness and appointed her to several highly visible working groups at the Justice Department. Thanks in part to Marcus's shameless boasting about her accomplishments, she'd become the darling of the New York congressional delegation and had even been rumored to be in talks with New York's billionaire mayor to run on a third-party ticket. Tara never seriously contemplated any of it, but when Charlotte Kramer called and asked to meet with her, she knew it was her opportunity to step onto the national stage. She also knew that she should say no. Tara was acutely aware of her limitations. Serving as an elected official in New York was one thing. She had enough privacy as the state's top prosecutor to let her public profile ebb and flow with the cases her office was working. The vice presidency was something entirely different. She had deep reservations about agreeing to meet with Charlotte. On the other hand, it had been years since the president had been unable to pull herself out of one of her lows. When Charlotte had called that day in August, Tara and Marcus were at the beach with Kendall. The president had been down more than twelve points in the polls. Now, as Tara stared at the antique map of the original colonies that hung in her office in the West Wing, she realized how foolish she'd been to have believed that Charlotte couldn't actually win.

Tara heard a knock on her door. She rose to open it.

"Madam Vice President?" It was Karen.

"Yes, Karen, I'm ready. Send them in."

Tara watched as eight men in dark suits and one woman in a navy skirt and jacket filed into her office. They seemed to be waiting for an invitation to sit, but she couldn't get her mind to communicate with her mouth fast enough. Karen stole a glance at her boss and took it upon herself to get everyone settled. "Madam Vice President, can I get you a latte or some tea?"

"Yes, Karen, a latte would be great. Thank you. Is Dale coming?"

"Yes ma'am. She ducked out to take a call from Ralph, but she'll be right in."

During the campaign, Ralph Giacomo had served as the president's senior advisor, a vague White House title that carries with it only as much responsibility and power as the president feels like awarding on any given day. He took advantage of the latitude it afforded him and cultivated a relationship with Tara that was as intimate as any bond between a politician and a trusted counselor. As a reward for helping Charlotte win a second term, he'd been named White House chief of staff. Ralph was less available to her now than he'd been during the campaign, but Tara was relieved that he'd insisted on being named Charlotte's chief of staff *and* senior advisor to the vice president. It was highly unusual for the chief of staff to hold a title with the office of the vice president, but Ralph made the case to the president that it would serve everyone's interest to have the president's operation synched up tightly with the office of the vice president, or the OVP.

Dale and Ralph were the two people Tara had come to rely on the most. Dale's role included responsibilities outside the scope of typical communications activities. She'd become a gatekeeper. She oversaw all scheduling decisions, travel and speech content, and press appearances. As Tara looked around at the faces of the policy team members, she wondered what they thought of her.

"Madam Vice President, you're going to be seated next to T. Boone Pickens, a former oil man who has invested hundreds of millions of dollars in alternative energy technology. He's one of the—"

"I know who T. Boone Pickens is," Tara interrupted.

"Right. I'm sorry. He'll moderate a discussion at a company called Wired Wind. They are trying to figure out how to take the power generated from wind and other alternative sources and distribute it more efficiently. Mr. Pickens is going to introduce you to several other entrepreneurs who are on the cutting edge of wind, solar, and nuclear energy development and transmission. We've drafted some questions for you to pose to each of them. Would you like to practice them?"

They were staring at her like she was a kindergarten student. Why would they think she'd need to rehearse their scripted questions? Why were the questions scripted in the first place? She wanted the meeting to end. Tara scanned the room and noticed that Dale was watching her intently from the back of the room.

"Madam Vice President, perhaps we could table the logistics until the day of the event and use today's time to discuss any remaining policy issues?"

"Yes, yes, Dale, thank you, that's a good idea."

The policy team looked a little disappointed, but they obeyed. Tara got through the rest of the meeting by staring at the plate of cookies and trying to decide which ones to eat once everyone left. When the last of the experts finally left her office, she sank into her couch and let out a loud sigh.

"How are you holding up, Madam Vice President?" Dale asked.

"I think I'm a little under the weather."

Dale nodded sympathetically. "It's been grueling. And with all the travel coming up, it's going to get worse."

The thought of things getting worse tightened the imaginary vise around her head.

"How's the Mideast trip shaping up?" Tara asked.

"Good. The plan is for you to be in Afghanistan to boost troop morale before the spring fighting heats up. You'll make stops in Saudi Arabia, Jordan, and Dubai. Ralph believes the trip will cement your foreign policy credentials and show you as a real partner to the president on national security issues."

Tara forced a smile on her face.

"That sounds like a smart thing to do."

"Let me know if there's anything else you need, Madam Vice President."

As soon as Dale left her office, Tara picked up the plate of uneaten cookies and devoured them. She rested her feet on the coffee table in front of her and shut her eyes for a couple of minutes. She didn't feel any better. Tara reached for the phone and dialed Marcus.

"I need to come home right now," she whispered.

"Honey, you can't do that again," Marcus warned.

Tara felt a lump forming in her throat. "I'm exhausted."

"Shhh. You're okay. Have you had anything to eat?"

"Yes. I had some soup for lunch." She declined to mention the four chocolate chip cookies she'd just polished off.

"Good. You don't want to let your blood sugar get too low. Why don't you have Karen get you some coffee or tea and I'll bring Kendall by for a visit?"

Tara brightened a bit. "We can all go home together after your visit."

"We'll see about that. Do you have anything else on your schedule today?"

Tara stood up to check her line-by-line schedule for the day.

"It says that I'm invited to attend a briefing for the president on foreign aid in the Roosevelt Room at six P.M."

"You should go to that."

Tara felt tears of frustration forming behind her eyes.

"We'll see how I feel," she said. "When do you think you'll be here?"

"I'm on my way to pick her up from school right now. We'll come straight to the White House."

"Thank you, Marcus. I'm sorry to bug you. I know you have your own things to deal with."

"You don't have to thank me—this is what I'm here for. We're going to get through this together. Next week will be better. You'll see."

"I didn't think it would be like this," she said quietly.

"You're doing great."

"No, I'm not. I screw something up every time I step out of the house."

"Come on, baby. You're the most admired woman in America. Doesn't that tell you something about the job you're doing?"

"But it isn't real. The person they admire isn't me. It's the idea that I'm them."

He sighed, and Tara could tell he was starting to lose his patience.

"Honey, please do me a favor and try to hang in there until we get there. Will you do that for me?"

"Yes. I don't know what's wrong with me."

"We'll see you soon."

Tara picked up one of the magazines on her coffee table. There she was, smiling back at herself from the front porch of the Naval Observatory, the official residence of the vice president. Marcus had his arm around her shoulder, and Kendall was standing in front of them. The headline read: "America Feels at Home with the Meyers." She shook her head back and forth and ran her finger over the picture.

"What have we done?" she whispered.

CHAPTER FIVE

Dale

The vice president nailed the event at Wired Wind in Michigan. In the weeks that followed, the West Wing eagerly dispatched her to similar events in Ohio, Wisconsin, and Iowa. Creating new jobs in the energy sector was one of the cornerstones of the president's economic recovery strategy. Previous presidents had harped on the national security imperative of lessening America's dependence on foreign oil, but eventually people figured out that most of that imported oil comes from Canada and Mexico. President Kramer turned the debate on its head by turning it into a jobs crusade.

It was clear to Dale that the vice president had done her homework on the obstacles that alternative energy companies had when it came to delivering their products to a hungry American market looking for cheap energy. She'd won rave reviews from the industry and in the business press, and Dale hoped that her boss was finally building up some confidence.

The vice president had turned in a couple of shaky performances early on that seemed to rattle her to her core. On a trip to the education department to greet workers, she'd been stumped by a question from an employee about merit pay for teachers. And on a visit to New Orleans, she'd stumbled on a question about hurricane preparedness. Dale suspected that the constant scrutiny was taking a toll, but the public remained fascinated by her. The media covered her every move, and the press contingency at vice presidential events rivaled the president's press corps in size and star power.

Despite her popularity, Ralph was afraid that Tara was becoming a one-trick pony with the energy events. He asked Dale to pressure the advance team and the State Department to push her trip to the Middle East up by a few weeks.

Dale had fallen asleep the night before with the speech the vice president would deliver in Jordan and a set of highlighters in her lap. She forgot to call Peter back, and she woke up to three texts he'd sent to make sure she was okay. She knew she was testing the limits of his patience and understanding. Now, as she balanced her BlackBerry on the steering wheel, she made a mental note to search for flights to San Francisco as soon as she got into the office. She'd already slammed on her brakes once to avoid rear-ending a garbage truck, and she didn't need to start her day by running down an early-morning jogger or crashing into one of her colleagues. As far as she could tell, those were the only people on the streets of downtown Washington at five-thirty in the morning. She slowed down as she neared the final traffic light. Once she was fully stopped, she skimmed her e-mails. Ralph had sent her three 911 messages. She'd be inside the White House complex in less than five minutes. Whatever it was could wait. Just as she was about to lower her BlackBerry into her lap, her phone rang. "Hello?"

"It's the Situation Room, ma'am. I have Mr. Giacamo for you."

"Thanks."

Dale held the phone to her ear as she turned onto E Street. She still didn't have a hard pass, the official "all access ticket" to the West Wing. The hard pass signaled to the Secret Service that a complete background check had been turned in by the FBI. Without it, you were treated like a visitor, at best, and a possible threat by the paranoid Secret Service agents. It didn't help with Dale's transition from reporter to staffer that she had to wear a scarlet "A" for appointment around her neck every day. But the most cumbersome consequence of lacking the coveted hard pass was that the Secret Service had to look up her name and clear her every time she entered the eighteen acres. Dale handed over her driver's license and pulled over next to the K-9 units.

"Do you have an appointment, ma'am?" one of the agents asked.

"No. Unfortunately, I work here. I have driven through this exact gate at this exact time every day for months now." He took her license and retreated into a small shed.

"Dale, are you there?" Ralph was still on the phone.

"Yes, I'm here. I'm trying to get into the office. I still don't have a hard pass."

"Come straight to my office when you get here. The vice president wants to cancel the trip."

"What? Why? We leave in three days."

"Not anymore. I was on the phone with both of them until two in the morning."

"Both of them?"

"The vice president and Mr. Meyers. I'll fill you in later. We need to work on a statement for the press. And have someone check on your hard pass. Even the interns have theirs by now."

Dale hung up and looked out at the agent who'd taken her license.

"I'm sorry to be a pain, but I really need to get in there. Is there anyone I can call?"

"You're all set, ma'am. Pull through the first gate and shut off your engine for the dogs."

"I know. Thank you."

She waited for the giant metal pillars to disappear into the ground, and then she drove carefully toward the first checkpoint. She popped the trunk of her BMW convertible and leaned back against the headrest. The light on her BlackBerry hadn't stopped flashing since she'd hung up with Ralph. It was probably the White House correspondents checking in before the morning shows. She rubbed her neck and waited for the giant German shepherd to complete his check of her car. When the agent waved her through she restarted her motor and drove slowly toward the third and final gate. While she waited for it to open, it struck her that she had achieved pariah status. Her former colleagues in the press didn't trust her, and her new White House colleagues hated reporters. It was like being back in high school when none of the cliques would have you—not even the nerds.

Dale parked her car on West Exec, the driveway that separated the West Wing from the Old Executive Office Building, and rushed into Ralph's office.

"There you are. Sit at my computer," Ralph ordered.

Dale sat down and tried to ignore the crumbs of food and discarded wrappers on his desk. His seat was warm. She cringed and did a quick calculation as to whether Ralph would notice if she reached into her purse for her Purell.

"Let's get this done so I can show it to POTUS before senior staff," Ralph urged.

"Ralph, slow down. Why isn't she going on the trip? Is she sick again? What's going on?"

"Dale, this isn't a reporter briefing. Write first and we'll talk later."

She felt her cheeks flush. Every time she thought she was achieving a status that would afford her the privilege of having all the facts, someone made it clear that the curtains were still drawn tightly shut.

"Yes sir. Should it be a statement from the press secretary or a statement from the chief of staff?" Dale asked.

"I was thinking more along the lines of a statement from the vice president. Something about regretting that she has to postpone her travels and that she looks forward to rescheduling later this year."

Dale typed up the statement with Ralph hovering over her shoulder. She worked quickly. He read the draft and approved it with a few minor changes.

"Add something about their kid being sick."

"Kendall."

"Huh?"

"Their daughter's name is Kendall," Dale said.

"Right. Add it."

She turned to look at him.

"What?"

"Is Kendall really sick?" Dale asked.

Ralph contorted his face into an expression Dale could not decipher. She sat quietly with her hands in her lap. The vice president hadn't said anything about Kendall being sick the day before.

"Do one version of the statement with some language about the kid being sick and one without," he barked.

Her gut told her that their daughter had nothing to do with the trip being canceled. As Dale typed, she felt as if she'd just crossed a line into a darker side of public service. On this side, the truth was easily subverted with two drafts that were strikingly similar but were separated by the fact that one was a lie. She printed out both versions and e-mailed them to herself before she stood up.

"Wait at your desk for any changes from the president." He ran out of his office and toward the Oval Office. Dale walked straight to the ladies room in the West Wing and washed her hands before heading back to the OEOB to inform her staff.

As soon as she walked into her office, Ralph was on the phone for her.

"Get this fucking thing out as soon as the morning shows go on the air. Use the version with the sick kid. Make sure you wait until after the White House correspondents have done their live shots."

"That will infuriate them."

"Perfect."

"Ralph, I'd feel better dropping this bombshell if I could speak to the vice president about it," Dale persisted.

"She specifically directed me to handle it, so we are going to handle it, Dale. You can talk to her later."

Dale knew that she'd have to pick her fights, but she had a terrible feeling about the statement. She skimmed it one final time and left it with her assistant to release at 7:15. She printed off ten copies for her staff and headed down the hall to face them. They'd been working around the clock to prepare for the vice president's trip, and now all that work would be for naught. Dale tried to paste a cheerful smile on her face. Her staff took the news better than she thought they would. None of them seemed particularly surprised. She rushed to the senior staff meeting and took her seat on the couch just as Ralph was making the announcement that the vice president was postponing her trip. Dale kept her head down and pretended to be taking notes. She raced for the door as soon as the meeting ended and spent the morning in her office catching up on paperwork and turning down interview requests for the V.P. She was about to head out to pick up a salad when the V.P.'s press secretary ran into her office.

"We have a situation."

"What's wrong?" Dale asked.

"The press has staked out Kendall's school."

"You're kidding."

"No. Sidwell just called the press office to let us know."

"What did you say?"

"I thanked them and told them I'd call them right back."

"Good. Tell them to follow whatever their normal policy is for dealing with the press and ask them to refer questions about Kendall Meyers to us if they don't mind."

"Dale, they were calling because Kendall is in school today. She isn't sick."

Dale pressed her lips together.

"Don't do anything. I'm going over to see Ralph to find out what the hell is going on."

CHAPTER SIX

Charlotte

Brooke and Mark were in town for the Cherry Blossom Festival. It was Brooke's favorite time of year in D.C. They came for a long weekend at the beginning of April each year to see the magnificent blooms. Brooke and Mark were Charlotte's best friends in the world. They'd all gone to U.C. Berkeley together. When Charlotte met Peter, he'd joined their tight circle, and the four of them had experienced all of the ups and downs of marriage and parenthood together. Until, of course, Charlotte became governor of California and then president. Brooke and Mark lived in Atherton and were regular visitors to the White House and Camp David. Charlotte loved them like family. They were the only people with whom she could be her true unpresidential self. They didn't see a president when they looked at her. They just saw their old friend.

"That's some spunky veep you got yourself, Char. We saw her with Kathie Lee and Hoda last week," Brooke said. She was wearing a Chanel sweater and tight jeans, and when she put her feet up on the coffee table, Charlotte noticed the red soles of what were obviously new Christian Louboutin shoes.

"It's only been three months. She's still settling in," Charlotte conceded.

"I'll say. She giggled and mugged for about five minutes, and then they brought out her husband and kid. They all looked at each other while Kathie Lee Gifford talked about how hunky Marcus was."

"What else are you supposed to do in those interviews?" Charlotte asked.

"You never even *did* those interviews," Brooke noted.

"I think Tara is finally starting to find her footing," Charlotte said.

"Aren't her approval numbers way down this month?" Mark asked.

"Her numbers are down, but they had nowhere else to go. She was at eighty-five percent and now she's at about sixty. I'd kill for those numbers."

"No, you wouldn't. You love being disliked by nearly half the country. It speaks to the martyr in you," Brooke teased.

"Char, what's the real story with her canceling her trip last month? The press really ripped her," Mark said.

"I don't know why everyone is so damn cynical these days. What difference does it make whether the kid was ill enough to miss school or just worried sick about her mother going to a war zone?"

Brooke raised an eyebrow. Mark swatted her and made a tsk-tsk sound. She ignored him and pointed at her empty wineglass. Mark stood to get the bottle of chardonnay out of the ice bucket. He filled Brooke's glass and topped off Charlotte's.

"Char, honey, I can see how it would take her some time to get used to life in a fishbowl," Mark said. Charlotte could see that Brooke still wasn't satisfied.

"What does Melanie think of her?" Brooke asked.

"We don't talk about it."

"Mel is settling in nicely at the Pentagon," Mark offered.

"I'm sure she enjoys bossing around men in uniform," Brooke added.

"No doubt. Only Melanie would find it a bore to boss around the leader of the free world."

Brooke and Mark chuckled.

"Actually, I think she was afraid of losing herself if she stayed here any longer," Charlotte explained.

"Let's face it. She and Tara would have killed each other. Mel would never have had the patience for her unpresidential appearance and little blunders, and Tara would have tired of Melanie's disapproval. It's for the best that she went to DOD," Brooke added.

Charlotte nodded and took a long sip of her wine.

"Peter said he's going to be seeing you soon to talk college apps for the twins," Brooke said. She could always read Charlotte well enough to know when it was time to change the subject.

"Thanks for reminding me. I need to set that up."

Their twins had just completed their junior year in high school at boarding school in Kent, Connecticut, and Charlotte and Peter would be joining the ranks of anxiety-ridden parents in the fall as they endured the waiting game for college acceptances. Penelope wanted to head west to Stanford or UCLA, and Harry wanted to stay on the East Coast. It felt like just yesterday when Charlotte had fought the decision for the twins to attend boarding school. And now they were leaving for good. She was haunted by the feeling that she'd missed out on something she would never be able to recapture. Her kids had grown into savvy, worldly, and good-natured teenagers, but she couldn't claim much of the credit. She'd done her best to be there for all of their "big" moments, but that's not when the important parenting takes place. What she'd missed was the daily mothering that Brooke probably took for granted with her kids, but that Charlotte pined for each and every day that she woke up hundreds of miles from where they were at school. She did her best to shake off her guilt about being a third-rate parent and turned back to Brooke and Mark.

"How's Peter doing?" she asked.

Brook and Mark shared a look.

"What?"

"I don't think things are going well with Dale now that she's with the vice president," Brooke said.

"Oh god. He probably thinks I hired her to spite him."

"Char, is it ever strange having her here?" Brooke asked.

"No, I mean, it's not like we run into each other all the time and talk about how Peter likes his eggs cooked. I have a job to do. She has a job to do. And when we end up in a meeting together, it's completely fine. You know, I was the one who reached out to her during the campaign to try to help her at the network."

"I remember. You offered her the interview with Tara."

"Right. We coexist just fine. She had nothing to do with what happened between me and Peter."

"I know, I know. We've heard this a million times," Brooke replied. "It's true."

"Char, I think it's time for you to get out there again," Mark suggested.

"Date?"

"Yes. You could use a man around here," Mark argued.

"For what?" Brooke deadpanned.

Charlotte laughed.

"What do you have in mind? Match.com? Single white female seeking man with several tuxedos of his own and a talent for hosting teas? Must love dogs?" Charlotte joked.

"That describes half of my gay friends from San Francisco perfectly," Brooke giggled.

"I'm serious, ladies. Brookie, don't turn this into a joke. Char, I want to set you up with one of the guys I go heli-skiing with," Mark offered.

"A man in the throes of his thrill-seeking midlife crisis is not what I need."

"I resent that comment," Mark protested.

"Let's go eat. I'm starving," Charlotte said. She took her friends by the arm and led them into the dining room for dinner.

CHAPTER SEVEN

Tara

Tara had ignored the first two knocks at her door, but this one sounded different.

It was more like banging than knocking.

"Who is it?" Tara asked. She stood and wrapped the down comforter around her. She loved the bedding at the Four Seasons. Tara was in Miami in advance of the Cuban Independence Day celebration. At first she'd refused to make the trip, but when she saw "RON Four Seasons Miami," White House shorthand for "reside over night at the Four Seasons," she'd acquiesced.

"Madam Vice President, it's Walter. I have the president on the line for you. It's the second time she's called."

"Uh, okay," Tara said. "Put her through."

"I've been trying for ten minutes, but your phones are unplugged or disconnected," Walter said, with practiced patience.

"Oh, right, hang on a second." Tara threw the comforter to the ground and grabbed one of the phone cords she'd pulled out when she checked in several hours earlier.

"They're connected now. You can put her through."

The familiar voice of the Situation Room operator came on.

"Please hold for the president," he said.

"Hello?" Charlotte said.

"Madam President, hi, sorry about that," Tara apologized.

"Don't worry. We all need peace and quiet sometimes." The president spoke in kind tones that Tara noticed a lot of people seemed to be using with her lately.

"Is everything okay?" Tara had a decent rapport with the president, but a Sunday-afternoon call was more than a little unusual.

"Everything is fine," Charlotte said. "I'm leaving for Afghanistan tonight and I wanted to give you a heads-up. I'll be back on Thursday, but I didn't want you to wake up to the news without first hearing from me."

"Thank you, Madam President, thanks so much. Please stay safe," Tara said. "And have a great trip. I can't wait to hear about it when you get back."

"Thank you, Tara. You have a good week, too."

Tara hung up and felt the sinking feeling she always got when the weight of the job sank in. The president was traveling to the war zone. If something happened, people would expect her to fill Charlotte's shoes. Tara sat back down on the bed, picked the down comforter up off the floor, and wrapped it tightly around her. She rocked back and forth and tried to pull herself together. She was expected at a cocktail reception to thank the campaign's big-dollar donors in an hour. It had been four months since the inauguration, and no one suspected anything. The public saw cheerful Tara, or feisty Tara, or hardworking Tara. They saw the Tara who fired up the crowds at political events and helped Charlotte win reelection against all the odds. On the covers of *Redbook* and *Good Housekeeping*, the public saw a smiling mother and wife who ran the country in her free time.

Tara looked at the stack of briefing materials on her desk. One was for the fund-raiser that evening and the other held her remarks for the Cuban Independence Day speech the next morning. On the floor was a stack of paperwork from her staff that seemed to grow no matter how hard she worked to get through it all. In her suitcase were three books she wanted to finish about fighting counterinsurgencies so she could participate with greater confidence in national security discussions. Tara decided to tackle the pile after a shower. She loved the large marble bathrooms at the Four Seasons.

By the time she stepped out of the shower twenty minutes later, she was feeling better. She wandered around her room in her towel, feeling optimistic about the week ahead. "I can do this," she repeated to herself over and over.

Her good mood evaporated instantly when she turned to her closet to get dressed.

Tara pretended she didn't care about the comments in the press about her "god-awful" taste in clothes, but the truth was, she was trying harder than ever to get it right. She was born without the girl gene that told her which colors were in fashion and which styles were right for her. Night after night, she'd try on the expensive suits and dresses that the president's advisors purchased for her during the campaign the previous year. But the longer she stared at her reflection, the more convinced she became that the suits were purchased to make her look dowdy and unattractive so Charlotte would look better by comparison. She pulled off the wide-legged linen slacks and tailored blazer that she'd packed for her trip to Miami, rolled them into a ball, and threw them on the floor of the closet.

Now that she was agitated again, she decided to relax a little longer before getting dressed. She lay on the bed and flipped to the back of the romance novel she'd snuck into her briefcase. *All He Desires* looked like something she'd already read, but Karen swore it was a new release. These days, Tara loved nothing more than to crawl into bed with briefing papers, a bag of potato chips, and a romance novel. She'd leave the romance novel off to the side as a visual cue: the prize that awaited her once she finished her "homework."

With just fifteen minutes until she was expected at the reception, Tara folded down the corner on the page in her novel and lay back looking at the ceiling.

"Four months down, three years and eight months to go," she said out loud.

CHAPTER EIGHT

Dale

D ale shook her head at the television. When the vice president was "on," there was nothing like it. Miami's powerful Cuban community had a new savior. The vice president was greeted by a ten-minute standing ovation that only grew louder when she delivered the first three lines of her speech in Spanish. She hit all the hot-button issues with precision and fired up the crowd with promises to make it easier for Miami's dissident community to travel to Cuba and send money to relatives. Dale breathed a sigh of relief. The vice president had sent alarming e-mails all through the night with questions about policy, translations, and other changes to her speech. By morning, the vice presidential speechwriting team looked like they'd been dragged behind a truck. Dale was afraid more of her staff would quit. She showered them with praise and listened to all their complaints about working for the vice president. She hoped that if she absorbed every last gripe and offered her heartfelt gratitude for their service they'd be less likely to gossip about Tara's mounting eccentricities with their West Wing colleagues and any friends in the press.

"What the fuck—the speech is to commemorate Cuban Independence Day, it's not the goddamned State of the Union," one of them had groused.

"She's a perfectionist," Dale had said.

"She's off her rocker," another speechwriter had said.

"Come on guys, she's under a lot of stress. She'll settle down. You did a great job. She loves the new speech." Dale had tried to soothe her staff, but they were at the end of their ropes. Now, Tara was basking in the adoration of the crowd. She'd be in a good mood for the rest of the day. Dale stood to walk over to the West Wing to pick up her lunch.

"Dale, Mr. Robbins is on the line. He says it's urgent," her assistant, Jimmy, said.

"I'm starving," Dale begged.

"It's the third time he's called today. I'll pick up your lunch if you talk to Robbins." Michael Robbins was one of the most aggressive reporters in town.

Dale glared at Jimmy.

"Fine." She picked up the phone and sat back in her chair.

Jimmy closed the door behind him, and Dale took a deep breath as she listened to the theories being presented to her on the other end of the line. She turned off her televisions and prepared for combat.

"Come on, Michael. You're kidding, right? You are not seriously writing a story about the vice president's weight gain, are you?" Dale asked. Her voice was even, but she had to work at it. Weight-gain stories were not Michael's bag—not by a long shot. Dale was certain that the vice president could lose or gain half her body weight and Michael would not notice. He was an I-reporter—the last of a dying breed of investigative reporters who chased down the darkest leads about the people in power. It was never a good thing when he called.

He was trying to manipulate the situation by getting her to confide in him, but Dale had used the same tricks with her sources during her reporter years.

"Dale, no one was more overjoyed about your addition to the inner circle than me, but it takes about two seconds on the Internet to find a diagnosis for an obsessive compulsive disorder that includes sudden weight gain as a symptom," he said, with an air of confidence that annoyed Dale.

"A man can gain ten, fifteen pounds and no one says anything. The vice president gains five pounds during her first year in office and you're giving me a hard time? What is this really about?" she said.

"You tell me," he said quietly. "I've got three West Wing sources who say she cancels sixty percent of her events, two who say she stares into space during policy briefings, and one who says she hasn't seen the inside of the Oval for over a month. I have two very senior congressional sources who describe a meeting with their boss in which she blurted out inexplicable answers to his relatively simple questions about what her judicial philosophy was, and I have a member of the Senate Foreign Relations Committee who swears on his life that she stared blankly at him for several minutes before abruptly ending a meeting she had requested when he asked her if the White House was forcing Israel to compromise on settlements. Do you need me to go on?"

"Please do."

"Well, there are her local media appearances. I'm sure it falls to you, Dale, to explain them away as honest mistakes that anyone could make, but flubbing a question about Yucca Mountain in Nevada, drawing a blank on government assistance for the auto industry while in Michigan, and staring silently at the reporter who asked her about the fence while she was on a trip to Arizona starts to look more than a little disturbing, wouldn't you say?"

"Michael, everyone has a learning curve," Dale insisted.

"I would be able to accept that, but we both know that someone gave her a briefing paper on the policy debate that's raged for years about disposing nuclear waste in Nevada, and someone must have mentioned that there are a good deal of people in Michigan who are still hurting from the shifts in the auto industry, and surely you filled her in on the emotions that still run high in Arizona on the topic of illegal immigration."

He was right. Dale had prepared talking points for the vice president on all those issues. And the vice president had screwed up her answers anyway. Dale sighed.

"What do you want, Michael?"

"I can paint a pretty disturbing picture with or without you, Dale," he said.

"Michael, she is fine. Any suggestion to the contrary has been knocked down each and every time it's been raised. The White House is going to take your sniffing around on this again very seriously," Dale said.

He was silent.

She wasn't going to speak first.

"Dale, you better hope for your sake that you're right, because you only get to play this card once. You know that," Michael said.

She hung up and a chill ran through her body. There it was. The call she'd been dreading. She was surprised it had taken the press so long to ask. Tara's behavior was increasingly erratic. She often canceled events at the last minute, she'd gained at least twenty pounds and looked more haggard every week, and her work habits were so bizarre that only a couple of her most senior advisors were allowed face time with the vice president.

Dale dialed the Situation Room and asked the operator to track down Ralph.

As she held for him, Dale looked out her window and watched the legislative affairs team pile into a car for the short ride up to the Capitol. For the first couple of months that Dale worked at the White House, every small detail fascinated her. She'd covered the White House for nearly four years, but as a reporter, she'd barely scratched the surface about the inner workings of the place. As her job with the vice president grew more challenging, the wonder she'd felt in those early days and weeks was replaced by anxiety and fatigue.

The operator either couldn't locate Ralph or he was ignoring her call. Dale hung up and looked over at the growing stack of invitations to events, speeches, and appearances that the West Wing had asked her to take to the vice president. She hadn't been able to go through any of the scheduling requests because the vice president hadn't been in the right state of mind to plan ahead.

Dale opened her desk drawer and pulled out a jar of peanut butter. She looked around her office and found a box of graham crackers. She laid the graham crackers out on a napkin and started spreading peanut butter on them. She'd been famished lately. She'd had a bagel with her coffee when she pulled into the White House complex at 5:30 A.M., but she was hungry again. The last thing she needed was to gain the freshman fifteen—a phenomenon that afflicts many White House staffers who succumb to candy bowls and unhealthy fare on the road. She ran her hand across her stomach and was relieved to find it as flat as ever.

Dale pulled her hair into a ponytail and looked out her window toward the West Wing to see if Jimmy was on his way with her grilled cheese sandwich and tomato soup. She had a meeting with the deputy national security advisor at one o'clock to discuss options for rescheduling the vice president's overseas trip. Dale used to look forward to meetings in the West Wing, but her White House colleagues barely concealed their discomfort when she joined their meetings. The West Wing assumed that OVP was being difficult, but no one ever probed. No one dared to ask the one question that was on all of their minds: *What is the deal with the vice president?*

She was engrossed in her e-mail when Jimmy arrived with her lunch. When she looked up and saw the tray of food, she devoured her sandwich and soup and guzzled a bottle of water in less than five minutes. With one minute to spare, Dale popped an Altoid in her mouth, grabbed her binder and BlackBerry, and ran out of her office for her meeting.

CHAPTER NINE

Charlotte

Charlotte had no idea why she was nervous. Peter had been her husband for nineteen years. They'd raised two amazing kids, juggled two successful careers, managed four homes, and cared for two sets of aging parents on two coasts together. Surely they could get through dinner, she thought. She went back into her bedroom on the second floor of the East Wing residence to change again. She pulled off her black Chanel sweater and put on a sheer Dolce and Gabbana blouse that Brooke had given her for Christmas. She turned to walk back out to the Yellow Oval where she was supposed to meet Peter for cocktails, but when she caught a glimpse of herself in the mirror, she stopped in her tracks.

"What do you think you're doing?" she asked her reflection.

She yanked the blouse off and put the sweater back on, shaking her head and muttering to herself the whole time. The black sweater was covered with brown fur from its brief stint on the floor of her closet. The dogs were sitting in her closet staring at the rare spectacle of their master changing her clothes multiple times and talking to herself.

Dinner was Peter's idea. She'd returned from Afghanistan the night before and would have loved nothing more than an early night of reading in bed with the dogs curled around her. But Peter thought they needed a strategy for college applications for their children, and if there was one thing that would always bring them together, it was their children.

In some ways, things were easier between Charlotte and Peter now that they were separated than they had been in years. It wasn't that she had necessarily forgiven him for the affair, but she was able to acknowledge, to herself at least, that she'd left Peter years before he fell in love with another woman.

Charlotte looked up at the security monitor in her closet and saw that Peter had arrived. She stopped and watched him for a minute. Her ability to analyze people and situations dispassionately was one of the skills she relied on most as a politician. It hadn't always served her as well in her personal life. As she observed Peter, she was struck by how attractive he still was. He'd started training for triathlons the summer before, and while he was thinner than when they'd been together, she could see from the way he moved that his body was all muscle. His hair was longish and a dirty blond. He'd worn it shorter during her campaigns, but she thought it looked better now. The lines around his eyes and mouth had deepened, but he looked good. An usher from the East Wing approached him and escorted him up the stairs. Charlotte grabbed a lint roller and ran it over the front of her sweater.

"Get a grip," she said to her reflection before turning to walk out of her bedroom with the three dogs a few paces ahead.

"Char, you look great," he said, bending down to scratch the dogs' bellies.

Charlotte laughed as the dogs made a pathetic and shameless play for his attention. Only Cammie, the oldest of the three dogs, stayed at Charlotte's side. She watched the younger dogs with disgust. Charlotte scratched Cammie's ears and made small talk while they stood in the Yellow Oval.

"How's San Francisco?" Charlotte asked.

"Good. Business is cooking. Thank God professional athletes haven't figured out how to write their own contracts," he said. Peter was one of the most respected sports agents in the business. He had a client base that spanned professional football, basketball, and baseball and a waiting list of people who wanted to switch from their agencies to Peter's. His secret was never letting supply catch up with demand.

"The kids said you guys are going to take the boat out over Memorial Day and do some waterskiing. Won't it be freezing?" Charlotte asked.

"Probably, but it's always such a sight to be on the lake when the mountains are still covered with snow," he said.

Charlotte tried to stop her mind from flashing back to their family vacations at Lake Tahoe. They'd spent winters skiing and summers boating. All of her happy memories of marriage and motherhood were set at Lake Tahoe.

"I haven't been there in ages," she said, wistfully.

"You should meet us out there some time," Peter offered.

"That would be fun." In a million years, she'd never disturb the tranquility and natural beauty of a place like Lake Tahoe with her entourage of security and national media. She could just imagine her thirty-car motorcade pulling into Squaw Valley and blocking traffic for miles in each direction.

"Are you hungry?" she asked.

"Very," he said.

They sat down to bowls of gazpacho followed by grilled halibut.

"Are you on a health kick?" Peter asked.

"No, but I thought you were." Charlotte laughed.

"Nah, I gave that up years ago."

"In that case, we'll serve dessert after all," she said.

The waiter brought out a tray of brownies and large bowls of ice cream and chocolate sauce.

Peter and Charlotte agreed that the nightmare scenario would be for Harry to be accepted to Stanford and for Penny to be rejected. He was ambivalent about getting into any schools on the West Coast, but she was desperate to leave the East Coast and move back to Northern California. They shared a laugh about which one of them would be tasked with calling the chancellor of Stanford University to request a trade of Harry's acceptance for Penny's if they found themselves in that situation. After they'd finished dessert and nearly two bottles of wine, Charlotte cleared her throat and looked across the table at Peter.

"This is probably going to come out in-artfully, but I would like for us to be friends, and I'm going to try to be here for you, as a friend," she said.

He was watching her closely.

"Thank you for saying that. I'd like that, too."

"So, in my capacity as your friend, I was wondering how everything is going with Dale," Charlotte asked, between large gulps of wine.

She knew him well enough to see that she'd surprised him.

"Everything is fine, Char, thanks for asking," he said, smiling at her. She breathed a sigh of relief that he hadn't actually taken her up on her offer to talk about his girlfriend.

"Should I open another bottle of wine, or do you need to get going?"

"I don't have to be anywhere," he said.

"Oh." Now she was the one who was surprised. She'd assumed that he would have planned to meet up with Dale after his dinner with her.

"What about you, Charlotte? Are you, or have you . . . you know?" He seemed flustered. She let him suffer for a minute longer while she stood to pour more wine into both their glasses. When she sat back down, she detected far more curiosity in his eyes than she would have expected.

"No. I am not dating anyone," she finally said. "The U.S. Congress isn't exactly a hotbed of eligible bachelors, and after reading the vetting reports on all of my appointees, I can safely rule out the executive branch." They both laughed.

"What about the judicial branch?"

"The average age is seventy-six. I do have a lead on an avid helicopter skier that Mark thinks I might like, but I'm skeptical that he'd make a suitable date for state dinners and what not."

He laughed again, and they slid easily into conversation about the twins' summer plans, and their work. Charlotte missed being able to turn to Peter for his reactions to things. He'd always had excellent political instincts. Charlotte wasn't sure if it was all the wine, or the combination of the wine with her jet lag, or the simple fact that she didn't have many people to talk to these days, but she was enjoying Peter's company much more than she'd expected to. She looked at her watch and was surprised to see that it was after midnight.

"I didn't realize it was so late," she said, standing.

"I should go," he said.

"We should do this more often."

"I agree," he said with a warm smile.

"Please do me a favor and tell those children of ours to call their mother more often."

"How about next Friday? I'll be in town for some client meetings," he said.

"Oh, you mean, for another dinner?"

"Yes, unless, by 'more often' you meant more than once every three years, not twice in one month. If I'm being presumptuous, just say so."

"No, no, that would be nice. I did mean it," she said.

"Friday?"

"I can't. My handlers have decided that June is the perfect time to dispatch me to useless international summits. I will be at the G-Eight."

"Of course. Standing me up for another summit. That was always your excuse." He laughed.

"Will you still be in town on Sunday?"

"I'll be in Connecticut to see the kids, but I could come down on my way back to California?"

"Only if it isn't too much of an effort. It would be good if we could work on the college stuff since we didn't really get too far tonight."

"It's no problem," he said.

"I'll see you next Sunday."

They stood there smiling at each other for a beat, and then he gave each of the dogs a final scratch before turning to go. Charlotte watched him pass the separate suite of rooms that had been his during her first term as president and head toward the stairs.

CHAPTER TEN

Tara

Tara rushed into her office, removed her coat, and unbuttoned her pants. It was getting more difficult by the day to get dressed. She looked at the desk in the middle of her office. It looked like it was in a different spot than where it had been when she left the day before, but that was impossible. She stared at the desk as though she were seeing it for the first time. There were neat stacks of newspapers, classified briefings, and her copy of the president's schedule for the day. She felt strange. Maybe she needed something to eat. Tara buzzed her assistant and asked for an egg sandwich with cheese and then walked over to the sofa and lay down. She suspected that her staff was starting to talk about her. She sensed their concern. Tara sighed and reached for the remote. She was flipping through the stations when Marcus threw open the door to her office.

"What are you doing?" he asked in a harsh whisper.

"What does it look like I'm doing?"

"Do you want me to answer that?" His eyes rested on her stomach.

"Damn it, Marcus. I'm working," she said, defiantly.

"I thought you were going to stay home today? Didn't we agree that it was a good day to work from home, Tara?"

"I came in to get some paperwork done."

Marcus looked around the room. Tara, with her pants unbuttoned, sat barefoot on her sofa with a *Project Runway* rerun providing the only sound in the room.

"And you've got Lifetime on for background noise?"

"I was looking for CNN to see if I could catch some of Charlotte's speech. I have to deliver a speech on her new jobs package tomorrow," Tara said.

He reached for the remote and changed the channel to CNBC.

"Her status report on Afghanistan probably won't deal with the jobs bill. You should be watching the business cables. Economic policy is your blind spot, and it's where someone in the press is going to trip you up with a question about banking regulations or something you've never heard of," he snapped.

At that moment, Tara's secretary walked in with her scrambled egg and cheese sandwich and placed it on her desk. Sensing the tense vibe, she rushed out and closed the door behind her.

"Were you going to eat *another* breakfast?"

"I'm hungry."

Marcus closed and rubbed his eyes while Tara watched him. Then he sat down on the sofa and took her hands in his.

"Everything is going to be fine, but I need you to promise me that you won't leave the house without telling me where you're going, okay baby?" He was holding her hands so tight now that she could feel her circulation being cut off.

Tara nodded her head.

"Do you understand how serious this is?"

She nodded again.

"Do you?"

"Yes." All she could think about was freeing her hands from his grip before he crushed her fingers.

"If anyone figures out what is really going on, you will be thrown under the bus faster than anyone can say 'Tara who?' No one will care that you're the heart and soul of this place. No one will remember that you're the only reason Kramer won. You will be G-O-N-E gone. Do you understand?" he said.

Tara nodded.

"Good girl."

"If I leave you here for a few hours, you'll tell the staff you're catching up on reading, right? You won't wander over to the press office or anything looking like that, right? No offense, but you look like hell."

Tara nodded again. Finally, he freed her hands.

Marcus stood and threw her breakfast tray in the garbage.

"We'll work out together tonight, and then I'll make protein shakes," he said. "Sound good?"

Tara felt like one of those dolls with a bobbing head as she nodded again.

She stood at the window rubbing her hands until she saw Marcus climb into the SUV that had chauffeured him down to the White House from the Naval Observatory. He had extended his leave of absence from the FBI to help with Kendall, but Tara wished he'd go back to work. As soon as his car started moving, Tara retrieved her egg sandwich from the trash.

CHAPTER ELEVEN

Dale

D ale e-mailed the final text of the speech her boss would deliver that day to the teleprompter operator. She hadn't had a
chance to go over the speech with the vice president the day before
because, according to her secretary, the vice president had been buried in paperwork. Dale put her multiple BlackBerrys into her purse
and shoved three newspapers in on top.

She ran into Karen on West Exec.

"I heard she was in for a few hours yesterday. How was she?" Dale
asked.

"I didn't even see her. She came in, went straight to her office,
ordered breakfast, lunch, and a plate of cookies from the Mess, and
then left three hours later without telling anyone."

Dale tried to keep her worry off her face.

"She must have had a lot of work to do."

"I'm sure," Karen agreed.

They boarded the vans that would take them to Andrews Air
Force Base. From there, they'd travel on Air Force Two, a smaller
and lower-tech version of Air Force One, to Pittsburg, where the vice
president would deliver the keynote address at the national small
business conference, held every year in June and one of the biggest
events on the calendar for a very important political constituency for
the White House.

The vice president was already onboard when they arrived at Andrews. She was in her cabin with her door closed. When Dale walked

by, she could hear the vice president on the phone, having what sounded like a heated discussion with someone. Dale couldn't make out anything she was saying over the sound of her television.

Dale took her seat in the first row behind the vice president's cabin and glanced at the menu card displayed on the tray in front of her. Next to the menu card was a handwritten note that read "Welcome aboard, Dale" and a travel advisory detailing the flight length and weather at their destination. One of the White House economic advisors sat down next to Dale.

"Do you think we'll get to brief her once we're in the air?" he asked.

He was eager to impress the vice president with his vast knowledge of the intricacies of macro- and microeconomic policy. Dale was planning on telling him to keep his briefing focused on the jobs plan, but she wasn't in the mood to engage one of the wonks in a debate before she knew for sure they'd get to meet with the vice president before they landed.

Dale sighed as she looked out the window. "I hope so."

The flight crew served drinks while Air Force Two took off. As soon as they were in the air, Dale unbuckled her seat belt and stood.

"Should I come with you?"

"No. I need to talk to her about next week's trip first."

"Should I come up in five minutes then?"

"I'll send someone to get you. Don't worry. I'm not going to brief her on economic policy without you."

Dale walked to the vice president's cabin and knocked gently. One of the members of the flight crew winked at her. Dale was afraid the vice president wouldn't be able to hear her over the sound of the engines. She was getting ready to knock again when the door opened a crack. The vice president peeked out.

"Come on in," she said.

"Good morning, Madam Vice President. Do you have some time to go over the speech? I brought a couple of the speechwriters on the trip to make any changes you want, and there's an economic policy guy back there if you have any questions about the president's jobs package."

"Thank you, Dale. Thank you so much. I'm, um, I'm sorry you

and I keep missing each other. I saw your messages about the things we need to go over. I thought maybe we could do some of that on the flight home," Tara said.

"Don't worry about it, ma'am. We can get to it any time. Let's just focus on today's speech."

"I know things are piling up. I know that, Dale. And I know I put you in a really bad position by not getting through all of the overnight memos that you prepare for me. It's just that. . . I mean, what I'm trying to say is that I'm sorry I can't do better," Tara said, looking down at her hands.

"Madam Vice President, you're doing great," Dale said gently.

The vice president was so quiet and still, Dale was afraid she was going to start crying.

"Madam Vice President, is everything okay?"

The vice president looked up. Her eyes were glassy, but she wasn't crying.

"You can call me Tara. In fact, please call me Tara," she said.

"I can't do that around the staff, but when we're alone, I will try," Dale said.

"Good. What's the speech about today?"

Dale swallowed. "The president's jobs package. Didn't you see the briefing?" she asked, as the color drained from her face.

"I'm teasing you. Yes, of course I read the briefing. I also watched the treasury secretary's testimony on the package yesterday." She stood up and crossed the cabin to pull something out of her briefcase. She handed over a messy stack of pages.

Dale breathed a sigh of relief.

"These are my changes to the speech. Nothing major, I just toned down some of the policy language so people who run businesses out of their homes understand what the heck we're saying."

"Great. I'll get these to the writers. Do you want to meet with the policy guy?" Dale already knew the answer.

"Hell, no. He'll confuse the heck out of me."

"You got it," she said. "You're going to do great. Try to have fun today. It's a very friendly audience."

"Oh, let me show you the two suits I brought so you can tell me which one is more appropriate." Tara retrieved a garment bag from the closet in her cabin.

Dale had avoided the clothes issue. Everyone who had ever tried to encourage Tara to embrace a more presidential look had been banished. She didn't think the vice president looked bad in what she was wearing—a beige skirt, albeit skin tight, and an oversized black blouse. She was pleasantly surprised by the two relatively simple suits that Tara pulled out.

"Either one will look great," she said.

"Can I try them on for you? You can tell me which one looks better. I've gained some weight because I haven't had time to get to the gym, and things don't look quite right these days."

"Sure."

Tara stepped into the bathroom to change. Lately, Dale couldn't believe that the feisty, irreverent candidate she'd met on the campaign trail was the same insecure, shy, and deeply rattled woman who'd just sat before her apologizing for not getting through her nightly reading. When Dale had interviewed her during the campaign the year before, she'd made news by rebuffing the president's advisors. She'd slammed them for second-guessing her preference for winging it on the campaign trail. In fact, candidate Meyers had been downright bullish about the superiority of her "gut instincts" over the calculations made by Charlotte's political professionals and their opinion polls. Tara had nearly blown up the campaign by creating so much discord. For a reporter on the front lines, it had been delicious. Now, as one of the vice president's closest advisors, Dale was perplexed and disturbed by the dramatic changes in Tara's behavior. Since Dale had first observed her, she'd always had a knack for cutting through the noise and speaking directly to people in a manner they both understood and responded to emotionally. Recently, she had also developed a tendency to badly botch the simplest public appearances and friendly press interactions. Dale felt as if she was walking on eggshells when she was around her. She didn't want to push her to do more than she could handle, but Dale knew that the light public schedule Tara had adopted in recent weeks was raising eyebrows.

"Are you ready for option one?" Tara asked from behind the door.

"Any time."

Tara stepped out of the bathroom in black pants, a bright pink blouse, and a black jacket. The blouse strained across her chest and the jacket didn't button. Dale cringed inwardly but forced a smile.

"That pop of color will look great on television," she said.

"You think so?" Tara asked. "Do you want to see the other outfit?"

"Absolutely." Tara returned to the bathroom, and Dale sat on the sofa in the small cabin and started to massage her neck and shoulders.

She'd agreed to join the White House staff because her career as a journalist was, if not over, then at a crossroads. Dale thought about e-mailing Peter to tell him about the day she was having, but they'd been trying to wean themselves off each other. The relationship that had nearly doomed Charlotte's prospects of reelection was dying a slow and near-certain death unworthy of the drama and turmoil it had created. When Dale agreed to move back to D.C. to serve as the vice president's senior communications advisor, Peter had assured her that he'd always be there for her when she could get to San Francisco.

"What does that mean?" she'd asked.

"It means that I love you and I'll always be here for you when you make your way back here, but you know as well as I do that I can't move back to D.C., rent a condo, and live with you while you begin your White House career," he said.

"Why not? We did it after the accident," she'd shot back.

"That was different."

"How?" she'd challenged. But she knew the answer. After the accident, he'd thought that they were beginning their lives together. Then she'd made her own priorities perfectly clear by leaving San Francisco to cover the campaign for the San Francisco station. When Tara offered Dale a job after the campaign, and told her she'd always regret it if she passed up an opportunity to serve her country, she'd accepted it without even discussing it with Peter.

Tara emerged from the bathroom in a black dress that fell effortlessly over her new curves. She looked better than Dale had ever seen her look.

"You look incredible."

"There's a jacket that goes with the dress. Do you want to see it with the jacket on?" Tara asked.

"Certainly."

She slid the matching black jacket on and stood in front of Dale the way a child stands before her mother before heading out to school.

"What do you think?"

"It's fantastic. Definitely wear this one."

"Thanks, Dale."

"Listen, I need to get your edits to the speechwriters so they can load them into the teleprompter before the speech, so I'm going to get out of your way. Is there anything else you need?" Dale asked, rising to leave.

"No, no, thank you, Dale. You're way too kind."

"I'll bring you a draft of the new speech once they've made your changes."

Dale made her way back to her seat and smiled as sweetly as she could at the economist.

"I'm sorry about that. She said she spent some time with the president and felt completely comfortable with the plan. She didn't want to muddy the waters with a briefing before the speech, but maybe on the way back you two can visit."

His face fell.

"I'm not briefing the vice president before her speech?"

"No, I'm sorry."

"Then why am I even on this trip?"

"For the hot meal," Dale pointed at his clean plate and the empty bread bowl. She saw Karen smile.

Dale stood to talk to the speechwriters. She handed them the vice president's edits and asked them to double-check the teleprompter to make sure the new version was loaded as soon as they landed. As they began their descent, Dale stood to use the bathroom quickly. When she got back to her seat, she put on her seat belt and powered up her BlackBerry and cell phone. By the time they got down to ten thousand feet, her messages started coming through.

They landed and boarded the cars for the short motorcade ride to the convention center. When the vice president took the stage, she seemed surprised by the warm reception. She kept looking over at where Dale and the rest of her staff were standing. When she looked in Dale's direction, Dale smiled and gave her a thumbs-up sign.

Once the applause died down, Tara straightened her jacket, cleared her throat, and began speaking. Dale was following the vice president's text on her own copy of the speech. Her delivery was passable—not smooth, but not halting, either, and the crowd was paying close attention. When she got to the section about business tax cuts, the audience was on its feet. Sending less money to the federal government was always a crowd-pleaser with small business owners. Tara looked like she was starting to enjoy herself. She looked up and laughed at a woman in her seventies holding a "Tara Meyers for President" sign. When the applause died down again, she looked from side to side where her teleprompter panels stood, but she didn't start speaking. Dale felt her own breathing quicken. "Come on, Tara, come on. Find your place," she said under her breath. Tara looked down at the stack of pages on her podium. She flipped through them but couldn't seem to find the right page. She looked up again—desperately looking at the teleprompters. Dale raced toward the back of the room where a frazzled teleprompter operator was covered with sweat as he tried to bring the machine back on line.

"It just went down," he said.

"Do we have a backup?" Dale asked. She was starting to panic. She looked up, and the vice president looked like she would rather melt away than stand there any longer. Her eyes were scanning the room. Dale knew she was looking for her, but for once, she didn't have any ready-made solutions. Tara started to fiddle with the microphone mounted on the podium. The crowd was growing uncomfortable with the silence. It wasn't just television audiences who had grown accustomed to flawless, made-for-television performances from politicians.

Dale felt a bead of sweat run down her back. She considered screaming at the teleprompter operator, but there was no point. He was lying on the ground frantically untangling the wires.

Dale looked up again, and Tara's eyes were locked on her, searching for guidance about what she was supposed to do next. Dale forced an exaggerated smile onto her face and made a circular motion with her hand to signal to Tara that she needed to keep things moving. Something in Tara's mind clicked. She stepped out from behind the podium, tossed her speech into the air, and headed toward the audience. A few members of the audience clapped nervously. Someone from the White House communications office handed her a wireless microphone.

"You guys ready to leave the script behind and get down to business?" Tara asked, taking a seat on the edge of the stage.

The crowd clapped more enthusiastically now, and a few of them whistled. Dale exhaled for the first time in what felt like thirty minutes but was probably more like two.

By getting out from behind the podium, Tara was transformed into a charismatic talk-show host. She hopped off the stage and made her way from table to table, mixing personal finance advice with insults for Washington and the lobbyists. She brought the crowd to its feet on several occasions with thunderous applause. And when she called on a woman who'd recently lost her job as a realtor, the room grew so quiet Dale could hear the lights hum.

While all eyes were on the woman, Dale watched the vice president. She was listening with her whole body. Her shoulders slumped when the woman spoke of bouncing from shelter to shelter after losing her home to foreclosure. She spoke of the humiliation of moving her children from school to school and showing up at the employment center every day to search for work. Dale saw Tara switch off the microphone and stand perfectly still, as though listening for just a few moments with all the force she could muster could make some of the woman's pain go away. When the woman finished speaking, Tara wiped a tear from her eye, walked over to her, and without switching her microphone back on, spoke to her for a couple of minutes. The audience remained quiet. After their private conversation, Tara turned her microphone back on, returned to the stage, and stared straight into the cameras.

"That, my friends, is what the politicians who you send to Washington are supposed to prevent. The pain that Lucy Thompson and her two daughters have known should not be possible in the most prosperous and technologically advanced nation in the world. And that, ladies and gentleman, the story of Lucy Thompson, is exactly what President Kramer had in mind when she tore up the playbook and crafted this new jobs bill," Tara said. The entire crowd was on its feet with a standing ovation. When it ended, Tara hopped back down for a few more questions.

Dale leaned against the wall and tried to compose an e-mail to the head of operations about buying a teleprompter that wasn't in use during World War I. She felt one of her phones vibrating in her purse. Dale was about to hit "ignore" but she recognized the number as the Situation Room operator.

"Hello?" she whispered with her hand over her mouth.

"Dale, Ralph here. Tara is bringing down the house. Was the prompter going down a stunt or did it really break?" Ralph asked.

"That was real. I'm glad you enjoyed the drama. It took five years off my life."

"It looks great. Tell her I was watching and thought she did a fantastic job," he said.

"She'll appreciate that," Dale said.

"Listen, I got your message on Monday, and I want you to know that I understand how challenging your job is sometimes, but we really need you to keep things together over there. You can handle this, Dale, I know you can."

"I appreciate your confidence in me, but I don't know if you are aware of how things are on our side of the complex. I think she's having a really hard time with some aspects of the job."

"I'm watching her on three cable channels right now and she looks fine to me. I'm going to show the clip of Tara with the homeless lady to Charlotte. She could stand to show a little more empathy in her speeches on the economy," Ralph said.

"Look, she's had a great event here, but I'm worried about her. Something isn't right," Dale said.

"Shhh. Don't ever talk about this stuff around the rest of the staff. Use your personal phone when you call me on any issue related to this topic. And from this point on, absolutely no e-mails about Tara, understood?"

"I understand. What do you want me to do about Michael Robbins? He has three calls in to me and I can't get him to hold his story on the V.P. forever."

Ralph was silent. Dale thought she'd been disconnected.

"Ralph?" she asked.

"Dale, this is why you were hired. Handle it."

CHAPTER TWELVE

Charlotte

Charlotte walked with her secretaries of defense and state toward the conference room where the bilateral meeting with the Russians that had been added to her G8 schedule at the last minute would be held.

Their group was quite a sight. Three middle-aged women—a blur of Armani power-suits, perfect blowouts, and sensible stilettos—walked in tandem toward the meeting room where they'd stare down Russia's old guard.

"Can we bluff a little bit on the new sanctions language?" Charlotte asked her secretary of state, Constance Friedman, a longtime career diplomat whom Charlotte had promoted to the top diplomatic post during her first term.

"Depends on how much brinksmanship you want to play with them," she said.

Charlotte smiled and quickened her pace.

"Do Russian men speak any language other than brinksmanship?" Charlotte asked.

Her secretaries of state and defense chuckled. Diplo-humor had a small but faithful audience, especially at international summits that showcased the imagery of multilateralism but rarely produced any breakthroughs.

"I think you can mess with them a little bit by telling them the other nations are on board already," Melanie whispered just before they entered the meeting room. Constance nodded in agreement, and Charlotte's eyes twinkled.

"Good morning, Madam President," the Russian president, Andrei Stanimir, said. Melanie and Constance greeted their counterparts and sat down next to the U.S. translator. On the other side of the table, the Russians sat in an identical formation.

Charlotte dispensed with the niceties. The Russians didn't appreciate them anyway.

"I don't imagine you enjoy the bloviating that goes on at these things any more than I do," Charlotte said.

Stanimir watched Charlotte carefully.

"No, I do not," he said.

Charlotte tucked her chin slightly and looked up at him.

"What do you say we break with tradition this week and actually get something done?" Charlotte asked, her eyes never moving from the Russian president while the translator spoke into his ear.

After a brief delay, his face relaxed into as much of a smile as a former KGB officer could muster.

"I'm relieved that you're not here to pressure me into some feel-good aid package for Africa or something," he said.

"I'd never waste your time with something like that, Mr. President," Charlotte said.

"Well then, what do you have in mind?" the Russian leader asked.

"You know as well as I do that the UN Security Council's sanctions vote on Iran is toothless without Russia's vote," Charlotte said. The Russian leader leaned back in his chair and smiled at his Russian colleagues.

"Yes, I know it's a familiar topic for you, and I do apologize if you and your colleagues have grown weary of the issue, but the fact is that your country is propping up a man who, frankly, represents a greater danger to his own citizens and his neighbors than he does to the United States. Yet my country understands the importance of dealing with the threat Iran poses to global security. It would appear, Mr. President, that you either don't understand the threat or are comfortable with your role as an enabler for a belligerent and dangerous Iranian regime," Charlotte said.

"Two questions, Madam President: Did you come here to lecture us, and are you finished?" Stanimir asked.

"Not quite. We hoped that you would take the opportunity presented to you this week to send a stronger message to Iran," Charlotte said.

The Russians exchanged bored glances.

"Madam President, we have stood with the United States of America on many occasions, but of course you are experienced enough now to understand that sanctions have no effect on the regime—they simply harm the Iranian people," he said.

Charlotte leaned forward and kept her eyes locked on his.

"That's why we're pairing the next sanctions vote with new Security Council language that makes it crystal clear that the global community has been ignored and disrespected by the Iranian regime for the last time," Charlotte said.

"I see. And how do you intend to convey this latest ultimatum to the Iranians?" the Russian president asked.

"We've already circulated language committing all Security Council members to military action. As a last resort, of course," Charlotte said calmly.

"And the other nations have agreed to this?" the Russian defense minister asked.

"Yes," Melanie and Charlotte replied in unison.

"I find that hard to believe," Stanimir said.

"Then go ask them yourself. I was asked to bring the language to you since we already had this meeting scheduled. No one thought it would be fair to present the new language to you when we're all seated together with a full press contingent filming our every move," Charlotte said.

The Russians didn't hide their irritation. When the translator finished, they pushed themselves away from the table and moved to the back of the room to huddle. Charlotte, Constance, and Melanie sat in silence. They had succeeded in boxing in the Russians, but, of course, Charlotte was bluffing. The U.S. hadn't shared the new language with any of the other allies yet. If Russia signed on, the others would fall into line. There would be consequences for playing games with the

Russians, but if Charlotte could get a strong enough statement out of the UN Security Council, she could convince Israel to delay taking matters into its own hands.

The three women watched the Russians carefully. The defense minister was agitated. The Russian president was listening to his aides with dwindling patience. After another minute of deliberation, the defense minister stormed out of the meeting room. The president and his foreign minister returned to the table and sat down slowly. Stanimir looked at Charlotte with unblinking, ice-blue eyes that gave Charlotte a bit of the creeps but otherwise failed to unnerve her.

"Madam President, you came to a friendly discussion prepared for negotiations. We were caught unprepared. That is our fault. It will not happen again. Perhaps you will be more focused on the problems facing the world and less focused on your personal travails in your second term," he said. The insult was designed to knock Charlotte down a notch.

"We came with the expectation that Russia is always prepared to negotiate," Charlotte said, smiling evenly.

"Russia will support the new sanctions language if the United States will call off the public relations machine that works around the clock to slander and harass the Russian businesses who are simply bringing products and services to a hungry Iranian economy. Do we have your word that the attacks on our businesses will stop?" he asked.

"Mr. President, I do not have the power to stifle the private activities of American citizens. The right to protest policies that our citizens disagree with is the bedrock of our democracy," Charlotte said. She kicked Melanie under the table. She couldn't believe the Russians were about to sign on to the military language that would finally put some muscle into the sanctions against Iran.

"I trust you will use your influence and extensive powers of persuasion then, Madam President, to discourage such negative attention for Russia's most vital businesses," he said.

"Of course, Mr. President."

"Very well. I have another meeting to attend, but I am pleased that we were able to spend some time together today, Madam President."

The defeated Russians and their translator left the room in single file. As soon as the door closed behind them, Constance stood up and did a little dance.

The sight of the normally stoic diplomat frolicking around the room made Charlotte laugh.

"It's a good outcome, right?"

"That was incredible. We need to celebrate," Constance said.

"Madam President, I think the technical term for what you just showed him might start with a b and rhyme with walls," Melanie said.

"We'll pay for it down the road, but at least we'll get a good result out of this trip. How about a celebration drink in my room tonight?" Charlotte said.

"Sorry, I have a working dinner with the Japanese foreign minister, and we all know how long that will drag on," Constance said.

"I'll take you up on it," Melanie said.

As Charlotte walked back to her room, she thought about how much had changed since her first term. Her status as the newly reelected American president with unprecedented levels of popular support from the American public was widely noted—and envied—in the vanity-soaked halls of the G8. While Charlotte enjoyed her peers' newfound admiration, it didn't have the same impact on her that it might have had four years earlier. She was on more solid ground now. She'd learned how to ride the political storms and trust the voters with the truth—no matter how unpleasant. That was how she'd won reelection. It was how she'd survived the public revelation of Peter's romance with Dale and smoothed over her new vice president's early gaffes. And it was how she planned to bring the other leaders to the table to avoid a military conflict with Iran.

She spent the rest of the day having productive discussions with her counterparts from France, Italy, Germany, and Great Britain. The Brits thought it was hilarious that she'd fooled the Russians. After ten grueling hours of sit-downs and press availabilities, she returned to her room. Charlotte was changing out of her suit when she heard Melanie at the door.

"Come in," she shouted from the bedroom. Melanie walked in and took off her shoes before sinking into a sofa.

"These things are brutal," she said.

"I know. The greetings take up more time than the conversations. Welcome to diplomacy," Charlotte said.

"What are you doing in there?" Melanie asked.

"Changing," Charlotte said. She emerged in leggings and a long sweater. "Do you want to borrow something more comfortable?"

"One glass of wine and I'll forget I'm in a suit," Melanie laughed.

"How's Congress treating you?" Charlotte asked.

"There are some old codgers who will never come around, but I'm making progress."

Melanie had managed to win over even her most skeptical critics with her depth of knowledge about current military operations and her stamina and enthusiasm for the job. It didn't hurt her credibility on Capitol Hill or around the world that she had Charlotte's ear on all matters.

"Let me know if I can help," Charlotte offered.

"I will. How was Afghanistan?"

"Good. I spent some time with General Ackerley and the top intelligence and state department folks. They're running a tight ship."

"We're still losing too many guys," Melanie said, shaking her head.

"I know. Every time I get the report in the morning I hold my breath until I know that Will wasn't among them."

Will was Brooke and Mark's nineteen-year-old son. He'd enlisted when she'd been reelected.

"He's a smart kid," Melanie said.

Charlotte nodded. "A lot of smart kids end up dead over there," she said.

Melanie was silent.

"Sorry to be such a downer. Listen, why don't you and Brian come up to Camp David next weekend? We're going to celebrate Brooke's fiftieth birthday. She's so pissed she's fifty that she wouldn't let Mark do anything. We're flying all the kids out and a few of their friends from home, and we're going to surprise her."

"I'd love to see that! Are you sure you have room?" Melanie asked.

"Of course," Charlotte said. They ordered from the room-service menu and settled into the sofa with their glasses of wine.

"How's Tara doing?" Melanie asked.

Charlotte sighed and took a sip of wine before answering.

"Fine, I'm told."

"You're told?"

"By Ralph. He says she's doing great, which is obviously an exaggeration, but I still think she'll get there," Charlotte said.

"Mmmn hmmn," Melanie said.

"Mmmn hmmn, what?"

"Nothing. I hope Ralph is right."

"Me too," Charlotte said.

"Do you think you'll get the Security Council votes on Iran?"

"I don't know. Why don't you set up some meetings in New York when you get back? Go meet with some of the UN ambassadors. Tell them I sent you personally. It would be really great to get that vote. It would strengthen our hand on everything else."

"Yeah, of course," Melanie replied.

"I feel good about things, Mel. You know I never say that. I hate to jinx myself, but I really feel like we have a shot at doing some big things."

Melanie held up her glass, and Charlotte leaned over to touch hers to Melanie's.

"To second terms," Charlotte said.

"To less-eventful second terms," Melanie added.

CHAPTER THIRTEEN

Tara

"Twenty-two, twenty-three, come on Tara, two more," Marcus demanded.

Tara looked up at her husband and barely recognized the man sitting on her feet screaming at her.

"Two more sit-ups, Tara, that's all I ask," he barked again. The exertion of his yelling caused a blood vessel in his temple to pulse visibly.

Tara stifled a laugh as she contemplated what her Secret Service agents must think of their strange new protectees. She lay back on the floor and covered her face with her hands.

"Don't touch your face—do you know how much oil and bacteria is on your hands after a workout?"

She ignored his instruction about removing her hands from her face. Marcus dug his knees into her feet and tightened his grip on her lower legs.

"Dammit, Tara. Finish something, for once. Two more sit-ups."

She was missing a National Security Council meeting because Marcus had insisted that she start carving out time to take better care of herself. She'd agreed, and now, an hour and a half later, in what felt like a grim reenactment of a *Biggest Loser* episode, the decision felt ridiculous.

"Marcus, please get off of me," she said calmly.

"Not until you finish two more sit-ups."

"Marcus, I need to get to the office. I know you're trying to help me, and, God knows, I need the motivation, but right now, I need to go to work," she repeated.

"Not until you finish what we started."

"Marcus, you're being crazy."

"You disgust me," he said harshly before digging his knees into her feet one last time and then pushing himself up with a rough shove. She could hardly feel her feet.

"I'm going to go shower and get dressed," Tara said quietly.

While she was still struggling to her feet, Marcus had hopped on the treadmill and was running at what looked like ten miles an hour. He didn't look away from his reflection in the mirror as she limped from the gym in the basement of the Naval Observatory and climbed the stairs to her bedroom. It had been nearly a month since she turned in the performance at the Small Business Conference that had earned her praise from the audience and had bought her some much-needed time with the press and among her skeptics. The *Washington Post* had written that Charlotte was the brains of the White House, and Tara its bleeding heart. She'd taken it as a compliment. The pressure to continue to connect like that was starting to eat away at her. She was frustrated that the moments in which she was speaking with authority about something were the ones that were never being filmed by the press. On the other hand, when the prying eyes of the press corps that now seemed to shadow her every move were present, she stumbled, misspoke, and put her foot in her mouth every time, without fail.

She turned on the shower and stared at her reflection in the bathroom mirror. She pulled out the adult acne medicine Marcus had purchased from one of the home shopping channels and started rubbing the lotion on her face. It burned so much that her eyes watered.

"How did this happen?" she wondered aloud. Of course, she knew exactly how it had happened. She'd made a deal with the devil when she'd decided to keep her condition a secret and pursue a life in public service. And that devil had a name: Marcus. He'd become the unofficial enforcer of her secret, and he took the responsibility as seriously as the Secret Service took their oath to protect her physical safety.

As the bathroom filled with steam, she reached for the phone and asked to be connected to her personal assistant.

"Hi, Karen," she said.

"Madam Vice President, is everything okay?"

"Yes, yes, everything is fine. I'm on my way in. I had to take care of some things at Kendall's school this morning," she said.

"Oh, you were at Sidwell?"

"No, no, just a phone conference, a conference call, I mean, you know, with teachers and the principal and everything," she said. Of course she couldn't say she'd been at the school when she hadn't— other parents would have noticed her fifteen-car motorcade. She squeezed her eyes shut and opened them again. The lies were getting hard to keep straight. She blamed the weight gain on a rare thyroid disorder and her breakouts on the change in climate from New York to Washington, D.C. Her frequent absences from work were because her daughter was having a tough time adjusting to a new school. And when Tara was conspicuously absent from Kendall's school events, she blamed her job.

"Hey, Karen, do we still have the hair and makeup gals on staff?" Tara asked. She used them so infrequently that they'd been placed on standby and only reported to the White House in advance of major appearances.

"Yes ma'am."

"Do you think you could send them up to the residence right now?" Tara asked.

"Yes ma'am. They'll be there as soon as I can get a car to take them."

"Thank you, Karen. I'll see you soon," Tara said.

She hung up and wiped a circle of the mirror clean so she could see herself.

She stared at her reflection again and remembered when she first experienced the depths of her own dark mind. She'd been studying abroad in Venice, Italy, with one of her favorite law school professors. For the first couple of weeks of her European stint, everything had gone reasonably well. She'd noticed that her sleep patterns were a little off, but figured her body clock was adjusting to the new time zone and the hours that the locals kept. Tara had never been out of the country before, but instead of taking in the sights and pleasures of Venice, she had obsessed over her studies. Her seminar was on European trade law, and the class schedule was unpredictable, which caused Tara great anxiety. She'd pull all-nighters trying to digest the unfamiliar material, and then she'd show up only to have her professor abandon the day's lecture and quiz to take the students to a museum or a three-hour lunch outside the city. While her classmates had seemed to love the spontaneity of the summer session, it threw Tara into a tailspin.

She had a particularly vivid memory of showing up for class after a grueling week of studies to find a note on the door from her professor asking the students to meet him for a walking tour of his favorite piazzas. Tara had fought back tears of frustration while the other students ran home to dump their book bags. As they wandered around Venice, Tara had stood back from the small group of girls who pressed their faces in the windows of the shops and the guys who'd tried to get their attention. She'd ignored the insights from her professor's Italian friend who was conducting the tour, and thought about how long it would take her later that night to rememorize the cases she'd studied the night before. When she had finally returned to her flat, she'd refused a rare invitation from her roommates to join them for dinner and had pulled her books out to start studying again. By this point, Tara was completely strung out from the long nights of studying and the uncertainty of the timing of their oral and written exams. The next morning, she'd heard her roommates showering and figured they were heading off for a day of sightseeing or shopping. It was Saturday, and that was the one day Tara allowed herself to sleep in and take in a tourist attraction before she started studying. She'd held her pillow over her face while her roommates had banged around in the kitchen, and she'd willed herself back to sleep after they'd left.

When she woke up around two P.M., she'd been surprised to hear the cars whizzing past her window. Their neighborhood was usually quiet on weekends. She'd dressed slowly and wandered out for a coffee and a pastry. Her adherence to the Weight Watchers points system had lasted only until she took her first bite of the flat, tasty Italian version of pizza. She was certain she consumed a day's worth of points at every meal in Venice, and she had the expanding waistline to show for it.

She'd gulped her milky coffee down and had asked the woman at the pastry shop what was going on that day to explain the traffic. Tara's Italian was so poor that the woman had answered her in English.

"It's not that busy for a Friday," she'd said.

Tara stopped breathing. She'd missed class. She'd thought it was Saturday. She ran from the bakery to the school and threw open the door just as the students were filing out. Choking back tears, she ran to her professor.

"I thought today was Saturday. I'm so sorry I missed class. Did I miss the exam? I missed the exam," she cried.

"Easy, Tara. Relax. You can take it next week. It's not a big deal," he promised.

"No, no, I can't put it off another week. I can't believe I missed the test."

"Don't worry, Tara. It's no problem. We'll do it after class on Monday," he said. "Get some sun this weekend. You look exhausted."

She didn't stop crying until she got back to her flat. She locked herself in her room and vowed to study all weekend so she'd nail the test on Monday. She remembered drinking several Italian espressos and going out in the middle of the night looking for more, but that's where her clear and sequential memories of the episode stopped. She remembered the sound of her door being kicked in by one of the neighbors. Tara recalled a scratchy blanket being thrown around her and remembered being shoved into the backseat of a cab. The cab must have taken her to the emergency room.

According to her records from the Italian hospital, her roommates became so concerned about her on Sunday night, after not seeing or hearing from her all weekend, that they broke into her room and found her lying naked on the floor with textbooks and notebooks open all around her.

Tara suspected that the "rescue" undertaken by her summer roommates was not entirely motivated by concern for her well-being. The admitting physician at the hospital had noted in her file that she'd soiled herself, and in the steamy Venice summer, it was quite possible that Tara had been stinking up the small flat they'd all shared.

Tara hadn't had any sense of how long she'd been in the hospital, but she remembered feeling like everything had finally slowed down. People's voices had the low, slow sound of a video playing in slow motion. She didn't understand anything anyone said to her, but it wasn't unpleasant. She'd felt uncharacteristically relaxed. Eventually, an English-speaking doctor had come to talk to her. He'd told her that she'd been there for ten days, during which they'd observed her and kept her mostly sedated while they waited for some of the drugs to normalize her brain chemistry. He'd described her state as catatonic when she'd arrived, but after a few days, she'd started responding to the medicine. They had asked her how long she'd been depressed. She remembered thinking that everyone felt down from time to time and that her sustained periods of the blues were nothing out of the ordinary. The doctors had asked her if she remembered a time when she wasn't down. She couldn't. They'd thrown around terms like bipolar disorder and manic depression and had recommended several prescriptions to help her.

The doctors had surmised that her condition revealed itself because of the triggers created by the dramatic change in her surroundings and routine. The English-speaking doctor suggested a return to a more supportive environment and a less stressful career path. But Tara's mind was made up. She'd done internships at the Manhattan D.A.'s office and could not imagine doing anything else with her life. The law was neat and clean. Everything else about Tara's life had been messy and chaotic. She'd wrapped herself in the law's rigidity and steeped herself in its arcane ways. She was made for a career in the law, and she was determined to make New York her home. On top of that, she was certain that she wanted to work as a government prosecutor. She was confident that those jobs were available only to the mentally fit. Perhaps a private practice would accommodate an attorney with a history of mental health issues, but Tara had learned enough about the profile of a government prosecutor to know that if it were ever discovered that she suffered from depression or bipolar disorder or anything along those lines, she was finished.

Besides, Tara didn't have a supportive environment to return to. She hadn't spoken to her family since she'd left years earlier for what they'd thought was a job in upstate New York. Tara had secretly applied to and been accepted at Albany University when she was eighteen years old. She'd received a full scholarship. Her mother, six brothers, and two sisters all lived within a few miles from where they'd all grown up in Michigan's remote Upper Peninsula. Her father had died of a heart attack when she was eleven years old, just weeks after the bank had foreclosed on his auto supply store. The last she'd heard, her mother was bedridden from complications associated with diabetes. Tara was the only person in her family to go to college, and she was certain that they would not understand why she'd followed college with law school and a career in public service. Her plan was never to find out how they felt about her life choices. She had not seen any of them in nearly two decades.

Before she had checked out of the hospital in Venice, she'd asked the doctors for a supply of the drugs that would last her a few months. She had lied and said she didn't have health insurance.

"America is so uncivilized. The lawyers don't even have health care," one of the Italian doctors had muttered under his breath as he filled a small shopping bag with her various prescriptions. Once she was back in the States, Tara rationed the drugs—taking only about a third of the prescribed pills so they'd last longer. She had no intention of seeking any further psychiatric care in the States when they ran out, and she'd hoped that the patient-doctor confidentiality laws would ensure that her hospitalization in Italy would remain a secret.

After graduating from law school near the top of her class, she went to work in the Manhattan District Attorney's Office. She rose through the ranks, impressing the prosecutors with her work ethic and knowledge. Tara made the jump to the U.S. Attorney's Office a few years later. That was where she met Marcus. He was an FBI agent who had recently joined the prestigious counterterrorism unit after working undercover for three years to bust one of the biggest illegal drug rings in the Northeast. Tara desperately wanted to join the U.S. Attorney's elite counterterror unit, which worked hand in hand with the FBI, but those were the plum cases, and she didn't have the political connections or the years of experience necessary to get that assignment. She rarely spoke to anyone at the office, but the attorneys had occasion to collaborate with the investigators, so she and Marcus crossed paths from time to time. Marcus was more than happy to boast about the cases he was working to an attentive young lawyer. And Tara was desperate enough to learn as much as she could about the counterterrorism unit that she listened to his stories about his years undercover. Over a long, hot New York summer, Marcus even convinced Tara to come to a few Yankees games with him.

Marcus and Tara became a couple. They shared an ambition born from a desire to erase their pasts with professional accomplishment. Ten months into their courtship, Marcus took Tara to dinner at Felidia, a fancy Italian restaurant on New York's Upper East Side.

"Tara, I think you are brilliant."

"You do?"

"Yes. You don't treat any of the cases you work on like they are simply files; you treat each and every one of them like an opportunity to right a wrong. It's very admirable," he said.

"Thank you."

"You are very special. I think you will go very far in this business." He smiled at her a little shyly.

She was so happy that someone recognized how much she cared about her work. Her eyes welled up with tears.

"What's wrong? What did I say?"

"Nothing. It's nothing."

He watched her closely.

"You're very kind to say those things, Marcus."

"They are true."

She took a deep breath and fought back more tears.

"I don't think I'll get very far at all in this business if anyone finds out the truth."

Marcus's eyes widened.

"When I was in law school I was hospitalized."

She couldn't look at him, but she forced herself to continue. The secret was suffocating her. She had to tell someone.

"I was hospitalized for depression."

He barely blinked while she detailed exactly what had happened during her summer abroad. She didn't spare him a single unflattering detail. She felt more and more unburdened with every passing second. When she finished, he was looking at her with complete adoration.

"Thank you for sharing that with me," he said.

She felt drained, but she smiled at him and then finished her cold ravioli dish.

A week later, he proposed.

Tara shook her head. "Why do you want to be with me?" she asked.

"We're good together," he said, taking her in his arms. "And I love you. Besides, you need me."

She nodded and tried to ignore the fact that relief was the primary emotion she felt that day, not love or affection for Marcus. They were married eight weeks later at City Hall. A few of their colleagues from the office were there, but neither invited any of their family members. After the wedding, they both threw themselves back into their work. Whenever Tara's load at the office became too grueling, Marcus buffered her from outside demands. He became her protector and her gatekeeper.

Now, in the steamy bathroom in the Naval Observatory, more than fifteen years later, Tara looked down at her feet. Bluish bruises were beginning to form where Marcus had been kneeling on her. Tara felt guilty about not finishing the workout. He had sacrificed so much for her over the years.

She reflected on how promising things had seemed in New York all those years earlier. Even then, Marcus had enjoyed Tara's success more than his own. He'd encouraged her and supported her and shielded her when the stress was too much. When local Democrats urged her to run for attorney general in New York, he'd been the one who assured her that they would keep her well enough to handle the job. When the White House had called, she knew she should say no. But Marcus would have none of it. "We can do this," he'd promised. "We have it under control."

Her symptoms had worsened with the move to Washington, D.C.

The relocation and the intense scrutiny in her new job had brought her to new lows. Many mornings, she'd lie in bed with a headache so debilitating, she couldn't move. If she stayed in bed for a couple of days, usually the clouds would begin to lift. But the stress, all of the time in bed, and her constant cravings for sweets and other starches had taken a toll. She had gained twenty pounds and had a wicked case of adult acne.

She heard a knock on the door. The hair and makeup folks must have arrived. She hadn't showered yet.

"Tara?"

It was Marcus. She froze.

"I know you can hear me. Listen, someone sent the hair and makeup folks up here by mistake."

She remained silent.

"I told them you didn't need hair and makeup today because you were working from home." Marcus had taken it upon himself to determine each day whether she was of sound enough mind to make an appearance at the White House. Increasingly, he thought the risk of criticism for missing work or canceling events was less than the risk of someone figuring out that Tara suffered from serious and debilitating swings of depression and despondency. That's why he had allowed the hair and makeup girls to leave thinking that the right hand didn't know what the left hand was doing. He'd much rather that than to have anyone on the White House staff see her in the throes of one of her low periods.

She waited for him to walk out, and then she stepped into the shower where her tears disappeared in the hot water cascading over her face and body.

CHAPTER FOURTEEN

Dale

Dale set the out-of-office wizard on her e-mail and reached down to turn off her computer. It was one A.M. She was confirmed on a six A.M. flight to San Francisco later that morning. She packed up three issues of the *Economist* and walked out of the Old Executive Office Building to where her car was parked on West Executive Drive.

She was spending the weekend in San Francisco with Peter. They'd both agreed that it was time to figure things out. The phone had proven itself an inadequate substitute for face time. Dale was always distracted when he called during the day and exhausted when he called at night, so they never made much progress in determining the status of their relationship. At best, their romance was on life support. Dale felt sick to her stomach about the worst-case scenario: the possibility that Peter was actually over her. She'd placed so much distance between them—geographically and otherwise—that she feared he'd finally given up.

Before she pulled out of the White House, she noticed that the lights were still on in the White House residence. It was out of the ordinary for the president to be in D.C. on a Friday night. She almost always traveled to Camp David, a short helicopter ride from Washington, on the weekends.

Dale shook her head slightly as if to shake off the notion that her boyfriend's ex-wife, the president of the United States of America, was probably up watching television or reading in the next building.

She put her car into reverse and backed slowly out of her parking spot. She waved good night to the guard and drove out of the White House complex. As she passed through the empty streets, she thought about how insane it would have seemed to her if someone had suggested a year earlier that she'd be part of the same administration her secret affair had nearly toppled. Luckily for her, Charlotte hadn't seen it that way. In fact, after the accident in Afghanistan and the subsequent loss of Dale's job at the network, Charlotte had been one of the only people who'd understood that losing her job was as traumatic for her as the physical injuries she'd suffered. When she'd been offered the position on the vice president's staff after the election, it had been made clear to her by Ralph that Charlotte had approved the appointment herself. Dale's presence was undoubtedly a reminder of the drama that surrounded Charlotte in her first term, but the public's fascination with Tara had, so far, provided enough of a distraction from Dale and Charlotte's shared history.

Dale left her packed bag in her car and went upstairs to her apartment to catch a couple hours of sleep. She woke to the blinking light of her BlackBerry, checked it for important messages, showered, and rushed to the airport. She parked her car in hourly parking and e-mailed herself the exact location so she'd be able to find it Monday morning when she returned on the red-eye.

As she settled into her seat in first class for the five-and-a-half-hour flight, she reveled at the thought of being out of cell phone and e-mail range. She'd never been one of the members of the press corps who'd thought the White House staff had it easy, but she hadn't truly appreciated how hard everyone, from the unpaid interns to the chief of staff, worked.

Whatever anxiety she had about seeing Peter after more than six weeks of strained phone conversations and three postponed weekend trips evaporated when she saw him standing at the gate waiting for her. His blond hair was lighter than usual, and he looked tan and fit. She felt flabby and pale in comparison. He pulled her into an embrace, and she buried her head in his chest. She wrapped her hands tightly around his body.

Peter pulled away and looked down at her crumpled face.

"What's wrong?" he asked.

"I'm just happy to see you," she said. She stared into his eyes. They were the color of a teal blue Crayola crayon.

"You look exhausted," he said, examining her face.

"And after six hours in the air, this is a well-rested me," she said, smiling through her tears and leaning in for another embrace.

"But you're having fun, I hope?"

"I wouldn't say that," she said, rolling her eyes.

"You better be," he teased.

She felt guilty about complaining about the job that had jeopardized their life together.

"It's fine, really. I feel good about being able to contribute, you know?" she said.

"I do," he said.

She wasn't sure if he meant he knew because he'd endured Charlotte's need to pursue politics, or if he was just trying to sound understanding, but she didn't want to ruin their reunion with another explanation of her decision to take the White House job instead of settling down with him in San Francisco. They'd had that conversation many times before, and it never ended well.

"Listen, since it's still early in the day, I thought we could head out to Stinson Beach and do a little hiking and then maybe have lunch in Tiburon. How does that sound?" he asked.

"Perfect," she said, squeezing his hand as they walked toward where his car was parked. Since he and Charlotte had separated, he'd scaled back on Secret Service protection. He still had a protective detail for public events and when he traveled with the kids, but the Secret Service allowed him to drive himself, and they no longer stayed overnight at his house.

Dale looked over at Peter as he drove. She couldn't read his face. She was surprised that he didn't want to head home first. Their normal routine was to fall into bed together before anything else. Maybe things really had changed between them.

They pulled into the parking lot at Stinson Beach, and despite her worry about whether Peter was going to cut things off once and for all, she felt calmed by the sight of the waves crashing on the beach.

She was glad he had suggested the hike. She pulled her running shoes and a fleece jacket out of her bag and put them on while Peter patiently watched.

They walked hand in hand for a while, and when the trail narrowed, Peter allowed her to lead. After about forty-five minutes, she stopped and turned around to face him.

"If your objective was to make me realize that I'm a total idiot for moving to D.C., you have succeeded." She leaned in and gave him a kiss on the lips.

He smiled and kissed her back.

"Come on. I didn't have any ulterior motives. I thought it would be nice to get some fresh air," he said, turning away from her and looking out at the fog that had settled like a blanket on the surface of the Pacific Ocean.

They hiked for another hour and then returned to the car.

When Peter took a different road than the one they'd come in on, Dale figured he was taking a scenic route or a back road. After about ten minutes he turned down a steep driveway and drove toward a charming beach house on a cliff overlooking the Pacific Ocean.

"Where are we going? Does one of your players live here?" she asked.

"I want to show you something," he said.

"A house?"

"Yes. A house."

He turned off the ignition and got out of the Land Rover. Dale sat in the car for a minute racking her brain to figure out what he was up to. When she opened the door, he was standing by her side of the car.

"Come check out our new beach house."

"What?" she asked. She was trying to keep the alarm she felt out of her voice.

"I thought it would be more 'us' than the city. And we've never really had a place that we made into a home together," he said.

Now Dale was afraid to get out of the car. She was afraid of letting Peter pull her back to him—back to San Francisco.

"You bought us a house? I don't even know how much time I'm going to be able to spend out here," she said.

"I know. I just thought it would be nice to have a place to get away to. At least get out of the car and check it out." He was starting to sound exasperated.

Dale stepped out of the car and walked toward the front door. The homes in Stinson Beach were quite different from the manicured mansions and quaint Victorians in Pacific Heights. Peter was right. It did feel more like them. Wildflowers grew in patches all over the front yard. The wood-shingled house looked like it could be pushed off the cliff by a forceful wind. She could see straight through the house to the ocean below. Peter opened the front door with a key he had on his key chain.

"Welcome home," he said.

Dale walked inside and couldn't help but smile. There was no furniture, but the interior had been recently renovated. The smell of fresh paint hung in the damp air and the windows still had the manufacturers' stickers on them.

"Did you do the renovation?" Dale asked. Before he answered, she knew he had. The understated elegance of the place was pure Peter.

"Without you around, I have an abundance of free time these days."

"I guess so," she said, admiring a bay window in the kitchen.

"Let me show you around," he said, taking her hand.

Dale followed him from room to room and noticed his attention to every detail. There were floor-to-ceiling windows everywhere, pale wood floors the color of sand, and walls the color of candlelight. In the master bathroom, Peter had placed a bathtub and shower in front of a window that overlooked the ocean. The rest of the house felt like one endless space.

"What do you think?" he asked.

"It's exquisite," she said.

Peter looked nervous.

"Do you really like it? I was afraid you'd feel too exposed, especially in the bedroom, but it's not like people can see us from the ocean," he said.

"No, no. It's perfect. It would be a crime to cover any of these views," she said, pressing her forehead against the window. She took a deep breath and tried to relax, but the thought of Peter buying, remodeling, and surprising her with a home was too much. His generosity smothered her with a new layer of guilt about taking a job three thousand miles away.

Peter came up behind her and put his arms around her waist. Dale stiffened.

"What's wrong?"

"Nothing. It's perfect," she said. And it was. She tried again to relax but her mind was racing. On top of the guilt she felt about being a shitty girlfriend, she hadn't had BlackBerry service since they'd arrived at Stinson Beach hours earlier. She could only imagine how many unreturned messages she had on her e-mail and cell phone.

"I was so scared that you'd hate it," he said.

"Why would you think I'd hate it?" she asked defensively.

"For one, the cell service out here sucks," he said.

"Really?"

"I've seen you turn your BlackBerry on and off half a dozen times. You know it sucks," he said.

She spun out of his embrace and faced him.

"You think I'm obsessive and unbalanced for checking my Black-Berry during the one weekend in two months we've had together, but what you don't understand is that I am hanging on by a thread at work," she said, her voice rising.

"Dale, I don't think you are any of those things. I love you, and I love that you're here, and I thought this place would help you relax. I can see that I was wrong," Peter said.

"It just feels like you're building a life for us here at the same time that I'm starting a new career thousands of miles away," she said.

"I live here," Peter said. He turned and left the room. She heard him closing doors and turning off lights.

"Come on," she pleaded, following him to the entryway.

"I thought you might enjoy an escape on the rare occasion when you can make it out here to visit me. I'm sorry you took it as a threat to your professional trajectory, or whatever it is I've offended by buying you a goddamned house."

Dale was so tired. She tried to think of what she could say to fix the mess she'd created—again—but she was at a loss. She knew she should just let him go so she could find someone normal—someone who would have the right reaction when her boyfriend surprised her with a beach house. She knew she was hurting him by dragging things out. She wanted to tell him how much she loved the beach house. She wanted to rewind the last twenty-five minutes and walk back into the house for the first time with joy and gratitude on her face. If she had it to do over, she'd burst into tears of happiness as he explained how he'd painstakingly hand-selected everything from the heated floors in the bathroom to the eight-burner stove in the kitchen. Then, they would rip each other's clothes off and make love on the floor in the master bedroom. They would lie there afterward and debate where to put the bed. She wanted to make everything okay, but it was too late. She'd hurt him too deeply this time.

When they climbed back into his car, he didn't look at her. They pulled into the garage at his home in Pacific Heights twenty minutes later and she put her hand on his.

"I'm sorry," she said.

"It's my fault. I should have told you it belonged to a friend. You would have enjoyed it more."

The rest of the weekend was strained. The incident at the beach house had forced all the pain and disappointment they'd caused each other into the open and now it hung between them like the cold, heavy fog that was draped over the city that weekend. On Sunday night they went for a walk along the Marina.

"Do you want to get some dinner before your flight?" he asked.

"I'm not that hungry, but if you want to eat, I'll eat," Dale said.

"I'm not hungry, either."

They walked back to his house and sat on the couch next to each other. After a few minutes of silence, tears started to slide down Dale's face. Her grief was a tangle of regret and remorse so bottomless, she couldn't begin to imagine how she'd get over it. Peter had loved her so intensely for so long that she didn't know who she was without seeing herself through his affection. He'd nursed her when she was hurt, and he'd been her sounding board and her lover and her best friend for three years.

She was terrified.

And despite the fact that he was sitting next to her, she knew he was really gone this time. His heart had broken into too many little jagged pieces at the beach house to be put back together again. Her silent tears soon became sobs that racked her body. Peter's arms were around her. He stroked her hair and held her tightly. They sat there until the sky had gone from gray to black. They stayed there until they both knew it was time to drive to the airport for Dale's red-eye flight back to D.C.

She pressed her body as close to his as she could.

"I love you," she said.

"I know."

"I hate saying good-bye to you."

"I know."

"Can I come back next weekend so we can finish talking about things?" she asked.

He didn't say anything.

"Is this how you want things to end?" she asked.

"I don't want things to end, but we both know that it won't happen. There will be a speech or a press dinner or an event added to Tara's schedule. Something will come up and you won't be here next weekend or the weekend after, and things will continue to drag on like this."

She didn't say anything.

"I can't do this anymore," Peter said. "And not because I don't love you enough. I love you too much. I need tonight's good-bye to mean good-bye. I need to try to get over you."

Dale squeezed her eyes shut. She couldn't believe he was doing this. She was afraid if she moved or spoke that he'd push her away and get in the car to take her to the airport, so she just held still and tried to memorize everything about him.

CHAPTER FIFTEEN

Charlotte

Charlotte made her morning walk from the White House residence to the Oval Office much more slowly now that Ralph was her chief of staff. It wasn't that she didn't appreciate Ralph. He tried hard, and he was the only person who could have presided over the West Wing during Tara's transition from statewide officeholder to vice president.

The press had called Ralph the "Tara-whisperer" and the staff adopted it. Every complaint about the vice president wound up on Ralph's desk and it usually fell to him to bring her up to speed on sensitive political issues or emphasize the importance of *not* canceling on certain members of Congress. These were not normal responsibilities for a White House chief of staff, but Charlotte appreciated his ability and willingness to finesse Tara's unpolished edges. She knew that the tensions between Melanie and Tara would have boiled over and become public if she'd remained in the chief of staff post.

Charlotte understood that Ralph was the best person for the job, but she missed Melanie's ability to anticipate her reactions to everything and everyone. During her first term, she had looked forward to their early-morning meetings more than any other part of her day. They'd meet in the Oval Office, go through the schedule for the day, discuss what had been in the papers, and catch each other up on any good gossip.

With Ralph, Charlotte found that the later she arrived, the

shorter the meetings. The odds of the national security advisor or press secretary stopping by increased with every minute, and Samantha had a standing order to usher them in, even when Ralph was still inside. Charlotte scanned the overnights and read all the names from the list of those killed and injured in action in Afghanistan the day before. She looked carefully to make sure Will was not among them. The report had always been the most sobering part of Charlotte's day, but now it held the potential to rip her world apart. At first she'd called Brooke and Mark each day to let them know their son was safe. After a few weeks, Brooke had admitted that the daily call created more tension and anxiety than it prevented, so Charlotte had stopped calling.

She stood and walked out to the reception area.

"Can I send Ralph down?" Samantha, asked.

"Not yet, Sam. Not until I have one more cup of coffee."

"He's been calling since six forty-five," Sam pleaded.

"What time is it?"

"Seven-thirty."

"Oh, all right, but after ten minutes, come get me," Charlotte said.

"He is going to flip."

"I know; do it anyway." Charlotte turned on her charcoal-gray heel and returned to her desk to wait for Ralph. She smelled him before she saw him. Whatever he'd ordered for breakfast, it had come with a side of bacon. She buried her face in her steaming mug of coffee and cursed Melanie for leaving.

"Good morning, Madam President."

"Morning, Ralph. What have you got for me today?"

"Rasmussen has your job approval up to fifty-six after shoving it up the Russians', uh, sorry—"

He stopped suddenly. Ralph's mind was such a crass place that some things didn't get fully translated before he opened his mouth.

"It's all right. Make sure the press knows I'm more comfortable with my poll numbers in the thirties and forties than the fifties. What else?"

"Uh, we're going to make a hard pivot to jobs and the economy this week and stay on it through the summer. We have back-to-back empathy events starting tomorrow," he said. He thrust a schedule in front of Charlotte's face.

"Empathy events?"

"Yeah, you know, it's more like a misery tour, actually. We're going to visit the places that have been hardest hit by the economic downturn. You know, the same towns we always visit in Michigan and Ohio, but we're going to package your travel this time so we can showcase how in touch you are with Middle America."

"That sounds positively stirring, Ralph," Charlotte deadpanned.

For a second, he couldn't tell if she was being sarcastic. Out of pity, she rolled her eyes to make it clear that his cynicism wasn't doing it for her first thing in the morning. Ralph was about to put a new spin on the empathy tour, but Charlotte interrupted him.

"How is Tara doing?"

Ralph looked surprised.

"She's great. She had an amazing event on the jobs package last week."

"I saw that. Quite a tragic story—that homeless woman—and Tara handled it brilliantly. But how is she doing personally? Is the family settled? Does she seem comfortable with the things we've put on her plate? Is it too much? Not enough?"

"I think so."

"You think so, what?"

"I think she's really happy with everything."

"I'd like to be sure of that Ralph. Please put a weekly lunch date for me and Tara back on my schedule," Charlotte demanded.

"Yes ma'am."

"I'd like them to start immediately."

"Yes ma'am, we'll start them next week."

"Let's throw caution to the wind, Ralph."

"Ma'am?"

"Let's make the good people of the scheduling office scratch their heads as they try to figure out how something got on my schedule without seven planning meetings, two rounds of polling, and twenty-three signatures on it."

"I'm sorry?"

"I want to have lunch with Tara today."

Ralph's mouth hung open for a fraction of a second. He recovered and groped for his Blackberry.

"Yes ma'am." Ralph turned to go.

"One more thing," she said.

"Madam President?"

"No staff."

"Madam President, I strongly suggest having someone there to take notes about the issues discussed," Ralph protested.

"This one is not negotiable. She needs to know that she can come to me with anything that's on her mind."

Charlotte watched his Adams' apple pulse wildly.

"Yes ma'am."

"Thank you, Ralph; I appreciate it. I'll go over the materials tonight for the empathy tour. I'm looking forward to it."

"Thank you, Madam President." He turned and nearly ran from the Oval Office.

Charlotte stood to stretch her legs and get more coffee.

"Is anyone else looking for me?" she asked Sam.

"Craig Thompson from leg affairs said he needs ten minutes and the speechwriters want to come down and discuss the speech for the 'jobless in Detroit' event. They are concerned that it reads too much like a campaign speech."

"Send Craig down first and see if the speechwriters want to come down afterward." Charlotte sighed. She needed to find a way to get through to Tara and figure out how she could help steady her. Once the press determined there was enough evidence to cement a narrative of Tara as an unreliable and inadequate number two, it would be hard to shake. In some ways, the press had painted Tara into a corner by placing her on the working-mother pedestal on one hand, and scrutinizing her every misstep on the other. Charlotte wasn't as troubled by the increasing frequency with which Tara canceled public events as she was by the growing concern that the hot lights of Washington were starting to expose weaknesses she'd never seen before. While Charlotte had been prosecuted by the press for all manner of sins, they'd never accused her of being overwhelmed by the responsibilities of her office. She returned to her desk and tried to push her growing concern about Tara out of her mind. In her six months as vice president, Tara had developed a deep emotional connection with a large swath of the electorate. Among her most ardent supporters there was a sense that she was being singled out for unnecessarily harsh criticism. Charlotte was grateful for this reservoir of goodwill toward her running mate, but the stream of anecdotes about Tara's inability to navigate the most casual and friendly of policy discussions suggested that the problem was something much deeper than a lack of preparation.

CHAPTER SIXTEEN

Tara

"Y ou look nice," Marcus said.

"Thanks. I'm having lunch with Charlotte today. Her assistant, Samantha, just called Karen."

Tara saw surprise cross Marcus's face, but he didn't say anything.

"It's just a weekly thing that she wants added to her schedule."

"Uh-huh," Marcus raised an eyebrow.

"What?"

"Nothing. Let me know how it goes. I'm going to take Kendall to camp today so I can talk to her counselor."

"Why? What's wrong?"

"I'm sure everything is fine." Marcus smiled tightly. "Don't worry about Kendall. Focus on your lunch with Charlotte."

Tara wondered sometimes if he manufactured assignments like the meeting with Kendall's counselor to highlight his role as their daughter's primary caregiver. One of his favorite ways to cut Tara down from the rare good mood was to hoard information about Kendall that he deemed threatening to her fragile mental state. It drove Tara crazy, but it was an effective trap. If she pushed to know what the problem was, he'd refuse to share any information with her until she was beside herself. Then, if she became agitated or hysterical, he'd say "See, I told you that you couldn't handle any additional stress. Let me worry about Kendall." She tried to spend as much time as she could alone with Kendall, but it was difficult. When she wasn't at work or working from home, Marcus was always lurking around a corner or listening from the next room when she and Kendall spent time together. Afterward, he'd offer advice on how to speak to her more "effectively." She tolerated his meddling out of fear that he'd leave her someday and take Kendall with him. She could survive anything else—any indignity that Marcus could imagine—but she could not endure losing Kendall. Kendall was her miracle.

They hadn't planned to get pregnant, and with her bouts of depression taking on a life of their own, she was worried that she'd pass her badly wired brain on to a child. But she'd missed a period and had taken a pregnancy test to be sure she wasn't pregnant. She was dismayed when it said that she was. She'd been on the pill since she was twenty-four. After she'd told Marcus, they'd pored through everything they could find on the Internet about the chances of passing her depression on to their child. There were many studies that suggested a genetic link, but it was also possible that their child would be fine. In the beginning, Tara was terrified that Marcus would pressure her to terminate the pregnancy. With every passing day, she grew more attached to the life growing inside her. It was the only time in her adult life that she'd felt completely okay—happy, even. She'd eaten all the right foods, and been sure to sleep and exercise. And when Kendall was pronounced healthy by the doctors who delivered her, Tara had cried tears of joy that she thought would never stop.

When Kendall was an infant, Tara would watch her all day and all night for any signs that something was wrong. She'd rush her to the pediatrician at the slightest sign of anything out of the ordinary. Seven years later, Kendall was a perfectly normal, healthy, happy child. She had friends, teachers adored her, and she was a smart, charming, funny little girl. Tara snuck into her room every night, after Marcus was asleep, to watch her daughter while she dreamed.

Now, as she watched Marcus lift Kendall into the SUV for the short ride to camp, Tara wondered if she would ever be able to unwind all the lies she'd told and live an ordinary life with her daughter. She doubted it. Tara watched Kendall lean toward the front seat to give the Secret Service agent a high five. Tara smiled, and then tore herself away from the window to finish getting ready.

During the ten-minute drive to the White House, Tara noticed people fanning themselves while they waited for the bus. It was the beginning of July, but the heat had already settled itself over D.C. She flipped through her briefing papers and made some notes on a memo from the White House Council of Economic Advisors.

"Who is the Council of Economic Advisors?" she wrote on the front page of the hundred-page report. She scratched it out before they pulled into the complex.

She said hello to everyone as she walked into her office and took a seat behind her desk. A perfectly stacked pile of the day's newspapers lay in the center. She opened the *New York Times* and read through each article. She pored through the *Wall Street Journal* and *Washington Post* next. Each paper had vastly different takes on the prospects of the upcoming Mideast peace talks. Tara realized that she didn't know the first thing about what her own administration was doing to restart the peace talks, and she had no clue which newspaper had gotten closest to the truth in their varying reports. She was about to call Karen to ask her to bring in someone from her national security team when the door to her office opened and Karen appeared.

"The president is ready for you," she said.

"It's early, right? I mean, lunch was at twelve-thirty and it's just eleven-forty-five."

"I think lunch with the president is whenever the president is hungry, Madam Vice President," Karen said.

Tara took a deep breath and walked slowly toward the door of her office.

"Right."

"You look nice," Karen said.

"Thanks."

Tara followed a single Secret Service agent from her office toward the Oval and stopped in front of Sam's desk.

"Madam Vice President, please go in. She's waiting for you in her private dining room," Sam said.

"Thank you, Samantha."

Tara crossed the Oval Office and knocked on the door to the president's private dining room.

"Come in," Charlotte called from the other side of the room.

When Tara entered, Charlotte was crouched in front of the DVD player.

"I wanted to play your speech at the Small Business Conference and ask you about it because I was just so moved by that woman's story when I saw it on the news, but I can't get this damn thing to work," she said.

"You don't need to watch it again. I was terrible that day. The teleprompter went down and I froze."

"You were magnificent, Tara. The whole thing was incredibly moving," Charlotte insisted.

Tara blushed.

"Madam President, thank you, but I was just trying to make the most of the situation."

"Charlotte. Please call me Charlotte."

"Okay."

"Please, come and sit down, Tara. Make yourself comfortable."

As soon as they were seated, a waiter appeared to take their orders.

"Do you know what you want?" Charlotte asked.

"Uh, sure, just give me one second."

"I'll have a Cobb salad with extra bacon and extra dressing," Charlotte said. "Tell those guys that I do not have a cholesterol problem and to stop being so chintzy with the good stuff. Oh, extra blue cheese, too," she added.

"Yes, Madam President," the waiter said. "And an iced tea to drink, ma'am?"

"I'll have iced coffee today. I'm really mixing things up, aren't I?" she joked.

"Yes ma'am. And for you, Madam Vice President? Have you decided?"

"Yes. I'll have a mixed green salad with some grilled chicken. And if it is possible, I'd like to have the dressing on the side."

"Of course, Madam Vice President. And to drink?"

"I'll have a Diet Coke."

He left the room and Charlotte turned to Tara and smiled warmly.

"I'm really glad we were able to schedule lunch. Ralph told me how hectic things have been for you with the travel, and of course you have a young daughter who you must miss terribly when we pull you away for all these stupid events in the battleground states. I don't know why Ralph is already so campaign-obsessed. I mean, the midterms are nearly two years away and he has us crisscrossing the heartland every week. I'm going to talk to him. Anyway, I can see how this could become a real bitch session if I don't watch myself. How are you? Is Kendall having a nice summer? Is Marcus still at home? Do you love that?"

Tara laughed.

"We're doing fine. Kendall loves her camp counselor and Marcus keeps busy, and I'm just trying to read everything and learn everything so I don't say something stupid or ask an idiotic question at a cabinet meeting or something." Tara's voice cracked.

Charlotte put her hand on her arm and leaned closer.

"Tara, what is it? What's wrong?"

"Nothing, nothing. I'm just so honored that you asked me to be your vice president, and I can't believe we won, and now we have this great opportunity to really make a difference. These are happy tears." She felt like an idiot. She was falling apart in front of the president.

"Are you sure?"

"Yes. I just wanted to say that I can do better. I'm going to do better."

"You're doing great," Charlotte declared.

Tara shook her head and fought back more tears. Marcus would kill her if he found out she'd broken down at lunch.

"Listen, I should have done this sooner. I asked you to lunch today to find out what I could do to support you and your family and help you block out the assholes in the press and the old farts on the Hill and all the other jerks who'd love to see us trip in our high heels and fall on our faces," Charlotte said.

Tara wiped her eyes and smiled.

"Thank you. There are some really old ones up there."

Charlotte laughed.

"It's incredible, isn't it? The Senate is turning into a senior citizen community."

Tara smiled and wiped her eyes with her napkin.

"And I mean it about the press. Ignore them. I spent my first term reading every nasty thing they wrote about me. I thought I was tough enough to handle it, but it's not about being tough enough. No one is tough enough for what they write about us. You just have to remember that they get paid to knock us down, and the ones who knock us out completely get paid the most."

"I'll keep that in mind," Tara said. She didn't know what, specifically, had prompted Charlotte's warning about not reading the papers, but she made a mental note to sit down with Dale and find out what the press had been reporting about her lately.

After lunch, Tara walked back to her office and sat down at her desk. Charlotte had been so lovely to her. Tara kept replaying her comments about ignoring the press. She picked up the phone and asked Karen to send Dale over. Minutes later, Dale appeared at her door.

"Good afternoon, Madam Vice President," she said.

"Hi Dale. Come on in. Listen, I was just wondering, how has our press been lately?"

"Excuse me?"

"I don't get a chance to read every little story about myself or watch every package, and I assume you do, right?" Tara asked.

"Of course, Madam Vice President."

"So, how's our press?"

"Are you referring to the coverage of the White House as a whole, or your coverage specifically?" Dale asked.

"For Christ's sake! I want to know what the hell they are saying about me that would prompt Charlotte Kramer to invite me to lunch to tell me not to worry about the press!"

Dale's face changed from confusion to something Tara hadn't seen before. It looked like pity mixed with surprise.

"Madam Vice President, I've tried to include a representative sample in the overnight memo I send to the Naval Observatory each night. Have you been receiving those?"

"Not regularly," Tara lied. She received Dale's memo every night. She always placed it on the top of her stack of reading material, but most nights, she fell into bed without touching the memos from her staff.

"I'm sorry. That explains a lot. I was told that the memos were getting to you, but I'll get to the bottom of where they are ending up. To be honest, your press is quite mixed. You still get rave reviews in the women's press. In fact, *Good Housekeeping* is doing another profile on you. This one is focused on your marriage and how you and Mr. Meyers share the parenting responsibilities when it comes to Kendall. I think it will be nice," Dale said.

Tara didn't look up.

Dale continued.

"But the Washington reporters are a cynical bunch and they were all really critical when we canceled the first overseas trip in the spring," Dale said, apologetically.

"Critical? They were critical that I stayed home because my daughter was sick?" Tara replied.

Dale stared at her blankly for a moment.

"Um, some of them had sources at the school who said she was in school that week, and the others just sort of strung the canceled trip together with other occasions where we backed out of things at the last minute. Unfortunately, once they convince themselves of a certain narrative, it's even harder to change the story line," Dale said.

"Isn't it your job to kill, whatever it is you call it . . . a narrative . . . that isn't true?" Tara snapped.

"Yes ma'am," Dale replied calmly. Tara thought Dale was speaking to her the way she'd speak to a tantrum-throwing child.

"It is my job to make sure you and the president get the best press that is possible. Perhaps we can start meeting once a week to discuss some of the inquiries and opportunities we have each week to shape the stories that the friendlier reporters are working on," Dale suggested.

Tara was trying to focus on what Dale was saying, but her ears were ringing and her face felt hot. She was angry at herself for trusting a reporter to be her communications advisor. Why did she think she could count on one of "them" to be loyal to her? She should have brought someone from the Attorney General's Office in New York. They may not have understood the ways of Washington, but at least they would have protected her. She noticed that Dale had stopped talking. She wasn't sure how long the silence had hung between them, but she turned her gaze from the window back to Dale. Her fury mounted as she took in the designer dress that seemed to hang on Dale's thin frame and her tasteful heels and jewelry. Tara was sure she put effort into downplaying her looks. She hardly wore any makeup and her hair was pulled into a loose ponytail on most days.

As Tara stared at Dale's puzzled face, she decided Dale was enjoying her humiliation at the hands of the press pack she was once a part of.

"Get out," Tara growled.

"I'm sorry?"

"Get out," Tara roared.

"Madam Vice President, what's wrong?"

"I knew I couldn't trust you to handle my press. I should have listened to Melanie, but I felt bad for you. I thought you'd been screwed by the network, and by the uptight handwringers around the president. But I was wrong. Now, get out," she screamed.

The color drained from Dale's face, but she remained composed. Tara clenched and unclenched her fists while Dale rose slowly and slipped out of the room. Tara imagined her rolling her eyes or shaking her head at Karen on her way out. Tara put her head in her hands as she weighed the odds of her entire staff finding out about her outburst. She didn't care. Charlotte's staff would probably hear about it as well. Maybe it would even make the papers. Tara's hands were shaking and she felt light-headed. The walls of her office looked like they were swaying. She pulled out the emergency cell phone she'd kept despite the Secret Service's warnings, and dialed Marcus. When he picked up, she could barely form words.

"Tara, what is it? What's wrong?" he asked.

She tried again to speak, but all that came out was a sob.

"Tara, I'm coming right now to get you," he said. "Whatever you do, do not pick up the phone and do not leave your office for any reason."

CHAPTER SEVENTEEN

Dale

By the time she got back to her office, Dale's cheeks hurt from the effort it took to keep a placid smile on her face during the walk from the West Wing. She wrapped her arms around her body as she paced her office and replayed the surreal display she'd just witnessed from the vice president. Dale couldn't believe the vice president hadn't seen any of the stories. For three days straight, the *Washington Post* had done a "Tara Meyers Watch" on its front page. The paper had only pulled it down when Dale promised invitations to the White House holiday party for all of the *Post*'s bloggers the following December. MSNBC had created a nightly feature spoofing the vice president's frequent absences called "Where in the World Is Tara Meyers?" And *Saturday Night* Live had recently aired a skit in which the president ran all over the West Wing looking for the vice president under desks and in broom closets. Clearly, the vice president's penchant for canceling events was above Dale's pay grade, but she could not understand why Ralph or the president didn't simply call her in and tell her to knock it off.

And the coverage would have been even worse if not for Dale's willingness to cash in on her relationships with her former colleagues. She had single-handedly kept the most aggressive investigative reporter in the country from writing a story questioning the vice president's mental and emotional stability.

"Damn, damn, damn," Dale mumbled. She was furious at herself for taking the job in the first place. It wasn't like she could crawl back to the people who'd offered her correspondent positions after the election now. She'd spent six months spinning and shading the truth about the vice president to the very people she used to align herself with professionally.

What was I thinking? she asked herself over and over as she continued to pace. She wanted out of her job, but it would be impossible to quit without becoming part of the story again. Besides, she owed it to the president to suck it up and make the best of it. Dale took a deep breath and tried to slow her pacing. She reminded herself that no job was perfect. Her position had its drawbacks, but it had been tolerable because the vice president seemed to appreciate her discretion. Dale had really tried to look out for her, but their meetings were so infrequent that the only method she had for communicating with the vice president was the memo she compiled each night. She'd tried to include the most relevant news articles—the ones that were shaping the overwhelmingly negative story line about the vice president's performance, but she also always tried to include something positive. A flattering piece from a woman's magazine or a local paper, or a letter to the editor from someone who'd seen her speak was always part of the clip pack that Dale sent over. Now it was clear that the vice president hadn't been reading her memos, and after the scene that had just played out in the West Wing, Dale wondered if the disgruntled members of the OVP had been right all along.

Dale had always found it strange that none of the staff from the campaign had sought positions in the White House, and half of the new team that had been assembled had left for other jobs in the administration. While Dale assumed that everyone who worked as a spokesman told little white lies about their boss, she was pretty sure they didn't cross the lines she'd been asked to cross. The first time she'd misrepresented the truth to a reporter, she was traumatized. She'd half expected alarms to go off and a truth squad to arrest her in her apartment later that night. But no one said anything. And hadn't Ralph been explicit in ordering her to handle the press and wave them off questions about the vice president's uneven performances? Or had she simply interpreted it that way? She shook her hands out next to her body and took a deep breath. *How did I end up here?* she asked herself. When the vice president had started unloading on her, she'd been tempted to tell her about all the stories that would have been written if she hadn't laid her body down on the tracks. Dale shivered a bit when she thought of the blank, glassy look that had come over the vice president. Dale had never seen anything like it. Tara's entire body had started shaking with rage.

Dale leaned over and pulled her phone off her desk.

"Is he there?" Dale asked Ralph's assistant.

"Yes, but he's in a meeting, Dale. I'll have him call you when he gets out," she replied.

"It's an emergency," Dale said.

"I think he's dealing with something of an urgent nature himself, Dale."

"This is of the *most* urgent nature," Dale pleaded.

"Hang on," the assistant said.

While Dale held for Ralph, she thought about how Peter had been right about one thing. There's no way she would have been able to leave town to visit him again. Dale would have canceled on him, he would have been disappointed, she would have felt awful, and they would have been back at square one.

"What the fuck happened in there?" Ralph asked, jolting Dale from her thoughts about Peter.

"Did the vice president call you?"

For an instant, Dale was scared that she was in trouble.

"The assistants hear everything. Mine talked to Tara's, blah, blah, blah. Plus, Marcus Meyers called me."

Dale slumped in her chair. "Why did *he* call?"

"He said Tara's not herself today and wanted to make sure she hadn't upset you. What did she say to you anyway?"

"Ralph, it was inexplicable. She called me over after her lunch and asked me what people in the press were saying about her and then went through the roof when I told her that her coverage was mixed. She started screaming and shaking and she told me she never should have hired me. I'm more than happy to submit my resignation right now, Ralph. I think she needs someone she's more comfortable with," Dale said.

"That's nonsense. She doesn't have any fucking clue what she needs. I've got to go downstairs for an NSC meeting, but come over to my office around five-twenty, Dale. It's time to read you in."

"Read me in to what?" Dale asked.

"I can't tell you over the phone. It's classified," Ralph said.

Dale couldn't tell if he was joking.

"I'll see you in a couple hours," she said.

"Don't be late."

"Ralph, I've got nowhere else to go."

She thought she heard him snort. Dale hung up and rubbed her throbbing head. She couldn't remember the last time she'd eaten. She didn't feel like another meal at the Mess. She looked around her office for Aleve. She swallowed three with the remains of her morning coffee and looked at her watch. What was she going to do for the next three hours?

Ralph's assistant looked surprised when Dale walked in at four forty-five.

"Did he ask you to come over?" she asked.

"Yes," Dale said, omitting the fact that he'd asked her to wait until five-twenty.

The assistant looked skeptical.

"Is he in there?" Dale asked with her hand on the door.

"Yeah," she said.

"Is he alone?"

"No."

Dale was getting annoyed.

"Who is he in with?" she asked.

"Mr. Meyers," the assistant said.

At that instant, the door flung open and Ralph stood in the doorway.

"Dale, just the person we were looking for. Come on in and make yourself comfortable."

CHAPTER EIGHTEEN

Charlotte

Charlotte took the dogs for a walk, read a stack of memos from her national security team, and downed two glasses of her favorite pinot noir and she still could not relax. She looked at the clock on the television. It was after eight P.M. If she walked back to the West Wing the press would think something unusual was happening. She picked up the phone and asked the operator to connect her to Melanie.

"Hi. Did you read the memo on our troop request?"

"Yes. Very well argued," Charlotte said.

"That's what you say when you're going to reject something."

"We can discuss it tomorrow, but I want you to know that however this turns out, you made the best case possible."

"Uh, thank you, Madam President. And I appreciate the call. Is everything all right?"

"I think so."

"Do you want me to stop by?" Melanie asked.

"No, no. I'm sure you and Brian are in for the night and that you don't want to be bothered with the neurotic concerns of a woman who lives alone with dogs."

"Seriously, I'll be right over if you want," Melanie offered.

Charlotte sighed. "I had lunch with Tara and she seemed really off, but it's probably that it's all still new for her, right?"

The line was quiet.

"Mel, I'm asking you to give me a reality check. Can you put your personal feelings aside for five minutes?" Charlotte pleaded.

"Madam President," she started. Charlotte knew that Melanie was choosing her words carefully. "You know that I'm not the right person to ask. It's been six months. The press isn't completely out of line. That said, it is Ralph's job to make sure that she has a structure around her that guarantees her success and stability, so if that's not happening, you need to call Ralph and have him fix things," Melanie said.

"You're right. I'll call him now. Thanks, Melanie."

"Of course. Call me back if you want. And I'll see you tomorrow at the national security council meeting."

Charlotte hung up and dialed Ralph. She rarely called him after hours.

"Madam President, good evening. Is everything all right?" Ralph asked.

"Yes, just fine. I hope I'm not getting you at a bad time."

"No, I'm just finishing up a meeting. Do you need me to come over to the residence?"

"No," she said, a little too quickly. "I wanted to reiterate my concern for Tara. She was quite emotional at our lunch today and I worry that the intense scrutiny is eating her alive."

"You're right about that, Madam President. The press treatment of her is horrible and it is getting into her head."

Charlotte was surprised by Ralph's admission. His typical response when she was worried about something was to try to convince her that she was overreacting.

"What's the plan to get the press out of her head?"

"She's going to take them on," Ralph said triumphantly.

"I don't think that's a good idea right now, Ralph."

"Listen, I was worried about it, too, but I've had meetings today with Dale, who thinks it's a good idea, and with Marcus Meyers, who says that the best way for Tara to excise her demons is to stare them down."

"Dale thinks it's a good idea?"

"She does now," Ralph said.

"Who does she think Tara should do?"

"All of them."

"No way, Ralph. She's not up to it," Charlotte said.

"That's what I thought, but Marcus took the plan to Tara and she said 'Let's do it,' so we're a go."

"Ralph, I'd really like to see her slow down. I don't think she's up for a grilling from all the networks," Charlotte pleaded.

"Not a grilling, Madam President—she's inviting the three morning anchors to breakfast with the Meyerses. The whole family will be there. She'll demystify the working mother thing. Marcus will be by her side, and we know how much the voters like Marcus. And that kid . . . the kid is cute as hell, and Tara and Marcus green-lighted the kid being in the interviews, so it's going to be great."

"Ralph, I saw her eight hours ago and it didn't seem as if she was up for this kind of scrutiny."

"Dale is going to make sure the interviews are all soft and friendly with no hostile questions permitted," Ralph boasted.

"Dale can't be expected to do that, Ralph. We both know that any correspondent or anchor is going to ask her about canceling her overseas travel and the quotes from anonymous White House sources about her being clueless about foreign policy and all the other nasty comments. Tara is too raw right now to let those kinds of questions roll off her back," Charlotte said.

"Dale said that if the interviews do not meet the vice president's expectations or achieve the strategic objective of relaunching her image, she'll resign on the spot. That's how confident she is that this will work out."

Charlotte stifled a laugh. Ralph was a fool. Dale probably offered the guarantee because she *wanted* to resign. Charlotte sighed.

"Thanks, Ralph. Oh, and tell Dale that if the interviews don't work out, her punishment will be that she has to stay."

Ralph guffawed and hung up. It sounded like he'd taken a bite of something large and messy. Charlotte sighed again. The dogs lifted their heads and looked at her with fleeting worry. She scratched their ears, and they went back to sleep. She thought about calling Melanie again, but didn't want to bother her. The person she really wanted to ask about Tara was Dale, but while she'd mostly forgotten the indignity of the scandal, she and Dale didn't have the kind of relationship that would support a nine P.M. phone call to discuss the vice president's state of mind.

She needed to talk to someone. She dialed Peter.

"Hi. It's Charlotte."

"I know."

"How are my evil teenagers?"

"They were excellent when I last spoke to them, but it's always possible that everything has changed overnight."

She laughed.

"Can you believe they are going to college next year?"

"No. When I pick them up this week it will be the last time they come home for the summer. Next year they'll be graduating."

"I feel like I've missed so many of these years, and now it's over. They're practically adults and they'll hardly need us anymore. Not that they've needed much from me anyway, but, you know, it's nice to feel like they might still turn to me for something. Now they are on their way into the world. It terrifies me."

"Charlotte, have you picked up a newspaper lately? Kids don't move out anymore. They are officially called the boomerang generation because they always come home. You can expect to live with them again. We both can."

"Well, I can see Harry coming home, but Penny is ready to spread her wings."

"You want to bet?"

"Sure. What should we bet? You want to take the controls of Air Force One for a flyby of Soldier Field?"

"That would be a blast, but I'm pretty sure you'd be accused of no fewer than twenty-five different infractions."

"How about dinner?"

"The loser cooks dinner for the winner. You're on."

They talked about the kids for a few more minutes and then hung up.

Charlotte felt better. Peter was warmer to her than he'd been in years.

She poured another small splash of wine into her glass and tried to quiet her racing thoughts. Ralph was going to be the death of her. She racked her brain for candidates for a new chief of staff.

CHAPTER NINETEEN

Tara

Madam Vice President, it's no secret that behind closed doors, lots of folks in Washington are saying that the job is too much for you to handle. Would you like to respond to those charges?" Dale asked.

Tara felt her face redden and nostrils flare. She didn't respond. Dale leaned closer and went at her again.

"Madam Vice President, is the vice presidency too big of a step from your previous position? Are you, as your critics in both parties have privately suggested in recent weeks, in over your head?" Dale stared emotionlessly at Tara.

Tara was fighting the urge to walk out of the room. She clenched and unclenched her hands and then took a deep breath and closed her eyes for a second. She blew the air out and sat up straighter. She looked Dale directly in the eye, smiled, and stuck out her chin.

"Caroline, I'm really glad you're here having breakfast with me and my family. And I appreciate this opportunity to answer my critics. There's no doubt about it. The vice presidency is a big job, and an important one. It's one I've been preparing for my whole life. Whether it was during college when I worked two jobs to pay for part of my tuition and all of my living expenses, or in law school when I managed a Starbucks during the day and studied all night, or as a young attorney in the Manhattan District Attorney's Office, or even during my time in the U.S. Attorney's Office; I have always risen to the challenge. I'll readily admit that I had a rough start, but, Caroline, what you and your viewers need to know is, um, what you need to understand is that I, uh, I, what I'm trying to say, Caroline is . . . what? What the hell is it that I'm trying to say? Damn!" Tara groaned, collapsing back into the sofa and covering her eyes with her hands.

"That I'm a fighter," Dale prompted.

"That's right, that's right. Caroline, you need to understand that I'm a fighter," Tara said, still slumped back on the couch.

"And that there's never been a challenge I haven't been able to meet," Dale prompted, again.

"That there's never been a challenge I haven't been able to meet," Tara repeated.

After a beat of silence, Dale continued.

"That when life has thrown obstacles in my path, I've figured out how to adapt."

"That when life has thrown obstacles in my path, blah, blah, blah," Tara said, making clear she didn't plan to recite the rest of the answer they'd prepared.

"I've spent my entire life working for justice and fighting for others, all while doing the best I can as a wife and a mother. At the end of the day, the American people can rest assured that I'll always do my best and that I'll always fight with everything I've got for their families," Dale read from the large index card.

She slid the five-by-seven-inch card back into the stack she was holding in her lap and sighed. Tara searched her face for signs of frustration, but all she could detect was sympathy.

"Madam Vice President, you were doing great," Dale said.

"No I wasn't. I can't believe I let you talk me into this," Tara complained.

Dale folded her hands neatly on top of the stack of index cards and readjusted her crossed legs. It was starting to infuriate Tara that she couldn't get a rise out of her. She was fairly certain that the interviews hadn't been Dale's idea. Marcus had told her that Ralph insisted the interviews were the only way to salvage her reputation and spare Charlotte the embarrassment of watching her vice president implode. Tara wasn't sure if the idea originated with Ralph or Marcus, but she suspected Dale had objected.

And now it fell to Dale to play the enemy. She had prepared three different sets of questions and answers based on her best guess of what the three morning anchors would ask. Tara rubbed her neck and thought for a minute about what she should wear. She thought about how nice it would be to do the interviews in fuzzy slippers and pajamas.

"Madam Vice President, would you like to take a break?" Dale asked politely.

"No, no. Let's keep going."

Tara watched Dale organize the cards into neat piles and considered apologizing for her outburst the week before. She wasn't sure how exactly she'd phrase it.

Dale, I'm really sorry I turned into a sociopath the other day. Don't worry . . . it won't happen again.

Tara smirked at the thought.

"What?" Dale asked.

"Nothing," Tara replied.

When Dale had arrived at the Naval Observatory hours earlier, she'd acted as though nothing out of the ordinary had transpired between them. They'd been sitting in the living room for what felt like hours now, and as Tara watched Dale jot additional talking points in the margins of the index cards, she wondered what Dale was thinking. She seemed even more serious than usual. Tara wanted to ask her what was wrong, but she worried that *she* was what was wrong. On the one occasion she'd been inside Dale's office, she'd noticed that there were no photos of family or friends. Tara suspected that there wasn't much in Dale's life other than the job. Suddenly, Tara wanted to know everything about her. She wanted to ask how she'd kept an affair with the president's husband out of the news and why they weren't together anymore. Tara didn't know for sure that Dale and Peter Kramer had split, but she suspected that was the case. *US Weekly* and *People*, Tara's other secret indulgences, hadn't run any recent photos of the two of them together.

Just as Tara was mustering the nerve to say something to Dale about how much she appreciated her help, her eyes wandered to Dale's two-thousand-dollar Valentino purse thrown carelessly on the ground. As

Tara took in the black cashmere sweater from Chanel that was strewn across the chair behind her, she was overcome with familiar feelings of inadequacy. She looked down at her own bulging stomach and wrapped her lime green cardigan more tightly around her body.

At that moment, Kendall came running in.

"Hi Mom!"

"Hello there, sugar pop! Where have you been?"

"Dad picked me up from school and took me to tennis camp, and then we went for ice cream at Thomas Sweet."

"Ice cream for dinner?"

"No, it was pizza night at tennis camp, so I had pizza for dinner and ice cream for dessert," Kendall beamed as she wrapped her arms around Tara's neck.

"That doesn't sound very healthy, sweet girl. You don't want to be fat like mommy, do you?" Tara asked.

Kendall was confounded by the question. She pulled Tara closer and gave her a kiss.

"I love you, Mom."

"I love you, too, sweetie," Tara said.

Kendall kissed her again.

"What was that one for?"

"Daddy says you need good luck tomorrow," she said.

"Daddy's right. Did you say hello to Dale?"

"Hello, Dale," Kendall said.

"I'm sorry, do you mind if I tuck her in? I haven't seen her all day," Tara asked Dale.

"Of course not," Dale said.

Tara followed Kendall to the kitchen.

"Did Dad tell you what was going to happen tomorrow morning, sweetie?"

"Sort of."

"Some nice people from the television stations are going to sit with us and talk to us for their shows while we eat breakfast," Tara explained.

"Cool!" Kendall said cheerily.

"And you don't have to talk to them if you don't want to, but if they ask you questions about your new school or your friends, it might be nice to mention how much you like Sidwell and your teacher, Mrs. Beckinsworth."

"Beckworth. And there's no guarantee that Mrs. Beckworth will be her teacher next school year," Marcus corrected.

"That's right. Mrs. Beckworth," Tara said.

"I knew who Mommy was talking about," Kendall said. Tara felt something far deeper than maternal love each time her daughter leapt to her defense.

"It's important that Mommy get all of her answers right tomorrow, that's all honey," Marcus said.

"She will," Kendall insisted.

"Thank you, my sweet girl," Tara said, holding her arms out for a hug.

As Kendall moved toward Tara, Marcus scooped her up.

"Time for bed, sweetie. Mommy needs to study."

Tara fought to keep the flash of pain off her face, but Kendall caught it.

"I want Mom to put me to bed."

"She can't tonight. She has that pretty lady over to help her get ready and she can't leave her waiting," Marcus said.

"Dale had a couple of calls to make," Tara offered.

Marcus placed Kendall back on the floor.

"Fine. I'm going downstairs to work out."

Tara took Kendall's hand and headed up the stairs toward her bedroom.

"You might see lights outside your window tomorrow morning. That's just the crews getting set up," Tara explained.

"Like a movie?" Kendall asked.

"Yes, a little bit like a movie." She laughed.

"Will there be any famous people?"

"No, just us."

Kendall squeezed Tara's hand and Tara stopped for a moment to look at her.

"Do you know how much I love you?" Tara asked.

"I know, Mom. I love you, too," Kendall said, holding tightly onto Tara's hand.

CHAPTER TWENTY

Dale

D ale felt the last shred of resentment she'd harbored since the week before dissipate as she watched the vice president leave the room clinging to her daughter's hand. Tara Meyers was doing the best she could, and the fact that her best wasn't cutting it was not lost on her. Being in the same room with Tara was like sitting with someone strapped to an explosive device. The clock was ticking, and unless the situation was handled delicately, the whole thing would blow up.

Dale prayed that they would appear normal to television viewers the following morning. Tara's grit had held up her approval numbers so far, but she didn't have much time left to convince Washington's ruling class that she hadn't been swallowed whole by the job. As she watched Kendall cling to her mother's hand as they climbed the stairs, Dale cringed inwardly at the thought of a seven-year-old waking up to the sound of news crews setting up to film her and her parents sharing a family meal the next morning on national television.

While she was working at the network, she'd never doubted that she was part of a noble and vitally important profession. Now that she saw how the prying eyes of the media could undo a family's peace, she felt something much closer to disdain for her former vocation.

Dale stifled a yawn and stood to refill her coffee cup. She'd hardly slept since her meeting with Ralph and Marcus the week before. Between preparing for the vice president's media blitz and trying to process what she'd been told that night by Ralph, she was becoming immune to her favorite sleep cocktail. One Ambien and two

Advil PM's had never failed to put her to sleep and keep her asleep for at least six hours before. But now she was a member of a very small club of White House officials who knew that the scene playing out at the Naval Observatory was anything but normal.

What had Ralph said the other night in his office? That Tara suffered from temporary anxiety disorder? Dale stirred two heaping teaspoons of sugar into her coffee and looked around for the cream. What the hell did temporary anxiety mean? And how was it different from permanent anxiety? How did they know her paralyzing anxiety was a temporary condition? How was Dale supposed to handle press for someone who spiraled into anxiety-induced tantrums when things became too stressful? And if she couldn't handle the press, how was she going to handle the real challenges facing the administration? Dale's head started to pound. She gulped the black coffee and wandered back to her chair.

Dale had sat in her office for hours that night scouring the Internet for information on the terms Ralph had dropped to see if they were technical ones. Marcus had sat quietly in a chair facing Ralph's desk. He'd barely looked up at her. At certain points, he'd nod to show agreement with something Ralph was saying, but otherwise he just sat there with his fist pressed under his chin.

She had put her notepad away the second Ralph started throwing around words like "mental toughness" and "psychic wellness." It sounded like bullshit, and she had a feeling that what he meant but could not say, and would likely never admit, was that he suspected she was having some sort of breakdown. Sitting there, in Ralph's West Wing office that night, steps away from the Oval Office, sirens had started blaring in her mind.

Weren't there competence issues involved? And legal issues? Shouldn't someone other than Ralph be quarterbacking the situation? Like a doctor?

And shouldn't the president know? Or did the president know?

Dale couldn't think of anything to say to Ralph or Marcus that night, so she'd simply nodded and said "yes sir" when either one of them addressed her. About an hour into the three and a half hour conversation, Ralph had informed her that he and Marcus wanted

Dale to arrange three favorable interviews for the vice president the following week.

"That'll give you plenty of time to prep her. Marcus will take charge of her psychic wellness as we've been discussing." Marcus gave Ralph a sideways look.

"He's going to get her into the gym to work off some of her stress," Ralph added while reaching down to pick up the last bite of his cheeseburger and shove it into his mouth. An uneaten turkey club sandwich sat in front of Marcus. Dale hadn't ordered anything.

She'd opened her notebook and had written "three interviews" on a blank page. It wasn't that she was afraid she'd forget her assignment. She needed to do something with her hands so she wouldn't sit there with her mouth hanging open. As she was getting ready to appeal the interview strategy with a concise list of reasons why it was a very bad idea, the president had called for Ralph.

She heard Ralph promise the president that Dale could negotiate ground rules for the interviews that would strictly forbid any probing or difficult questions. Her insides froze when he'd offered those assurances. It would be impossible to negotiate those conditions. She'd sat in her office in the OEOB until three A.M. that night staring at the lights that were still on in the residence. She'd even fantasized about calling the president to beg her to intervene.

Now she heard someone approaching the living room and braced herself for another tedious session with the vice president. She willed herself to project positive and supportive energy to boost Tara's confidence. When she turned around, Marcus was standing in the room in padded biking shorts and a long-sleeved Lycra top. He teetered on his spinning shoes.

"Good evening, Mr. Meyers. Nice to see you again," she said, standing.

"Evening, Dale. Please don't get up. Have you ever tried spinning? Best workout that exists. I've been trying to get Tara on a bike for ages but she refuses. It would do her a world of good," he said.

Dale smiled politely.

"Maybe you can say something to her?" he suggested.

Dale was getting ready to protest when he changed the topic.

"How's she doing?" he asked.

"Fine."

"Seriously?"

"We have more work to do, but she's going to be fine."

"I hope so. What do you want her to wear?"

Marcus had put his leg on top of the couch and was stretching his hamstrings.

"Excuse me?"

"Tomorrow. For the interviews. What should she wear?"

"Oh, I don't know. Something she's comfortable in. She's in her own home."

"She's a little large at the moment so there aren't a lot of options, but I'll see what I can dig up."

Dale was more than a little surprised that Marcus was her self-appointed stylist.

"I'm sure there are people who can bring some things over," she offered.

Marcus smiled and shook his head.

"We've tried that. They all end up on the bottom of her closet."

"She could pick some things out—things she feels comfortable in."

"We're going to get her back into her size tens soon, and then down to the size eights after that."

He patted his own flat stomach.

As Dale tried to figure out if it was less awkward to look at him or to avoid looking at him while he limbered up, she reached the conclusion that he was a complete jackass.

"What time do you want her up?" he asked.

"Oh, I was going to ask her when she wanted to meet tomorrow. I'll go over the newspapers, bring her any guidance from the NSC or the White House on anything breaking overnight, and then we'll do a final run-through."

"Just tell me when your go time is and I'll have her down here," he said.

"I guess five A.M., so we aren't too rushed. Is that too early?"

"No, of course not. She can do this, you know. I mean, she just needs to get through this adjustment period and she'll be fine," he said. It was the first nice thing he'd said about his wife all evening.

"I think she's doing just fine now," Dale said.

"What are you guys talking about?" Tara asked, appearing suddenly in black sweatpants and a matching hoodie. She was wearing socks but no shoes and Dale hadn't heard her come down the stairs. She wondered how long Tara had been listening.

"How you are going to knock these interviews out of the park tomorrow, baby," Marcus said with a phony smile.

Tara walked to his side and said something Dale couldn't hear.

He nodded and said, "I've got it. You get back to your prep. You need it."

Before he left the room, he grabbed a roll of fat from around Tara's stomach.

"After we conquer the morning shows, we're going to focus on this," he said, looking at Dale while he spoke.

Tara looked mortified, and Dale could hardly keep the horror off her face. She couldn't decide which one of them was more shocking: Marcus for being so mean, or Tara for standing there and enduring his abuse. Dale felt like hurling her empty coffee cup at him.

"Dale here doesn't have an ounce of fat on her, do you, Dale?"

Dale looked at Tara sympathetically and tried to think of something funny to say to deflect Marcus's verbal assault.

"I have a mouth full of cavities and stringy brown hair. I'd kill for your wife's perfect teeth and gorgeous head of hair."

Tara smiled gratefully and Marcus let go of her. Dale continued. "Mr. Meyers, while we are honored by your company, we have a lot of work to do tonight before we can all go to bed," Dale said.

"No problem. It's time for me to spin off a cool thousand calories. The music doesn't bother you does it? Helps distract me from the pain."

"No," Dale said. Her eyes were on Tara as he made his way down the stairs in his spinning shoes. As soon as the door closed behind him, Dale heard him turn up the volume on the stereo. Eminen started blaring from the lower level.

Tara looked like she might cry.

Dale wanted to tell her to ignore the asshole she was married to, but she knew better than to insert herself. Tara had taken a seat on the same sofa where she'd been sitting before. She looked like she was trying to pull herself together.

"I have an idea," Dale said.

Tara looked up.

"Shoot the prick?" Tara said, with such a straight face that Dale was too stunned to say anything.

She laughed.

"Insanity defense," Tara added with a sly smile.

Dale laughed it off but filed it away in her I-can't-believe-this-is-my-life file.

"That wasn't what I was going to say."

"I know what it must look like." Tara sighed.

Dale waited for her to continue. When she didn't, Dale spoke.

"Madam Vice President, the American people are trying to figure you out. People are mostly interested in you because you seem too normal for politics. That makes you more intriguing and appealing, in a lot of ways, than President Kramer," Dale said.

Tara contemplated this.

"That's why I tried to work some of your struggles—with weight, with motherhood, with work—into the answers. I think that's how we dig out of this little hole we got you into. Let the American people inside the struggles and maybe they'll help pull you out."

Dale was trying to sound reassuring. She didn't like what the meat grinder was doing to Tara. She prayed that the vice president would regain some of the grit she'd displayed during the campaign.

"Can I tell you something?" Tara asked.

"Sure."

Dale thought for a second that she'd confide in her about whatever was going on.

"I am such a huge fan of Caroline Carter. I've watched *Wake Up, America* since I was in college and I feel like I know her, you know? You must think I am so lame. I mean, you know all these people."

"I don't want to shatter your image of her, but Caroline is dumber than my shoes," Dale said.

Tara looked crushed. Then she started to laugh.

"Take that back, Dale. I won't let you take away all my heroes."

Dale laughed and breathed a sigh of relief that Tara's sense of humor had returned.

"How about another round with the index cards? No theatrics. We'll will just go through all of the questions and answers until you're comfortable with the content?" Dale asked.

"Let's do it," Tara replied.

CHAPTER TWENTY-ONE

Charlotte

G ood god, sometimes I understand why they have so many enemies," Charlotte complained.

"They are a pain in the ass, but they're our pains in the ass," Melanie replied.

Charlotte, Melanie, Constance, and a herd of foreign policy advisors had joined their Israeli counterparts for a working dinner to discuss options for dealing with Iran's nuclear threat. The Israelis had renewed their request for bombs that could reach Iran's underground facilities and Charlotte had renewed her opposition, but, privately, she wondered why. If it became a foregone conclusion that the Israelis would attack Iran, shouldn't she ensure that their mission had a chance at success? Especially if lives were on the line and Iran's neighbors were secretly rooting for Israel to successfully thwart Iran's nuclear ambitions?

Charlotte sighed and looked at her watch. It was after nine P.M. She'd wanted to call Tara and wish her good luck in the morning but Ralph had said that Tara was hunkered down with Dale. Charlotte had had a bad feeling about the interviews all day. She'd snapped at her budget director and barked orders at her economic advisors during a meeting on the mid-summer employment picture. At the NSC meeting, usually the highlight of her day, she was unfocused.

She said her good-byes to the Israelis and convinced Melanie to come upstairs for a drink. They settled into their normal spots on the Truman Balcony with glasses of iced tea and a plate of lemon bars between them. The dogs were licking powdered sugar off the floor.

"Madam President, is everything okay? You fidgeted through the entire meeting, and I've never even seen you wear a watch, but tonight I saw you take it off your arm and place it on the table in front of you to supervise the passage of time. What's going on?"

"Nothing. I'm fine," Charlotte said.

"If you're fine, then I'm glad I don't sit down the hall anymore."

Charlotte sighed.

"You have your own problems, not to mention your own massive agency to run."

"That's never stopped you before."

"You're going to tell me that you told me so."

"You're worried about Tara's interviews tomorrow. What do you hear about how her prep is going?" Melanie asked.

"Ralph says it's going well."

Melanie opened her mouth to say something, but stopped herself.

"You don't think Ralph is giving it to me straight. I know. But what choice do I have?"

"You could call Dale. She may not be our favorite person on the planet, but you did allow her to be hired onto your senior staff. You certainly have the right to have a direct line of communication with her. Her title is deputy assistant to the president."

"I know." Charlotte stood up and paced the length of the balcony. Two of the dogs watched her walk back and forth while the oldest jumped onto the spot where she'd been sitting and curled up in it.

"Call her," Melanie urged.

Charlotte stopped and looked out toward the Washington Monument for a few seconds before she turned to Melanie with a determined look in her eyes.

"You're right. She's smart and she's not interested in seeing Tara humiliate herself."

"Or you."

"Right."

The irony wasn't lost on either one of them. Dale hadn't been worried about humiliating Charlotte when she had had an affair with her husband.

Charlotte picked up the phone and asked the Situation Room to reach Dale. They called back with Dale on the line in seconds.

"Hi Dale, it's Charlotte Kramer."

Melanie leaned forward to listen to Charlotte's end of the conversation.

"Listen, I was wondering how things were going there. Is Tara, I mean, do you think she's going to be ready for the interviews tomorrow?"

"I see. You're with her now, aren't you?"

"Dale, would you mind calling me when you leave, no matter what time it is? And please tell her I called about another matter, and that I wish her the best of luck."

Charlotte hung up.

"Was that as awkward for you as it was for me?" Melanie asked.

Charlotte smiled and sat back down. She pulled the sleeping dog into her lap.

"She was either surprised as hell that I called or worried as hell about Tara, I couldn't tell and she couldn't talk. Damn it. Ralph is out of his mind to do this to her," Charlotte fretted.

Melanie murmured in agreement.

"Did I tell you about our lunch? Tara looked like a woman on the edge last week. She came into the Oval like a tightly wound bundle of nerves. It was like she was on a White House tour or something. She was looking at all the crap in the Oval Office like she'd never seen it before. She was oohing and aahing over everything. I wanted to shake her. When I told her not to let the press bother her, she looked like she'd been slapped. I simply wanted her to know that I've stood where she's standing—that I'd been ridiculed and examined, and I'm still here. I wanted to boost her self-esteem and confidence and I think I shattered it."

"That's impossible. It's nothing you did. Tara doesn't seem rooted to me. That husband of hers always looks like he's working some angle, and Ralph is always shielding her from the press and the rest of the staff, so she's completely isolated. It seems as if she's searching for something to anchor herself to. Once she finds it, she'll settle in. You did."

"What was my anchor?"

"The dogs."

Charlotte raised her eyebrows and smiled.

They both knew that Melanie had been the unflappable, stabilizing influence around which Charlotte had oriented herself during the turmoil of the first term.

"These dogs are something," Charlotte said, rubbing Cammie's belly.

Melanie smiled and leaned back in her chair. "Should we have some wine?"

"Yes, I'm sorry. I don't know why they brought us tea. Hang on."

Charlotte called an usher and a bottle of their favorite Cakebread Chardonnay appeared.

"How are things with Brian?"

"Good. Really good. Too good." She smiled.

"That so?"

"We're going to the Inn at Little Washington this weekend. He's been acting a little strange and I have a feeling he could be planning to propose, but everyone gets engaged there, so it makes me think that there's no way he's going to propose."

"Hell, if he doesn't marry you, I will. I need a wife like you can't believe."

Melanie laughed.

"I'll tell him that if he doesn't move fast, you've offered me the entire East Wing."

"Call me right away if it happens, Mel. I'm so happy for you. Do you want to get married here? That would be nice. Or at Camp David?" Charlotte asked, suddenly excited about the prospect of a White House wedding.

"No, I think I'm too old for a big wedding, aren't I?"

"You're thirty-seven."

"I'm thirty-eight. I told Brian he should find someone who has ovaries that didn't spend their best years under the artificial lights of the West Wing."

"You're ovaries are fine. Plus, they do incredible things these days with IVF and what not. You'll be fine. Do you want to have kids?"

"I just sort of figured that someday I'd have them."

Charlotte beamed at her. She felt proud and jealous and sad and happy all at the same time.

"You and Brian are incredibly lucky to have found each other and grabbed on to each other. Don't screw it up," Charlotte said.

"I know." Hugging wasn't part of their relationship, but if it were, this would have been an occasion for it. Instead, Charlotte repeated her offer.

"I'm serious about the White House wedding," Charlotte said.

"I'm not even engaged yet." Melanie laughed.

They finished two glasses of wine each and the plate of lemon bars.

"I've missed our two-course meals. Wine and dessert. There are at least two food groups in there, right?"

"At least," Charlotte said.

Charlotte wanted to ask Melanie to do something that she knew Melanie would not want to do. It fell squarely outside her responsibilities as secretary of defense, but there wasn't anyone else she could ask. She turned to face Melanie.

"Uh-oh. What?" Melanie asked.

"Why do you say it like that?"

"Because you have that look."

"What look?" Charlotte asked.

"The 'try to forget I'm the president of the United States of America' while I ask you to do whatever you're about to ask me to do," Melanie said.

Charlotte crossed her arms across her chest and laughed.

"I hate that you can read me like that. But you're right. I want you to do something for me."

Melanie looked as if she was bracing herself.

"I'm listening," she said.

"Reach out to Dale. Take her to lunch. See what she knows about Tara," Charlotte pleaded.

Melanie smiled.

"What?" Charlotte asked.

"Nothing."

"Will you do it?"

"Do I have a choice?"

Charlotte smiled. She was pleased with herself. If Melanie opened up a line of communication with Dale, she'd have a source of information independent from Ralph's spin.

She walked Melanie out of the residence and returned to the sofa on the balcony to work on the speech she'd deliver in China later that week. She couldn't think about anything other than Tara's interviews the following morning. She thought about calling Billy Moore, the news director at one of the networks, to plead with him to go easy on Tara, but she knew it wouldn't make a difference. Besides, she didn't want to raise the stakes by showing how concerned she was.

She looked at the clock and wondered if Dale would call her back. She went back to her speech and crossed a huge section out with a thick black Sharpie. The speechwriters were experiencing some turnover—something that never happened under Melanie's rule—and the new writers hadn't developed the necessary camaraderie and brainmeld that is essential for successful presidential speechwriting. She sighed and prepared to cross out an entire page, but decided against it. She'd call the writers into the Oval Office the next morning and share her concerns. She flipped impatiently through her "Read" file and then placed all the paperwork on the ground.

Charlotte was anxious. Not just about the interviews the next morning, but about her decision to put Tara on the ticket. At the time, she'd been so eager to shake up the status quo that she rushed the selection process once Neal agreed to step down. And while she wouldn't have admitted it to anyone on her staff, she thought it was a long shot, at best, that she'd win a second term. Lately, she'd had a nagging feeling that she'd done something irreversibly reckless.

CHAPTER TWENTY-TWO

Tara

Tara knew she was flying too high.

She was dropping "y'alls" and "all y'alls" like she was at a goddamned rodeo. Her affinity for those infectious southern contractions was owed to a charming college student from the University of South Carolina named Lacey who'd worked as a summer intern in the U.S. Attorney's Office. She couldn't explain why or exactly how she'd adopted Lacey's southern drawl, but it had stuck.

God, she felt strange. It was as though she'd ingested helium gas and was floating above the ground, speaking in a squeaky, high-pitched voice and watching the activity below. She touched her face and was immediately convinced that her smile took up too much space. Her mouth felt big, and she was doing strange things to make it appear smaller. The interviews hadn't even started yet, but already the conversation around her was going too fast at times and too slow at others. She felt like she was watching a badly dubbed movie in which the dialogue lagged behind the action.

Tara watched Marcus make a latte for one of the anchors. He was always so pleasant with strangers. She looked over at Kendall, who was sitting at the table watching the crews check their cameras and microphones. She didn't look upset or uncomfortable, but Tara could tell she was sleepy. She felt awful about waking her up before five A.M. More than anything else, Tara was angry at herself for letting Marcus talk her into the massive production unfolding in her kitchen.

She flipped through the small stack of index cards Dale had left her the night before. Before Dale left around 11:00 P.M., Tara was able to put most of the responses into her own words, but now, as her eyes moved over the cards, she felt as if she'd never seen them before. She inhaled sharply and walked out to where the crew was gathered on the patio. A few of them were smoking. They all held paper cups of coffee. Tara smiled at them and then stared down at the cards again so no one would try to talk to her.

It was still dark out but the sun would be up by the time the interviews started. It was already warm and quite humid. D.C. didn't cool down at night the way New York did. Tara looked at her underarms and saw that she'd sweat through the cotton dress she'd painstakingly selected for the interviews. She felt her chest tighten and she turned to walk back inside to change.

She ran into Dale in the front hallway.

"Good morning, Madam Vice President. Are you ready?"

"I think so," Tara lied.

"You look nice," Dale smiled.

"I look fat."

"No, you look great."

"It doesn't matter. I have to change anyway. I stained this dress already." Tara turned to head upstairs, eyeing Dale's sleeveless black linen dress with envy. She'd paired it with open-toed heels that looked like they cost a fortune. Tara looked down at her feet as she lumbered up the stairs. She was wearing espadrilles that made her feet look as wide as they were long.

"Did you have a chance to go over the newspapers, Madam Vice President?" Dale called after her.

"Not yet. Anything in them?"

"A couple stories that they could ask you about. Do you want to go over them?"

"Sure, come on up and tell me about them while I change."

"Yes ma'am."

Once upstairs, Tara disappeared into her closet.

"I thought this was breakfast with the family? Light and friendly chitchat over eggs and pancakes?" Tara complained.

"It is, but it's also a newscast, and there are just a couple stories that you should know about," Dale replied.

Tara felt her stomach tighten as she pulled down and swiftly rejected a yellow-belted sundress.

"What are they? What are the stories?"

"Do you want me to read them to you?"

"No. I want you to tell me what they would ask me and what I should say," she snapped.

Tara hated herself for the way she was speaking to Dale, but her brain was full.

Dale held up her BlackBerry and started reading a story about a friendly fire incident from the night before in Afghanistan. Tara was having a hard time focusing.

"I said I didn't want to hear the story. Friendly fire in Afghanistan. What's the talking point?"

"I'd suggest that you express your deep sympathies for the loss of life, state your commitment to the safety of every American, coalition, and Afghan soldier on the battlefield—fighting for a free and safe Afghanistan—and say that the president is committed to doing anything in her power to reduce and ultimately eliminate any loss of life."

"Fine. Next."

Tara saw Dale swallow and noticed that she hadn't looked up from her BlackBerry since she'd come upstairs.

"The other story they could ask you about is in the *Washington Post* style section. It's about whether high-profile women are held to different standards than men when it comes to their appearance."

"Why would they ask *me* about it?"

"Well, I haven't seen it, but there is a photo of you that accompanies the article."

"A photo?"

"Yes."

"Why?"

"Apparently, the caption reads 'Fair Game? Vice President Meyers has packed on the pounds since being sworn in.'"

"Oh god. What does the photo look like?"

"I left my house at four A.M. and the papers hadn't been delivered."

"Jesus Christ."

"Madam Vice President, we talked about this. Just brush off any questions about your weight with the line we practiced about how countless women battle unwanted pounds. Talk about how you're trying to find balance between work, family, and taking better care of yourself, but you're not perfect."

"We talked about it before there was a photo of me in the style section," Tara barked.

Dale didn't say anything.

"What else?"

Dale looked down at her BlackBerry again.

"Those are the biggies," she said.

Tara had pulled on a shirtdress that strained at the chest a bit, but was an otherwise reasonable selection. She smoothed her hair and walked toward the door.

"Madam Vice President," Dale said.

"Yes?"

"You're going to do great."

Tara managed to mutter "thanks" before she walked back down the stairs.

CHAPTER TWENTY-THREE

Dale

Dale had a half a dozen other stories to go over with the vice president, but she didn't want to blow her circuits with too much information. She only mentioned the ones she was certain the anchors would ask, but now she was fretting about skipping the others. She felt her phone vibrate.

"Hello?"

"Did you go over the bankruptcy bill with her?" Ralph asked.

"No. I didn't get much further than the friendly fire story in Afghanistan," Dale replied.

"Why not?"

"Trust me. I could barely get her attention with a story about U.S. deaths in Afghanistan. I wasn't going to push my luck by trying to cram something in her brain about the bankruptcy bill passing out of the Senate Finance Committee."

"It's a big deal."

"If you'd like to come down here and prep her, I'll tell her you're on your way."

"No. I'm sorry. I'm sure you're doing your best. Good luck."

"Thanks." Dale hung up before he could say anything else.

When she'd called the president back the night before, she'd had half a mind to tell her that her vice president was hanging on to the edge of a cliff with her fingernails. But she fought her impulse to be the bearer of bad news and concluded that the president was the one person who should not know anything until it was clear what they were dealing with. There had been a moment when she thought Charlotte was going to ask her what the hell was wrong with Tara, but it didn't happen. The president was professional and gracious and sounded relieved when Dale said she believed that Tara was adequately prepared for the interviews. That was last night. Now, the vice president was in a bleary-eyed pretantrum state of mind over something. Her weight? Her outfit? Her husband? Dale wasn't sure.

As Tara and Marcus took their seats at the breakfast table, Dale positioned herself off to the side of the kitchen. She watched Marcus engage in casual banter with the sound technician who was putting a microphone on his shirt. Once he was hooked up, he talked Kendall through the process. She seemed to enjoy the attention. Dale watched Tara stare off into space while her microphone was being attached to the collar of her dress. The vice president didn't even look up when the man reached into her dress to tape the wires to the inside of her dress with electrical tape.

Dale moved to where a producer was checking the shot and examined it herself in the monitor. Tara was sitting on one side of the table and Marcus and Kendall on the other. Between them, there was a bountiful bowl of fruit, some type of egg dish, and a stack of toast. A selection of jam and butter had been placed beside the toast along with a platter of pastries. There was a carafe of orange juice on the table as well as something that looked like grapefruit or pineapple juice, and their mugs had been filled with steaming coffee.

A producer approached Dale.

"We have three minutes until the top of the show. We'd like to start with a live shot of the family and then we'll get to the interview at about three minutes after the hour. Does that work for you?"

"Sure," Dale said.

"Do you want to give the family a heads-up that we're going to take a live picture at the top? Maybe they can start eating then so it looks like the interview comes in the middle of their meal?"

"Sure," Dale said. She'd always been uncomfortable with the stage-craft of interviews like this.

Dale walked up to the table and knelt down in front of the vice president.

"Your mic is hot," she said to Tara.

The vice president stared at her blankly.

Dale pointed at her microphone.

"It's on, I just wanted to remind you."

Tara nodded.

"In about two minutes, they are going to take a live shot of all of you and start their broadcast with it, and then Caroline will join you at the table and start the interview at a couple minutes past seven. Got it?"

Tara nodded again.

"And, uh, they'd like you guys to start eating."

"Goodie," said Kendall, reaching for one of the huge pastries. She placed it on Tara's plate and smiled.

"Mommy loves these," she said.

Marcus made a face that Dale could have killed him for. Tara's face registered the blow like a slap. She took a few seconds and then turned to Kendall.

"Thank you, baby. That is one of my favorite treats," she said. "I'm going to save it for later because I think I'd better start with fruit today."

Dale could tell that Kendall thought she'd done something wrong. She leaned over to grab the pastry off Tara's plate and knocked the coffee cup into her lap.

Two members of the crew came rushing over with paper towels and even the anchor looked over with concern. To Tara's credit, she simply smiled and covered her lap with a napkin.

"We're fine. Everyone can relax," Tara said.

"I'm sorry, Mom," Kendall said quietly.

"Don't worry, sweetie pie," Tara replied. She rubbed Kendall's shoulder and glared at Marcus.

"Just another breakfast with the Meyers family," Tara said, loud enough for everyone assembled to hear. A few people laughed. Tara piled her plate with fruit and refilled her coffee. Dale breathed a sigh of relief and returned to her perch on the side of the kitchen. Tara usually liked for Dale to stand in her line of sight to offer time cues. For example, she'd hold up her hand when there were five minutes remaining, and she'd tap her watch a couple times to signal that the interview was almost over.

In the past, Dale had also been able to channel reassurance from across a room. If there was ever a time when her telepathic powers would come in handy, this was it.

Dale watched as the anchor was having her perfect hair and makeup touched up for the third time since she'd arrived. One person dabbed Caroline's flawless forehead with a puff while a second sprayed an invisible flyaway into place. A third person reapplied lip gloss to her perfectly glossed lips. Dale looked down at her fingernails and tried to remember the last time she'd had a manicure. She ran her fingers through the ends of her ponytail and made a mental note to schedule a haircut for the next time she was in New York.

She watched Caroline take one last look at her notes before making a big production about pouring herself orange juice and taking a dry piece of wheat toast from the bread basket. She put three strawberries on her plate next to the toast and then looked at Tara for the first time. Seconds later, the floor director pointed at the camera in front of Caroline and the newswoman flashed her toothy smile.

"Thanks for waking up with us, America. Today, in a *Wake Up, America* special, we are having breakfast with Vice President Tara Meyers and her gorgeous family."

"Good morning, Madam Vice President. Thanks for having us."

"Thanks for joining us for breakfast, Caroline. I'm so happy that we get to do this. I've been a fan of yours for years," Tara said warmly.

"Oh, that's awfully nice of you. I want to get right at it, Madam Vice President. Some of your critics think the job is too much for you to handle. Are they correct?"

Tara glanced at Dale briefly.

"I'm so happy that you asked me that question, Caroline. And I appreciate this opportunity to answer my critics. There's no doubt about it. The vice presidency is a big job, and an important one. It's one I've been preparing for my whole life. Whether it was during college when I worked two jobs to to help pay my tuition and expenses, or in law school when I managed a Starbucks during the day and studied all night, or as a young attorney in the Manhattan District

Attorney's Office, or even during my time in the U.S. Attorney's Office—I have always risen to the challenge. I'll readily admit that I had a rough start, but the American people can rest assured that I'm in the fight for them and their families each and every day," Tara said, smiling confidently as she recited the answer exactly as she and Dale had rehearsed it.

CHAPTER TWENTY-FOUR

Charlotte

Hurry up, girls. Do your business," Charlotte ordered.

The dogs ignored her and continued to sniff the grass in the exact spots where they'd peed the night before.

Charlotte had cleared her schedule until nine A.M. so she could watch the interviews from the residence. She'd decided to run the dogs out quickly after the first two interviews. She was eager to get back inside before the last one started.

The first segment had gone smoothly enough. Tara looked nervous, and Charlotte could tell the answers were rehearsed, but at least she hadn't frozen up or said anything off the wall. Charlotte hoped the bar in the public's mind was as low as hers. The second interview went better than the first. Tara repeated the same answers, but because the material was more familiar, she sounded less scripted doing so. Charlotte was beginning to think she'd been unnecessarily harsh on Ralph.

"Time's up, girls. Cammie, you're going to have to hold it until we go to work in a little bit." Charlotte walked briskly from the South Lawn back to the residence with the dogs a few paces ahead of her. She hoped none of the press had seen her out there in her workout clothes. That would set off a round of stories about how she'd added a workout to her morning routine, which couldn't be further from the truth.

Charlotte poured herself a second cup of coffee and sat back down at her desk in the study on the second floor. The third interview would air at eight A.M. when the audience was made of up almost entirely of women viewers. Charlotte hoped it would be the easiest. The regular anchor was out on maternity leave, so the woman with the title "newsreader" was conducting the interview. Charlotte didn't know her and had never been interviewed by her, but she seemed pleasant when she read her two-minute news bursts at the top of each hour.

"Good morning, Madam Vice President," she said. Her voice was so loud that Charlotte reached for the remote to lower the volume.

"Good morning. Thanks for joining me and my family for a little breakfast." Tara looked more relaxed.

"Whose idea was it to invite all of us here for these interviews and why did you think something like this was necessary?" the newsreader asked.

Charlotte turned the volume back up and waited for Tara to answer.

Tara stared at her for a few seconds too long.

Uh oh, Charlotte fretted.

"I wanted all of you to have a chance to get to know our family a little better," Tara finally said.

Atta girl, Charlotte said to herself.

"That's really nice, but we've been trying for months now to spend some time with you so that our viewers could get to know you and your family. I'm just wondering if these interviews have anything to do with the spate of stories that have run in various papers recently speculating that you're having problems with the adjustment to Washington."

"No, of course not, Maria," Tara said quickly.

"Marie," she corrected.

"What?"

"My name is Marie, not Maria."

Tara's eyes darted around the room.

Who cares what your stupid name is? Charlotte fumed.

"Marie, I'm so sorry about that. We just thought it was a good time to have y'all over for a bite and a chat about whatever was on all y'alls' mind today," Tara said with a forced smile.

"But what I'm asking is why *now*?" Marie pushed.

"No time like the present!" Tara chirped, a little too enthusiastically.

"Madam Vice President, how are you holding up?" Marie asked.

Tara looked around the room again.

Come on, Tara, just get back to your message points, Charlotte silently urged.

The wheels in Tara's mind were churning so furiously that Charlotte half expected to see smoke rising from her head.

"No doubt, the vice presidency is a big job. And I wouldn't deny the fact, Marie, that I have had a rough start. But what your viewers need to know is that I have always risen to the challenge, whether it was when I was in college or law school or the U.S. Attorney's Office, and I have fought the fights that need to be fought."

Tara sounded like she was reading from cue cards that were just out of her line of vision. The network switched to a wide shot of the breakfast table. A slow-moving fly hovered above the egg dish, and the fruit salad and pastries looked as if they were sweating as much as the vice president. Marie looked as though she'd just stepped out of the air-conditioning, which she probably had.

"I heard you say that earlier this morning, and I'm just wondering what fights you waged in college and law school. Were you involved in many causes or political campaigns?"

"No, I meant that I fought my way through school and scraped by, and then fought my way into law school, and then fought my way into the DA's Office and the U.S. Attorney's Office." Tara was starting to sound exasperated.

Damn, Charlotte thought. *Why couldn't she just do one interview? This young reporter has been sitting in a van somewhere watching Tara offer the same answers to the previous anchors. She's showing them the benefits of going last.*

"What you're saying is that your ambition is what has always powered you through difficult times?"

"No, I mean, I guess. I don't know. I just wanted to do well, you know?"

The reported nodded and stared down at her notepad.

"What issues has President Kramer entrusted you with?"

"What do you mean?"

"Your predecessor took the lead on most of the domestic issues to allow President Kramer to focus on the wars in Iraq and Afghanistan.

I'm curious what your portfolio looks like, particularly in light of the economic challenges we're facing."

"I, uh, I work on everything."

"There's nothing specific that the president turned over to you and said, 'Do whatever you think is best—I'll follow your lead?'"

Tara looked stumped. After taking what felt like five minutes to think about the question, Tara shook her head. "None I can think of," she said.

In the wide-angle shot the network was running, Charlotte noticed that Marcus was shifting uncomfortably in his seat and even Kendall looked unnerved.

"I ask you this question, Madam Vice President, because one of the criticisms of you among members of Congress is that you often seem stumped by their policy questions, and I'm wondering if perhaps that's because the president has asked you to focus on a few key areas and leave the rest to her?"

Tara stared blankly at Marie.

Charlotte picked up the phone.

"Please get Ralph on the line for me."

"Yes ma'am?" he replied seconds later.

"I want this to stop. Now."

"Yes ma'am. I don't know what happened. Dale assured me that these would all be like the last two, and—"

"Stop. Just stop. Meet me in the Oval Office in twenty minutes."

When she hung up, she was breathing heavily enough to pique the dogs' interest. "Shhh," she said to them when all three came closer. She returned her attention to the television set. Cammie leaned against her while she watched.

"I'm sorry, what was the question?" Tara asked.

"It's okay, we can move on. Madam Vice President, I have a few more questions for you, and I have to ask you a favor. Your folks have been giving me 'wrap it up' signals practically since I started, but I wonder if you might indulge our millions of viewers with a few more minutes of your time."

Tara looked like she was in shock.

"Sure," she said meekly.

"Can you tell our viewers what the most difficult thing is about making this move with your young family to a city you don't know, and taking on the responsibilities of the vice presidency for a president you hardly know who is a member of a political party you don't belong to."

Tara stared at Marie for so long that the reporter asked if she needed the question repeated.

"Marie, I would have to say that the most difficult thing is, well, moments like this, when I have no idea where to begin to answer that question."

"Your honesty is refreshing, Madam Vice President. Why don't you start by telling us how it is to be part of a Republican administration?"

"It's great. I mean, I was always really in the middle, and Charlotte and I agree on just about everything."

"Can you name one area where you disagree?"

"No, nothing comes to mind."

"Madam Vice President, have you and the president ever discussed abortion?"

"No. I mean, I know she is, I mean, no. We haven't discussed it." Tara looked like she didn't even realize she was still on television.

"If a Supreme Court seat opened, could you support someone who thought *Roe* was wrongly decided?"

"No," Tara said.

"Okay, well, I have more really good questions, but I just noticed that your staff is about to cut the power to our camera. Thank you so much for your time. This is Marie Mendes, reporting live from the Naval Observatory, the official residence of Vice President Tara Meyers and her family. We'll be right back."

As soon as it ended, her assistant, Sam, appeared in Charlotte's study in the residence. Charlotte felt like she was a hundred years old.

"Hi, Sam. I'll be in the Oval Office in ten minutes. Is there anything I need to deal with before I walk over?"

"You have some urgent calls, ma'am. The Speaker called and wants to speak to you right away and the press office wants to see you immediately to get guidance on what to say to reporters who are asking if you were watching the interviews. Oh, and Melanie called and offered to come over."

"Did you see it?" Charlotte asked.

"Yes ma'am," Sam replied.

"Was it as bad as it seemed?"

"I don't know, ma'am. Do you want me to get Melanie on the line?"

"Sam, come on. It was awful. You thought it was a disaster, didn't you?"

"She looked a tad uncomfortable, ma'am," Sam replied reluctantly.

Charlotte knew that whatever had gone awry in her first term was going to feel like a joy ride compared to what was about to unfold. Until the interviews, questions about Tara's abilities and competence could be brushed away as partisan sniping. But now that she'd laid bare her insecurities and obvious uncertainty about her role and function as Charlotte's number two, there were few palatable options for a comeback.

"Please get Melanie on the line," she asked Sam.

The phone rang seconds later.

"Was it as bad as I think it was?" Charlotte asked Melanie.

"Yes."

"What happens now?"

"I'm not sure."

"What's your best guess?"

"I need to think about it."

"Call me back when you've worked out the best- and worst-case scenario."

"I will, Madam President, I will."

Sam had picked up the other phone in the study.

"Ma'am, the secretary of state is on the line to confirm that you are still planning to depart tonight for the Asia trip. Would you like to speak to her?"

"No."

"Ma'am?"

"Tell them you'll call them back when you know whether I'm still going on the Asia trip tonight."

"Yes ma'am."

CHAPTER TWENTY-FIVE

Tara

Tara watched the night turn from a seemingly endless dusk to Washington's version of darkness. The sky never turned completely black in D.C. She'd never paid much attention to the weather before, but summer in Washington was unlike any she'd ever experienced. Tara had decided that Washington's inability to fade to black was due to its toxic combination of humidity, heat, and proximity to swampland. It was only a few hundred miles farther south than New York City, but the climate was more similar to the sticky, oppressive heat of the Deep South than the occasional humidity and thunderstorms typical of summertime in the Northeast. In Washington, everything wilted, even the people. Tara had felt uncomfortably hot for as long as she could remember. The more she strained to remember a time when the weather wasn't unpleasant, the further back she had to go. She settled on Inauguration Day as the last time she remembered feeling cool. It felt like a lifetime ago, but it had only been six and a half months.

The heat had depleted her physically almost as much as the previous seventy-two hours had depleted her mentally and emotionally. The *Washington Post* described the interviews as "a PR disaster of unmatched magnitude." The *New York Times* ran a mushy editorial about Marie Mendes's "plucky gumption" and said the interview would have "Woodward and Bernstein–sized consequences." In hindsight, she never should have agreed to do them. She'd let Marcus and Ralph guilt her into biting off more than she could handle.

Tara had managed her limitations for more than a decade and a half by taking on only what she could manage, never any more. It hadn't helped that Ralph and Marcus had suggested that her future, and Charlotte's political fortunes, hinged on the success of the interviews. Tara had been paralyzed by the stakes, but in reality, it was summer and no one outside of Washington was paying attention to the clumsy execution of her official duties. They were now, though. She sighed and stroked Kendall's damp hair. It was even humid inside with the air-conditioning running. Tara stared at the fireflies outside Kendall's window and berated herself again for not listening to her gut about the interviews. She could have simply ignored the nasty news stories, studied harder, pushed herself to connect with the people who showed up at her events, and shown a bit of expertise on law enforcement issues when they arose. It wasn't like Charlotte was pressuring her to run with any of the administration's legislative items. Hell, Tara didn't even know what their legislative agenda looked like. Tara looked down at Kendall as she snored. She'd slept in Kendall's room for the last three nights. The first night, it had been for Tara's benefit, but after Kendall came home from summer camp in tears over something one of her friends had said, Tara had taken up temporary residence in her daughter's room. Kendall wouldn't tell Tara what had been said, but the camp director had called to say that some of the children had been unkind. The self-loathing that Tara felt for everything she'd imposed on the people around her was at once debilitating and satisfying. She deserved it, but she also knew that none of them would be able to move on until Tara let it go. She and Kendall were working through it, and for once, Marcus didn't try to get between them. He'd been uncharacteristically hands off in the days since the interviews. Instead of his normal hovering, he stayed as far away from them as possible.

While Kendall slept, Tara allowed herself to wallow. Shame had always been her motivator. The stupid reporter had asked about her ambition, but it had never been about the pursuit of accolades or accomplishment. No one had ever been there to celebrate her successes. But the shame was always right on her tail, threatening to catch her if she let herself go even just a little bit.

If she were a normal person under medical supervision, she would have gone to the doctor and explained that when she moved to D.C., she went from feeling like she was drowning at times, to something far worse. She would explain to a doctor that for the last six months, she woke up on most days feeling like someone was holding her head underwater and forcing her to take huge gulps of liquid, and that the harder she choked, the more she wished for the days when she simply felt like she'd been drowning. She'd describe lows so debilitating that she'd pull herself along the walls of the house and prop herself in Kendall's doorway to get through the night. She'd explain that when none of these things worked, she'd wake Kendall up and smother her face with kisses. Maybe a doctor would have been able to do something for her. But Tara had opted out of proper medical treatment for her illness when she first decided she wanted a career in public service. Medical records were always the subject of intense media interest. Any public person who didn't turn over records that would otherwise be protected by a patient's right to privacy was always viewed with great suspicion. It's not that Tara had any inkling that she'd wind up in the White House, but she'd paid enough attention to politics to know that mental illness was an immediate disqualifier. So, instead, she'd allowed Marcus to create a structure to insulate her from stress and other triggers. And it had worked fine in New York, but Washington didn't lend itself to the highly shielded existence she'd grown accustomed to as A.G.

She looked up when Marcus appeared in the doorway to Kendall's room.

"Hi," she whispered.

He started to say something. She placed her finger over her lips and rose slowly from the bed.

"Where have you been?" she asked as they walked downstairs toward the kitchen.

"I played basketball then went for a run on the Mall."

"Do you want something to eat?"

"No thanks. I'm not hungry."

Tara felt more unsure of herself around Marcus when he was polite than when he was mean.

"How's Kendall doing?" he asked.

"She won't tell me what her friends said to her. She said she doesn't want to hurt my feelings. I told her that as long as she still loved me, there's nothing anyone could do to hurt me."

She thought he looked pale.

"Are you feeling all right?" she asked.

"Yeah, yeah. Don't worry about me."

Tara watched Marcus unpack his gym bag. He placed his sweaty clothes on the kitchen floor and removed his basketball shoes from the bag to air them out. The closer she examined him, the more worried she felt. He looked as though he knew that they were in over their heads. She took a deep breath and was getting ready to say something to him about how they were all going to be okay when the phone in the breakfast room rang, jolting her out of her thoughts. Marcus leapt for it.

"Hello?"

He held the phone out for Tara.

"It's for you. It's the Sit Room."

The Sit Room rarely called this late.

"Hello?"

"Madam Vice President, I'm sorry to bother you, but a meeting is being convened in the Sit Room in about twenty minutes. Are you able to come in?"

"Certainly." She wasn't even sure who she was speaking to.

She hung up and turned to Marcus.

"What's wrong? Is it Charlotte?" Charlotte was in Asia.

"I don't know. They asked me to come in for a meeting."

They shared a knowing look.

"I don't think it has anything to do with us," she said quietly.

She saw Marcus swallow.

"Right."

"I'm going to head upstairs to change. Will you stay in Kendall's room in case she wakes up?"

"Of course."

"I'm sure everything is fine," she said, with more confidence than she felt.

Exactly twenty minutes later, she was escorted into the conference room of the Situation Room on the ground floor of the West Wing. The White House was never a noisy or chaotic place, but it felt quieter than usual to her tonight. The guard stationed at the door stood when she entered.

"Good evening, Madam Vice President," he said.

She smiled and nodded at him. She walked into the Sit Room and was directed to the conference room where she was surrounded by familiar faces on the monitors that hung on the walls. On one screen, she recognized a few senior Justice Department officials, and on another, she saw a group of FBI agents from New York's counterterror unit. The New York police chief was on another screen. In the center screen, a satellite feed was open with the word *Beijing* taped on a piece of paper on the bottom of the screen. Someone from the president's traveling entourage would be joining them as well, Tara figured.

The CIA director and the director of national intelligence were seated at one end of the table. The attorney general, the deputy national security advisor, and the undersecretaries of state and defense were on the other end. Ralph was seated in a chair behind the chairs at the table and a few other White House aides who Tara recognized but couldn't name were sitting next to him.

"Thanks for coming in, Madam Vice President," the deputy national security advisor said.

"We are waiting for POTUS, the secretary of state, and the SECDEF to join us from Beijing and then we'll get started. I think everyone knows why we're here," he said.

Tara had no idea why she was there. Her eyes were glued to the center monitor where Charlotte, Constance, and Melanie had appeared while the deputy national security advisor was speaking. They looked like they were in a hotel room.

"Good morning from Bejing," Charlotte said with a wave. "Melanie and Constance are still here for meetings with their counterparts, so I asked them to stay for the call.

"Good morning, Madam President," the deputy national security advisor said. "I want to make sure that Tim is with you as well."

Tim was the president's national security advisor.

"We're all here," Charlotte said. "Thanks for coming in, Tara. I hope we didn't pull you away from anything. You look like you were having a peaceful night at home."

For some reason, it didn't dawn on Tara that they could see her, but they were on video teleconferencing systems as well.

"No problem at all. I'm happy to be here, Madam President."

"We have a bit of a delay over here. Why don't you guys take the lead from there," Charlotte suggested.

"Very well, Madam President, Madam Vice President. As you all know, we are monitoring a situation that has the potential to result in a more sophisticated and audacious attack than anything we've seen on U.S. soil. Ever," he said.

Usually, that sentenced ended with "since the attacks of 9/11." As daunting as the topic was, Tara finally felt like people were speaking a language she understood.

"Madam Vice President, you'll be familiar with the case. Youseff Bordeaux is someone we've been watching for a number of years now. His brother was prosecuted by the U.S. Attorney's Office in Manhattan for a failed plot to blow up the Brooklyn Bridge. I believe you were an assistant U.S. attorney at the time."

"I remember Youseff. He was extremely helpful. We dropped a conspiracy case against him because he helped us put his brother away for life. He lives with his wife and kids in New Jersey and works as an IT consultant for at-home eBay business owners."

"He *lived* with his wife and kids in New Jersey. He sent them to Yemen eight months ago. He quit his job and has become expert at covering his tracks. As soon as we obtain a court order for a wiretap, we lose him."

"That's surprising. Even back then, he was completely Westernized. Whatever he's up to, there have to be clues in his e-mail or on the Web sites he visits. He was an early fan of chat rooms. He used them to raise money for his brother's defense. We could never tie him to the plot, but despite his willingness to help us prosecute his brother, I had my suspicions about which way he'd go after."

"You were correct to have suspicions. And it's pretty clear which way he went, Madam Vice President. We believe that he is connected to several of the recent homegrown plots in the northeastern United States. Thankfully, his associates aren't as good as he is at covering their tracks. All the attacks I mentioned were thwarted and they've generated some of the best leads we've had in years to the financial system and the communications networks that these loose affiliates are running. We found Youseff's cell phone number in the phone left behind by the Christmas tree bomber. Youseff sent another would-be attacker a slew of links to bomb-making Web sites. Thank God, his buddy couldn't follow instructions very well. The guy's device blew up his kitchen before he could detonate it," said the FBI director.

"Sounds like he's their new DIY expert," Tara said.

"DIY?" asked the deputy secretary of state.

"Do-it-yourself. The new terrorist entrepreneurs recruit young, unconnected nobodies and connect them to a help desk of sorts—someone like Youseff who then serves as an advisor to aspiring terrorists. It's efficient for the ringleaders: no risky travel or importing weapons on commercial flights. And it's like the terrorists' version of a talent competition. Dozens of young guys start out in the early rounds, each of them seeking glory in the eyes of their heroes and idols at the top of the terror networks in Yemen, Afghanistan, and Pakistan. By the final round, only a couple of them are still standing, and they are the ones who move up and become the leaders in the U.S. The really scary thing is that they're not motivated by religious zealotry; it's more akin to the allure of a gang and the competition among all the rookies to make it to the big leagues by pulling off an attack," Tara said.

"The vice president is exactly right. And unfortunately, the religious connections are what we started tracking after September 11. We don't have any technological advances, other than the monitoring programs, over these guys anymore," said the head of the NSA.

"We're looking for a mentor to young, Web-savvy terrorists?" Charlotte asked.

"That's about right, Madam President. The bigger concern I have is that he's disappeared completely in recent weeks. This is the longest we've gone without a hit on his cell phones or e-mail addresses from the other suspects we monitor," the CIA director said.

Tara was staring at his picture. She remembered everything about his face. Even after his brother's investigation and trial were over, she'd thought about him for months. Youseff had given her the evidence she needed to make his brother's conviction a sure thing. She'd had no reason not to trust him. But even then, she'd sensed that the deal he'd done with her office had been a chess move, a step toward a larger objective. She remembered presenting his attorneys with the deal. They'd wanted twenty-four hours to review it. He'd insisted on signing it right then.

"Tara, any guesses?"

"I don't know, Madam President. But it's not a good sign that we've lost track of him."

"Do we think there's any connection to the actions we're taking to isolate Iran?" Charlotte asked.

"I don't think so, Madam President, but we'll run down everything," the CIA chief answered.

"Why are we more worried about this particular suspect than we are about all the homegrown cells in every major city in the country?" Melanie asked.

"It's not that we're more worried, Madam Secretary. We have teams watching all the homegrown cells that are on our radar. As you know, we have a pretty good record lately of pulling the plug on these guys before they launch anything successfully. The concern we have with Youseff is that he's been here long enough to have planned something spectacular for next month's anniversary of the 9/11 attacks."

"I'm having a hard time grasping how he could have planned something spectacular without our knowledge. Haven't we been watching him?" Melanie challenged.

"We were. And his disappearance from every one of our surveillance methods, and the fact that it's now been several weeks without any sign of what he's up to, is what triggered tonight's emergency meeting."

Melanie didn't look satisfied, but Tara thought they were wise to convene the group. Youseff had the knowledge, the connections, and the familiarity with the U.S. to plan something big. He was the perfect point person for whatever attacks were envisioned for the September 11 anniversary. And he'd had ample time to build a team and plan. Youseff had been in the United States for nearly two decades. Tara racked her brain to try to remember any other details about the case. If she could show Charlotte that she was actually good at something, maybe she could survive.

CHAPTER TWENTY-SIX

Dale

In Dale's fantasy, she screamed, "Write whatever you fucking want" into the phone at the combative, hostile journalist. In reality, she was about to make her twenty-third call of the day to speak, off the record, about the vice president's "rough patch" to a reporter who, more likely than not, would be sympathetic and embarrassed by the questions she had to ask.

"It was bad staff work," Dale would offer to the reporter on deep background.

"We didn't prepare her for process questions," she'd say. "You can use that on background from an official deeply involved in the interview planning, if you want," she'd say.

But no matter what she did to take the fall for her boss's less than stellar performance earlier in the week, the impression of the vice president as unprepared, unpolished, and unstable had been cemented in people's minds.

Dale stared at the stack of pink message slips on her desk. In three days, she'd barely made a dent. She glanced at her e-mail. Her in-box was daunting. She shut down her desktop computer and threw her BlackBerry and phones in her purse. She was looking for a rubber band to wrap around her phone messages when her private line rang.

"Hello?"

"Dale Smith. Michael Robbins."

Damn, she thought. *Why couldn't I just let that one go to voice mail?* She sat down and turned her computer back on.

Dale and Ralph had been charged with damage control. The White House press secretary, who was now traveling with Charlotte in Asia, had offered a statement before they left simply stating Charlotte's continued confidence in her vice president and in the vice president's team. Dale was the one who had to do all the heavy lifting with the press while Ralph worked to salvage Tara's credibility on the Hill. Neither of them was making much headway. One of the networks had aired a poll in which sixty-nine percent of the public claimed to have "serious concerns" about the vice president's ability to carry out her official responsibilities. Only twenty-two percent of people claimed to know what any of those official duties were.

"How can I help you tonight, Michael?" Dale asked.

"I'm sorry to pile on."

No you aren't, she thought.

"No worries. We all have jobs to do. I get it. How can I help you?"

"The leadership in the house is calling for an independent counsel."

"To do what?"

"To investigate your boss."

"Investigate her for what?"

"Come on. Be careful, Dale. You're gonna get subpoenaed. Be careful what you say here. This isn't a game anymore. People go to jail for perjury. I don't want to put you in a box. If you can't help me, just say so, but don't lie. I'm giving you good advice, Dale."

She was silent.

"You still there?"

"Yep. They haven't subpoenaed me yet."

"I'm glad to see you still have your sense of humor."

"I aim to please."

"I'm getting pushed to update my reporting on the stuff we talked about at the beginning of the summer."

Dale thought she'd try playing dumb.

"What stuff? I can't remember what happened a week ago, Michael. Refresh my memory."

"Come on. The weight gain, the rumors about her erratic behavior, missed events, long absences, lying about the kid being sick to get out of overseas travel."

"Seriously?"

"Yeah. Seriously. Your boss is in big trouble, Dale. This isn't going to be fun. Do you want to talk to her about what I'm working on and see if she has any comment?"

Dale sighed louder than she'd planned to.

"She isn't going to have anything to say for your story. Is there something else I can do for you at ten-thirty at night?"

"That's it. The story will be online in a couple hours. I wanted to give you a heads-up."

"Thanks."

"I have some numbers if you need them."

"What kind of numbers?"

"Criminal lawyers."

Fuck you, she thought.

"Let's keep our fingers crossed that it doesn't come to that," she said.

"Dale, I think it's about to," he said.

"I've got to run," she said, slamming the phone down harder than she'd intended. She placed her head in her hands.

"Hey, don't break that. It'll take them a week to replace it."

She looked up quickly. Her door was open. She didn't think anyone else was around.

"I promise you I wasn't eavesdropping. I was walking by and heard the crash and stopped to make sure everyone was okay."

Dale still hadn't said anything. She was trying to remember who else she'd spoken to on the phone with her door open.

"You do know who I am, don't you?"

"Greg."

"Craig."

"Shit. I'm sorry. I sit next to you in senior staff every morning. I'm not this person."

He smiled.

"None of us is."

She smiled back.

"As penance, why don't you come have a glass of wine with me at Capital Grille. You look like you need it."

"So I can tell you all about meltdown Monday?"

"If you'd like. Or we can just drink wine so that next time I stop to make sure you haven't been buried alive by a falling bookshelf, you get my name right."

She looked around her office. It looked like a hoarder had taken up residence in the gracious space she'd been given next to the vice president's ceremonial suite. There weren't many more calls she could return at ten-thirty. She'd hardly left her office all week. A glass of wine wouldn't hurt anyone.

Dale considered calling Ralph before she left, but she could tell from the motorcade parked on West Exec that they were still in whatever meeting had been convened in the Sit Room. She should be worried about why the vice president was in the Sit Room on a Thursday night, but she had her hands full. Maybe they'd raise the threat level and the government would seize the phone lines so she wouldn't have to return any more press calls. Dale took a deep breath and looked up at Craig. She'd heard that he was quickly becoming one of the president's most trusted advisors. As a Republican president with the first-ever Democrat for a vice president, Charlotte's relationship with Congress was of unprecedented difficulty. Craig was widely credited with keeping the Republicans satisfied on issues like defense and spending while also cultivating the highly partisan Democratic Speaker of the House on issues like immigration, education, and health care. *People* magazine had included him in their "Most Beautiful People" issue, and Dale noticed right away that he was uncharacteristically well dressed for a government staffer.

"I'd love a glass of wine," she said.

She placed the phone message from Annie McKay, Melanie Kingston's executive assistant, on top of her stack of messages and left the pile in the center of her desk. Dale looked at the four pairs of shoes under her desk and slid into the Manolo Blahniks. As much as she didn't want to be hit on by anyone she worked with, getting a drink with one of her more attractive colleagues was the best offer she'd had in ages.

Dale agreed to ride the one and a half miles to Capital Grille with Craig only because the White House was located halfway between the restaurant and her apartment. She'd have to come back in the direction of the White House anyway. Dale watched Craig approach a black two-door BMW on West Exec. She had expected a sensible, if stylish, SUV and was pleasantly surprised by the sleek sedan. He drove fast and smiled at her when they pulled up to the valet. When he placed his hand on her lower back to guide her toward a table in the bar area, she was embarrassed by how much she enjoyed the contact. He ordered dry martinis for both of them and a bottle of expensive red wine.

"What happened with you and Peter Kramer?" he asked.

She took a large sip of her martini.

"Don't you want to know about what happened Monday morning at the V.P.'s residence?"

"I'm much more interested in what happened with you and Peter. You guys looked so good together. It looked real. Tell me it was real."

"It was real." Dale was caught off guard by her emotions. She took a few more sips of her drink. "Will you excuse me for a second?" She started to get up.

He placed his cool, tan hand on hers. "Now I'm the ass. I didn't mean to upset you," he said.

"You didn't upset me." She managed a small smile, and they sat there quietly while she drained the rest of her martini.

"Peter is incredible, and it was really, really good for a while. He's got an amazing amount of patience, but I fucked it up," she confessed.

She found encouragement in his friendly, interested eyes.

"Do you know why we broke up? He bought me a beach house. A fucking beach house in Stinson Beach. It hung over a cliff and it was perfect and beautiful and he had a tub put in the bathroom because I love hot baths. And when he took me to this beach house—this amazing beach house—I freaked out. And that's why I am no longer with Peter. I was too crazy for him. Too. Fucking. Crazy."

The bartender filled two fishbowl-sized glasses with the warm, woody red wine. Dale gulped hers.

"Aren't you glad you stopped to save me from my bookshelves?"

"Very." He smiled a perfect smile and glanced briefly down at his BlackBerry.

"Will you excuse me for two seconds?" he asked.

Dale watched him take a call on his BlackBerry. She didn't remember the last time she'd had this much to drink. She planned to ask him to put her in a cab when he returned.

"You seem like a very nice person," Dale said when he sat down again.

"I'm not that nice. You are feeling like a not-nice person because you got my name wrong and you've had a bad stretch, but we're not that different. I keep to myself like you do." He finished his glass of wine but did not appear to be feeling the effects of the large amount of alcohol they'd consumed in a rather short period of time.

"You don't go out with all the other White House staffers?" she asked.

"Do they all go out together?"

"I don't know. I always assumed they did. I had such a different impression of the place when I covered it. There's a real sense of intrigue when you're on the outside looking in. When you're inside, it's nothing like you expect."

"No?"

"No."

"Well, maybe it's our expectations that mess everything up. I mean, other than watching the vice president go up in flames on Monday, it's been a decent week, hasn't it?"

"Funny you should ask. Just before you walked in an investigative reporter offered me the numbers of a few criminal attorneys he knows."

"And who said the press hates Republican administrations?" She laughed into her wineglass.

"Gimmie the ninety-second version of the Meyers shit show."

"Oh, god. Where to start. First off, she is totally paralyzed by the job. She has such dramatic mood swings that sometimes she totally nails a speech or an event, and everyone thinks she's great and they put things on her schedule, and then she has a meltdown and they have to wipe her schedule clear until she can peel herself off the ceiling. Marie Mendes just happened to catch her on a bad day."

"Look, I hear the same thing from the members of Congress who catch her on those bad days. They usually call me afterward to complain, or, if they aren't completely self-absorbed, to ask if she's all right. Mind you, there is a very small universe that actually shows concern," he said.

"What do you tell them?"

"I usually take it upon myself to concoct some excuse about her having the flu, or her kid calling her just before she stepped into a meeting, or something weighing on her back at the office, but it was bound to catch up with her. You can fool some of the people some of the time . . ."

"But you can't fool all of the people all of the time," Dale completed the cliché.

They sat together without talking and watched a group of young congressional staffers try to convince a bartender to serve them burgers even though the kitchen had closed twenty minutes earlier.

"Was it Michael Robbins?" Craig asked after a couple of minutes had gone by.

"Huh?"

"Was it Robbins who offered you the criminal lawyers' numbers?"

"How did you know?"

"I've known him for years. He's been stirring up the independent counsel story for weeks. I have some very good sources of my own on the Hill who tell me he's been drumming up sources to confirm his theory about the independent counsel request all summer," Craig said.

"Why?"

"Things get slow for investigative journalists when everyone plays nice. Scandal is better for their business, even if they have to create it."

"Great. How much worse will my job get if the independent counsel investigates Meyers?"

"Things would get worse, but you'd survive, and at some point, it doesn't matter, does it? I mean, your boss is going to be under the microscope the entire time you work for her. But you still have a job to do, and you just do it. I don't know that any of these jobs were ever fun, but they all suck now. You do them for as long as you can endure it and then you move on."

"That's depressing."

"Nah. People think working at the White House is the dream job, but it hasn't been that for a long time—if ever."

"Why do you do it?"

"That, darling girl, I will tell you next time . . . when you are buying the drinks. It's time to get you home so you're bright-eyed and bushy-tailed at senior staff tomorrow morning."

Dale groaned. Craig paid the bill and Dale noticed that people watched them walk out together. He didn't touch her again on the way out, but when they pulled up to her apartment, he hopped out of the car to open her door and gave her a quick peck on the cheek. He was a sophisticated guy, and while she wasn't expecting him to try to come upstairs, she thought he might at least ask to see her again. *You're an idiot*, she thought. *He'll be seated next to you in six hours at the senior staff meeting*. She thanked him for the rare night out and went inside. Dale wandered around her apartment, which suddenly felt huge and lonely. She crawled into bed and dialed Peter's cell phone number.

"Hi," he said. The sound of his voice opened up a piece of her heart that she'd shuttered since she left San Francisco.

"Hi," she croaked.

"What's wrong?" he asked, with all the concern he had always shown her.

"I miss you." With that simple admission, she fell apart.

He listened to her as she told him about getting screamed at by Tara the week before and the meeting in Ralph's office and the references to the vice president's mental state and the interview strategy and creepy Marcus and the interview prep. When she got to the morning of the interviews, he interrupted her.

"You don't have to relive the interviews unless you want to. I saw them."

"And then the president asked me and Ralph to do damage control so I've been on the phone for three days, saying god knows what, and the hardest thing is that I don't actually know what's what anymore." She left out that she was so lonely she ached all the time, and decided not to tell him that she missed him desperately and wanted to hop on the next flight to San Francisco and never return to D.C.

When she stopped talking and crying she could hear him breathe. It sounded like he had his hand over the receiver.

"Oh god, are you with one of your players?" she asked. "Or the kids? Are you with the twins?"

"No, no. I'm just finishing dinner. It's fine. It's always fine. I'm sorry you have to deal with these things. I wish I could do something."

His words sounded forced. Dale realized her mistake.

"I'm sorry I called you. I just, I didn't know who else . . . I'm sorry. I don't have anyone else to talk to."

Once she said it, she felt even worse for leaving the impression that she only called Peter because she didn't have anyone else to talk to.

"You can always call, Dale. Listen, it's after two A.M. there. Why don't you try to get some sleep? If you want to talk more tomorrow, I'll be in the L.A. office."

"You're right. It's late. Thanks Peter."

"Hang in there," he added.

She hung up and felt too sad to cry any more. Calling Peter had crystallized how completely alone she was. Dale took an Ambien and set her alarm clock and her BlackBerry for five A.M.

CHAPTER TWENTY-SEVEN

Charlotte

"A re those bedsheets over the windows?" Charlotte asked. She and Melanie were still sitting in the room from which they'd participated in the call with the Sit Room. Constance had left already for a breakfast with the Korean foreign minister.

"I believe the technical term, Madam President, is pipe and drape," Melanie quipped.

"And why are they hanging over the windows?"

"Why do you think?"

"To reduce the glare on the laptops?"

"Guess again."

"I can't contemplate the alternative."

Melanie laughed.

"It is humbling to learn that the best antispying measures we've got are the same ones ten-year-old kids use to build forts, isn't it?" Melanie teased.

"Jesus. If people had any idea."

"Most of the information the host countries get during these trips is obtained from our trash. The Secret Service puts shredders in every hotel room now because people were leaving their line-by-line schedules with each and every one of your movements in the garbage cans at hotels."

"Seriously?"

"Yep."

Charlotte couldn't stop staring at the blue pieces of fabric stapled and taped over the windows. "That's just incredible."

Melanie watched in amusement.

"Thanks for staying an extra day. I know you have to get back to testify on the Hill," Charlotte said.

"No problem. I had some good meetings here. It was definitely worth the trip."

"What did you think about the call?" Charlotte asked.

"I'm not sure it was worthy of convening a call across several continents. Youseff is AWOL. The bureau lost him and they are trying to cover their asses so the CIA doesn't throw them under the bus if something happens."

"Do you think something will happen?"

"It's always a possibility," Melanie said.

"The bureau and the agency agree, for once. Doesn't that make you nervous?" Charlotte probed.

"A little, but it's just as likely that they're both wrong," Melanie said.

Charlotte made a disapproving face.

"I thought Tara sounded good," Charlotte offered.

"Mmmn."

"You didn't?"

"What do you want me to say, Charlotte? I think she cost you a lot of credibility and goodwill with her interviews this week. It's probably wise for me to keep my views to myself at times like this."

"Why? Because otherwise you'll tell me that she was a stupid choice and that I was craven and impulsive to put her on the ticket?" Charlotte was standing now.

Melanie seemed stunned by Charlotte's rare display of anger. She didn't react right away.

"Look, Melanie, you were there. You know that I did it for Neal as much as I did it for myself. If I'd had any idea that she wasn't up for it, I wouldn't have picked her." Neal McMillan was Charlotte's first vice president. He'd offered to step down so Charlotte could shake up the campaign by putting a Democrat on the ticket and running on the first ever "unity ticket," a concept that had long been contemplated by presidential candidates, but had never before been attempted.

"Charlotte," Melanie started quietly. "She was never even vetted. Some oppo research guys Googled her and watched videos of her on YouTube."

"What are you talking about?"

"It doesn't matter now."

"Melanie, she was vetted. Ralph said the lawyers gave her the standard questionnaire and asked her all the questions we asked Neal four years earlier."

"That's not exactly how it went down. They knew you wanted her selection to work out, so they figured out how to get to yes. But look, you shouldn't worry about it now. You've got to make the most of it. You have to stand by her. If people catch any whiff of the White House cutting her loose, she's dead," Melanie said. "And so are you," she added.

"Why are you telling me this now?" Charlotte asked.

"Please just forget I said anything. It wasn't my place. I'm sorry."

"As I recall, you were the one who demanded that the whole thing be kept a state secret," Charlotte complained.

"That's correct. It's as much my fault as anyone else's."

Charlotte sighed deeply. After a couple minutes passed, Melanie stood to go.

"Madam President, I'm going to the gym. I've got a couple hours before I have to head to the airport and I was going to run on the treadmill. Do you want to come?"

"No thanks. I think I'll call the kids instead."

"It's the middle of the night in Connecticut," Melanie said.

"Oh, right. Well, I'll send them an e-mail," Charlotte said.

Melanie didn't push her.

"I'll call you when I get back. You know where to find me if you need me," Melanie said.

As soon as the door closed behind her, Charlotte dialed the number she'd recently rememorized. It was about only about eleven P.M. in California.

"Hi."

"Hi," Peter replied.

"Is it too late?"

"Not at all. How are you?"

"Are they still talking about the interview?"

"They certainly are."

"Wonderful."

"How are you holding up?"

"I don't want to think about it. Tell me something about my children that I don't already know. That shouldn't be hard, right?"

"Penelope could use a little motherly doting."

"Why? What's wrong?"

"She's just going through a little something. I'm not sure exactly what, but she's been moody lately."

"Do you think she's all right?"

"She's seventeen. Penny's fine. Char, I was trying to distract you. I didn't mean to make you worry."

"No, I'm glad you said something. I'll call her later today. I think it'll be morning in Connecticut around the time I'm wrapping up my last meeting."

"She'll like that."

Charlotte was quiet.

"Charlotte?"

"I'm here," she said.

"Maybe it's the delay, but you sound strange."

What she wanted to say was that she'd heard things hadn't worked out between him and Dale and she was sorry. She had been wrong about them. She'd thought he and Dale would eventually marry, and she saw enough of herself in Dale that she'd mostly made peace with the whole thing. But she'd be lying if she didn't admit that she was intrigued by the news that Peter was unattached. She'd had a recurring daydream over the past several weeks. She would arrive back at the residence after a long day of meetings and public events and tedious policy debates and tell someone about her day. Then that someone would pour her a glass of wine and put his strong hands on her tight shoulders. Just as the fantasy would start to please her immensely, Peter's face would come into focus. She always halted the daydream at this point and told herself that he was simply the last man she'd been in a relationship with. Peter cleared his throat and started to speak, snapping Charlotte out of her thoughts. Before he could get anything out, Charlotte interrupted.

"Maybe we can have dinner again when I get back?"

"I'd like that," he replied.

"I was going to use the college applications as an excuse again, but I'd just like to see you again."

Peter chuckled.

"Are you laughing at me?"

"Not at all. It's just that I forgot how direct you can be. I like it," he assured.

"I'll call you when I get back," she promised.

She hung up and wondered what the hell she was doing reeling Peter back in.

CHAPTER TWENTY-EIGHT

Tara

Tara walked back to her office in the West Wing to study the file. She noticed several missed calls from Marcus and felt her stomach tighten at the thought that something might be wrong with Kendall. She dialed their home phone number.

"Marcus, it's me. Is Kendall okay?"

"She hasn't stirred since you left."

Tara was relieved.

"I'm going to do a little reading here. I'll be home in an hour or so."

"It's late," Marcus warned.

"I know. I'll just be a half an hour more. We have another meeting in the morning and I'll be better able to absorb this stuff tonight than in the morning."

He agreed, and she hung up just as Ralph walked in.

"Great job in there, Tara," Ralph said.

Tara was embarrassed that he felt he had to praise her performance at an internal meeting.

"Thanks. And thank you for including me, especially during a week when I've caused nothing but embarrassment for the president."

"Tara, you've got to shake off those interviews. The first two interviews were great, and frankly, those networks have much bigger ratings. Marie was a bitch. Dale should have flagged that one when she saw that Marie had been assigned the one-on-one. I'm really sorry."

"It's not Dale's fault. Marie got under my skin and I let her stay there," Tara said.

Ralph nodded and shrugged and snorted all at once, leaving Tara with the impression that he'd said all that he came to say about the interview.

"The A.G. asked me to give this to you. He said it's got some notes in it from your days in the U.S. Attorney's Office about Youseff."

"Thanks."

She opened the file and read her own notes from the case. She'd always been so precise in her case notes, often typing up several drafts before they were perfect. Tara had viewed those files as sacred. She'd been much better suited for the law than she was for politics. If only she'd figured that out sooner.

Tonight, she felt strangely invigorated. The White House was nearly empty, but it didn't feel lonely or odd to be in her office at such a late hour. Her Secret Service agents were just outside her door, and the White House Mess had reopened to serve the senior staff snacks and beverages in the Situation Room. There was a cheese plate and a couple of bottles of water waiting for her on her coffee table when she entered. Tara thought about how she might have been able to manage things better if she'd had more moments of quiet. She wondered if it was too late.

CHAPTER TWENTY-NINE

Dale

D ale balanced a Big Gulp–size cup of iced coffee on top of the binder that held her schedule for the day and the detailed schedules of the president and vice president. She dreaded going to senior staff more than usual. A morning-after encounter with someone you've slept with is awkward, but facing someone who takes you out, gets you drunk, and doesn't even try to kiss you is humiliating.

She took her seat and moved her body as far away as possible from Craig's side of the sofa. He walked in at 7:32.

"Morning," he said smiling at her. She could smell his fresh breath before he even sat down. He looked a million times better than she felt. Despite brushing and flossing her teeth three times, she was sure she still had martini breath.

She smiled at him with her mouth shut, and as soon as the staff meeting ended, she raced toward the vice president's office. Ralph had beaten her there and was standing in the receptionist's area.

"Just the person I was looking for. Dale, with POTUS gone for five more days, the vice president is going to take the lead on the homeland security portfolio. She's heading over to DOJ for a briefing as soon as she gets in, and then she'll go up to Manhattan to get briefed by the JTTF leads. I need you to travel with her, and I'd like for you to assemble a small press pool to cover her meetings."

"Won't this look like an overreaction to her interviews? The White House working double time to repair her image after V.P. fails to name a single issue the president has asked her to manage?" Dale objected.

"I don't need your reporter's cynicism right now. It would have been helpful earlier in the week, but today, I need a can-do attitude. Can you do that?"

His sarcasm stung. Dale had an urge to call her former colleague from the network, Brian Watson, and leak every stinking nugget she had on Ralph and everyone else.

"No problem." She forced herself to smile.

"Thank you, Dale. The V.P. will be advising the president on whether to raise the threat level, and the president will be looking to her for any other recommendations in our national security posture."

She stared at him, dumbfounded.

"What is your problem?" he asked.

"Nothing. I've got my marching orders, sir."

He pulled her into the stairwell.

"I'm concerned that you aren't one hundred percent committed, Dale."

"I think I've proven that I'm pretty damn committed these days, Ralph. Don't you think?"

"But you don't agree with the strategy?" Ralph pushed.

"In my opinion, the vice president is still a little fragile," Dale said.

"Bullshit. She's fine. She had a bad day on Monday. Nothing more. It happens to everyone. We need to start treating her like a grown-up and she'll act like one. No more coddling her, Dale. It's not like it's worked for her anyway, has it?"

Dale felt like she'd been slapped again. She mumbled something about needing to make some calls to get the press pool organized and practically ran down the stairs.

She collided with Craig in the West Wing basement. "Whoa!" he exclaimed, holding out his arms and catching her. Seeing him made her want to run away faster, but he had stopped her in her tracks, literally.

"Where are you going?" Craig asked.

"New York. The vice president is going to catch her some terrorists," she joked.

"Seriously?"

"Seriously. That doesn't sound like an overcorrection to you, does it?"

"It explains why I'm taking Ralph to the Hill to brief the House and Senate Homeland Security committees."

"President Kramer asked us to run damage control, not to oversee crisis creation," Dale complained.

"This is only the second time in about two years that we've gone to the Hill to brief the committees on a specific threat," Craig said.

"Do you think they're really worried?"

"These meetings are usually for CYA purposes only, so it's anyone's guess. But I'd pack a gas mask, just in case."

"You think they are simply covering their asses?" Dale asked.

"Maybe. Wanna have dinner when you get back?" Craig asked.

Dale was at a loss to come up with an excuse. He looked amused by her attempt.

"I'd love to, but—"

He cut her off.

"Don't turn me down yet. If eight o'clock comes around and you're hungry, come over. If not, no big deal."

He flashed his warm smile and she felt the same butterflies she'd felt the night before when he walked into Capital Grille with his hand on her back.

"I'll let you know," she promised.

Dale accompanied the vice president to the briefing at DOJ and rode in the limo with her to Andrews Air Force Base where Air Force Two was waiting to take them to New York. They would be in the city for less than two hours.

"Madam Vice President, is it okay if I brief our press on the flight up about who you're meeting with in New York?"

"Whatever you think," Tara said. She hadn't said much and Dale wondered if she was still upset about the interviews.

"Madam Vice President, for whatever it's worth, the buzz about the interviews has started to die down."

"I don't care about that, Dale. I regret that I reflected poorly on the president and my family, but I don't care about it for any other reason.

And I know it wasn't your fault. I let it happen. It's done. We should put it behind us."

Dale nodded and returned her gaze to her BlackBerry. Annie McKay from Melanie Kingston's office had called her again. She added a note in her calendar to call Annie from the plane. She glanced up at the vice president. Tara looked at her and offered what looked like an apologetic smile. Dale looked away. Tara's moments of self-awareness threw Dale off the most because they forced her to consider that she truly understood just how badly things were going for her.

Dale went to the back of Air Force Two and briefed the press while the plane took off. She braced herself against one of the reporter's seat backs and shook her head apologetically at one of the Air Force Two stewards who gave her a disapproving look when she refused to take a seat during takeoff.

By the time they landed in New York thirty minutes later, there was a Politico story titled "Can Tara Meyers Get Her Groove Back?" It included quotes from unnamed administration sources and Hill staffers debating whether she could recover from her dismal interview earlier in the week by showing off her law enforcement acumen.

Dale forced a smile onto her face as the press filmed them boarding the motorcade for the siren-led ride into the city.

She watched crowds of irritated commuters and annoyed New Yorkers go by in a blur. At a stoplight, she stifled a laugh. She thought she saw Tara smile, too. A man in a brightly colored shirt was holding up a sign that read: "Come Back to New York, Tara, Home of the World's Most Famous Fruits and Nuts."

Tara was greeted by the mayor and police chief, and after a wave to the cameras gathered for her arrival, she was ushered inside the NYPD's counterterrorism unit.

Dale's sense of dread grew as she sat through two hours of briefings on the loosely knit terror cell (the most dangerous kind, according to the experts gathered that day) led by Youseff Bordeaux, the brother of a terrorist who'd tried and failed to blow up the Brooklyn Bridge. This was the case Tara had helped prosecute years earlier. By the time they made their police-escorted return to the airport for the thirty-minute flight back to D.C., Dale's head was pounding.

"Dale, do you think I should come to the back of the plane with you to show the press that I'm still standing?"

Dale contemplated this. It was risky and she worried that it would look like they were trying too hard. Besides, most of what Tara knew about the terror threat was still classified, so there wasn't much leg to show on the day's briefings.

"Let me go back there today. It's been a long week and I think I can wrap it up with some general comments about the briefings we just did and your plan to brief POTUS tonight," Dale said.

"Whatever you think is best," Tara said.

Dale boarded the plane and walked straight back to the press section.

"Dale, any comment on Wadsworth's call for an independent counsel?" asked the wire reporter. Congressman Wadsworth headed the Government Affairs Committee.

"We'll cooperate with our friends in Congress on any and all matters," Dale said, as instructed by the White House counsel.

"Who was in the briefings today, Dale?" asked the reporter from the *Washington Post*. Dale scrolled through her e-mail and found the list of participants and read it to the press, stopping to spell several of the names and promising to check on a few of their titles.

"Dale, the *Wall Street Journal* is running a story about Vice President Meyers's roller-coaster ride of a week—from being humiliated on live national television on Monday to briefing the president on the latest terror threat by Friday. Any comment?"

"Welcome to the circus."

She instantly regretted her quip, but it was too late. By the time they landed, the cable channels were playing circus music as background to the live shot of Air Force Two landing. Dale rushed to the front of the plane.

"Madam Vice President, I'm so sorry. I don't know why I said that."

The vice president looked serene.

"Best line of the week, Dale," she said.

Tara boarded her limo and Dale hopped into the staff van that would ride behind it. She was exhausted, and she had hundreds of e-mails in her in-box that she hadn't responded to because her Black-

Berry had been confiscated during the briefings in D.C. and New York. She planned to order a bowl of tomato soup from the Mess and spend the evening catching up.

The staff van pulled onto West Exec around eight P.M. Dale walked up to her office and turned on the television. MSNBC was still playing circus music.

"After a disastrous start, the vice president ended the week on a high note, apparently taking the lead for the White House on a looming terror threat. It might be that with the president attending to vital state business in Mongolia, and the rest of the cabinet on vacation, there wasn't anyone else available, but Vice President Meyers will be briefing the president on a terror ring she once helped prosecute later tonight we're told by the vice president's senior counselor Dale Smith. When asked about the vice president's tumultuous week, Smith quipped, 'Welcome to the circus.' Not exactly what most Americans had in mind when they elected Charlotte Kramer to a second term, but, hey, we'll take it."

Dale hit mute and searched for the Food Network. She powered up her computer and stared at her phone log from the day. She drove her assistant crazy with her message system. She liked an old-fashioned pink slip for each call so she could stack them up and sort them into piles, but she also liked her calls logged in a Word document so she could look for patterns in the messages and maintain a record of each day's calls. Tonight, there were pages of detailed phone messages waiting for her. She stared at them and couldn't find a single one she felt like returning. She dialed Craig's cell phone.

"Does your dinner offer still stand?" she asked.

She could hear Radiohead playing in the background.

"Absolutely. Give me your ETA and I'll have dinner on the table," he said.

"I'll be there in twenty minutes. Will you e-mail me the address again?"

Dale hung up and walked down the empty hall toward the bathroom. She brushed her teeth and splashed water on her face. She examined her face in the mirror. She looked tired. There were new lines around her eyes that she constantly tried to convince herself were from dehydration, but she was pretty sure they were there even when she remembered to drink water. She pinched her cheeks and contemplated foundation and some blush, but reapplying makeup felt like too much effort. She pulled her long, chestnut-colored hair into a ponytail.

Dale drove out of the White House complex and turned right on 17th Street. She followed it around Dupont Circle and merged onto Connecticut Avenue. She had to navigate around large groups of tourists. It was August, and in August the visitors to Washington, D.C., outnumber the locals. She thought about stopping to buy a bottle of wine, but she didn't pass a single place that would carry anything nice enough.

She made a right turn a couple of blocks before the Washington Hilton, as he'd instructed, and then she went through two stop signs. The homes were mostly redone townhouses—the sorts of places that Dale would want to live in if she ever committed to a city long enough to make a life for herself. She stopped in front of his address and looked up. The elegant brownstone was dripping with character and charm. There were boxwood hedges in the tiny garden in front of his building and a chandelier hung in the window half a flight above the street level. It looked nothing like Dale's sterile apartment. It looked like a home.

She rang the bell and felt a twinge of anxiety. Breaking out of her routine made her nervous.

Craig was barefoot when he greeted her. He was wearing jeans and a white linen shirt with the sleeves rolled up. Dale noticed that tomato sauce had splashed on his face.

"I'm glad you decided to come," he said.

"You're a mess." She pointed at the sauce below his eye.

"I can't make anything worth eating without getting it all over myself. Come on in. I was about to put the pasta on."

"It smells amazing," she said. And it did. Dale hadn't been around anyone who knew how to cook since the last time she was with Peter. She tried to remember the last meal they'd cooked together but she couldn't recall what they'd made.

"I hope you like garlic. I went with the Sicilian version. Garlic, onions, peppers. Is that going to be okay?"

"It sounds delicious."

She pushed thoughts of Peter from her mind and joined Craig in the kitchen. He handed her a glass of wine and refused to let her do anything. In exactly eight minutes, he drained a steaming bowl of penne in a colander over the sink, dumped it into a ceramic pasta bowl and covered it with his rich, orange-red tomato sauce. He took out a hunk of Parmesan and grated a generous portion over the pasta. He twisted a salt grinder over it and then a pepper grinder and then placed it on the table. A Caprese salad was on the table along with a pitcher of ice water and two bottles of Chianti.

"Dinner is served."

"Where did you learn to cook?"

"There are some things a self-respecting adult has to teach himself, my dear," he said. "I went to Italy one summer and took a five-day cooking class."

Dale took a bite. "It's incredible. On the nights that I actually eat a meal that could be called dinner, it's either take-out or involves something from the freezer."

"You shouldn't eat that crap. Make a salad instead. It takes five minutes."

"I don't ever have anything in my fridge."

"What are you, eleven years old? Go to Whole Foods or Dean and DeLuca on your way home and buy a salad. You'll feel like a new person," he said, smiling at her.

"Okay, Dad," she said.

"Ouch."

He didn't ask about her day, and she was relieved to talk about something other than the vice president. He told her about his art collection while they ate and drank. At some point, he brought out a homemade tiramisu that Dale devoured.

"Your mother did all of those?" Dale asked, pointing to a series of watercolors of Yosemite National Park.

"Yes. She painted until she started making money at it. Then she stopped. She said that the day it turned into a job, she didn't have another creative brushstroke in her."

"Really? Does she still paint?"

"She paints again but refuses to sell any of it."

After dinner, they migrated to the den. She told him how she and Peter met, the lengths they went to so as not to be discovered. They laughed about what the Secret Service must have witnessed over the years. He didn't offer any personal information aside from the stories about his mother's paintings and Dale didn't probe.

They'd polished off two bottles of wine.

"Shall I open another?" he asked.

"I shouldn't."

"Why not? It's Friday. I'm not going to let you drive in this condition anyway. You can stay here."

Dale gave him a slightly confused look.

"I should get out of your hair. I don't want any of your, you know, your other friends to get the wrong idea. I don't want to make any trouble for you by straggling out of here in the morning."

He started to laugh a low chuckle.

"Impossible," he promised.

"You'd be surprised. I have a special knack for messing things up for people."

"Dale, I can't believe I have to tell you this. I thought you'd figure it out yourself."

He sat there looking at her and it was like she was seeing him for the first time.

"Oh my god. I'm such an ass. Don't say it. I'm sorry I'm so stupid. I swear to you, once again, I am not this person."

He laughed. "I haven't had to tell a woman I wasn't into her in a long time."

"Wow. I had no idea. Does Kramer know?"

"She does. I told her when she offered me the job three years ago. She was getting a whole lot of shit at the time from the right for being to the left of the Democrats in Congress on gay marriage. I told her that if she ever changed her position, it would be a deal breaker for me. She's been great on all those issues, and she and I have never talked about it again. I don't think she told anyone, not even Melanie."

"Is it a secret?"

"Not really, but I do make an effort to keep people guessing. It isn't anyone's business."

Dale nodded in agreement.

"No. It isn't."

They talked about art and food and Italy some more and then Dale started to feel sleepy.

"Maybe I'll just drift off right here, if you don't mind," she said, snuggling under the most luxurious cashmere blanket she'd ever touched.

"You're welcome to stay here or you could sleep in the guest room. It's pretty comfy, too. I left some pajamas in here that I've never worn."

She pulled herself from the sofa and followed him to the guest room. In the center was the most inviting bed she'd ever seen. It looked like one of the display beds in the window of Frette linens. There was an antique chest of drawers on one side of the bed and a nightstand piled high with biographies of presidents and other famous Washingtonians. She pulled the tags off the Burberry pajamas.

"Thanks for these," she said. He blew her a kiss and closed the door behind him. She washed her face and brushed her teeth with the toothbrush and toothpaste he'd left for her and then collapsed onto the softest featherbed she'd ever laid on.

"Oh my god," she called out.

"I told you. Sleep tight," Craig called back from his room.

"Night," she yelled.

She slept more soundly than she had in weeks. When she woke up, she groped for her BlackBerry and was astonished when she saw that it was after ten A.M.

She dressed and wandered into the kitchen. Craig had made coffee and there was a plate of biscotti, croissants, and muffins in the middle of the table.

"Will you marry me?" she asked.

He smiled.

"I'm glad you slept well."

"Did you work out?"

"Just went for a quick run," he said. "You were sound asleep."

"Who are you?"

He laughed and filled an oversized mug with coffee for her.

"Milk?"

"Yes, please."

She drank her coffee and polished off a croissant and half a blueberry muffin while he watched her eat.

"Dale, I have a confession to make."

"What?"

"I wasn't just passing by your office the other night."

"No?" She reached for the other half of the blueberry muffin.

"No. I don't expect you to know this, but my office is in the East Wing—the other side of the complex."

"Oh." She did not know that leg affairs sat in the East Wing.

"Why were you in the OEOB?"

"I was out on West Exec with the smokers, and I saw your light was on. I'd noticed that you looked distraught in senior staff. The interview thing was obviously a disaster, and I had read a while back that you and Peter were no more. You seemed really upset and it didn't seem like you had made any friends on the White House staff yet, so I wanted to make sure you were all right."

She stopped chewing.

"I was about to walk in when I saw you turn off your computer and then your phone rang, so I walked down the hall and started doing laps around the OEOB. On one of my loops, I heard what sounded like you wrapping up a conversation, so I was getting ready to knock, and that's how I happened to be standing there when you slammed the phone down."

"I see."

"Are you mad?"

"No."

"Good."

She stood up walked over to where he was standing in the kitchen.

"I have to go," she said.

He looked worried.

She grinned.

"And not because you stalked me in the OEOB. I have a very important day ahead of me. Either I will buy new clothes, or I will find the laundry room in my building and wash my dirty clothes."

He laughed and walked her out to her car.

She started to pull out of her parking spot and noticed a few of Craig's neighbors standing outside talking with coffee cups and newspapers in their hands. It all seemed so civilized. She rolled down her window and shouted his name.

"Thanks for last night," she said, mischievously and loudly enough for a few of his neighbors to notice.

He laughed.

"Peter Kramer was a fool to let your skinny ass go," he said. Now his neighbors were craning their necks to see what was going on.

Throwing her head back with laughter, she honked and then drove away slowly. She had a smile on her face all the way home. Dale had found something that was rarer in Washington than an honest pollster. A friend.

CHAPTER THIRTY

Charlotte

C harlotte woke up in Korea with a crippling sinus infection. It was only the sixth day of her ten-day trip. She felt like an ax had been slammed into the center of her head and her chest hurt when she breathed. The air in Mongolia had been too dirty for human inhalation. Charlotte pushed herself out of bed to study her schedule for the day. She was to tour a memorial that had just been completed to honor the victims of North Korea's attack on the island of Yeon-pyeong in 2010. Two Korean marines had been killed and dozens of people injured. Her visit was meant to underscore America's new, tougher line on North Korea. She would travel by helicopter with a small press pool that would film the solemn ceremony. Charlotte was heartened to see that Tate Morris, the White House correspondent for CBS news, would accompany her. He was irreverent, funny, and smart, and while he never held back when the cameras were rolling, she'd spent enough time with him on international flights to know he'd be decent company for the day.

With her line-by-line schedule for the day in her hands, Charlotte lay back down in bed and shut her eyes. The last time she had woken up feeling this bad was during her reelection campaign almost a year earlier. She'd been traveling through Ohio with Tara. Melanie and Ralph were in the front of the bus and they were all enjoying the news of a postconvention bump in the polls. She had initially believed that she was simply run-down from all the rallies and speeches, but it was soon clear that she was sick. The White House doctor had given her

600 milligram tablets of Motrin for her headache and a powerful decongestant. She'd guzzled hot tea and waited to feel better. After the first rally of the day, Melanie had walked to the back of the bus with the news that had knocked Charlotte to her knees. Roger Taylor, her closest advisor, had shot himself.

Officially, Roger had served as the defense secretary during her first term, but he'd been much more than that. Roger was her best friend, her intellectual soul mate, and her constant companion. When he took his life, Charlotte felt responsible. He'd been disgraced by an investigation into his decision to switch the helicopter that he and Charlotte were traveling on in Afghanistan. The switch had resulted in the original helicopter staying on the landing strip long enough to be targeted by insurgents. The helicopter had gone down and the news crew traveling with Charlotte was hit. Dale Smith, who'd been having an affair with Peter that everyone thought Charlotte was unaware of, had been among the journalists injured in the crash.

Charlotte didn't often indulge her feelings of regret and remorse over her administration's handling of the investigation into Roger's actions in Afghanistan, but this morning, she made an exception. She'd stood by and watched him fall from grace. In hindsight, that had killed him before he ever lifted the gun and pulled the trigger. She moved her hands to her chest. It ached every time she unpacked Roger from her vault of painful memories. She missed him more than usual lately. She wondered what he'd say about the current terror threat. Her mouth formed the beginning of a smile as she remembered the way he'd go on and on about the homegrown terror cells with his booming voice and wild hand gestures. She knew exactly what he'd say about Youseff and his associates. "Blast the shit out of them, Char. Play the game the only way they understand it: with brutality."

She rose gingerly from the bed and moved slowly into the bathroom to shower. Charlotte was relieved that Melanie had left the day before. She was tiring of Melanie's visible show of disapproval about Tara. Charlotte had done what she had to do to make sure all of them had a job to come back to on November 7. It wasn't unreasonable for Charlotte to have assumed that Tara was up for the job—she was a statewide elected official in New York, for Christ's sake. Charlotte took a quick shower and then steadied herself against the sink while she combed out her long blond hair. Her makeup and hair folks would be in shortly. She felt dizzy, but she wasn't entirely sure if it was her illness or the picture of Tara that was emerging from all corners of her administration that was to blame.

On the flight over, Charlotte's CIA briefer had mentioned that the vice president hadn't shown up for her morning briefing for more than two weeks. After arriving late for the classified briefings for several days in a row, the CIA director had dispatched the vice president's briefer to the residence as a convenience. The vice president hadn't shown up for any of those briefings, either, so now her intelligence briefings were put into memo form and left with her assistant. A couple days before her morning-show meltdown, Craig Thompson, the White House director of legislative affairs, had lingered after a policy meeting in the Oval Office to ask Charlotte to make a discreet phone call to the Democratic senator from New Jersey whom Tara had mistaken for the independent senator from Connecticut.

And after much prodding, Sam had reluctantly confided in her that Tara's assistant often went days without seeing the vice president. Sam said that Marcus would usually call around nine A.M. to say whether Tara would be in or not. And her head of political affairs had asked for a private meeting to discuss the fact that requests for Tara to appear at fund-raisers or political events had dropped off precipitously.

All this was on top of a near-revolt from the policy folks, who were irate that Tara canceled almost all of her policy briefings. In isolation, some of the behaviors were understandable, but taken together, the developments were disquieting.

Charlotte choked down some toast that had appeared while she was in the bathroom and then took one of the 600 milligram tablets of Motrin. She dressed in a black pantsuit and skimmed the event briefing while her makeup was applied. She shut her eyes and tried to rest for a few more minutes while her hair was blown out.

Marine One was parked a short distance from her hotel, and she greeted Tate and his crew warmly once they were on board. He covered his mouth and refused to shake her hand.

"I don't want to infect you. I've got the goddamned croup or something," he said.

"Me too," she replied.

Charlotte instructed the White House medic to load him up with the same drugs he'd given her. Disarmed, Tate took longer than he might have otherwise to ask about Tara.

"Madam President, I've got to ask. Off the record, what's going on with the vice president?"

"Oh Tate, come on. You remember what it was like when you first made it to the network or whatever the equivalent is to a leap like the one she just took. The White House is a zero-tolerance place for mistakes. There's no time for a learning curve. She was thrown into the fire, and so she's making all of her mistakes in full view of all of you and the public," Charlotte explained.

"I can accept that there are things she doesn't know, Madam President. But I think that what people can't figure out is why the hell you don't tell her to stop canceling shit, excuse me, events, appearances—the things she could control. It would go a long way toward making her appear steadier, Madam President."

"Thanks, Tate. I'll keep that in mind."

He smiled.

"Sorry, Madam President. I'm sure you get lots of advice these days."

"And I appreciate all of it. Are you going to get on the air tonight with a piece on the memorial ceremony?"

"Honestly, I doubt it, but I'm going to pitch it. Off the record, any intelligence about what the North is up to? They obviously know we're coming today."

"Yes, and I have a bad feeling that they like the fact that we're drawing attention to their destruction, but it's still the right thing to do."

"Of course, Madam President."

They were quiet while Marine One landed on the small island. The crew got off first so they could film Charlotte. She thought about calling Ralph quickly to suggest that Tara keep a normal schedule in the wake of the interviews, but one of the military aides cued her to get off the helicopter. She took a deep breath and smiled as she stepped off Marine One and was greeted by the Korean president.

CHAPTER THIRTY-ONE

Tara

Tara had planned to wait to speak to the president when she returned from her trip, but she couldn't put it off any longer. She'd watched the live footage of the president in Korea, and she knew that the president's public events for the day were over. Her hand shook a bit when she asked the Sit Room to connect her to the president at her hotel.

"Madam President, I'm so sorry to bother you. I hope I'm not getting you at a bad time."

"No, it's no problem."

"How are you feeling, Madam President?"

"I feel a little better. Thank you for asking. What's wrong, Tara?"

"I have a bad feeling about Youseff. It feels wrong. The people we are watching aren't talking, and they are always talking. If they knew we were listening, they'd be talking anyway. They wouldn't go silent. It feels wrong," she said.

"Did you talk to the director?" Charlotte asked.

"Yes, they don't know what to make of it, but I just wanted to tell you myself that I think something is about to happen. It's too quiet."

"Tara, you need to get Ralph to move everyone to the Sit Room so we can talk as a group. I can get back on the line right away, but I need you to work through the NSC to run down whatever you want to run down. The FBI can bring people in. The NSA can analyze more of what they've been listening to. We can get more wiretaps approved, but you need to tell the team what you think. Do you understand?"

"Yes ma'am. Of course. I will do that."

"Will you promise me you'll do that as soon as we hang up?"

"Yes," Tara pledged.

She stood and walked down to Ralph's office.

She opened the door and stood just inside the doorway. The staffers assembled in his office disbursed.

"Madam Vice President, to what do I owe the pleasure?" he asked, rising to greet her.

"What meeting was that?" Tara asked.

"Oh, it was our regular meeting on the farm bill. We always threaten to veto it, but no one ever vetoes the farm bill, so we were talking about whether there isn't a way to make it a little better for our friends, but I just—"

Tara felt the room start to spin. *No*, she urged herself. *Not now.*

She steadied herself and sat in the chair in front of Ralph's desk.

"Ralph, I just spoke to the president."

"Just now? How? Did you call her?"

"I still have a phone," she snapped.

"I didn't mean it that way. Of course you can call the president whenever you want. How's she feeling?"

"She's worried. And so am I. Youseff isn't doing any of the things he should be doing. I think something is about to happen and it scares me that the White House chief of staff is in a farm bill meeting."

His face turned red and he pushed his lips together.

"Tara," he said, through clenched teeth. He was trying to intimidate her, but there was nothing Ralph could do to her. She was married to the scariest man she knew. Tara stood up and looked down at him.

"You think because I screwed up the interviews that you can treat me like some silly and irrelevant nuisance, but that isn't how this is going to work from now on, Ralph."

For his part, Ralph was seasoned enough to know how to put out a fire. He switched tactics.

"Madam Vice President," he soothed, "I understand this is an area you know a lot about, and I really appreciate your input—everyone does—but the FBI has been tracking these guys for months. We're on top of it as much as we can be. And as you know, these scares usually, thank God, lead to nothing."

She glared at him. In that instant, she hated him more than she'd ever hated Marcus. At least Marcus never second-guessed her judgment in the one area she knew something about.

"I told the president that I thought something could be imminent," Tara said.

At this, Ralph's composure evaporated. He slammed his fist on his desk.

"Damnit! Don't ever do that, Tara. We never tell the president, even if we know something is going to happen. How does she answer questions now about what she knew and when she knew it?"

Tara stared back at him, confused. She hadn't thought of it that way.

"Because, if for some reason, you happen to be correct and something happens, how do we answer the questions about what the fuck the president was doing in motherfucking Mongolia?"

"She's in Korea now," Tara corrected.

"Wherever the fuck she is!" He was shouting.

"I'm sorry. I did what I thought was right."

He was breathing heavily now. She focused her gaze on his chest, which was rising and falling quickly.

"Tara, I'm sorry for my anger. It's not you. There's just a lot going on. Why don't you give me half an hour and I'll convene a meeting in the Sit Room," Ralph said. He was pacing back and forth behind his desk now.

"Thank you," Tara said. She forced herself to look him in the eye one last time before she turned and walked out of Ralph's office and back to her own.

CHAPTER THIRTY-TWO

Dale

D ale and Craig were leaning against the wall outside of the Mess drinking large cups of coffee. They watched one of the waiters refill the bowl of M & M's.

"Do you know that there are more germs in that bowl of M & M's than on a bathroom door?" he remarked.

"That's disgusting. I eat those every day."

"You shouldn't. Come to Capital Grille with me tonight," Craig said.

"It's Monday."

"You don't drink on Mondays?"

"It's eight-thirty in the morning."

"What does that have to do with anything?"

"Shouldn't I be at home chopping vegetables for my healthy salad?" she teased.

"I'll put an extra olive in your drink. That will count as today's veggie," he said.

She laughed. "Fine."

"Oh, shit, I've gotta go," Craig said, looking down at his Black-Berry. "The Speaker's office just heard that we're raising the threat level. Do you know anything about that?"

"No, but the vice president picked today to start coming to the office before noon, so I should get back to my desk to see what inspired assignments land on my desk. I'll e-mail you if I hear anything."

"Thanks. Same here." Craig walked out of the West Wing basement and into one of the cars that would take him up to the Hill. She watched some of the young female staffers watch him walk out, and she smiled to herself. Sometimes she worried that she was sharing too much with Craig about the vice president, but it was nice to have someone to talk to about the lunacy of her job. Peter had never really been interested in talking to her about work. It was fun to have a work husband. Besides, Craig spent more time with the president than any other senior staffer these days. He must have earned her confidence by being discreet and trustworthy.

She ordered a fresh cup of coffee and walked across the driveway to her office. Once inside, she turned on the TV and was comforted by the insipid banter. Surely nothing too dire could be under way if the hosts were debating whether the president was more or less focused on her job as a single mother. She finally returned Annie McKay's call. According to Annie, Secretary Kingston was bringing over some of the more senior women in the administration for a series of lunch discussions. She wanted to include Dale. The invitation was curious, but Dale agreed to the first date Annie proposed. She was adding the lunch to her calendar when her private line rang. She considered letting it go to voice mail since it was usually Michael Robbins, but the number looked like one of the numbers in the Sit Room. Reluctantly, Dale picked up on the fifth ring.

"Hello?"

"Dale, I need you in the Sit Room immediately." It was Ralph and he didn't sound happy.

"What is it?"

"This time it really is classified."

CHAPTER THIRTY-THREE

Charlotte

Thank you, everyone, for gathering so quickly. Tara, go ahead and get us started. What do we know?" Charlotte said from the secure video conference that had been set up on board Air Force One. The plane was more secure than Charlotte's hotel room, so they'd traveled to the airport to participate in the call. The secretary of state and national security advisor flanked her.

"Madam President, I've asked the FAA administrator to be here with us, as well, and I'm going to turn it over to him in a moment. I want to ask CIA Director Dorfman to speak first. Director?"

"Madam President, the vice president has been convinced since our first meeting a couple of days ago that we were missing a piece of the puzzle. We've been looking at Youseff and all of his known associates in the U.S. Our reason for concern, as we've discussed, was that he'd gone completely dark, or so we thought. We hadn't spent any time on his wife and kids because we believed they were sent to Yemen so he could focus his efforts here in the U.S. Well, we went back and looked at the family again. We worked with the Yemeni government to approve wiretaps and to do some other monitoring. I'll cut right to the chase. We learned that Youseff's kids are actually his nephews. He's been raising them as his own children with the promise that together they'd avenge their father's—Youseff's brother's—capture."

"In hindsight, that's not at all surprising," Tara said.

A few of the other participants nodded.

"Where are we now, Director? Do we know where he is?" Charlotte asked.

"That's the bad news. The answer is no. At least we have a new strand of information and live conversations in Yemen to monitor."

"What's the good news?" Melanie asked.

"The good news is that the nephews left Yemen a few days ago and they are probably about to try to enter the U.S."

"Why is that good news? Couldn't we get the Yemenis to detain them?" Melanie objected.

"As you know, we could have, but it was the agency's recommendation that we not do so. Youseff's nephews were careful. They haven't discussed a specific plot and they never reveal their location. It would have been impossible to hang on to them. But don't worry. We have all of the airports in the U.S. and the Homeland Security agencies on high alert."

"Let me get this straight, we discover Youseff's kids are really his terrorist brother's kids, and we listen to enough conversations to believe that they're intent on revenge for their father's capture, but we don't think we have enough to ask the Yemenis to detain them?" Melanie protested.

"Melanie, you know that the Yemenis would have hauled them in if we'd asked them to, but then they would have been freed, eventually, and they would have disappeared. If we capture them here, we send them to Gitmo and throw away the key if we deem them unlawful combatants," noted the undersecretary of defense.

Melanie still seemed unsatisfied and the CIA director looked uncomfortable with the reference to Gitmo. He turned to face the video-teleconferencing equipment and addressed the president.

"We'll find them, Madam President," he promised.

"I know you will," she said.

"Madam President, would you like to go through the operational readiness rundown so you know what everyone is doing? We believe that an attack is likely timed to coincide with the arrival on U.S. soil of Youseff's nephews," the FBI director offered.

Charlotte rubbed her eye sockets with her thumbs and contemplated taking another Motrin. She looked at the faces in the Sit Room.

They were all watching her, waiting for her to say or do something. She wondered what they'd do if she just sat there and said nothing. Before she could find out, Melanie started in on a list of questions.

"Before we do that, I'm wondering if we've alerted the airlines yet," Melanie asked.

"The FAA is doing that now," Ralph replied.

"Have we alerted law enforcement about the potential change in the threat level?"

"Melanie, we were waiting to make sure that we had a consensus recommendation to raise the threat level, but they've been receiving regular bulletins from the Department of Homeland Security about the threat," Ralph said.

Melanie nodded.

"I'm sorry, have we already made the determination to raise the threat level? Wasn't that the purpose of this call?" Charlotte asked. "And why would we assume they'd use planes again? I'm interested in Tara's thoughts on this."

"Madam President, I don't think it will be planes. Not because it isn't possible, we all know it is, but that's not how Youseff operates. He's an innovator, and this is a family affair. I think they'll try something novel," Tara said.

"Like what?" Melanie asked.

"First of all, he'd probably hit a soft target because it's less hassle and it offers the same degree of psychological devastation—perhaps more. It could be a suicide bombing or a chemical attack, or maybe just a mass shooting."

The group was quiet again.

"Should we go around the room on the decision to raise the threat level?" Charlotte asked. One by one, she asked everyone in the room to weigh in. Everyone was in favor of elevating it.

"Obviously, we'll cut our trip short to get back there as soon as possible. What's your best guess on timing?" Charlotte asked.

"Madam President, with the nephews' departure from Yemen and September 11 right around the corner, I think we have to assume that something could be imminent or under way," the CIA chief replied.

"Right," Charlotte said. "I'm not happy about being halfway

around the world at the moment. We're going to take off and head straight home as soon as we get off the call."

Normally, someone on her national security team would caution against doing something that would cause diplomatic irritation, but no one spoke up.

"May I play devil's advocate for a moment?" Melanie asked.

"Of course, Secretary Kingston," the CIA director replied.

"Is it possible that there is nothing under way? I mean, is it still possible that nothing is happening?" Melanie asked.

"It is always possible, Melanie. But in my view, that is the less likely scenario at this point," the director said.

Charlotte kept her eyes on the camera that was beaming her into the meeting in the Sit Room and reached into her pocket for another 600 milligrams of Motrin.

"Melanie makes a good point, but let's all proceed as though an attack is expected. Tara, Ralph will go over the evacuation plan for your family. Ralph, I'll call Peter and the kids as soon as we get off to let them know they could be moving at any time. All of you should make plans to locate your families in a place where you won't worry about them any more than necessary and where you can be in touch easily. We'll reconvene in a couple hours from the air. Keep your heads about you and just do your jobs, people. This is why you're all here. I believe in each and every one of you. Does anyone have any questions?"

The room was silent. The gravity of the moment was slowly sinking in.

"Thank you, everyone. We'll speak again soon," Charlotte said.

CHAPTER THIRTY-FOUR

Tara

A small group stayed behind in the Situation Room after Charlotte signed off. Tara was so engrossed in their discussions that, at first, she didn't notice that Melanie was sitting across the table watching her.

"Madam Secretary, is everything all right?" she finally asked.

Melanie cleared her throat and stood up quickly.

"I was just listening to what you all were saying and trying to figure out if this guy is the type who would be more satisfied by all this than he would be by mass murder," she said, gesturing at the staffers hovered over computer monitors and the stacks of classified briefing materials on the table. She stared at Tara for what felt like forever and then turned to leave the room.

"Madam Secretary," Tara called after her.

Melanie turned with one hand on the door.

"Fifty-fifty," Tara said.

"Sorry?"

"There's a fifty percent chance he'd be more excited by all this than by an actual attack," Tara said.

Melanie nodded. They both knew it didn't change anything operationally, but Tara suspected she'd just passed an important test.

Melanie nodded at the CIA director on her way out.

"I'll see you at the tank briefing," she said.

Tara hadn't noticed a briefing at the Pentagon on her schedule, but things were changing by the minute.

She wrapped up her conversation with the intelligence officers and returned to her office. Dale followed a few steps behind Tara as she climbed the flight of stairs to the main level of the West Wing. During the meeting, Tara had turned to look at the row of staff members sitting behind her and had noticed that Dale seemed to be transcribing everything everyone was saying. She hadn't said anything since they left the Sit Room.

"What did you think?" Tara asked her. She was out of breath.

"I'm not sure I understand what Secretary Kingston was getting at," Dale said.

"She wants to make sure we're not exposing the president to accusations that she is overreacting or hyping the anniversary of September 11 to rebuild support for the Afghanistan mission," Tara said.

"Do you want me to type up my notes from the meeting? Or work on some talking points for you for later?" Dale offered.

"I'm fine for now, but I'm sure your calls are piling up. Why don't you check in with your press contacts and let me know what you're hearing. Once the news breaks, we'll want to be able to confirm what meetings and briefings I've attended. You've got good notes on all that, right?"

"Yes ma'am," Dale said.

"Good. Once I make certain that I'll be at the Pentagon briefing, we can add that to the list," Tara said. Dale nodded and turned to walk back to her office.

Tara closed the door to her office, sat down at her desk, and dialed Marcus.

"How's it going?" he asked.

"I'm doing fine," Tara whispered.

"Really?" Marcus whispered also, even though he was home alone.

"Yes, really. I feel good. Better than at any other point I can remember since I got here," Tara insisted.

"I'm really happy to hear that. Maybe this is the beginning of something better. I'm going to stay close to home. Call me if you need anything."

"I will."

"You can do this, Tara. You know these issues better than anyone else there," he said.

It was the nicest thing he'd said to her since they'd arrived in Washington. She felt a sudden flood of affection for him as she hung up. She stood to walk down the hall to Ralph's office to find out when the Pentagon meeting was taking place and to make sure she had a seat at the table. Tara was afraid that if Melanie was in charge of the invitations, she'd be left off the list.

She wondered if she should plant the seed with Ralph that Melanie was undermining her in the meetings. Ralph had history with Melanie, and it wasn't good. Tara was certain that Ralph would never take Melanie's side on any dispute, but she wanted to be sure. Tara saw an opportunity to recast her image internally, at least, by showing her White House colleagues she wasn't a complete idiot. She wasn't going to screw it up.

Tara barged into Ralph's office without knocking.

"Ralph, did you think Melanie's line of questioning was appropriate for a meeting like that?" she asked.

He didn't seem surprised to see her standing in his office, but he seemed to mull her question over before answering.

"It didn't strike me as too off base for Melanie," he said.

"I think it's important that the president have the benefit of multiple perspectives, but I think some members of the national security team probably find her dominating tone a little off-putting. I don't know if it's the kind of feedback the president would seek out from you, but I wanted to mention it."

"Yes, of course, Madam Vice President. I'll pass it along to her. Thanks."

Tara smiled to herself as she walked back to her office. She was sure that Melanie had provided a constant stream of criticism about her performance to the president over the past six months. It felt good to return the favor.

During the campaign, she had desperately sought Melanie's approval, but the harder she tried, the more Melanie seemed to distance herself from Tara. Marcus thought Melanie was a bitch. He'd called her a typical Washington spinster who'd been married to the job for so long that she hated any woman who had a husband and kids and any semblance of a life outside of work. Tara suspected that there was more to Melanie's disapproval of her than that, but at the moment, she was immensely pleased with herself. She'd managed to get invited to the briefing and to knock Melanie down a notch or two. *Not bad*, she thought to herself, *not bad at all.*

CHAPTER THIRTY-FIVE

Dale

D ale couldn't decide what was more disturbing—that there was a terror threat serious enough to drag the president home from halfway around the world, or that her boss was in charge of the federal response. She tried calling Craig on his cell phone, but it went straight to voice mail. Dale remembered someone in the Situation Room mentioning that the Homeland Security committees would be briefed immediately. Craig was probably in those briefings. Dale watched from a window in her office as a groundskeeper neatened the flower beds in front of the formal entrance to the West Wing. She felt a growing sense of dread. A few reporters were hanging out on the driveway in front of the West Wing where they always held an informal "stakeout." The press was being kept in the dark about the nature and seriousness of the threat, but they weren't stupid. And it was only a matter of time before the Hill started leaking.

Dale knew she should take advantage of the small window of free time that had presented itself, but she couldn't focus. Her mind was racing. She hadn't been handed any formal assignments in the Sit Room, but she figured that someone would be expected to compile a "ticktock" of the day's events. She would be ready. Everything that everyone had said in every meeting she'd attended over the previous twenty-four hours was detailed in her notebook. She had created a precise record of who was in each meeting and who had been given responsibility for any follow-up. She'd taken the notes with an eye toward the kinds of questions she would have asked back in her reporter days, often jotting her own questions in the margin. She noticed as she flipped through her notes that she'd circled Melanie's question about whether Youseff would be more pleased with the knowledge that he'd brought the White House to its knees than by carrying out an attack. She'd written in the margin "he could be fucking with us," which she started to cross out but decided to preserve, at least until the end of the day.

Dale could hear a group of staffers talking and laughing in the hallway outside her office. The vast majority of White House employees were completely unaware that a lunatic was planning to finish what his brother had started years earlier. Dale glanced at her BlackBerry and felt sorry for her former colleagues in the press. She knew exactly what kind of turn their day was about to have.

Dale desperately wanted to talk to someone. She tried Craig one more time. When he didn't pick up, she called Ralph's office.

"He's down at the Mess. Do you need me to pass him a note?" his assistant offered.

"No, it's not urgent," she replied.

She watched the groundskeeper for a few more minutes. He was on his hands and knees now with a spray bottle and cloth. It looked like he was washing the leaves. Dale dialed Peter's cell phone.

"Hi," she said when he picked up on the first ring.

"Are they taking care of you?" he asked.

"Yes. I've been in the Sit Room all day with Tara. What a nightmare, huh?"

"I'm glad you're in there," he said.

"I'm beginning to believe that ignorance really is bliss."

"I don't remember you spending much time in the dark before," he said.

"True enough. Are you with the kids?"

"I'm going to pick them up now," he said.

She sighed. "I can't believe this is happening."

"Stay close to Tara. Go wherever she goes. There's always a press person in the room during a crisis like this, so you'll be fine. If she gets evacuated, go with her."

"Peter, I don't know if she is up to this."

He was quiet.

"Peter?"

"You need to go see Charlotte as soon as she gets back."

"Oh, right, good idea. She's going to be managing a White House on high alert for a terror attack. I'm sure she'll want to visit with me about the vice president," Dale said. Her tone was more snide than she'd intended.

"What do you want me to say to you, Dale?" he said. He sounded irritated.

"I didn't realize that I'd compromised your sense of spousal loyalty by confiding in you."

She could hear him take a deep breath.

"Dale, if you're seriously concerned about Tara's abilities, you need to go talk to her as soon as she lands. If you don't say something to her, I will," he warned.

It was the first time he'd ever threatened to divulge something Dale had told him. "I shouldn't have said anything," Dale said.

"Listen, the kids are here. I've got to go. Take care of yourself."

He hung up without saying good-bye.

Dale tried to remember the last time he'd called her and she couldn't think of a single instance since they broke up. She printed out her call log and wrote some notes on her notepad to guide her on-the-record comments about the meetings. The plan was for the press office to confirm that the president had cut her trip short and was on her way back to Washington as soon as the first press calls came in after the Hill briefing. Dale looked up at her televisions and noticed that CNN was airing its "breaking news" graphic. She picked up her land line and got ready to start reading out the vice president's schedule of meetings on the threat.

While she was holding for NBC's White House correspondent, she saw a text from Craig.

"Play down V.P.'s role. Members r asking who's holding down the fort in POTUS' absence. Say that POTUS in regular contact with her nat security team. The intvu's are still fresh up here."

Crap, Dale said under her breath.

"I heard that," her assistant said. He'd appeared in her doorway.

"You have been put in charge of the president's arrival on the South Lawn at twelve-thirty A.M." he announced.

"You're kidding, right?"

"Nope. The press office called and said that since you are the most senior press officer who isn't traveling with the president, you have been named the action officer for the arrival. Oh, and they added that they are ready to assist you in whatever capacity you need."

"How about in the capacity of being in charge of the president's arrival?"

"Except that one, it would appear."

"Lovely," she sighed. Being named the action officer was supposed to convey authority, but it usually meant that someone else had off-loaded the assignment.

"What can I do to help?" he asked.

"I don't know yet. Want to take a walk over to the press office with me to find out exactly what an arrival entails?"

"Absolutely!" he exclaimed. He was a little too enthusiastic for Dale's mood.

CHAPTER THIRTY-SIX

Charlotte

The Motrin and coffee finally kicked in, and Charlotte felt more like herself. She finished a round of calls to a few of the allies and then asked for another update on the intelligence. She was having a hard time understanding how the agencies had let Youseff slip off their radars in the weeks before September 11. Charlotte had worried all year about the tragic milestone. She called her personal steward and asked how long until they landed at Andrews.

"We're flying around some weather, Madam President. As soon as we get back on course, it should be seven hours," she was told.

"Thank you," she replied.

Charlotte stood and started pacing back and forth in her cabin. She was furious at herself for coming on the Asia trip. She'd never agreed to international travel at this time of year before. There was always an uptick in the chatter. It was little consolation, but Tara had seemed very sharp on all of their calls, and had actually injected a greater sense of urgency into the deliberations. In fact, her astute read on Youseff was the reason Charlotte was heading home. Charlotte walked back to her desk and sat down.

She picked up the phone and asked the Air Force One operator to connect her to Peter. She wanted to make sure the kids were not too unsettled by the news. Penelope reacted particularly badly these days whenever any aspect of Charlotte's job got in the way of her life, which she constantly made clear was completely separate from her mother's life. Charlotte made a mental note to set aside some mother-daughter time when things settled down.

"Charlotte?"

"Hi, I wanted to see if the kids were grumpy about having to change all their plans."

"Nothing I can't handle." Peter sounded relaxed.

She could hear the twins talking loudly in the background. He made it seem easy.

"Thank you for this. Are you all heading to L.A.?"

"I don't know yet. What do you think? I didn't know how far to take them."

Her hands went to her chest. She felt it tighten with an intense desire to protect all of them from harm.

"Char?" he asked.

"I'm here. I think you guys should go to San Francisco. Nothing ever happens there except earthquakes." She tried to sound light.

Peter didn't laugh.

"You sound worried, Charlotte," he said.

"I am a little worried," she admitted.

"Are you worried about the threat or is it something else?" Peter asked.

"Isn't the threat enough?" She hadn't succeeded in keeping all of the edge that she felt out of her voice.

"Is it Tara?"

She sighed loudly.

"Char, I think you and Dale should compare notes."

It was funny. She felt comfortable asking Peter about Dale, but hearing him utter her name still packed a punch. She didn't say anything for a few seconds. Peter was the most sensitive person she knew, and if he wanted her to confer with Dale, it was probably a good idea.

"Char?"

"Peter, do me a favor and stay away from the bridges if you take them to San Francisco," she said.

"Don't worry."

"I'll worry less knowing that you're all together. Let me say hello to them."

She talked to Harry for a few minutes and just as he handed the phone to Penelope, Charlotte's national security advisor barged in.

"Madam President?"

"Can it wait?" she asked, covering the phone with her hand.

"I don't think so," he said.

"Penny, I've got to call you back," she said into the phone. "I'm sorry, honey."

"What is it?" Charlotte asked. She was annoyed.

"Melanie asked that we interrupt you and put her through right away."

Charlotte nodded her approval for the call to be put through.

"I'm worried that we're being too reactive," Melanie said without preamble.

"In what way, exactly?" Charlotte asked.

"The White House is embarrassed on Monday by the vice president's disastrous interviews, and by Friday she's your point person on a looming attack. Even if it's all true, it stinks."

"What do you suggest I do?"

"I'm not sure we need to make such a public show of escalating our defenses in response to the terror threat."

"If something happens and they attack us for not being on a protective footing, we say, 'Sorry everyone, we were worried about the press calling us fakers'?"

"I'm not saying that, Madam President, I'm just saying we should consider toning down the public appearances of Tara going in and out of the JTTF and DOJ and the breathless updates about your location and ETA. It feels contrived."

Charlotte was exasperated now.

"Melanie, it would have been helpful if you'd made these points in the meeting, when I could have done something about it."

"I'm sorry. I've been sitting here watching the coverage and it gave me pause. I felt like I needed to say something to you. It's only a matter of time before Congress accuses you of wagging the dog."

Charlotte squeezed her eyes shut and held her hand over her mouth.

"Madam President?"

"I'm here."

"What do you want me to do?"

"Stay in contact with Ralph until I get back."

"I'll do it."

"Thanks, Mel. See if he can tone down the arrival or something."

"I'll call him right now," Melanie promised.

"Thanks."

Charlotte hung up and stared at the darkness outside her window. She thought about the last time she and Roger were together in her cabin aboard Air Force One. She thought about his insistence that she never let the enemy alter her behavior. "When you do that, they're winning," he'd said. She thought about his letter and she wished he were there to offer her guidance and to steel her for the fights she knew lay ahead.

CHAPTER THIRTY-SEVEN

Tara

Tara lifted her head and wiped the crumbs off her blouse. She was lying on the couch in her office waiting for Air Force One to land at Andrews Air Force Base. The networks and cable channels were showing the same live shot of an empty runway that they'd been airing for the last thirty minutes. Tara closed her eyes and focused on the sound of her own breathing. She'd taken a yoga class once where all they did was listen to the sound of their breathing. It was supposed to sound like a whale. Tara only remembered feeling like a whale.

Now she had to face the fact that despite her careful efforts to pace herself, she had hit the wall. She'd been in the Roosevelt Room around dinnertime when she felt herself starting to slip. Dale was briefing the senior staff on the interagency public affairs system that had been set up to centralize all press relations at the White House. Press secretaries from DOD, CIA, FBI, DOJ, DOT, NSA, and the State Department were all sitting together at card tables in a room down the hall from the Situation Room so that everyone would speak off a single set of facts.

Tara was listening to the briefing and taking a few notes one minute, and the next, she felt like the room had been plunged underwater. Suddenly, everyone was speaking in voices that were so distorted, it took all her concentration to understand what they were saying. She had pushed herself away from the table and walked slowly back to her office. She'd considered calling Marcus, but there wasn't anything he could do. She'd locked her door and asked her secretary to hold all calls while she caught up on some reading. That had been nearly four hours earlier.

She pulled her notebook from the table in front of the couch and tried to organize a single page of notes in case Charlotte asked her for an overview of the day. She had started the day so strong. She'd been one of the most vocal participants in the Situation Room in the morning. Then she'd headed over to the Pentagon for a briefing. While she was on her way back to the White House, she'd received a call from Dale informing her that news of the terror threat had leaked from Capitol Hill and that they would begin confirming Tara's participation in the briefings. At six-thirty, the networks had led their newscasts with stories about the credible terror threat facing the country. The cable channels were wall to wall with analysis and very few commercials. They'd all shown video of Tara over the previous days, walking into and out of briefings in New York and Washington, D.C.

During Dale's briefing, the senior staff was given instructions about how to handle press calls. Tara started to highlight that section but then scribbled it out. Charlotte wouldn't care how press calls were being routed.

She sighed and strained to think of some new kernel or fact that she could offer about Youseff. *Don't prove your uselessness in there*, she said to herself. She put her hands over her face and rubbed her eyes until they burned. She missed Kendall. Tara hated missing bedtime. She felt off balance when she went an entire day without seeing her daughter.

Keep it together, she said to herself. She repeated the mantra over and over. She noticed tears streaming down her face only when they landed on her notes and blurred the ink. *What is wrong with you? Charlotte has kids, too, and she isn't running around Air Force One crying about it*, she said to herself. Tara squeezed her eyes shut and tried to regroup. She looked up when she heard the device on her desk that notified her of the president's whereabouts beep for the first time in days. After three long, low beeps, she heard the familiar alert: "All cars, all stations, Wayfarer arriving Andrews Air Force Base. Wayfarer arriving."

CHAPTER THIRTY-EIGHT

Dale

L isten up, people, can I get your attention, please?"

Dale was shouting at the top of her lungs at the large group of reporters gathered on the South Lawn for the president's return to the White House. No one was listening.

"The expression 'herding cats' was obviously invented by someone who was trying to organize reporters," she said to her assistant.

He handed her a bullhorn that the advance guys had brought to the site. She refused it but stood on a box that one of the correspondents would use later to make herself taller for a live shot.

"Listen up, guys. Air Force One just landed at Andrews. The president is about fifteen minutes out," Dale announced. "We'll leave the lights up and let you do live shots from out here for one hour after she lands. That's it, everyone got it?"

"Who is traveling with her on Marine One? Do you have the manifest?" one of the reporters yelled.

"I don't have it, but you'll see for yourself when they get off the helicopter."

"Thanks a lot," a couple of reporters groused.

Dale had covered dozens of presidential arrivals. On days like this, she was convinced that her new responsibilities were karmic payback for her disregard for all the White House staffers who helped her do her job when she was at the network.

At Ralph's direction, Dale had first planned to open the arrival to the smaller and more manageable press "pool," but when she learned from a junior press aide that she had a full-scale revolt on her hands from the White House Correspondents' Association for trying to limit access at a moment of national importance, she'd relented and opened the arrival to all press. She hoped Ralph wouldn't scream at her in front of everyone. Dale waded through a section of foreign reporters to get back inside the Diplomatic Room to talk to the Secret Service. As she stepped over a photographer from Japanese TV, she heard the familiar flapping of the propeller. She turned to watch the first helicopter that always accompanies Marine One hover above the Ellipse for a moment and then move away as the president's chopper neared the South Lawn. The trees started to buckle in the wind and leaves blew everywhere. Reporters shielded their eyes, but Dale stared straight at the helicopter as it landed gracefully in the center of the South Lawn. She forgot about the reporters and watched for the president to disembark. She felt an immense sense of relief that the president would resume control of the terror investigation. The president stepped off the helicopter and nodded in the direction of the press before walking briskly into the Oval Office.

Dale shooed some of the reporters away and pointed them toward Charlie Higgins, the White House press secretary. He had sauntered off the helicopter and wandered over to the rope line to talk to a few of the reporters. She'd never liked him. When she covered the White House, she had found him lazy and unresponsive. Now that she worked at the White House, she knew he didn't even read the newspapers. He relied on staff to tell him what was in them. But that wasn't why she was annoyed tonight. Dale was eager to get down to the meeting in the Situation Room.

"Hey, Charlie, they're all yours," she yelled.

He cocked his head to the side in a way that reminded Dale of a puzzled golden retriever. Dale couldn't tell if he'd forgotten that Dale worked on the White House staff, or if he was surprised that she'd been asked to help with a presidential event.

She rushed to the Sit Room and took a seat in the back row. When she looked up, she was almost directly in the president's line of sight. She listened as the president gave Ralph a hard time about the grand spectacle on the south lawn. "It was an arrival, not a royal wedding."

Ralph apologized, and amazingly, made no effort to shift the blame to Dale.

Charlotte's eyes were bright and she showed no signs of weariness from the eighteen-hour flight. She had on a crisp white blouse, a black jacket, and black slacks. She greeted everyone with a curt smile and asked for an update. She turned to Tara who had her head buried in her notes.

"Madam Vice President, do you want to start, or should we recap the intelligence?"

Dale held her breath until the vice president started speaking.

"Madam President, why don't we start with an operational update?"

"That works. Hank, where are we?" Charlotte asked, turning to the head of the FBI.

Dale's view of the vice president was mostly obstructed. When the secretary of state stood to refill her coffee Dale examined her for the first time since the meetings earlier in the day. She looked disheveled and tired. The conversation in the room sounded exactly like the meeting they'd had six hours earlier. After about thirty minutes, the president went around and asked everyone to argue a theory that they did *not* believe applied to the investigation into Youseff. Charlotte was a fan of exercises that forced her team to think outside the box. She believed it was a small but important way to challenge conventional wisdom. Most of the participants suggested theories that differed only slightly from what they all believed to be going on. When they got to Tara, Dale braced herself.

"May I pass?" she asked. Dale thought her voice had trembled.

Everyone looked up.

"You've been holding down the fort, Tara. You may take a pass," the president said. Dale was struck by the fact that the president used the same expression that Craig had used earlier in the day.

The head of national intelligence started to make a joke but Charlotte interrupted him. Charlotte thanked everyone for their attendance and then stood up to signal that the meeting was over.

"We'll reconvene in the morning."

Dale noticed that the FBI director and the attorney general had shared an eye roll. Obviously, the only reason they'd had the meeting was to compel the press to report that the president had landed and attended immediately to the terror threat. Tara scurried out of the room so quickly that Dale couldn't get to her without climbing across the table, so she remained seated until the room started to clear out. A group of intelligence officials surrounded the president and spoke in hushed tones. Dale looked at her watch and was surprised that it was after one A.M. She wasn't tired. While she was underlining the list of attendees and checking it against her list from earlier in the day, an usher approached her and asked her to wait for the president in the Oval Office.

"Excuse me?" Dale asked.

"The president has asked if you wouldn't mind waiting for her in the Oval Office, Miss Smith," he repeated.

Dale swallowed.

"Yes sir," she said.

He smiled and directed her out of the Situation Room and up the stairs toward the Oval. They walked in through the doorway that Dale had only ever seen open for West Wing tours. Dale had never seen anyone actually walk through it.

"Right this way, ma'am," he said.

She had never been inside the Oval Office alone.

"Where should I wait?"

"Make yourself comfortable."

Yeah, right, Dale thought.

She sat at the edge of the sofa and waited for the president to return from the meeting downstairs. She looked around at the photos of the twins on Charlotte's desk. Peter had many of the same pictures.

Hearing the door open, she stood. It was the president's assistant, Samantha.

"Miss Smith, can I get you something to drink?"

Dale was about to refuse, but she thought it might be helpful to have something to do with her hands.

"I hate to bother you, but I would love some coffee."

"Cream and sugar?"

"Yes, both, please. And thank you."

Samantha smiled. "The president will be right in."

As the door behind Samantha closed, the door on the other side of the Oval Office swung open and Charlotte strode in.

"Thanks for stopping by, Dale. I know it's late." Dale was certain that the president had been awake longer than any of them.

"It's not a problem." She smiled nervously at the president.

"And I'm sorry to keep you here for another meeting after what has already been a very long day."

"Please don't apologize."

"Would you like some coffee? Or water? Or a drink? I have a full bar."

"Samantha is getting me some coffee," Dale replied. She watched Charlotte walk toward all the doors and make sure they were shut. Then she returned to the sofa and sat down across from Dale.

"How are you doing?" Charlotte asked.

"I was watching all the reporters swarming around out there during your arrival, and I thought how fortunate I am to be able to do something instead of just report on it."

Charlotte's expression was impossible to read, but Dale was trying hard not to bore her.

"Did Melanie reach out to you?"

"Yes ma'am. Her office called while she was overseas to schedule lunch."

"Good, good. I'm glad. We need to find ways to take advantage of all your relationships with the press. Melanie had some ideas about how to loop you in better."

"Sure, yes, anything I can do to help."

"One thing I've been hoping to get your perspective on is the vice president."

Samantha walked in with a silver tray holding two cups of coffee, a creamer, and a sugar bowl. She placed the tray on the coffee table between them.

"Thanks, Sam," the president said. She waited for her to close the door behind her.

"Dale, how do you think she's doing?"

"Madam President, I don't know how to answer that," Dale said.

"I think we both know that there's something out of the ordinary going on," Charlotte said with a raised eyebrow. Dale poured cream into her coffee and stirred it with the dainty silver spoon. She was afraid to look up. Dale couldn't lie to the president. She wasn't sure what she should say. Charlotte continued.

"I have my own theories. They were just hunches until I had lunch with her a few weeks ago. I'd really like to hear what you think is going on."

Dale swallowed her coffee in large gulps and tried to avoid the president's stare. She figured that Peter had said something to her, which meant that Charlotte and Peter were on much closer terms than they'd been before. She wondered, for a moment, if they were together again, and her gut ached. She cleared her throat and tried to write a headline in her mind. She pushed everything else aside and organized her concerns into a reasonable and credible set of facts and anecdotes for the president.

"Madam President, I share your concerns," she started.

Charlotte leaned forward.

As Dale spoke, the president's face went from curiosity to worry to resignation. Dale was relieved to be sharing her burden, but in the back of her mind, she wondered if she should reveal so much of what she'd seen to someone who could face serious questions about when it was made clear to her that the vice president was floundering. As Dale recounted the story of the vice president screaming about her press coverage, the president seemed to recoil. Dale was quick to broaden the anecdote to include other incidents. At one point, the president reached out and touched Dale's arm.

"Thank you for everything you've done. It is far beyond the call of duty, and I appreciate your discretion."

In that instant, Dale was more gratified personally and professionally than she'd ever been in her life.

CHAPTER THIRTY-NINE

Charlotte

A s Charlotte listened to Dale tick through the litany of early signs of a breakdown of some sort, her mind flashed, as it often did when she and Dale were in the same room, to thoughts of Dale and Peter together. She wondered if Dale had shared these same stories with Peter. She must have, Charlotte decided. He was the one who'd insisted she and Dale share information. She forced herself to listen carefully to what Dale was saying about the canceled events, the obsession with clothes and weight, and Tara's crushing fears of inadequacy about gaps in her knowledge of world affairs. Dale painted a picture that was every bit as grim as Charlotte had feared. Any hope she'd had that Tara was simply off her game evaporated.

Charlotte looked up and realized that Dale had asked her a question.

"I'm sorry?"

"Madam President, I don't know how much of this you want to hear," Dale offered.

"Keep going," the president ordered.

"Well, the next part gets into Ralph's role, and I'm not sure if I should talk about that."

"I think I can guess what his role was in all this, but go ahead. The tape recorders were removed with Nixon. This conversation is between you and me."

Dale took a deep breath.

"Ralph called me over to his office and Marcus was in there and they told me that she had mental toughness issues," Dale said.

"That sounds like something Ralph would say. What did Marcus say?" Charlotte asked.

"Nothing. He sat in Ralph's office and stared straight ahead."

"Did he seem worried?"

"I couldn't tell. Tara and Marcus have a bizarre relationship. I've been around the two of them and they seem to have their moments. I was at the residence helping her prepare for the morning shows and he spoke to her in a way that made me uncomfortable, but I can't really say what Marcus's role is in any of it."

The president nodded.

"What did he say to her that made you uncomfortable?"

"He made comments about her weight and her clothes, and he was incredibly rude and condescending to her."

The president nodded again.

"Madam President, I'm sorry that I didn't do more," Dale said.

The president was about to say something when Samantha stuck her head in. It was after two A.M.

"Madam President, I'm sorry, I have the FBI director. He said it's an emergency."

Dale stood to leave.

"You can stay," Charlotte said. She picked up the line on her speakerphone.

"Go ahead, Hank," she said.

"Madam President, we got him. We got Youseff."

"That's great news. Were you able to get any specific information about the plots he's involved in?"

"We haven't started questioning him yet, Madam President. That's the obvious next step. Given his relationships with the various domestic cells and the fact that he's been grooming his nephews, it's quite possible that he's already provided sufficient materials and technical support for the plots to be carried out without him. We can't take our foot off the gas."

"Keep me posted."

"Yes ma'am."

CHAPTER FORTY

Tara

Something was ringing and she couldn't make it stop. She looked around and Marcus wasn't in their bedroom. She stared at the clock in her room and it said 3:00. Tara wondered for a second if it was A.M. or P.M. She couldn't tell if she'd been asleep for two hours or twelve. It was still dark. The phone had stopped but now her ears were ringing. She couldn't decide which was worse. She was sitting at the edge of the bed with her feet dangling off to one side.

Marcus came into the bedroom.

"It's the Sit Room," he said.

"What time is it?" Tara asked. "Am I late?"

"It's three A.M. You were sleeping." He was speaking to her in kind, calming tones.

"I'll call back in a little bit. I need to sleep," she said. She started to lie back down.

"I think you need to pick up."

She held her hands over her face.

"I'm exhausted," she said.

Marcus sat down on the edge of the bed and watched her while he picked up the phone on her desk.

"Hi, this is Marcus Meyers. I have the vice president." He handed her the phone.

"Hello?" Tara nodded a few times and then looked up at Marcus while she spoke to one of the duty officers in the Sit Room.

"When do I need to be in? Okay. I'll be there. Thank you."

Tara handed the phone back to Marcus and covered her face with her hands again.

"What is it?" he asked.

"They got Youseff and we are reconvening at oh six hundred," she said. She still hadn't looked up. Marcus placed a hand awkwardly on her shoulder.

"That's great!"

She looked up at him with tears streaming down her face.

"I can't go back in there. I'm completely burned out."

"Shhh. You can do it."

"I can't do it anymore, Marcus. I can't."

"What do you want to do?"

"I want it all to stop."

"You'll feel better in a few days," he said.

"We keep saying that, but I don't. It's getting worse. I'm getting worse."

He put his head in his hands and didn't say anything else.

CHAPTER FORTY-ONE

Dale

Dale barely had time to drive home, shower, change, and get back to the office before her first meeting of the day. Much to the press secretary's displeasure, Ralph asked Dale to lead the team that would handle all of the press briefings on Youseff's capture. He'd told the press secretary that Dale had sat through all of the National Security Council meetings and therefore had a better handle on the intelligence, but Dale suspected that he wanted to micromanage the public relations effort, something that he'd have no qualms about doing with Dale at the helm. Placing her in charge was also a subtle way to reinforce his decision to place the vice president front and center as the public face managing the threat in Charlotte's absence.

Her first meeting of the day was with the CIA. She was getting a classified briefing on the intelligence that led to Youseff's arrest. It was her responsibility to work with the briefers on a version of the intelligence that could be unclassified and shared with the press. Craig was in the meeting as well. He would use the unclassified material for his briefings with congressional staff.

After the CIA meeting she rushed into senior staff. The president walked in at the beginning and thanked everyone for their hard work. Dale noticed that a few people had tears in their eyes when she praised them for keeping the country safe. Charlotte could be stirring, and Dale was surprised by how committed she felt to helping in any way she could. When the president finished speaking, the staff gave her a standing ovation. Afterward, Dale held a meeting with all of the public affairs officers from the agencies that had been dispatched to the White House. They decided to keep the centralized press room up and running through the end of the week. The White House was struggling with how to communicate the message to the public that Youseff's capture didn't mean that the threat had passed. To make sure that the administration didn't send any mixed messages, all spokespeople would still report to Dale. Her day was packed with meetings, press calls, and troubleshooting for her expanded staff.

Around four P.M., her assistant walked in.

"Ralph wants to see you," he said.

"Did they say what it's about?" she asked.

"*They* did not say anything. *He* said to tell you to come over at your earliest convenience."

"He?"

"Ralph."

Dale took a deep breath and glanced out her window toward the White House residence. Charlotte would not have betrayed her confidence by telling Ralph what she'd said the night before. Dale stood up and smoothed her skirt. She took a sip of coffee and put a few Tic Tacs in her mouth before she headed toward the West Wing.

A smiled formed on her face when she noticed Craig and a few of his colleagues standing in the doorway to the West Wing basement enjoying a cigarette break.

"Where have you been all day?" Craig asked.

Dale pulled him away from the group of staffers.

"I have so much to tell you," she whispered.

"I know, I know. You're the lady of the hour," he teased.

"I was in the Oval last night at two A.M. when the FBI director called."

"Why?"

"I'll tell you later. Where are you going to be?"

"I'll be here."

"I'll find you." Without thinking, she leaned in and hugged him.

Shit, why do I do things like that, she thought as she walked away and noticed the other staffers still huddled by the door.

Dale walked into the reception area of Ralph's office.

"Is he in there?" she asked his assistant.

"Go right in. He's been waiting for you," she said.

Ralph was behind a laptop that he kept next to his desktop for e-mails that were political or personal in nature. "Hey, what's up?" he asked without looking up.

"Not much," she said.

"Nice job yesterday. The president thought you were very impressive."

"Thank you. And thank you for falling on your sword over the size of the press contingent at the president's arrival."

Ralph picked up a nerf football from his desk and started tossing it up in the air. Dale watched him throw it a couple of times.

"That's my job," he said without looking at her.

"Well, thanks, anyway."

"Dale, how do you think everything is going?" he asked.

"Fine, I guess. How do you think things are going?"

Ralph tossed the ball up and waited for it come down before he spoke.

"Really fucking good. I think things . . ."

He threw the ball up again and waited for it to come back down before he finished his sentence.

". . . . things are about to be really good, Dale. The public loves it when the president catches the bad guys." He threw the ball up, and this time it came down between his desk and where Dale was sitting. She made no effort to catch it, so the football landed on the ground between them with a soft thud.

She stared at him. She had no idea what she was doing there.

"I just wanted to thank you for the role you've played in keeping things around here on track," he said.

"What do you mean?"

"Well, your work in keeping things quiet about OVP has made a lot of the good things possible, Dale. And we'll never forget it." He smiled at her.

He was almost as creepy as Marcus Meyers. She wanted to tell him to fuck off, but she flashed a cool smile instead.

"Happy to be of service, Ralph."

He stood up to pick up his football, talking a long, leering look at her legs while he was at it.

"Is there anything else I can do for you?"

"You're done so much already, Dale. I'm really glad you're on the team."

She stood to go.

"Thanks again, Dale."

She felt her heart racing, and she was sure that if she looked down at her hands, they'd be shaking a little bit.

She raced from Ralph's office and toward the stairwell. The president was coming up the stairs.

"Good afternoon, Madam President," Dale said, stopping herself from running into the president's Secret Service agent.

"You look like you're in a hurry."

Dale forced a smile.

"Racing back to my desk," she joked.

"Thank you for last night," the president said quietly.

Dale nodded. She thought she saw Charlotte nod slightly as well.

Dale stepped aside and leaned against the wall while Charlotte and her Secret Service agents passed.

She was still standing there when her assistant appeared.

"You're late for your next meeting," he said, thrusting her notebook into her hands.

"What's the meeting?"

"The National Security Council invited you to sit in on their declassified briefing for members since the vice president is out sick. Craig is saving you a seat," he said.

She headed back up the stairs to the Roosevelt Room. She hadn't heard from Tara all day. She took copious notes in the meeting and then went back to her office to return press calls and catch up on e-mail. The terror threat had actually streamlined her calls. Instead of having to track down a thousand different pieces of information for each individual reporter, they were all calling with the same questions. Around ten P.M. she texted Craig.

"Where are you?"

"Went to bed early. Call me on your drive home."

Dale shut down her computer and went out to her car. She looked up at the residence and noticed that there were more lights on than usual.

Dale started to head toward her apartment, but she didn't feel like being alone. She did an illegal U-turn on M Street and headed toward Craig's. She pulled up in front of his town house and noticed that the lights were out. She looked at her watch again. It was only 10:30. She rang the bell. A light went on in the bedroom and she could hear him moving around inside.

"Coming," he yelled.

"It's me, I'm sorry for waking you," she whispered loudly.

He opened the door.

"Hi," he said. He'd thrown on a black T-shirt and jeans.

"I didn't think that you'd actually gone to bed," she said sheepishly.

"Well, I'm up now. Do you have your emergency pack of cigarettes in there?" he asked, pointing at her car.

"I do!" she said. "I replenished them last week." She turned to get the pack of Marlboro Lights she kept in the glove compartment and noticed that the light in his bedroom was still on. She thought she saw someone looking out the window.

"Do you have company? Should I go? I should go," she said.

"Sit down and tell me about last night," he said.

"You can't tell anyone, ever, that I told you about it. Not even when you're one hundred years old and senile and you think the statute of limitations is up. It'll still be secret, okay?"

"Yes," he promised.

He sat on the front steps and lit two cigarettes. She took one and sat down next to him and started with the steward approaching her in the Situation Room and asking her to wait in the Oval. When she looked back at his bedroom, she noticed that the light was no longer on.

CHAPTER FORTY-TWO

Charlotte

A toast," Charlotte said.

"We already toasted everything at dinner," Penelope complained.

"One final toast," Charlotte pleaded.

"I'm going to bed," Penelope said.

"Fine, good night, sweetheart. Thank you for spending the night here," Charlotte said. Penelope blew her a kiss and disappeared to her room.

"What's her problem?" Charlotte asked Harry.

"She probably missed a party or something," Harry said.

"I'm sorry that I messed up your plans," Charlotte apologized.

In the three and a half weeks since they'd captured Youseff, his interrogations had yielded loads of good information about the domestic cells, but his nephews were still missing, which made the intelligence officials worried enough to leave the threat level elevated for the 9/11 anniversary and beyond. When they were on high alert, the Secret Service liked the kids to break up their normal routines. Charlotte had suggested that they spend the weekend at the residence and they'd reluctantly agreed.

"Don't worry about it. I'm going to go to my room. Night, Mom; night, Dad," Harry said.

Charlotte couldn't help but smile.

"Did you hear that? I haven't heard that in a long time." They hadn't all been together except for at school events since her Inauguration. Peter had been with Dale then, so they hadn't spent any time together as a family.

"What are you thinking about?" Peter asked.

"I was trying to remember the last time we were all together."

He smiled and rubbed Emma's muzzle. The dogs loved having a new person to suck up to. Cammie was at Charlotte's feet and Mika had followed Harry to bed.

"Do you want to have a drink on the balcony?"

They walked outside with the two dogs at their feet.

"Thank you, Peter," Charlotte said.

"For what?"

"For suggesting that I speak to Dale. It was a good idea."

Peter nodded and took another sip of his drink.

"I don't know what happened with you two, but I always wanted you to be happy," Charlotte told him.

He turned to look at her.

"Charlotte, I don't want to talk about Dale." His voice wasn't angry or hostile, just a little sad.

"Understood."

They sat there for a few minutes without talking. The dogs were sprawled on the couch between them. Charlotte was about to ask him something about the twins when he moved closer to her.

"This is nice, Char," he said.

She was feeling nostalgic, and she was also trying very hard to pinpoint whether that was *all* that she was feeling. With the kids applying to college, she felt like the entire family structure that had been a part of her life for so long would disappear entirely. She looked over at Peter. He had a tendency to exude whatever emotion he thought the person he was with wanted him to exude. It was what drew everyone to him. She was sure it was what had brought him and Dale together. She wanted to make sure he wasn't simply accommodating her need to feel connected to all of them again.

"Peter, do you think we would have made it if I hadn't, you know, come here and, you know . . ."

"Been president?" He started to laugh.

"Don't laugh. I'm trying to be serious," she begged.

"I know, I know. Let's see. Would we have made it if you hadn't become president? I don't know, Char."

CHAPTER FORTY-THREE

Tara

Tara was on her stomach reaching under the king-sized bed in their master bedroom for the last box she hadn't looked through.

"What are you doing?" Marcus asked, startling her. She thought he was downstairs working out.

"Jesus, you scared me."

She pushed herself up off the floor and wiped the dust off her stomach and thighs.

"What are you looking for?"

"Our holiday boxes."

"It's September."

"I know. I haven't seen them since we moved in."

He eyed her suspiciously for what felt, to Tara, like an eternity.

"Don't do anything stupid, Tara."

Stupid? Tara thought, shaking her head slightly. "We're way past that," she mumbled, under her breath.

"What?"

"I said we are way past stupid," she repeated. Marcus seemed to grimace as he turned to look out their bedroom window. Kendall was playing outside.

He pressed his lips together and filled his chest with air. He blew it out before he turned to face her again.

"What are you mulling in that head of yours, Tara?"

"Nothing," she said quickly.

"I don't believe you."

She sat down on the edge of the bed and examined him, as she often found herself doing lately. His hairline was quickly receding and he had even deeper lines on his forehead and around his eyes. He was so thin, his skin hung loosely from his cheekbones and jawline. His body fat must be down to one percent, she thought. He looked up and she averted her eyes.

"I have my first official physical exam next weekend," Tara said.

Marcus walked over to his nightstand and pulled out a stack of papers.

"I read back through the last seven or eight years of vice presidential physicals. The press typically releases a summary stating that you are in good health. I think they will probably want to release the results of your mammogram and your cholesterol and weight. Those are the things Charlotte releases each year. I was thinking you could ask them not to release your weight until, you know . . . "

"Right," she agreed, nodding. Every president since President Ford had released the results of his annual physical exam to the press and the public.

"Vice President McMillan did a colonoscopy each year, but I don't think they'll have you do one," he added.

"That's good." She tried to smile.

He stood on the opposite side of the bed, shifting his weight from one foot to the other.

She turned her body around from where she was sitting to face him. She searched his face for some sort of opening to share what she'd been mulling for days.

"Listen, I was thinking . . . maybe the doctors can do something. I haven't ever seen a real doctor. Well, except, you know, in Italy. Maybe there's something I could be taking," Tara offered.

Marcus sat down on the bed with his back to Tara. He untied his running shoes and pulled them off his feet. He removed his socks and placed them inside the running shoes. His breathing seemed to quicken a bit, but Tara couldn't see his face.

"You mean something that might keep you from falling into an abyss every third day? Or maybe some cure that would ensure that you could get through a workweek without having a meltdown? Or some miracle drug that would guarantee that Kendall never walks into the bedroom when you're in bed with the curtains drawn crying in the middle of the day?"

His voice rose with each question he barked at her.

"I just thought . . ."

He spun around and looked at her. "You thought that I hadn't considered how much a real doctor might be able to help you," he snapped.

She stared at her hands.

"I'm sorry. It just feels like things are sort of out of control right now."

"Do you think I haven't noticed?" He was barely in control of his voice. "Sorry," she said.

"I sit up every night and try to read everything I can find on the Internet, and every single fucking white paper I can find from all of the medical journals, and every goddamn article that pops online about this stuff," he insisted.

She looked up for an instant and noticed that his hands were clenched into tight fists.

"I'm sorry," she repeated.

"Tell me what you want me to do that I'm not doing. Do you not understand how desperately I wish I could help you?" He was pacing back and forth now.

She moved away from where he was pacing.

"Are you really that clueless that you don't know that I sit up here all day while you're at the White House, hoping, praying to God that you're going to keep it together for one more day, so Kendall doesn't have to watch her mother run out of town in disgrace?" He was yelling at her now. "I gave up everything, Tara. Everything. My job, my friends, my entire goddamned life. Do you think there is anything I enjoy about my life right now?" He made punching motions with his fist to punctuate each word.

"I said I'm sorry. I didn't know," she said. She was too startled to cry.

"You don't know anything." Marcus went into the bathroom and slammed the door behind him. Tara followed him and leaned against the door. She felt like she deserved his harsh treatment of her. It was her fault they were in this situation.

"Is that why you hate me so much?" she asked. He was silent. She slid down the door and sat curled up against it for a couple minutes. She wasn't crying, but her nose was running as though she was. She wiped it with her sleeve.

After a couple minutes, he opened the door and looked down at her.

"I don't hate you," he said calmly.

She looked up at him.

"I'm terrified for you, Tara, for all of us."

If she weren't afraid of causing Kendall sadness and shame, she would have found a way to disappear. Everyone would be better off. But the thought of Marcus raising Kendall was enough to get her off the ground. She needed a plan.

CHAPTER FORTY-FOUR

Dale

Dale pulled into her usual spot on West Exec and left the motor running while she took another sip of her coffee and glanced at the headlines on the front page of her *New York Times*. She considered reading the paper in the comfort of her car, but it was already 5:45 A.M., and there was a psychological advantage she felt when she was at her desk before six. She turned off the car and checked her BlackBerry for pressing messages before locking its keypad and tossing it into her purse. She made sure her lights were off and then turned to walk toward the OEOB. She glanced toward the West Wing basement and recognized two of Peter's Secret Service agents. During their three-year affair, they'd been incredibly generous toward her.

"Hey guys," she said.

"Hi there, Dale, how're you doing?"

"Good, good. Can you believe I work here now?" she whispered, flashing them a big smile.

She'd appreciated that they never appeared to judge her or Peter during the time they were together. As far as they were concerned, it was their job to keep Peter alive, not to get involved in his personal life.

They smiled back.

"Were you guys reassigned?" Dale asked.

The agents looked at each other and then back at Dale.

"No? What are you doing here?"

They looked uncomfortable. Dale realized her mistake.

"Oh, god. I know you can't say anything. I'm sorry. Nice to see you guys. Take care."

Dale nearly broke into a run as she made her way up the stairs toward her office in the OEOB. She closed and locked the door behind her and sat down at her desk. She was breathing hard.

Calm down, she told herself. *He could be here with the twins. Not at five-thirty in the morning, you idiot*, she countered.

The possibility that Peter and Charlotte would reunite had always haunted her. She'd often worried that their entire affair would be reduced to a road bump in Peter and Charlotte's long, complicated marriage. She stood up to get another look at the agents. They were gone. They must have moved back to the East Wing exit so they could get Peter out of the complex undetected.

Dale wanted to call him and ask if he and Charlotte were back together. She had half a mind to call Brian and leak the story to the network so they would confirm it for her. But Brian probably knew already from Melanie. *Oh god*, Dale thought. *I'm sure I'm a joke to all of them.* The silly reporter who kept Peter occupied while Charlotte adjusted to the rigors of the office. She gulped down the rest of her coffee and tried to focus on the vice president's schedule. Tara had a drop-by visit with the fall interns, a private lunch with a former colleague from New York, and a few policy briefings in the afternoon. Dale had her lunch with Melanie over at the Pentagon, which had been moved to four P.M. She wasn't sure if it was still even a lunch. She opened her set of news clips and tried to focus on the articles. It was pointless.

She needed to talk to someone. She e-mailed and texted Craig. "Call 911," she wrote.

Her phone rang almost immediately.

"What's wrong?" Craig asked.

"Peter is here," she whispered.

"In your office?"

"No, in the residence. I think he and Charlotte are sleeping together again."

"Why?"

"Why are they sleeping together?"

"No, why do you think they are sleeping together?"

"I ran into his Secret Service detail this morning."

"I wouldn't jump to any conclusions, but he was going to move on at some point. Surely, you recognized that when you rejected that Stinson Beach house."

"I know. I know. I just didn't think he'd replace me with someone who is even less available."

"It's not clear that he's done that, is it?"

Dale took a deep breath. "If they are together, I'd be happy for them."

"No, you wouldn't. That would be decidedly unhealthy."

"You're right. I would not be happy for them. Does that make me a bad person?"

"It makes you human, and I have had my doubts over the last few months."

"Oh, screw you." She laughed.

"Not for me, darling."

"I'm the only one in town, then."

"Touché."

Dale laughed.

"I'm running into Starbucks. You want another coffee?"

"No. Thank you, though."

"For what?"

"For talking me off the ledge."

"Are you officially off the ledge?"

"Yes, your work here is done. I'm sorry for the early-morning drama."

"Your attraction to chaos and dysfunction rivals mine. It's what I love most about you."

"My attraction to chaos is giving me crow's-feet. I'll see you at senior staff," she said.

She felt bolstered by her chat with Craig. She finished reading her news clips and reviewed a few speaking invitations for the vice president. She put some of the more interesting events on the top of her pile. Every time her mind wandered to thoughts of Peter and Charlotte together, she forced them out. Dale had plenty of work with which to distract herself. She was determined to help right the ship with the vice president. Tara had been out sick for nearly a week, and when she'd returned, she'd been uncharacteristically level-headed.

But instead of feeling comforted by the vice president's periods of stability, Dale was always most anxious at times like this. It felt too much like the quiet before the storm. Before her run-in with Peter's Secret Service agents that morning, she'd been thinking about checking in with Charlotte again. As Dale gathered her notebook and rose to walk over to the senior staff meeting in the Roosevelt Room, she determined that it was highly unlikely that the president would ever want to see her again. If she and Peter were making another run at things, the last thing she'd want was a reminder of how far Peter had strayed.

CHAPTER FORTY-FIVE

Charlotte

Charlotte pulled on a cashmere robe and tiptoed toward the bathroom. She was amazed by how unceremoniously she and Peter had started sleeping together again. They'd had their second sleepover the night before. Charlotte allowed herself a small smile as she stepped into the shower, but her thoughts quickly shifted to the day ahead. She'd be engaged in intense negotiations with the chairmen of the Senate Foreign Relations Committee about a scheduled troop drawdown in Afghanistan, and she knew Melanie would be disappointed if she didn't spend all of her political capital trying to get them to agree to delay the withdrawal.

She and Melanie were meeting for breakfast to discuss their negotiating posture. Charlotte contemplated, then rejected, telling Melanie about Peter. It wasn't entirely clear to her where things were heading. She was enjoying him more than she'd remembered enjoying him before their split. Charlotte dried herself quickly and pulled her hair into a high ponytail. She slipped into a simple black Carolina Herrera sheath and stepped into a pair of black heels. She allowed herself a quick glance toward where she'd left Peter and the dogs sleeping in bed before she scurried toward the West Wing.

Melanie was already in the Oval Office when she arrived.

"Morning," Charlotte chirped.

"What did you do?" Melanie asked.

"What?"

"You are never this cheerful in the morning. What's going on? Did you fire Ralph?"

"What are you talking about? I'm always like this."

Melanie eyed her from head to toe.

"Why are you looking at me like that?" Charlotte demanded.

"I'll figure it out," Melanie promised.

"Did you order breakfast yet?" Charlotte asked.

"I didn't know we were actually eating. Usually a breakfast meeting with you is six cups of coffee. I packed a Clif Bar."

"Of course we are actually eating," Charlotte insisted.

"Okay then. What do you want? I'll have Sam place our orders."

"I'll have scrambled eggs and toast with a side of fruit."

"I heard that," Sam said from beyond the door. "Melanie, you want the same?"

"Make mine egg whites, please," Melanie said.

"Done," Sam said, closing the door to the Oval Office.

"Did you see the *Washington Post*?" Melanie asked.

"No, why?"

"Oh, they have a mash-up full of blind quotes about how the administration is divided on the way forward in Afghanistan. Some guy is quoted saying he liked you better with balls than with a heart."

Charlotte smiled.

"That sounds like something Roger would say," Charlotte said.

"I thought the same thing," Melanie replied.

"Should I be troubled that people think I have a heart?"

"Not yet."

"How's your little romance going?" Charlotte didn't mean to sound mocking, but she couldn't help it. At some level, she felt like she'd been replaced as Melanie's sounding board and it bothered her at times like this. On the other hand, if Melanie were still her constant companion, there would be no way she could keep her new arrangement with Peter a secret.

"I'm sure this will come as a surprise to you, but he still seems to find me charming," Melanie said. If she'd detected Charlotte's edge, she didn't let on.

"What else are you hearing?" Charlotte asked.

"Nothing much," Melanie said, shrugging her shoulders.

"*Nothing much*? That's all I get from you these days? I liked you better when you were single" Charlotte had a look on her face that was part amused, part annoyed.

"And I *know* I liked you better when your approval rating was twenty-eight percent," Melanie replied dryly.

A waiter from the White House Mess wheeled in a cart with their breakfasts.

"You can leave those covered," Charlotte said curtly.

"Yes ma'am," he said.

Melanie remained seated on the couch and Charlotte walked back and forth in front of her desk.

"Do you know how isolated I am here, Melanie? I can't stand Ralph enough to even let him keep me in the loop. His assistant and Sam don't get along, so Sam never hears anything. I am on a god-damned island," Charlotte fumed.

"Madam President," Melanie started.

"Let me finish. You go off to DOD and leave me here with the 'B' team of speechwriters, the most vapid press secretary I've ever had in my entire career, and Ralph and all of his militant young sycophants. And when I ask you for a little peek at the outside world, you come up completely empty. You are going to have to do better than that," Charlotte said. She walked over to the couch across from Melanie, uncovered her plate of eggs and sat down.

Melanie was smiling.

"Sam has a boyfriend."

"No, she doesn't."

"Yes, she does."

"Impossible. Sam and I speak all day long."

"You speak?"

"Yes, we talk all the time." Charlotte knew she sounded defensive.

"Impossible." Now Melanie was the one who looked amused.

"Why is it so hard for you to believe that I actually talk to my staff?"

"Because you don't. And if you did, you'd know that she's head over heels in love with Frank from the staff secretary's office.

"Winnie's kid?"

"No, that's Arnie. Frank is no one's kid. I mean, he's someone's kid, but that's not how he got the job. I hired him as an intern two years ago and he did such a stellar job that now he's the deputy staff secretary."

"Aren't you smug today?" Charlotte chided, between bites of her fruit salad.

"What's Peter doing here?" Melanie asked.

Charlotte choked on a piece of cantaloupe.

"Was it something I said?" Melanie asked.

Charlotte laughed nervously.

"What makes you think Peter is here?"

"His motorcade is lined up at the East Gate."

"Really?" Charlotte wasn't thinking fast enough.

"What do you mean, *really*? Surely Peter isn't hiding somewhere in the residence. He didn't even do that when you were, you know, allegedly together."

Charlotte put her fork down and looked at Melanie.

"Would you think I was nuts if I told you we were sort of trying each other on again?" Charlotte asked.

"It depends on what you mean by trying each other on."

"I don't know exactly. I'm sure it'll amount to nothing. Forget I said anything."

"Forget that you mentioned that you're sleeping with your ex-husband? I don't think so. Madam President, I'm on a goddamned island over there at DOD. It's just me and all those big, mean old military guys. I mean, I come to you for a little peek into the private lives of the rich and powerful and you give me nothing. You are going to have to do much, much better than that." Melanie leaned back and smiled.

CHAPTER FORTY-SIX

Tara

Tara had canceled on Frannie three times over the summer, but now, she was looking forward to seeing a familiar face. Frannie Jones was one of the only people Tara had stayed in touch with from her early days in the U.S. Attorney's Office. Until Tara had left for Washington the year before, she and Frannie would meet for lunch about once a month to fill each other in on the latest gossip from their legal circles.

Frannie was one of the smartest prosecutors Tara had ever met. She'd been offered several fancy jobs at DOJ, but she'd turned them all down to remain an assistant U.S. Attorney in the Manhattan office. Tara suspected she was holding out hope that someday she'd land the top job as the presidential appointee as U.S. Attorney for the Southern District of New York. Tara made a mental note to talk to Ralph about judicial appointments. It would help Charlotte politically to appoint some conservative Democrats to the U.S. attorney positions.

Frannie had married a defense attorney with grown kids and had formed fast, easy bonds with them. Tara wasn't surprised that Frannie was the one accompanying her stepdaughter on college visits to American University and Georgetown. Tara was reading through her schedule for the rest of the week when Frannie appeared in her doorway. She rushed to the doorway to greet her.

"You are big time, my friend, so very big time," Frannie said. She looked around Tara's office admiringly.

"It's hard to believe, isn't it?"

"Not at all. You were destined for big things, Meyers. Do I have to call you 'vice president'? I just got used to attorney general."

"Please don't. Do you want to order lunch?"

"Sure. Do I get the grand tour afterward?"

"Of course."

They ordered salads and Diet Cokes. Tara rarely felt impressed with herself, but sitting there with her old friend made her feel happy that she could share part of her success with someone she'd known when she was starting out in government.

"Tara, it's really great to see you."

"It's great to see you. I was just thinking that it's been way too long. We should do this more often."

"I agree, but I have to confess that I had an ulterior motive for today's visit."

"Oh?"

"Tara, I need to tell you something."

"What?"

"Kirkpatrick has been asked to serve as a special prosecutor."

Brent Kirkpatrick was the U.S. Attorney for the Southern District of New York. He was also Frannie's boss.

"What's the case?"

"You."

"What?"

"Well, not you specifically, but the House and Senate Judiciary committees wrote a letter to the A.G. asking that a special prosecutor be appointed to investigate the raising of the threat level in August."

"Why?"

"Listen, Kirkpatrick knows I'm in Washington, and I'm sure he suspects I'm giving you a heads-up, so whatever you do, don't get me in trouble."

"I won't, but what does the threat level being raised have to do with me?"

Frannie stood up and started to fidget.

"I shouldn't be here, but I didn't want you to get blindsided by this."

"By what, exactly?"

"There are White House and administration sources that went to the House leadership over the summer with concerns about your job performance."

Tara felt her body start to overheat. She willed herself to stay calm so she could get as much information as possible from Frannie.

"What kind of concerns?"

"They claimed that you had a nervous breakdown or something and that the White House covered it up."

"What?"

"I know. Listen, you should be comforted by the fact that even the lunatics on the Judiciary Committee didn't bite. But then, when the White House raised the threat level in August, the sources came back and said that they feared for the safety of the country when they heard that you were the president's point person. They also alleged that the White House could have been creating a diversion with the whole terror threat."

"What are you saying?"

"Tara, your colleagues think the terror threat was raised to divert attention from you," Frannie said softly.

"From me?" Tara was indignant now. "The president would never play around with national security. And Youseff *was* a threat. The CIA just did a three-hour briefing on all of the intel they've obtained from his interrogations."

"Tara, please try to calm down. I'm telling you everything I know because I think it's motivated by politics and sour grapes and lord knows what else, but you can't do anything with this information or I'll be out of a job. I don't think the president has been briefed yet. And I'm not working on the investigation. They'd never ask me to. Kirkpatrick knows we're friends."

Tara looked out the window. In the distance, she could see a couple of the television correspondents filming live shots. She imagined the frenzy that would ensue once a special prosecutor started looking into the decision to raise the terror alert. She wondered if she could spare Charlotte the whole mess by resigning on the spot. She and Marcus could pick Kendall up at school and drive away that night. The thought comforted her. She turned to Frannie and smiled.

"Thank you so much for the heads-up. I am lucky to have you as a friend."

"Tara, I'm so sorry. Is there anything I can do?"

She couldn't believe the way things had spiraled out of control. If only she'd done a better job.

"There is one thing you can help me with. Since no one else knows, I can't really ask anyone else for help."

"Yes, yes, anything."

"I don't want you to have any exposure, so you have my word that I won't do anything until I'm informed through proper channels."

"I appreciate that."

"At some point, I'll need to offer my resignation."

Frannie didn't challenge her on the point.

"Will you help me draft a resignation letter so that when the time comes, I have something prepared?" Tara asked.

CHAPTER FORTY-SEVEN

Dale

She knew she should go home, but Dale wanted to see if he'd be back. She rose from her desk in the OEOB to stare out the window toward the White House residence every ten minutes or so. She wasn't even sure what she was looking for. If Peter were there again, he wouldn't stand in front of the windows and wave to her. His Secret Service detail would be more cautious this time, too. They wouldn't risk being recognized again after running into Dale the day before.

Dale strained for some scrap of evidence that he was there. At least then she'd know for sure that he'd erased her. She would know that he was back with his wife and their entire affair had become filler. The relationship that had defined her for so many years would be reduced to Peter's reckless phase, bookended by his marriage to his wife.

Dale knew at the time that she'd regret pushing him away in Stinson Beach. All he'd tried to do was grab on to whatever scrap she could make available for their relationship and she'd shut him out. She had practically pushed him back into Charlotte's arms. Dale turned from the window and resolved to stop torturing herself. She shut down her computer and dialed Craig on her way out of the White House complex.

"Hi. You busy?"

"I'm never too busy for you. Where are you?"

"I'm leaving the office now."

"I'd suggest we meet for a drink but it's after midnight."

"Yeah. I think I'm going home."

"You want to come over?"

"I don't want to impose."

"I had the housekeeper turn down the guest bed when she was here earlier."

"Really?"

"I had a feeling."

"In that case, I'll see you in a few minutes."

When Dale stepped into Craig's cozy town house ten minutes later, she was glad she'd avoided her own sterile apartment. He poured her a glass of wine and handed her a plate of cheese and crackers. Dale smiled gratefully and sank into his sofa. She noticed two dinner plates, two wine glasses, and several knives and forks drying in his dish rack next to the sink.

"Thanks," she said.

"Don't mention it."

"You don't have to stay up with me. Go to bed. I'm fine. I'm going to drink my wine and then stagger off to bed."

"I'll sit with you for a little bit," he said.

"Do you think he was with me because he couldn't be with her?" Dale asked after a couple of minutes.

"Does it matter?"

"I think it does. I mean, if he's with her, was he ever really with me?"

"We both know the answer to that. He was with you, and it was good. He's not with you now because you didn't want him."

"It's not that I didn't want him," Dale protested.

"Dale, it doesn't matter who he's with. You guys aren't together and that's what hurts. Don't get wrapped up in who he's with now. If he could have had you, he'd have been with you."

"It's just, this image of the two of them together keeps flashing in my mind, and it stops me in my tracks, you know?" she asked. She kicked off her shoes and sank deeper into the sofa.

"I'm sure Kramer felt the same way about you," he commented.

"Ouch."

"Well, it's not like she didn't have enough problems. And then you and Peter, I mean, you sort of owe her this, if they are even together, which we still don't know they are."

"What are you saying?"

"Come on, you don't see a little bit of the universe keeping things even?"

"You think I deserve this?"

"No, I just think you have this wonderful way of removing any sense of responsibility from the things that happen to you. You're totally charming about it and it's one of your most endearing traits, but I worry that sometimes you delude yourself into thinking you're just walking along and these terrible, senseless things happen to you."

Dale didn't like the direction he was going. She put her wineglass down and looked at him.

"Honey, I'm sorry if I've hurt your feelings. I'm going to stop now. I'd just hate to see your new relationship with the president damaged by any overly emotional reaction to your ex-boyfriend moving on. But that's all I'm saying. I'm done playing the shrink." He made a zipping motion over his lips to signal that he would say no more.

"Don't stop. Please, go on. You're on a roll," Dale insisted.

"Well, it's just that you talk about getting fired from the network like you were the casualty of cutbacks or something. You were the future of that network. They fired you because you were screwing the president's husband and you were their White House correspondent."

Dale felt her face flush. Craig continued.

"And Tara Meyers didn't sentence you to death when she hired you. She gave you something most people in this town would kill for—a second act. You got to come back at the top of the food chain in White House politics. Do you know how lucky you are?"

"I feel really lucky tonight," Dale groused.

"Look, the good things happen to you because you're really good, but the bad things don't happen to you because you're this innocent victim who keeps getting shit on. I don't mean to be harsh, but I feel the need to make sure that you see things as they are," he said.

"You're really illuminating them for me."

"Dale, I'll drink with you until you pass out every night, but you've got to get a grip on reality."

"On reality?" Dale challenged.

"Yes. Reality. Not nearly as exciting as the dramas around which your life revolves, but the real-life stuff that the mere mortals deal with."

She had finally had enough.

"What, like you are living in reality? What's the word for the kind of reality you live in? One in which you are literally hiding people in your bedroom at night and letting half the White House staff believe you are the town's most eligible straight bachelor?"

"Don't make this about me."

"It is totally fucking surreal to be lectured about reality by the straightest gay man in Washington."

Dale didn't want to stay in his home for another moment.

As she stood to go, he piled on.

"One doesn't have to be perfect to point out how hopelessly self-absorbed you are."

Dale threw off the blanket she'd been sitting under and grabbed her purse.

As she rushed down the stairs, she racked her brain to make sure she hadn't picked a fight with him. She was sure she hadn't. He'd just attacked her from out of the blue.

"Dale, don't leave. You just had two glasses of wine. Just go to bed. We'll talk in the morning."

She couldn't even look at him. She walked out the door and got into her car as quickly as possible. She lurched out of her parking spot and headed toward Georgetown. It was almost one A.M. and the streets were empty. She didn't see the police car pull out behind her until his flashing lights lit up the inside of her car.

The officer approached her car and leaned down to look in at her through the driver's side window.

"Step out of the car, ma'am."

"What's the problem officer?"

"Have you been drinking, ma'am?"

She looked up at him. "No. Why?" she asked.

"You were driving down the middle of the road."

CHAPTER FORTY-EIGHT

Charlotte

C harlotte sat behind her desk in the Oval Office until she heard the vacuum cleaners go on for the second time. They'd vacuumed around nine P.M., and Charlotte doubted that anyone had tracked any debris though the West Wing in the last four hours, but those sorts of details didn't much matter at the White House. Some people found the traditions outdated and redundant, but Charlotte understood what all presidents had understood about the White House. Things happened the way they did because the smallest of things, such as being able to rely on the cleaning crew making its rounds at the same time each and every day, can make a president feel in control of the minor details of her life.

Charlotte hadn't realized that the most difficult thing about being president would have nothing to do with the intricacy of policy problems or the nastiness of the political debates. The most difficult thing about being president was feeling utterly powerless.

She'd remained stoic that evening when her personal attorney informed her that a special prosecutor had been appointed by her Justice Department to investigate charges that the White House abused its power by raising the threat level to distract from its mounting political problems.

She'd had a feeling for a couple of weeks that things were about to unravel. News of the investigation had come almost as a relief. She'd known for a while that another shoe would drop. At least now she knew what it was. She and Peter had planned to have dinner again, but she had canceled. She'd asked Sam to hold her calls and keep everyone out of the Oval Office. The dogs had been fed and walked by the house staff. Charlotte wanted to be alone. As soon as news of the investigation got out, there would be no conversation, and no interaction that wouldn't be ensnared in its web. Charlotte wanted to remember everything about the presidency before this chapter began. She also wanted to collect her thoughts about everything she'd said and done during the period in question. Her attorney was meeting her again the next morning at six A.M. to start the process of preparing her for a potential interview. He would work to avoid Charlotte having to testify, but in the end, some compromise would be reached in which the special prosecutor would travel to the White House to interview her.

Charlotte was taking a mental inventory of every conversation she had ever had about Tara. She kept coming back to her discussions over the past ten months with Melanie. The investigators would take Melanie's deposition, and all of her misgivings about Tara would become public. Charlotte's thoughts shifted to Ralph. She should have known she was on the wrong side of the Tara divide when she found herself aligned with Ralph. She shook her head slightly, remembering when Ralph had started spinning her about Tara's abilities. It had started at the very beginning.

But Ralph wasn't to blame. She had placed her political ambitions ahead of her own better judgment when she picked Tara. The vice president's instability had become increasingly clear in the weeks and months after their inauguration. The bigger problem, as Charlotte saw it, was that the disastrous television interviews had confirmed any remaining doubts about Tara's fitness for office.

Charlotte closed her eyes and tried to connect to the presidents who'd sat at this desk before her—during wars, investigations, and personal failures. She wanted to feel strengthened and fortified by their tenacity. She wanted to be transported from this hour in her presidency to the lowest moment in anyone else's presidency. For whatever mistakes her predecessors had made, not one of them had ever acted with her audacity. Not one of them had ever exposed the country to the harm that she had by picking Tara as her vice president.

She didn't hear Peter walk in, but when he walked around her desk and put his arms around her, she let him.

CHAPTER FORTY-NINE

Tara

I don't know why I agreed to help you," Frannie said. They were in the guest bedroom at the vice presidential residence the day after their lunch meeting. Frannie had taken off her suit jacket and was squinting at the screen of a laptop. Tara had changed into sweats. Marcus and Kendall were downstairs making chocolate chip cookies. She'd felt compelled to tell Marcus the night before that an investigation into the raising of the threat level was about to be announced so that he'd leave them alone and keep Kendall distracted. Tara had insisted that Marcus disconnect the cable boxes. She didn't want Kendall to see the "Breaking News" alert about the special counsel. While she wouldn't understand the specifics, she had a highly evolved instinct for things that would bring more unhappiness to their home. Marcus had remained calm and thought they were upstairs preparing a response. He had no idea they were drafting Tara's resignation letter.

"You agreed to help me because you are a good person, you have known me a long time, and you know that I always try to do the right thing," Tara said.

Frannie rolled her eyes.

"And I don't have anyone else," Tara added.

Frannie smiled sympathetically but didn't look up from the computer. Tara had a hunch that there was more to Frannie's willingness to help than a sense of loyalty or friendship. Like many career law enforcement types, Frannie was easily convinced of her own moral obligation to help right a wrong. They'd worked side by side for several years and Tara had always felt like Frannie understood her at a deeper level than she let on. Tara was fairly certain that if Frannie had ever asked her directly, she would have confided in her about her debilitating periods of depression. Tara suspected that Frannie felt a sense of complicity for observing Tara from close enough proximity to know that something was wrong, but never asking what. Both women seemed to be operating from this shared assumption. It was the only explanation for Frannie's willingness to jeopardize her own career to help Tara end hers.

"Besides, your country needs you," Tara added.

"My country could kick my ass for this."

They'd met at the residence after Frannie's tour of Georgetown and Tara's lunch meeting with her domestic policy staff and were working on the resignation letter on personal computers. Tara was certain that any questions about whether she used federal equipment in an appropriate manner would be the least of her problems, but it made Frannie, a by-the-book government lawyer who Tara was certain was already feeling deeply conflicted about the role she was playing, feel more comfortable. If Frannie was shocked by Tara's request to help her draft a resignation letter, she was hiding it well. Frannie was unflappable, but Tara assumed she was still trying to digest the news that her friend and former colleague planned to resign as vice president rather than endure an investigation that would delve deeply into the reasons behind her uneven performance. Frannie was loyal, but not just to Tara. She was also a faithful servant of the letter and spirit of the law. The fact that she'd agreed, almost instantly, to help Tara extricate herself from her official duties, suggested that she knew something about the evidence that had compelled the appointment of a special counsel to begin with. All of this remained unspoken between the two of them, but it was emblematic of more than a decade of mutual empathy and trust.

"Tara, how do you want to handle questions about your health? Should we say that a previously undiagnosed condition worsened? Is that even true?"

"That it worsened, yes, obviously," Tara said.

"Spare me the parsing, old friend. Was there ever a diagnosis?" She was looking directly at Tara now with a prosecutor's unblinking, dispassionate gaze.

Tara stood up and locked the door to the bedroom. "It's pretty complicated," she said.

"From your perspective, I imagine it is. But these are yes or no questions in the court of public opinion, Tara. Was there a diagnosis? Did you seek medical attention?"

"I didn't seek it."

"Tara, what are you saying?"

"Look, I will tell you whatever you want to know," Tara promised.

Frannie shook her head. "I don't want to know any of this. You were my goddamn idol. I can't believe what I'm hearing."

"I can't believe it half the time, myself. It's good to know that I was good at something at one time."

"Good? You were the best."

Tara could hardly remember a time when she felt competent at work.

"Sometimes it's like none of that stuff ever happened. I can't tell you the last time a week went by in which I wasn't screwing something up and embarrassing myself and the president."

"There are a lot of people who remember all the good work you did in our office."

"If I'd had any sense at all, I never would have left that world. I was doing fine in New York. I could manage things. I could pull back when I wasn't feeling well. I had the space to gather myself and then dive back in when I was up to it. Here, there's no escape from the press. There are cameras everywhere. I can't wear an ugly sweater without ending up on *Access Hollywood*."

"Tara, if you want me to help you, you're going to have to give me the specifics."

Tara sat down on the bed and put her notebook down. "I had my first, uh, episode, if you will, while I was doing a summer session in Italy during law school. I was in the hospital for ten days."

"What happened?"

"I was in a strange, new place, I pulled a few too many all-nighters, and the whole unscripted and unscheduled approach to the course threw me into a tailspin."

"I know how you like your schedules and deadlines," Frannie said.

"In Italy, there wasn't any structure to speak of. I was a mess. The doctors sent me home with a shopping bag full of antidepressants and some other stuff and told me to find a psychiatrist and psychologist as soon as I got back to New York."

"And you never did, did you?"

"No," Tara admitted. "I stretched out the drugs and tried to monitor myself closely."

"And Marcus? You told Marcus, I assume?"

"Yes. Before we got married. He was amazing about it. When I was down, he'd try to shield me from the outside world until I felt better. It was easier once we had Kendall. We used her as an excuse too many times to count."

Frannie was trying to keep the disbelief off her face, but Tara could tell she was struggling to process the information.

"When we came down here after the election, I was feeling fine, and there was no reason to suspect that our system would stop working."

"Until it stopped working," Frannie interjected.

"It's so different here. The job is all-consuming. I have to answer for my whereabouts every hour of every day. And even when I stay home to try to get better, I fall deeper and lower because I know I'm missing out on things that I need to learn to be able to do my job. I went from bad to worse when we moved, and I can't pull myself out of it anymore."

"Have you tried medication?"

"It's funny, you can get five different kinds of sleeping pills, uppers, downers, and any other drug you can think of, but if you were to go into the White House Medical Unit seeking an antidepressant, eyebrows would be raised, at least if I were the patient. Frannie, you know that you can't be the vice president and be on antidepressants."

Frannie nodded.

"Frannie, it's really important that you believe me when I tell you that I was doing well. For a long time, I was completely normal. I could feel when things were sort of going off-kilter and I would get a little more rest or work from home."

"I believe you. But the move and the additional stress and the change in environment triggered another, what are we calling them? Episode? Breakdown?"

Tara nodded.

"It's not too hard to put it all together," Frannie said.

"I'm sure the special prosecutor will feel the same way."

Frannie sighed deeply and furrowed her brow. "What does the White House know?" Frannie asked.

"The White House has no idea about any of it, so they didn't cover anything up, if that's what you're getting at."

"Tara, don't be so sure. The investigation is going to examine every e-mail, every statement, every excuse ever made by everyone who worked closely with you. They're going to be hunting for any scrap of evidence that the White House was making excuses for every performance on your part that was less than stellar. And the president is going to be pressed to reveal what she knew and when she knew it."

"But no one knew anything, Frannie. I never told anyone. And that's why I'm going to resign before anyone gets in trouble."

"Is this why Marcus is still on leave from the FBI?" Frannie asked.

Tara opened her mouth to speak and Frannie interrupted.

"Wait, don't answer that. I can guess."

They worked in silence for a few more minutes, and then Tara walked over to the desk where Frannie was sitting. Frannie turned back to the computer and reread the last few sentences she'd written. Tara started to read over her shoulder. Frannie pointed at a paragraph.

"I'm writing this as though you're heading down the path of agreeing to cooperate with the special prosecutor, right?" Frannie asked.

"Yes, I think that makes the most sense."

Frannie nodded. "Makes things easier, I think."

"Is there any precedent for this?"

"Which part?

"Cooperating with the special prosecutor."

"Yes, a few years back the president and vice president met with the independent counsel on the leak that got the FBI agent killed in Michigan. Remember? During Harlow's administration?"

"That's right, of course."

Frannie resumed her typing. When she was finished, she cleared her throat and tapped the side of the computer to get Tara's attention.

"I decided to keep this short and sweet. I think this works as a letter and as a statement if you were inclined to read it on camera. Come take a look. Essentially, I have you take responsibility for not being honest with the public or the president about your mental health problems, which I don't get into at the top because people will be shocked enough. Then I go through your life of service, and your years as a prosecutor and enforcer of the laws of the land. I get a little fuzzy here, but I basically lay out your acceptance of whatever consequences come your way as a result of your actions."

"It feels very confessional," Tara said.

"Unless I missed something, I believe that's what the moment calls for."

Tara nodded. "Marcus is going to freak out," she said.

"Tara, I say this not as your friend and former colleague, but as a federal prosecutor. This is quite serious. I'm sure there's a record somewhere in Italy that says that you were diagnosed with bipolar disorder or severe depression and instructed to seek immediate medical attention. Don't be surprised if that doctor seeks some sort of dispensation from the patient-doctor confidentially laws and speaks out about it. It's not likely, but it's possible. And the public will not react lightly to the news that the woman who would be president if anything were to happen to Kramer is mentally ill. That will scare people. It may be grossly unfair, but we live in a country where we'd much rather a sex addict have his finger on the button to our nuclear arsenal than a mental case."

"Frannie . . ." Tara started.

Frannie interrupted. "Let me finish. None of this will be pleasant. This is the only path that allows you a glimmer of hope at preserving your legacy so that when Kendall googles all of this someday, she will see that even your critics thought you handled yourself with grace. Now, come read the letter all the way through before you say anything."

Tara sat next to Frannie and pulled the laptop closer to her face. She turned to Frannie when she finished.

"Thank you," she said.

She asked Frannie to save the letter to a flash drive she'd pulled out of her travel bag. It had her old speeches on it.

"I mean it, thank you very much."

"You're welcome." Frannie handed her the storage drive with the resignation letter on it. "Do you want me to delete the document from this laptop?"

"Yes, please."

"Done."

"What did you name the document?"

"I saved it as 'Top Secret.'"

Tara thanked her again and walked Frannie to her car. She knew that the difficult part lay ahead of her. She walked into the kitchen and sampled some of Kendall's cookies.

"These are yummy, munchkin," she said.

"Do you want some milk?" Kendall asked.

Marcus was leaning against the counter.

"Kendall, why don't you start your homework and I'll come in to check on your progress in a few minutes," he suggested.

"I want to eat cookies with Mommy."

"Why don't you make a plate of cookies and take them to your room and we'll eat them together when you finish your homework?" Tara suggested.

Kendall piled a plate high with cookies and walked upstairs to her room.

"What do you know about the investigation?" Marcus asked as soon as Kendall left.

"Frannie could get in a lot of trouble for telling me, so please don't share this information with anyone."

"Who the hell do you think I talk to these days?" Marcus hissed.

Tara shuddered a bit.

"Kirkpatrick is going to be named as a special counsel to look into allegations that the White House deliberately exaggerated the terror threat to distract attention from me," she said.

It took a moment for the news to sink in, but when it did, Marcus was furious.

"Fucking assholes," he said, through clenched teeth as he stomped around the kitchen.

"Marcus, I think I should resign."

Marcus had his hands on both sides of the kitchen sink and his back to Tara. She could hear him breathing heavily but he didn't say anything right away.

"Marcus?"

He spun around.

"Don't even think about it. If you think for a single goddamned second that I'm going to stand by and watch you take the fall for this, you are out of your mind. I will not allow our daughter to watch her mother drummed out of this town for something that was not her fault. You didn't select yourself as vice president. Do you understand me? I will take Kendall and leave the country to spare her the agony of witnessing your demise. Do you hear me?" He was shaking with rage.

Tara nodded her head.

"I understand."

CHAPTER FIFTY

Dale

D ale stood in the hall outside Melanie's office shifting from one foot to the other. She'd sat on a beige sofa in the waiting area for nearly half an hour, but once she'd read and reread the assortment of newspapers and newsmagazines, she'd grown impatient. She'd stepped into the hallway to check her cell phone messages and was listening to a long voice mail from one of the speechwriters when Melanie's assistant, Annie, stepped into the hallway.

"Miss Smith, I'm so sorry about that. The secretary is ready for you," she said.

"Thanks," Dale answered.

Annie led Dale back through the waiting area and into the formal office of the secretary of defense. Melanie was the country's twenty-fifth secretary of defense and the first woman to lead that department. As White House chief of staff, she'd been at the same "rank" as all the cabinet members, but some still saw her appointment as a political reward for one of President Kramer's cronies. Melanie had refused efforts by her allies to aggressively counter those attacks. She'd said at the time that she would let her performance speak for itself. So far, she'd proven that fifteen years in the West Wing was perfectly adequate preparation for the post.

Her new office lacked the splendor of the West Wing offices, but it was formidable. Dale noticed a small photo of Melanie and Brian dressed up for the White House Correspondents' Association dinner.

"Hi Dale, come on in. I'm sorry I kept you waiting so long," Melanie said. She was friendly but not warm. Dale still wasn't sure what she was doing there.

"It's no problem at all."

Melanie walked over to a small conference table and took a seat.

"How's everything going?"

Dale contemplated how to answer the seemingly simple question. "Honestly?" she asked.

"Up to you," Melanie said. Dale thought she saw a slight glint in her eye.

Dale stiffened.

"Dale, let's not waste our time bullshitting each other. I called you over here to see if you're all right."

Dale exhaled for the first time since she'd entered the office.

"I don't know."

Melanie was watching her closely.

"I think things are about to get really strange on my side of the river."

Melanie nodded. She looked like she was thinking about whether to tell Dale something. Dale had a feeling she knew what it was. On her way over, Michael Robbins had called to give Dale a "heads-up." He was hearing rumblings about a White House whistle-blower who alleged that the vice president had a nervous breakdown and that the White House had covered it up. Dale was watching Melanie now and waiting for her to say something. Melanie didn't blink very often, and it made Dale blink more than usual. She squirmed in her seat. Melanie made her nervous. Despite the sordid personal history between Dale and the president, Charlotte had always been nice to her. Melanie, on the other hand, had never let down her guard.

"Listen, Dale, it's probably best that we speak in hypothetical terms."

"Of course."

"Hypothetically speaking, if there were something really wrong with the veep, who would know?"

"Ralph, Marcus, obviously. Maybe Karen?"

"And would someone in your position know?"

"Someone in my position would probably see enough to know

that something was wrong, but I don't think the person who deals with the press would be fully read in."

"And how are we using the word *fully*?"

Dale leaned back in the chair and thought for a few seconds about how to answer the question.

"I guess I mean, hypothetically speaking, of course, that while the situation may now seem obvious, it was never explained to me. I just sort of pieced together one bizarre fact after another and figured it out."

Melanie pushed her chair back from the table and stood up. Dale watched her walk slowly toward her desk and sit down behind it. She wasn't sure if she should stay at the table or move to the chair in front of the desk. Melanie had her back to Dale. After a couple of minutes, she turned and faced Dale again.

"Dale, you and I have never spent much time together, but I know Brian has always had a lot of respect for you."

"It's mutual," Dale said.

Melanie smiled. She was obviously proud of Brian, which Dale thought was a surprisingly vulnerable reaction from her. "Believe it or not, Dale, Charlotte admires and respects you a great deal as well. She thinks you are a rare talent, professionally speaking, of course."

Dale wasn't sure if the joke was for her benefit or Melanie's, but she smiled back.

"Thank you. That means a lot."

Melanie leaned forward.

"Dale, I'm going to give you a piece of advice, for whatever it's worth, and you can take it or leave it."

"I appreciate any advice," Dale said.

"That place is about to become a snake pit. Everyone will have their own private lawyers. No one will be in charge. You're going to get press calls about things you never thought imaginable. You'll run around, trying to find answers to those questions, but you'll figure out pretty quickly that the whole place has been turned upside down. No one will give you a straight answer about anything. The newspapers will be filled with anonymous quotes from the personal lawyers who are trying to portray their clients in the best light and position them for deals."

"Deals?"

"You know, immunity, pleas, whatever. And Ralph will not go down quietly, if he is, you know, hypothetically speaking, the one who masterminded a cover up of whatever is wrong with the veep and gave out the orders. How is your relationship with Ralph?"

"Strained, at best," Dale answered.

"He pulled you into this?"

Dale nodded as dread filled every last muscle and nerve ending in her body.

Melanie opened the top drawer of her desk and pulled out a stack of business cards held together with a rubber band. "Old school, I know," she said. Melanie found whatever card she was looking for and picked up the phone. Dale could see that she'd dialed a 202 number.

"Is he there? Please tell him it's Melanie Kingston and it's rather urgent."

She didn't look at Dale as she held the line. Whoever she was calling picked up the phone in about three seconds.

"Jimbo. I'm sorry to pull you out of whatever you were doing, but I need a favor. What are you doing tonight? I need you to sit down with someone this evening. I think she's going to need your help. Can she come to your office around eight?"

Melanie wrote something down on the legal pad in front of her and underlined it.

"I'll tell her. Yes, you need to come to the house for dinner soon. I would love that. I will tell him. Thank you. Oh, her name is Dale. Dale Smith."

Dale held her breath and imagined a thousand things that Melanie's lawyer friend could have been saying at the other end of the line. Whatever it was, Melanie didn't react.

She hung up and tore the page off the legal pad. There was an address and instructions about how to get into a K Street office after hours.

"Jim Moffet is expecting you tonight at his office at eight. Do not tell anyone where you are going. Do you understand? Do not take a White House car and do not let anyone see you walk into the building. Tell Jim everything."

Dale was too stunned to say anything other than thank you. She exited Melanie's office and headed out to the town car that had brought her over the bridge from the District of Columbia to the Pentagon building in Virginia. The sky had darkened, and it was cold for October. Dale wished she had brought a coat. She hadn't loosened her grip yet on the paper Melanie had handed her, but as she settled into the backseat and asked the driver to take her back to West Exec, she unfolded it. Melanie had made an appointment for Dale to meet with the former deputy attorney general. He was now a very prominent attorney in town, best known for defending the former Speaker of the House for alleged campaign finance violations. For once, Dale didn't check her BlackBerry or phone for messages. She spent the entire ride back to the White House trying to figure out why Melanie would want to help her and how she knew so much about what was coming.

CHAPTER FIFTY-ONE

Charlotte

C harlotte read the statement for a tenth time. She'd crossed most of it out with her thick black Sharpie and scribbled edits in the margins. She had proceeded to edit her own edits, turning the document into a messy page of black hieroglyphics. The statement was only half a page, but it would be replayed more than any other words she'd uttered as president. She sighed and tried to decipher her new draft.

The plan was for her to read the statement in the Rose Garden in front of the White House press corps. Her personal attorney wanted her to say that she "welcomed" the investigation. Charlotte thought it was ludicrous, but she'd agreed to listen to him, for now at least. She left the word in the text. No president ever really wants the curtains lifted on the sometimes distasteful reality of a modern executive branch. The American presidency was not designed for twenty-four-hour cable news coverage and embedded journalists. It was designed for a different time—an era in which mystique and reverence for the country's leaders was believed to contribute to the public good at least as much as transparency and infinite debate.

Besides, the announcement would guarantee that her White House would grind to a screeching halt. All crises divert the attention of White House staff, but the appointment of a special counsel causes paralysis.

Charlotte sighed again. For most of the senior staff, the anxiety was already just beneath the surface. Charlotte had been warned in advance not to speak to anyone about their interviews. Her personal attorney was the only person she was allowed to speak to about the investigation without running the risk that the conversation would ultimately end up in the public record. Charlotte glanced at a memo outlining the steps that the small circle of advisors who knew about the special counsel had taken. A separate unit had been set up in the White House legal office to deal with the logistical coordination, such as document production and the scheduling of interviews, between the White House staff and the special counsel. A mid-level press person had been assigned to deal with all press calls. The press secretary would not field questions about the special counsel from the podium. Despite the steps to wall off the unpleasantness, it would pollute everything.

Charlotte looked up and noticed Sam standing in the doorway to the Oval Office.

"Madam President?"

"Yes, Sam, come on in."

"Mr. Kramer just arrived at the residence. Should I tell him you're on your way over?"

"Uh, in a minute. Let's try calling Melanie again, first."

"Yes, ma'am." Sam disappeared and then reappeared seconds later.

"Madam President, Annie said she was wrapping up a meeting with Senators Dean and Kirk."

"Mmmn hmmn."

"Would you like me to ask Annie to interrupt?"

"No, just ask her to have Melanie call me when she's done."

"Yes ma'am." Sam returned a moment later.

"Annie asked if Melanie could stop by on her way home. Should I tell her you have a dinner tonight?"

"No, no. Tell her that's fine. I'll wait for her here."

Sam stood in the doorway awkwardly.

"I'll call Peter," Charlotte said. Sam looked relieved.

Charlotte had Peter walk the dogs and pushed their dinner back to nine P.M. While she waited for Melanie, she flipped through a report from her director of OMB until her eyes glazed over. She signed a stack of photos of herself and was about to turn on the news when Sam opened the door for Melanie.

"Hi," Charlotte said. "You're busier than me these days."

Melanie offered a tense smile. "How are you holding up?" She sat down on one of the sofas.

"Oh, god, I'm completely fine. I'm just worried about the impact on our people and on our agenda. The first year of a second term is the only opportunity to get anything done."

Melanie nodded in agreement.

"How was your meeting?" Charlotte took a seat on the sofa across from Melanie.

"My meeting?" Melanie's face was blank.

"Annie said you were meeting with Dean and Kirk?"

"Oh, *that* meeting. It was good. I pitched them on procurement reform and they seemed interested." She recovered quickly, but, obviously, Melanie hadn't been meeting with Senators Dean and Kirk.

"Think they'll cosponsor a bill?"

"I hope so." Melanie averted her glance.

Charlotte was about to ask about Brian when Melanie raised the investigation.

"Listen, I've been advised not to discuss Tara or any of the conversations you and I have had about her from the time of her selection as your running mate onward. I'm going to have to testify about all of it, obviously." Melanie's voice sounded tight.

"I know, and I'm sorry. I know this takes you away from other important things," Charlotte acknowledged.

Melanie didn't dismiss Charlotte's apology as unnecessary. "Hopefully, this whole thing will blow over quickly. I've been thinking that maybe we shouldn't see each other outside of our official interactions until things settle down a bit."

It felt like a breakup. "You're right, of course." Charlotte didn't know what else to say.

"I probably shouldn't even be here. Brian is digging around on the report that surfaced during the last weekend of the campaign about her stint in rehab as we speak," Melanie explained.

Charlotte looked puzzled.

"Remember? The one that Tara assured us was false? Now it appears likely that I lied about it during the campaign, but hey, what's a little white lie between friends, right?" Melanie sounded angry.

"Melanie, you communicated what we knew to be true at the time."

"Don't worry. That's what I plan to tell the special counsel."

Charlotte pressed her lips together and decided to let Melanie blow off a little steam. She leaned back in the sofa and uncrossed her arms.

"Charlotte, you should also know that the *National Enquirer* just posted a story online quoting the wife of an Italian doctor who claims to have treated Tara while she was studying abroad there in law school. Did you know about any of this?"

"Jesus Christ, Melanie. The *National Enquirer*? Is that a trusted news source now?"

"Charlotte, they've been right about more things than you could ever imagine. And they chase the stories the mainstream press doesn't have the guts to pursue."

"I can't believe you're sitting here defending the tabloids," Charlotte countered.

Melanie stared out the window toward the South Lawn. She seemed to be trying to cool herself down before she spoke again.

"Don't think for a second that I fail to understand the gravity of this for your presidency," Melanie said.

"I don't think there's anyone who understands the gravity of the situation better than you, Melanie."

Melanie nodded. "This is going to be very complicated for me with Brian covering the story and everything I've done to distance myself from anything remotely political over at the Pentagon."

"I understand. I'm sorry, Melanie. I really am."

"I know you are." Melanie stood up and walked toward the door. She wore an expression of thinly veiled disgust. Charlotte fought the urge to feel offended. She understood that Melanie was reacting to a jumble of emotions that she probably couldn't articulate if she tried. In part, she was furious that she'd allowed someone like Tara to dismantle the image she'd worked so hard to salvage for Charlotte. It was as much about someone "undoing" her hard work as anything else. But Charlotte suspected she was also reacting to her own lifetime of misplaced priorities. Melanie felt as though she was owed exactly what she'd put into the job, but that wasn't how a life in politics was calculated. A lifetime of good and noble deeds could be erased with heartbreaking consequences in an instant. They'd both learned that lesson the painful way when Roger died.

Melanie turned to face her before she got to the door. "I wanted to tell you something else. Brian and I got engaged last weekend."

"That's wonderful!"

"I know the timing couldn't be worse, but I didn't want you to hear it somewhere else."

"Mel, I'm thrilled for you. I really am. And please congratulate Brian for me, too. He's very lucky."

"Thanks. We'll all celebrate after this has died down a bit. I've got to meet Brian at a dinner. I'll see you later this week at the NSC meeting?"

"Yes, you will. Thanks for stopping by, and congratulations, again."

"Have a good night, Madam President."

As Charlotte watched Melanie flee from the Oval Office she steeled herself for the ugliness ahead. Melanie wouldn't be the only one. Idealistic aides were the most loyal and hardworking, but they had a tendency to turn on you with a vengeance when they became disillusioned. Charlotte said good night to Sam and made her way slowly toward the residence where Peter was still waiting for her. As she neared the door that separated the West Wing from the East Wing, she noticed Melanie sitting on a bench near the back of the Rose Garden. She approached the bench and saw Melanie holding her BlackBerry phone. She had a strange look on her face—one that Charlotte had never seen before.

"Mel, what are you doing out here? Are you all right?"

"When did you figure it out?"

"Figure what out?"

"Come on," Melanie pleaded.

Charlotte sighed deeply. Melanie wanted to know how long she'd left someone who was unfit for office in a position of power. For the first time, Charlotte suspected that it was possible Melanie was recording their conversation for the special counsel or for Brian, or for someone else. She steadied herself and stood there for another minute. Melanie wouldn't look at her.

"Melanie, come inside," Charlotte urged.

Melanie was staring straight ahead. Charlotte walked closer and started to sit down next to her.

"Please don't," Melanie whispered.

Charlotte stood up and backed away immediately. They stayed that way for a few minutes, both women aware of the irreversible damage that had been done to their relationship by the events of the past year. Charlotte wasn't exactly sure what Melanie had expected her to do once Tara had started to unravel, but clearly, she hadn't done enough in Melanie's book. And for Melanie's part, she looked so broken that Charlotte's overriding instinct was to comfort her like she would one of her own children.

"I'll let your agents know you're out here," Charlotte finally said.

Melanie nodded. It looked like she was crying.

"Do you want me to call Brian and tell him you'll be late for dinner?"

"I just called him."

"All right, then. Good night." Charlotte turned and walk slowly toward the residence.

CHAPTER FIFTY-TWO

Tara

T ara was perplexed by the effect that the announcement of a special counsel had on official Washington. Appointing an outside investigator was the only politically viable way for DOJ to handle accusations of White House misconduct. The move seemed obvious and unavoidable to Tara, but that didn't stop the city from being swallowed whole by the news. As Frannie had warned weeks earlier, Brent Kirkpatrick, the U.S. attorney for the Southern District of New York, had been tapped to serve as the special counsel.

Tara sighed and studied her schedule for the day. In the aftermath of Charlotte's statement the week before, welcoming the investigation and expressing confidence that her national security team and senior staff had acted appropriately at all times, the White House became strangely automated. There were fewer meetings and public events, and the staff seemed subdued. Ironically, it was the slower pace that allowed Tara to finally get her sea legs. She made it through Dale's overnight memo each evening after work and read the white papers from the policy staff.

Tara also quietly started to get her affairs in order. If she followed through with her plan to resign, they would need a place to go where Kendall could continue her school year uninterrupted. Tara had no problem envisioning her life after the vice presidency. In fact, the thought filled her with tremendous relief.

The official scope of the investigation was to examine whether the White House deliberately exaggerated the threat of a terrorist attack to divert attention from its political problems. An unnamed member of Congress was quoted in the *Washington Post* the week before saying that the "scope of the investigation will be broad enough to illuminate exactly how this White House is operating." Another unnamed official told the *New York Times* that "the public has legitimate questions about what goes on behind closed doors, and about the basic competence of the people at the highest levels of government." Tara soon realized that Congress had used the elevation of the terror threat as a hook to justify conducting a fishing expedition. They weren't interested in gaining any deeper understanding of the threat posed by Youseff Bordeaux. If they were, they would have simply hauled Charlotte's national security team up to the Hill for closed sessions and beat the hell out of them until they shared all of the intelligence. This line of questioning would have ended their witch hunt in a hurry. The intel about Youseff was frightening enough to have left the threat level raised until his interrogations were complete and his known affiliates in custody. If anything, a case could be made that the White House shifted *off* of "high alert" too quickly after Youseff's capture, especially since his nephews remained at large. Tara believed that the plot had simply been delayed, not disrupted at all. But the veracity of the threat posed by Youseff wasn't what the White House's critics were after.

Tara turned up the volume on her television when CNN aired its ominous Breaking News graphic. The White House reporter had learned that phone records from Air Force One had been subpoenaed. Tara shook her head at the television in her office in the West Wing. She couldn't believe that such a routine move on the part of the special counsel's office warranted a Breaking News bulletin. Washington didn't make any more sense to her now than it had when she'd arrived nearly a year earlier. The same members of Congress who had demanded that an outside investigator look into the allegations of White House misconduct had missed the fact that she and Brent had worked together when they were in their mid-twenties. Now, Brent Kirkpatrick was well known as a hard-charging prosecutor who'd handled some of the biggest public corruption cases of the last decade. He was respected by members of both parties, and while he acted as though he was immune to the affection of his admirers, Tara knew better. His lifelong dream was to be appointed FBI director. Only a president can make that selection. Nothing catapults a prosecutor to prominence more quickly that treating the powerful like common criminal suspects. The irony, Tara mused, was that it was practically impossible for anyone at the White House to have actually committed a crime. The allegations of misconduct were purely political in nature, and the appointment of a special counsel even more so. A White House official would have to be found to have broken an existing criminal statute, and in Tara's years of experience, it was not a crime to change the subject. The investigation was ordered to embarrass President Kramer and flush out the depth of Tara's incompetence.

If anyone was actually indicted, the crime would be, as it always is in Washington, a cover-up. She hoped that her resignation would go a long way toward satisfying Kirkpatrick's desire to deliver a scalp. She'd do anything to spare the president the heartache of watching her West Wing implode. That's why it was so vital that she convince Marcus. He wasn't exactly coming around, but she was determined to convince him that it was the best thing for all of them. She just needed to come at Marcus from a different angle, one that made her resignation a no-brainer for all of them.

She massaged her temples and stared at the television. David Gergen was droning on about the history of special counsels and Wolf Blitzer was trying to look riveted. Tara muted the program and returned to her newspapers.

Soon, she was shaking her head again. Politicians loved to complain about unauthorized leaks to the press, but no single event in Washington generated more self-serving leaks than a special counsel's investigation. Given the government officials targeted by the investigation, the lawmakers responsible for a special counsel being appointed, the witnesses interrogated by the investigator, and the outside lawyers employed by everyone involved, there were enough sources spinning their version of events to fill three times the newspaper inches typically printed in Washington on any ordinary day.

And in those disparate versions of events, a few consistent themes came through more clearly than ever before. Charlotte Kramer had more political enemies than any president in recent history. A lot of her opponents were members of her own party who harbored deep resentment over her treatment of her former defense secretary. She had read about his suicide when Charlotte first tapped her as her running mate. Tara couldn't determine whether they'd been romantically involved, but it was apparent that they'd been extremely close. Tara was dismayed that several of the conservative columnists and talk-radio hosts were linking Charlotte's treatment of Roger to her treatment of Tara. Rush Limbaugh had gone on for the third straight day about Charlotte Kramer lacking character. The attacks from the left were almost as nasty. MSNBC ran a prime-time special the night before called *Impeaching the President: A How-To for New Members of Congress*.

Tara picked up the phone and dialed Marcus's cell phone.

"What if there was a way to resign with a guarantee that you and I are immune from any related investigations, charges, and inquiries now and in the future?" she asked with her hand over her mouth to make sure no one outside her office could hear her.

"We both know that's impossible." Marcus sounded wistful.

"Put that aside, for a second. Would that be enough?"

"I don't know," he said.

"We'd be able to go on with our lives."

"Don't do anything, Tara," he urged.

Before she hung up, she promised him that she wouldn't, but she knew better than anyone else in the West Wing how things would unfold in the coming days and weeks. She had to spare her family further humiliation. She picked up the phone and called Frannie's personal cell phone.

"Can you talk?"

CHAPTER FIFTY-THREE

Dale

A round seven-fifteen P.M., Dale walked out of the White House complex and traveled the three blocks to Jim Moffet's K Street office. The former deputy attorney general had agreed to represent her during their first meeting as a personal favor to Melanie. He didn't explain why he owed Melanie such a big favor, and Melanie hadn't offered any further explanation for why she'd intervened on Dale's behalf. Her best theory for Melanie's generosity was that Brian persuaded her to help Dale in return for the good fortune that had befallen him since Dale's career at the network abruptly ended and his blossomed. He'd been given the weekend anchor job that had once belonged to Dale. At the moment, she was so freaked out by the prospect of having to testify before a grand jury and the request for all of her e-mails and phone records that she didn't spend too much time thinking about why she had an attorney as seasoned and respected as Jim Moffet. She was simply grateful for the turn of events. She'd already received unofficial word from the special counsel's staff that she would be called in for one of the first interviews.

During a phone conversation earlier in the day, Jim had asked Dale to search for e-mails and phone records that would paint the picture he wanted to present of Dale repeatedly warning her superiors about the vice president's state of mind. She scoured her e-mails for the evidence that Jim requested, but, unfortunately, she'd heeded Ralph's advice not to use her White House e-mail account to discuss her concerns about the vice president. She'd found a few cryptic messages to Ralph and others and had printed them out, but a thorough search would take her days.

Now Jim smiled warmly at Dale and pulled out a yellow legal pad on which Dale noticed he'd scribbled some notes. "I spoke to the special counsel's office today and I have a better sense of what they want from you, Dale," he started.

She tried to listen closely as he described his conversation, but her mind kept straying. She could tell that with this, their third meeting, he had switched out of the listening mode that he'd been in during their first two sessions. The first night they'd met, Dale had started at the beginning and told him everything. He'd taken few notes. Mostly, he'd just listened and nodded and smiled sympathetically.

"Am I in trouble?" she'd asked.

"I don't think so. You did the job you were hired to do. And you called for help when you felt things were getting out of control," he'd said. She hadn't told him about her meeting with the president yet, and she wasn't sure if she should. What good would it do? The president wouldn't mention the meeting, so if she didn't say anything no one would know.

Her attention was brought back to Jim's readout of his call with the special counsel's office by the sound of someone knocking on his door.

"Come on in," he said.

A petite brunette holding three giant binders entered the room.

"Dale, I'm bringing in a colleague, Connie Taylor, to help on your case. She and I will both be available to you twenty-four hours a day, seven days a week. We are your team, and you can call on us for anything—big or small."

Dale looked up at Connie. She looked like all the women in the White House Counsel's Office—pretty, pale, thin, and primly dressed. Connie dropped her binders on the conference table with a thud.

"Have you debriefed her on the call with the special counsel's office?" Connie asked. Dale noticed that she only looked at Jim when she spoke. He nodded.

"I was just going over that. Why don't you sit in," Jim said.

Connie's face was expressionless. "Sure," she said.

"Dale did some preliminary document production, Connie. I thought we could go over that material together."

Connie sprang from the table to make copies of the e-mails Dale had pulled from her purse. While she was out of his office, Jim's assistant put a call through from his wife. As he spoke in low tones, Dale glanced down at her BlackBerry. Craig had e-mailed her more than a dozen times since their fight. She'd ignored all his messages. His harshness that night had taken her by surprise. She was used to disappointing the men in her life, but for some reason, she'd thought her relationship with Craig was on firmer ground. His latest round of apologies and pleas for forgiveness were so pathetic though, that they had succeeded in wearing her down.

She hit reply to one of the three e-mails he'd sent that day. She was too tired to be mad at him anymore.

"Stop with the apologies and I'll call you tonight," she wrote.

"Come to dinner?" he wrote back right away.

"It would have to be late," she typed.

"Any time."

"9:30 P.M.?"

Craig typed back a smiley face. Dale shoved the BlackBerry in her purse and looked up. Jim was looking at her intently and Connie had returned and was looking at her too. At one time, Jim Moffet had been very good-looking. He would have been exactly Dale's type. She wondered, for a moment, if he was happily married and if he found her at all attractive. In their meetings, he'd been incredibly doting toward her. He was constantly reassuring her that everything would be all right. It had reminded her of how Peter had always tried to take care of her. Dale realized that he must have asked her a question.

"I'm sorry, what did you say?"

"Do you have plans tonight?"

"What? No. I mean yes."

"No problem, Dale. Relax. My wife will be thrilled if your answer is yes. I haven't seen her all week. Let us digest the e-mails overnight and we will start with our first practice interview in the morning over breakfast. Does that work for you, Connie?"

Connie nodded and started stacking her giant binders on top of each other again.

"Thank you," Dale said.

"Get some rest tonight."

Dale wrapped her black cashmere sweater tightly around her as she stepped into the cool night. She folded her arms across her chest and kept her head down as she speed-walked across Lafayette Park and back through the Northwest Gate. She threw her purse into her car and drove out of the complex with one eye on the speedometer as she made her way onto 17th Street toward Dupont Circle. She couldn't handle getting pulled over again. The officer had eventually let her go home the last time she'd left Craig's, but not before an excruciating battery of questions and threats to haul her into the precinct for a blood and urine test.

Craig was standing in the open doorway when she got out of her car. She was expecting a hug and an apology, but as she got closer, she could see that he was exercised about something.

"Take the battery out of your BlackBerry," he urged, pulling her into the town house.

"What?"

He took her BlackBerry from her hands and removed the battery. "Do you have others?"

Stunned, she opened her purse and handed him her iPhone. While he laid out her disassembled electronics on the table in his entryway, Dale walked into the kitchen. An old U2 song was blaring from the stereo and several covered pots and pans simmered on the stovetop.

"Uh, how about a 'Hello, nice to see you, Dale,'" she mocked.

"Sorry. I'm really glad you came, and I'm going to apologize properly for the out-of-line shit I said to you the other night, but I need to talk to you about the investigation first."

"Okay," she said slowly.

"You have a lawyer, right?"

She nodded.

"Someone good?"

She nodded again. She didn't mention that Melanie had essentially placed her in Jim Moffet's hands.

"Listen, the special counsel stuff is going to be what it always is, and if you have a good lawyer and all of your e-mails and stuff, you'll be fine."

"I hope so."

"I promise. They are thinking much bigger than the special counsel. This is about to get huge." He sounded possessed.

"Who is 'they'?" Dale asked.

"The House Judiciary Committee. They are talking about impeachment proceedings for the president."

"What? For what?"

"For placing a fucking head case a heartbeat away from the Oval Office."

Dale started to pace back and forth in the kitchen. He was scaring her.

"How do you know?"

"That's the longer story that I planned to tell you tonight—over many bottles of wine."

"Tell me now. You're freaking me out."

He motioned for her to sit.

"Come sit down and relax."

"Relax? You pull the batteries out of my PDAs, tell me they're going to impeach the president, and then tell me to sit down and relax? Are you kidding?"

"I'm sorry. Okay, so the Speaker's office is calling the shots," he explained.

"Right. They got the Justice Department to appoint the special counsel. That's been in the paper. The Speaker is leading the charge for the Democrats. She called this Kramer's Watergate."

Craig nodded. "Right. The Democrats are still mad that Charlotte picked one of their rising stars to serve in a Republican administration, but now some of them are beginning to think they'll have the last laugh if it turns out she's schizophrenic or psychotic or something."

"I don't think she's schizophrenic."

"Gee, that's a relief."

"Stop it. I can't even believe we're having this conversation," Dale protested.

"This isn't even the worst of it."

"What makes you think they're considering impeachment hearings?"

"The Speaker's chief of staff is someone I know very well."

Dale opened her mouth to say something but the mixture of pain and shame on Craig's face stopped her.

Craig walked back into the kitchen.

"Langston Phillips?" she asked.

He nodded.

Langston Phillips had been one of Washington's most eligible bachelors for nearly a decade. He'd married a twenty-two-year-old Capitol Hill correspondent from CNN the year before and she was pregnant with twins. Dale's mind twisted and turned for a few seconds before she figured it out.

"You're with Langston." It wasn't a question.

Craig nodded.

"How long?"

"We've been together for nine years."

Dale walked over to the couch and sat down with her legs tucked under her body. Craig was still in the kitchen. He turned down the music and filled two glasses with wine.

"I'll have vodka," she said.

He left the glasses of red wine on the counter and pulled the bottle of vodka out of the freezer. They sipped vodka and he told her about his nearly decade-long relationship with the married chief of staff to the Democratic Speaker of the House.

CHAPTER FIFTY-FOUR

Charlotte

W hat do you mean she won't call you back?" Peter asked.

"I mean that when I call and leave a message, she doesn't return the message," Charlotte replied.

"Give me the phone."

"What? No. Why? What are you going to do? It's pointless. Melanie is too idealistic for her own good. You'd have to be to have worked for three presidents, don't you think?"

Peter nodded. "At least Ralph can't be accused of idealism."

Charlotte laughed.

"Do you think either one of them is responsible for the front-page story in the *Times* today?"

She sighed deeply. "I don't know."

The *New York Times* quoted unnamed sources who described "bitter divisions" among Charlotte's senior advisors during the terror scare in August. One source revealed that Ralph was furious at the vice president for what he saw as an "overreaction," and another source described DOD as "deeply skeptical" about the intelligence that lead to the elevated threat level.

"Are you hearing anything from the special counsel?" Peter asked.

"No. Our folks have been promised a heads-up if anyone on the staff becomes a target or a subject of the investigation as opposed to a witness, but I don't expect they'll share much more than that. It's surreal, isn't it?"

"Yes," he said.

They were sitting on the Truman Balcony under a blue wool blanket with 'Air Force One' stitched in one corner with gold thread. An early storm was stripping the fall leaves off the trees on the South Lawn. Cammie had her head in Charlotte's lap and the other two dogs were huddled near Peter. Charlotte stroked Cammie's muzzle and the dog moaned a little with pleasure. Charlotte had given up her after-dinner cigarette habit, but she still liked to have coffee out on the balcony. It was usually the only time, other than her walk from the residence to the Oval Office, when she breathed fresh air.

Charlotte glanced over at Peter and was surprised to catch him looking at her. He leaned over and kissed her softly.

"You must not have heard the news," she said.

"What news?"

"That I'm dead inside."

"No, I missed that."

"Rush Limbaugh announced that he'd finally figured out what kind of woman would let her most valued national security advisor fall on his sword so she could be reelected and then leave her vice president bleeding on the battlefield less than a year later."

"Rush Limbaugh said that you were dead inside?"

"Yes, and that I was the most frightening politician in the country and possibly on the world stage, and that Tara Meyers should dump on me and everyone who works for me before she becomes the second senior official to get hung out to dry."

"Char, you shouldn't listen to Rush Limbaugh."

"I don't. But my father does. And so does your father. And so do thirty-eight million others."

Peter smiled sympathetically and watched her closely.

"What are you thinking about?" Charlotte asked.

"Nothing."

"That's not your 'nothing' look. It's a something look. What were you thinking?"

"I was wondering if we could actually pull this off again or if we did too much harm the first time around for this to ever be more than what it is now, which, for the record, is pretty nice," he said.

Charlotte was quiet. She'd wondered the same thing, but her

compartmentalized mind had tabled those questions for a time in the future when she wasn't worried about being impeached. She stared at the Washington Monument for a minute before she started to speak.

"I think people are capable of doing extraordinarily brave things. I see it every time I'm in Iraq and Afghanistan. And I wonder why we don't do more extraordinarily brave things in our personal lives. Or, better said, why *I* don't do more extraordinarily brave things with my personal life, which, of course, presumes that I have a personal life, which, as you know better than anyone, I don't, and have not had in a couple of decades."

Peter looked slightly amused.

"I was thinking that if these eighteen- and nineteen-year-old kids—and you know, Will is one of them—if these kids can do these brave things, these things that defy my capacity for understanding, then why can't I find the courage to do some of the things that scare me?"

"That's a funny question coming from the most powerful person in the world," Peter noted.

Charlotte reached over and slipped her hand into his. He smiled at her and they sat there and watched the leaves swirl in the wind. Even though he was the one who'd had the affair, she felt as if she was the one who had more work to do in convincing him that she could be in a real relationship. She had to prove to him that she was able to let him love her this time. Their problem was never that Charlotte hadn't loved him. She'd always loved him. Their problem was that she never let him love her back, and if they were to have any chance at all this time, that would have to change.

Charlotte looked up when one of the members of the residence staff suddenly appeared.

"I'm sorry, Madam President. I have an urgent call for you from Craig Thompson," he said.

"Thank you."

She walked inside to pick up the phone in the Yellow Oval.

"Good evening, Craig," she said.

"Madam President, the Speaker's office just got a tip from a senior

Justice department source who claims that the vice president is meeting secretly with the special counsel tomorrow."

Charlotte swallowed. Peter was watching her through the window.

"Thank you, Craig. Please keep me posted."

"Yes ma'am."

Tara

Tara dressed carefully in the black dress and matching jacket she'd once tried on for Dale. She applied makeup and smoothed her hair with a round brush and the blow dryer before heading down-stairs. Marcus hadn't returned to bed after their last argument the night before. He'd come around on the meeting she'd arranged with the special counsel for later that day, but he was still concerned that they would take what they wanted and screw her out of her demands. He wanted to go with her but she'd insisted that she go alone. This was what had set off their final round of fighting. Marcus was so ac-customed to protecting her. Her need to be insulated and his need to be essential were the things that had kept them together all these years. If she went through with her plan to resign, there wouldn't be anything for him to protect her from ever again. Their entire partner-ship would become unnecessary. She was surprised that this thought made her feel as sad as it did, and she was relieved to see him sitting at the breakfast table with Kendall as though nothing out of the ordi-nary were taking place that day.

"Hi guys," she said.

Kendall was delighted.

"Hi Mommy." She came over and kissed her. "You look pretty."

Tara wiped grape jelly from Kendall's lower lip and kissed her on the forehead. Marcus watched them. She avoided making eye contact with him while she measured out a cup and a half of raisin bran and poured skim milk on top.

"Banana?" Marcus offered.

"Huh?"

"Do you want half a banana?"

"Oh, no, no thanks," she said.

She forced herself to eat a spoonful of cereal, but she had a hard time swallowing anything.

"Mommy, can we have meatballs tonight?" Kendall asked.

"Of course we can."

One of Tara's newer agents knocked on the door.

"Ma'am, we have the traffic stopped on Mass Ave. One of the guys thought you had an eight-forty-five meeting so they had us get the route ready early."

"No problem. I'm ready!" Tara jumped up from the table without finishing her cereal and kissed Kendall again before turning to go.

"Call me," Marcus called after her.

"I will," she said, without turning around.

As the motorcade pulled out of the Naval Observatory, Tara looked closely at the lone protester who had stood vigil on Massachusetts Avenue across the street from the residence every day since she'd moved in. One of her agents had told her that he'd been there through the previous two administrations. He held a sign that read "Stop the abuse" on one side and "Shame on the Catholic Church" on the other. Tara noticed a woman in a Prius with "No blood for oil" bumper stickers plastered across the front fender honk and hold out a "thumbs-up" in the direction of the protester. The man pumped his sign in the air and grinned widely.

Washington was full of people who had something to say and believed that it was the responsibility of people in power to listen. Tara could hear her agents speak into the radio about their location. She'd finally figured out most of their secret language.

"All cars, all stations, Albany en route sixteen hundred."

Albany was her Secret Service code name. Marcus was Amsterdam and Kendall was Andover. It was possible that they'd all been called by those code names for the last time. If her meeting with the special counsel went the way she hoped it would, she would no longer be the vice president by the end of the day. Her plan was to offer her resignation in return for immunity for all related criminal and civil charges against herself and Marcus as well as a pledge from the U.S. Justice Department that there would be no further investigation or inquiry into her mental health, prior treatments or diagnosis, or statements that she or Marcus made about her fitness for office. The deal would allow them to leave Washington with a clean slate.

She looked out her window at the empty stretch of road they would travel all the way to the White House. Traveling by motorcade had been such a thrill to her the first few times she'd watched as the police officers stopped traffic and her limo or SUV zoomed through traffic lights and swerved across several lanes, sometimes driving in the lane normally reserved for cars traveling in the other direction. Now it felt like another unnecessary imposition that she'd placed on people simply trying to commute to work. She leaned back and closed her eyes for the remaining minutes of the drive. It would all be over soon enough.

CHAPTER FIFTY-SIX

Dale

Connie was playing the role of the special counsel and Jim was coaching Dale's answers. Dale thought Connie was taking her role-playing a little too seriously. She didn't even break character when they took bathroom breaks.

"Miss Smith, can you tell us when you first became aware that there was something wrong with the vice president?"

Dale looked at Connie and then at Jim.

"How am I supposed to answer that? I mean, she started to skip meetings and would work from home for days on end almost right away, but I hadn't worked on the campaign, so I wasn't sure if that was normal for her, or if there was something going on," Dale explained.

"How about if you simply say that you were new to the administration, but her behavior struck you as a bit inconsistent pretty soon after you started working for her," Jim suggested.

Dale nodded and turned to Connie.

"I thought her behavior seemed a bit erratic from the beginning."

"Erratic how?" Connie asked.

"What do you mean, Connie?"

"I don't know who Connie is, Miss Smith, but I'd like to know how Vice President Meyers acted erratically, in your judgment."

"I'm asking you if you want me to name specific incidents, or just give my general impressions."

"Miss Smith, please share both the specific incidents and your general impressions with the grand jury," Connie ordered without looking up from whatever was on the page she was staring at in her oversized binder.

Dale was annoyed that Jim didn't discourage Connie's badgering. This was supposed to be a practice session.

"Well, Mr. Kirkpatrick. The vice president started to cancel meetings and postpone briefings and internal meetings with staff shortly after I started at the end of January. My impression was that I hoped it was just an adjustment period."

"Thank you, Miss Smith. Can you tell us what you did when she started to cancel meetings and postpone briefings?"

Dale looked at Jim again.

"What I did? I didn't *do* anything. I was a staffer. And I'd never worked in government before. I just tried to keep things together," Dale said to Jim.

"I'm sorry, Miss Smith, I didn't hear that."

"Let's take a break, Connie," Jim suggested. Connie looked bored.

"Dale, Kirkpatrick is going to come at you with dozens of formulations like the ones Connie just presented. He's going to ask you what your impression was of her behavior and then he's going to probe you about what action you took. His premise is, essentially, that the White House perpetrated a fraud on the public by keeping the vice president's problems under wraps and making her appear better than she was."

Dale felt sick to her stomach.

Jim put a hand on her shoulder. "You can do this. Let's pick up where Connie left off."

"Miss Smith, on May 18 of this year, you sent an e-mail to Ralph Giacamo telling him you needed to speak to him about the vice president. What was the purpose of that e-mail?"

"I was getting press calls about her missing events and canceling her first overseas trip and I didn't know how to handle them."

"And what did Ralph tell you to do?"

"He told me to handle it."

"Handle it?"

"He told me to handle the press calls. To just pass it off as no big deal that she'd missed the events."

"He used those words?"

"I don't remember what words he used, but he made it perfectly clear that I was to make sure the press stopped sniffing around about the vice president."

"I see. Thank you, Miss Smith."

Connie walked over to the table and opened up another one of her giant binders.

"Should we go chronologically or just do the e-mails?" she asked Jim. Dale was starting to find it amusing that she always spoke to Jim as though Dale was not in the room. The two of them decided to keep going with Dale's e-mails, and as Connie read through the stack of twenty or so that they'd selected as the best examples of Dale's growing concern about the vice president's condition, she forced herself to focus on offering the most direct and brief responses. She was beginning to understand that the best strategy was to answer the question in a way that discouraged further lines of questioning. As the questioning dragged on, she was having a hard time quelling her own rising sense of panic. Dale noticed several missed calls from her dad and felt guilty about not calling him back the last three times he'd called. She'd been intentionally vague with her parents about the legal jeopardy she was in. It didn't make any sense to worry them. How could she explain to them that she was, once again, about to play a prominent role in a very public scandal involving the president of the United States? They'd probably wonder if their daughter wasn't the problem. Dale was beginning to wonder the same.

CHAPTER FIFTY-SEVEN

Charlotte

Charlotte glanced at her watch. She'd asked Craig to stop by again. Prior to the investigation, it would have been nearly impossible for any member of the White House senior staff to spend so much one-on-one time with her without other staffers of equal rank feeling displaced. But the investigation had scrambled the normal sensibilities of the hierarchical White House staff. Besides, as her head of legislative affairs and her top liaison to Capitol Hill, Craig had information Charlotte couldn't get anywhere else.

"Madam President, I'm sorry if I kept you waiting. I was on the Hill when Sam called."

"Don't worry about it. I finished the Sunday crossword while I was waiting."

He laughed. They had an easy rapport. He'd never been the type of staffer to demand a lot of face time with her, which made him all the more appealing. And while she'd always relied on his deft touch with members of Congress, they'd never socialized or developed a personal relationship. In some ways, it made working with him now easier.

"They're talking about taking up the impeachment resolutions after your State of the Union."

More than anything, she liked that he got straight to the point. Impeachment had always worried her more than the investigation. As long as everyone testified truthfully, she was confident that a criminal probe by the special counsel would turn up nothing. An impeachment vote was another thing altogether.

Craig looked calm.

"Why after the State of the Union? Is Congress trying to show me some perverse sense of civility?"

"It's more likely that they need time over the holidays to organize themselves. And from their perspective, there's no reason to get ahead of the grand jury. You know how it works, right?"

"I think so, but I welcome a refresher civics lesson if that's what you're offering."

"Any crazy member can introduce an impeachment resolution. I think a few Democrats made noise about an impeachment resolution for you after the helicopter accident in Afghanistan during the first term."

"Yes, I remember."

"The House only needs a simple majority to approve an impeachment inquiry. If they get the vote, the House Judiciary Committee conducts an investigation. If they think they have an impeachable offense, they draft articles of impeachment."

"And then the House votes on the articles of impeachment, and with a simple majority vote, I'd be impeached and then stand trial in the Senate."

"Exactly. Now, the Judiciary Committee is going to want to wait and see what sorts of things start leaking out of the special counsel's office, because they're going to be calling the same witnesses and examining the same evidence."

"And your gut reaction is that they will go forward with impeachment?"

"I have been told that they have the votes in the House to proceed with the Judiciary Committee investigation."

"Jesus Christ," she said under her breath.

Charlotte neither liked nor understood the quixotic ways of Capitol Hill. That's why she almost always deferred to Craig and his staff when it came to negotiating legislation. Now, they'd be negotiating the terms of impeachment proceedings.

She was speechless.

Craig was standing in the center of the Oval Office. He didn't seem uncomfortable with her silence or concerned by how she might respond to his grim news. No matter how alarming the topic, Craig never rushed to react to anything she said. When he spoke, it was always to ask an important question or offer an insight that she typically hadn't thought of herself.

"What if I testified in front of the House Judiciary Committee or at my trial in the Senate?" Charlotte finally asked.

"No president facing impeachment has ever testified."

"I know."

He was quiet for nearly a minute.

"I could feel out the Speaker," he offered.

"If it leaks to the press, the offer is off the table."

"You're thinking that the optics of hauling you, the president of the United States, before the Judiciary Committee to testify in your own impeachment proceeding would be so historic that it would make it easier for them to justify *not* voting to impeach."

"Do you have a better idea?"

"It's impossible to know at this point if they have the votes to proceed to a trial."

"Are you suggesting I roll the dice with a Congress that agrees on nothing other than its belief that I'm the anti-Christ?"

"No ma'am."

"Let's feel them out."

"Yes ma'am."

"Craig," she started.

"Ma'am?"

"Thank you for your assistance."

He nodded dutifully. "I feel like I should tell you, Madam President, that there's always a chance that even if you testify . . ."

"That they'll vote to impeach me anyway. I know."

"Okay then."

"It's a risk, but only two American presidents have ever been impeached, and both were acquitted."

"And another resigned," they said, practically in unison.

Charlotte was leaning against her desk with her legs crossed. Craig was standing in front of one of the sofas. He never sat down, and it was rare that he even stood still.

"Madam President, if I may?"

"Please."

"I think your calculation about the symbolism is probably right. The public is confused by this entire mess. At this point, they think it's all politically motivated, and even though they sense that there's something wrong with the vice president, they don't blame you—yet. You'd go before Congress with a healthy public approval rating. That would make it harder for them to throw you out of office."

She considered this for a few seconds and then nodded, more to herself than to Craig.

"Make the call right away," she said.

"You mean right after the bill signing, right?"

"What? Oh, yes. How could I forget about the bill signing? Jesus. Isn't it strange how this place never stops spinning?" She laughed.

"You should take comfort in it. It means the place is tough. Just like you, Madam President."

She smiled.

"Thanks, Craig. This is the cancer research funding, right?"

"Yes, we supported a doubling in funding at the NIH. Senators Lucky and Messina are here for it with a group of cancer survivors who lobbied for the funding. There will be still photographers here, but no correspondents."

Charlotte nodded.

"Bring them in."

CHAPTER FIFTY-EIGHT

Tara

After sitting through three hours of briefings on the economy, Tara excused herself from the Roosevelt Room and ducked into the West Wing basement. She'd asked her Secret Service detail to take her the six blocks from the White House to the bureau in a dramatically abbreviated motorcade—the kind that could easily be mistaken for a cabinet secretary or visiting dignitary. She took a private elevator to the conference room and was greeted by one of her own agents who had advanced the location. She rose when Brent Kirkpatrick entered the room. He nodded at the agents and smiled at Tara.

"It's been a long time," he said.

They shook hands.

"Thanks for doing this," she said.

"Anything for an old friend. I've admired your quick rise, Tara."

"I've admired your work in New York. I know that's the job you always wanted and I'm happy for you that you finally have it. You must feel a tremendous sense of accomplishment, Brent."

He was trying to figure out if she'd offered a sincere compliment or if she was alluding to his larger ambitions.

"Thanks, Tara. I know you're busy, and I hope you won't find it unceremonious or rude if I get to the business at hand?"

"No, of course not."

"Frannie said you had a proposal for me?"

"I do."

"I'm all ears."

"I was under the impression that you'd been briefed on the details already."

"I just want to make sure my people didn't miss anything." He knew as well as she did that Frannie wouldn't have missed anything. He wanted to get her to ask him face-to-face. It was a classic negotiating tactic, and not a very elegant one.

"Are you going to make me ask you?"

"I want to make sure I understand exactly what you are asking us to do for you, Tara."

He should have been using her official title, but using her first name was part of his strategy to diminish her so that the arrangement was as one-sided as possible. She needed to change the dynamic in the room quickly. She signaled to her agent that she was ready to leave and stood up from the table.

"I shouldn't have come here. You had an opportunity here, too, Brent."

She was in the doorway before he called after her.

"Tara, I think we got off on the wrong foot. Please come back in here. I haven't slept in a week, and the White House is stonewalling with documents and witnesses. It's been a nightmare," he confided.

She remained standing.

"Please sit back down. I'm sure we can work something out."

"Madam Vice President," she said.

"Sorry?"

"I'm sure we can work something out, Madam Vice President."

"I'm sure we can work something out that is mutually agreeable, Madam Vice President," he said.

She sat back down and laid out her conditions.

"I have your assurance that my family will be immune from any related prosecution, investigation, allegation, and insinuation?" she asked.

"I can't do that, Tara."

"Yes, you can."

"What do you mean by related?"

"It doesn't matter what I mean. I need it in writing."

Kirkpatrick sighed and rubbed his chin while he contemplated her request. They both knew what she was asking. She wanted to make sure that Marcus could work as a law enforcement official again and that she could practice law. If they were ever charged with any criminal act, that would be impossible.

"Fine."

"How will the president find out?"

"As soon as you walk out of here, I will call her myself. Frannie will make sure of it." Despite Frannie's initial belief that she wouldn't work on the investigation, he'd pulled her in.

Not telling Charlotte was the part of the plan that bothered Tara the most. She felt she owed it to the president to resign face-to-face, but Frannie had convinced her that there was no way to keep her departure clean if it looked like they'd made some political arrangement. Tara had her family to worry about, and she couldn't do anything that would compromise the one shot she had at protecting them. They shook hands again. Brent could barely conceal his glee at having produced such a dramatic result. Technically, the president still had to accept her resignation, but as the SUV made its way back to the Naval Observatory, Tara knew that was a mere formality.

Brent promised to deliver the formal letter of resignation she and Frannie wrote to the president himself. Charlotte would have it before Tara made it home. Frannie had worked confidentially and quickly with the Government Services Administration while Tara was meeting with Kirkpatrick to arrange for movers to arrive at the residence that afternoon. They stopped at a traffic light and Tara watched a group of young women standing on the corner banging away at their BlackBerrys while they talked to each other without making eye contact. Her Secret Service agents were silent.

Tara glanced at the clock in the car. Kendall would be leaving school shortly and she wouldn't know that when Marcus picked her up, it would be the last time she'd see any of her teachers or friends at Sidwell. Tara felt a lump form in her throat. She reminded herself that she'd resigned to protect them from the ugliness that would ensue if the investigation had focused for weeks and months on Tara's performance as vice president.

CHAPTER FIFTY-NINE

Dale

"A re you sure you don't want me to come with you?" Craig asked for the third time.

"No, I'm fine. Jim and Connie are pros. Besides, I think you're probably needed around here."

They huddled close together on the balcony off of Dale's office in the Old Executive Office Building watching staffers walk to and from the West Wing. A crane that had been used to unload the White House Christmas tree the day before was parked on the North Lawn and a line of cars that had chauffeured members of Congress attending a briefing on Pakistan stretched from the entrance to the West Wing Lobby to the Northwest Gate.

"Is the veep here today?"

"I think so. She had meetings this morning, and it looks like her motorcade is still here," Dale answered.

"Poor woman," Craig murmured.

"I know."

It was slightly illogical, but Dale felt nothing other than pity for the vice president. The decision to serve as Charlotte's running mate had put things in motion that she never could have foreseen. Dale's appearance before the grand jury was scheduled for that afternoon. She'd prepped the entire day before with Connie and Jim.

"What's the maximum sentence for perjury?"

"Don't be an idiot. You're not going to perjure yourself."

"That's what every White House official thinks before they go into these things."

"Dale, just listen to your lawyers. You're going to be fine," he assured her.

"Want to have dinner tonight?" she asked.

"Yes. I want you to meet someone."

"Who?"

He smiled a coy smile.

"Not Langston?"

"Yes," he said.

"You told him that I knew?"

"Yes."

"Did he freak out?"

"Yes. He calmed down when I told him that anyone who slept with the president's husband secretly for three years was capable of keeping a dinner quiet."

Dale was still surprised.

"I'm looking forward to it."

"Me too. Good luck today, sweetheart. You're going to do great." He kissed her on the cheek.

"I'm scared."

"I know. But it's going to be over soon. I promise."

She watched Craig walk back toward the West Wing. Then she gathered her purse and coat and left to meet Jim and Connie at their office. They planned to travel together to where the grand jury met each day. When she arrived, Connie was friendlier than normal, which Dale found unnerving. Jim squeezed Dale's shoulder protectively. "I've got a car waiting for us downstairs," he said.

Dale nodded and followed them to the car. She didn't realize what a short ride it was to the D.C. U.S. Attorney's Office on 4th Street. She followed them into the nondescript government building and avoided the gaggle of photographers and cameras that were staked out in front. A few reporters shouted questions. Dale kept her head down. Connie disappeared once they were inside. She and Jim were ushered into a waiting room.

"Dale, it's really important that you let the grand jury see how torn you were between doing the job you were hired to do for the vice president, and going outside the chain of command to raise awareness about the concerns you had about the V.P."

"I understand."

"You did the right thing, by my read of the situation. Make sure the jury sees it that way. That's your job in there, Dale."

"Got it."

"Remember, you can come out any time to talk to me."

"Thanks, Jim. Thank you for everything."

"Good luck."

CHAPTER SIXTY

Charlotte

W hat are you hearing?" Charlotte asked.

"Dale is testifying before the grand jury today," Craig answered.

"I know. How's she feeling?"

"She's going to be fine."

Charlotte nodded. She and Craig were eating lunch in the private dining room off the Oval Office.

"The Judiciary Committee has a witness who confirmed that you were concerned about Tara even before Inauguration."

"That's not true."

"Maybe the witness is full of it. The committee claims to have notes from conversations *someone* had with you throughout the winter and spring about the vice president's decline."

Charlotte was quiet.

"Madam President, do you know who it is?"

Charlotte gazed at a spot on the carpet behind Craig's chair.

"Madam President?"

"I know that you think Melanie is the source, but I can't believe she'd do that."

"How much does she know?"

"She knows that I've been worried about Tara for a long time."

"Worried?"

"Concerned that she wasn't up to the job. Worried about the toll the scrutiny was having on her personally. Troubled about her inability to ignore the noise."

"Does Melanie know that you suspected Tara had mental problems?"

"I don't know if I ever used the term 'mental problems' with her, but she knows that I was deeply concerned."

"I'm sorry to drill down with you, but simply being worried about your vice president is a very different thing than having knowledge, or suspecting that your vice president has competence issues. Can you think of any instances when you might have told Melanie that you thought she was not fit to serve?"

Charlotte worked to control a flash of anger from showing on her face.

"No."

"Madam President, if I may; why *don't* you think it's Melanie?"

"Because she would never sabotage the office of the presidency."

"She hates Tara."

"And she hates Ralph, and she's mad at me for picking Tara, and she's feeling powerful over at DOD, but she wouldn't do it," Charlotte insisted.

"Madam President, people do irrational things when they're scared."

"She doesn't get scared."

He retreated from this line of argument.

"Madam President, do you want my advice?"

"You're here, aren't you?"

"Don't let them wait until after the State of the Union."

"What are you suggesting?"

"I think that if you offer to testify before the House Judiciary Committee right away, you have a whole lot more leverage. You would also put a full stop to the daily drumbeat of leaks and stories that threaten to suck the life out of everyone in this building."

"You're suggesting I testify before they vote on any single article of impeachment—to prevent a trial and preempt the whole thing?"

"Yes ma'am."

"Find out what the soonest date would be to pay our friends in Congress a visit."

"Yes ma'am."

As Craig was walking out of the Oval Office, Sam rushed in.

"Madam President, I have the attorney general on the phone. He said he needs to come see you right away."

CHAPTER SIXTY-ONE

Tara

T ara came down from the attic and went straight to the main level of the residence. Movers covered every inch of the kitchen, living room, and den like a swarm of bees. Marcus had asked them to stay downstairs until he and Kendall packed her room. Tara was looking for Walter, her favorite Secret Service agent. He was standing on the driveway observing the activity. He smiled kindly when Tara approached.

"How are you, Madam Vice President?"

"I'm fine, Walter. I don't think you have to call me that anymore."

He smiled sympathetically.

"Walter, can you do me a favor?"

"Sure thing."

"Can you make sure the president gets this?"

Tara pressed the letter into his hand and felt lighter almost instantly.

"Yes ma'am. Consider it done."

She smiled up at him.

"Thank you, Walter, for everything you've done for me and my family."

"It was my pleasure, ma'am."

She turned to walk back into the kitchen.

"Why don't you leave those out?" she suggested to a mover with a box marked "kitchen." Frannie had arranged for them to rent a house in Katonah that had been on the market for more than three years. Apparently, the owners were thrilled by the prospect of rental income, so they'd agreed to allow Tara to move in immediately.

Other than the sound of the movers taping, lifting, and dragging their huge boxes, the house was quiet. Tara had unplugged all of the televisions. She had no idea how the news of her abrupt resignation was playing, but she was sure it had broken, and she was comforted by the knowledge that Kendall wasn't watching. Other than dragging her out of the attic, Marcus was barely speaking to her. Tara walked upstairs where he and Kendall were carefully packing Kendall's clothes in one suitcase and her toys and books in another.

"Hi Mom. Did you pack already?" Kendall was trying so hard to be strong that it almost caused Tara to break down.

"I didn't. How about if we finish in here and then we move into my closet next? We can put all our things together in one suitcase. How does that sound?"

"Good. Daddy, you can go pack your suitcase. Mommy will help me now."

Reluctantly, Marcus left the room.

"Mommy, where are we going?"

"We're going back to New York. Does that sound good?"

"Am I going back to my school?"

"I want to talk to you about that. We are going to be living in New York, so you'll be going to a new school. Is that okay?"

"Am I going to see my friends again?"

"Once we get settled in New York, your friends can come visit us."

Kendall looked at Tara warily. "Why are we leaving today?"

"Remember when we left school in New York last year to come here?"

"Yeah."

"Well, we came here for Mommy's job. And now I don't have that job anymore, so there's no reason to stay here."

Kendall understood the situation at a much deeper level, but Tara didn't want to get into it with Marcus in the next room. Someday very soon she'd tell her everything.

"Things are going to be much better in New York, sweetie. I promise."

CHAPTER SIXTY-TWO

Dale

Miss Smith, what I'm having a difficult time understanding is how, on the one hand, you were the one raising a red flag about the vice president being overloaded, as you testified in this morning's session, while on the other hand, you were attacking journalists and unnamed White House sources who expressed similar concerns in your on-the-record comments."

Dale took a deep breath and forced a pleasant expression on her face. Connie told her that smiling looked arrogant and frowning looked unhelpful, but the questioning had gone on for four straight hours without a break. She was growing weary.

"Sir, I wasn't sure if I was simply being oversensitive, so I shared my concerns with the White House chief of staff."

"Ralph Giacamo?"

"Yes sir."

"He testified that you never expressed concern about the vice president's mental health to him."

"Well, I may not have said it in those words, but I called him and told him I was concerned about her."

"And he told you to, quote, handle it."

"Correct."

"And that's what you did, am I correct, Miss Smith?"

"For a while, yes."

"When was the next time you remember talking to anyone about your concerns about the vice president?"

"In August, the vice president did a series of interviews with the morning shows and they didn't go very well."

"I remember."

"After the interviews, people on the White House staff started talking about the vice president in a different way."

"And until those interviews, how many people on the White House staff did you talk to about your concerns about Vice President Meyers?"

"Just Ralph."

"And after?"

"Well, after, things started happening much faster."

"You accompanied the vice president to a series of briefings in August on the alleged terror threat, correct?"

"Yes."

"And did you think that was a good idea?"

"That I accompany her?"

"No, I'm sure that was a good idea. Did you think it was a good idea that she take the lead on the alleged terror threat?"

Dale inhaled sharply enough to get the attention of the grand jury.

"Miss Smith?"

"No. I did not think it was a good idea."

"Did you express that thought to anyone?"

"Yes. I told Ralph that I thought it would look like an overreaction to her disastrous interviews."

"So, you were worried about how it would look?"

"Yes, no, I mean . . . I was worried about how it would look and I was also worried that she wasn't up to it. I told Ralph that I thought she was too fragile."

"And what did he say?"

"He told me that my cynicism would have been more appropriate earlier in the week, or something along those lines."

"Ralph sounds like a peach."

"He has a difficult job."

"How was your relationship with Ralph?"

"Fine."

"Let me rephrase that. How is your relationship with Ralph Giacamo now?"

"I don't think he thinks much of me."

"And what do you think of him?"

"He has a different style than I do."

"Miss Smith, do you think there was a legitimate threat of a terrorist attack this summer?"

"I am not an expert, but I think there's always an increased threat before nine-eleven."

"And it didn't seem strange to you that the same week in which the vice president delivered an abysmal performance on morning television she was asked to be the president's point person on a terror threat?"

"I would not use the word *strange*. In fact, if you know Ralph, it was anything but strange."

Dale thought she saw a small grin on the face of Kirkpatrick's co-counsel.

"Let me rephrase the question, Miss Smith. Did you think it was a good idea to put Ms. Meyers in charge of the administration's response to the terror threat."

"She did an excellent job, sir. And it's important to understand that these sorts of things are always handled collaboratively. No single person can exert control over a national security situation. The entire national security team was present at every discussion."

"No single person can impact the course of our country's national security? You really are new at this, Miss Smith."

Before the judge could say anything, Kirkpatrick apologized and returned to his newly phrased question.

"Miss Smith, please tell us if you thought Vice President Meyers was up to the challenge of taking the lead on the terror threat over the summer."

"I believe I answered that, sir. She was quite impressive in the meetings in which I was present."

Kirkpatrick was getting frustrated.

"Miss Smith, did you feel any concern as a citizen when you first learned that Ms. Meyers would be placed in charge of the terror threat?"

Dale had been horrified by the prospect of Tara Meyers taking the lead. She thought about asking the judge if she could be excused to speak to Jim, but it would only prolong the inevitable.

"Yes," she finally said.

"Yes, what, Miss Smith."

"Yes, I felt concerned when I first learned that Ms. Meyers would be placed in charge of the terror threat."

Kirkpatrick looked smug as he walked back to his table and sat down.

"Thank you very much for your testimony, Miss Smith."

"Am I done?"

"For today. We'll start up again in the morning. You should plan to spend the rest of the week here with us, if that's all right with you, Miss Smith."

"Yes sir."

Jim and Connie were waiting for her when she exited the room.

"How'd it go?" they asked.

"I don't know. They said that I should plan on spending the rest of the week here."

Jim and Connie had odd looks on their face.

"What's wrong? Did I screw up?"

"No, no. You did great, Dale."

"What is it? Did they think I was lying about something? Is that why I have to come back?"

"No, in fact, Kirkpatrick's deputies came out and said you were even more helpful that they'd expected.

"What is it then?"

"While you were testifying, the White House announced that the vice president submitted her resignation and the president accepted it."

CHAPTER SIXTY-THREE

Charlotte

It was still dark out, but Charlotte couldn't sleep. She could tell by the way he was breathing that Peter was awake, too.

"Can I make you some breakfast?" he asked.

"I'm not hungry. Can I ask you something?"

"Of course."

"Why do you think she did it?"

"Tara?"

"No. I know why Tara resigned. She wanted to protect her family."

"Melanie?" he asked.

"Yeah."

"I don't know, Char."

Even Peter had stopped defending her. Most people believed that Melanie had provided both the special counsel and the House Judiciary Committee with the anecdotal evidence to justify their probes. While nobody presumed she had turned over a smoking gun, the conventional wisdom was that Melanie had been the whistle-blower who revealed that Charlotte had had her doubts about Tara's fitness for office since just after their Inauguration.

At this point, Charlotte didn't care about the impact on her political standing, but the collateral damage that had been done to her administration was unforgivable.

Charlotte turned on the bedside lamp and pulled her notebook into her lap. She had prepped most of the day before with her lawyers. They'd been briefed on exactly how the questioning from the House

Judiciary Committee would go. Craig had received assurances from the Speaker's office that the members would be respectful.

Brooke and Mark had offered to fly out to be at the residence when Charlotte came home. She'd told them not to bother, but Peter thought they'd cheer her up, so they were on their way. She'd told the twins not to leave school again, but Peter was flying them down as well.

"Thank you," she said quietly.

"For what?"

"For being here today."

She dressed before the sun came up and received her intelligence briefing in the residence. Her personal attorney met her in the Diplomatic Room and they proceeded to the motorcade before eight A.M.

Craig had gone to the Capitol ahead of her to take care of any last-minute logistics. Her entire advance team had spent the week at the Capitol negotiating camera angles and photo ops with the Speaker's press office. Charlotte felt like she was involved in the stagecraft for her own execution.

She entered the Capitol and went straight to the House Minority Leader's office where she'd wait until she testified. She didn't bring any White House staff members with her. Instead, she was accompanied by a dozen lawyers—most of whom worked in private practice in Washington, D.C., all of whom she'd met for the first time three weeks earlier. She leaned against the window. It was a blustery day, but the journalists outside the Capitol were undaunted. Hundreds of live trucks ringed the Capitol grounds. Charlotte was standing alone thinking through the responses they'd practiced. The committee had agreed to a single day of questioning. The whole thing would be over by dinnertime. One of the lawyers had turned the volume on the television up and was standing in front of it as though the reporter might know something he didn't. Charlotte shook her head and laughed to herself.

Craig had been counting the committee's votes all week. He was confident that if the Speaker went before the cameras to express satisfaction with the president's responses, the committee would vote to cut short all proceedings. As much as she was dreading it, going before the committee was a brilliant idea. Ralph would have advised against it. He would have enjoyed the brinksmanship of daring the House to vote on the articles of impeachment and proceed with a trial in the Senate. Charlotte was relieved that he'd asked for a leave of absence until he was cleared by the special counsel. Increasingly, Charlotte found that she didn't have the stomach for political brinksmanship. She wanted an end to the drama that had shaped her presidency so far. If she had an opportunity to continue as the country's forty-fifth president, she planned to spend her time getting things done.

One of her advance people appeared in the office and whispered in the ear of a Secret Service agent. Cliff appeared at her side and they traveled down the hall toward the committee room. Just before she entered, Charlotte shut her eyes and did something she hadn't done since the day the helicopter had crashed in Afghanistan. She bowed her head and prayed.

Tara

The first line of the pitch letter invited her to star in her own comeback story. Tara chuckled and typed a quick e-mail to her agent that simply read: "Thanks, but no thanks." She shook her head and dumped the fax into the garbage. Tara couldn't think of anything more undignified than appearing on a reality program, even if it was on the Oprah network.

She watched Kendall play in the front yard with one of her new classmates. Kendall had made a smooth transition to her new life. They'd moved into a small, charming ranch-style home in one of the better school districts in Westchester County and settled into an easy routine. Tara dropped Kendall off at school each morning on her way to the gym. After forty-five minutes on the treadmill or elliptical machine, she stopped off for a latte, shopped for groceries, and ran any other errands. Afterward, she'd head home to write. Tara was amazed by the size of the advance she'd been paid to write about her short time as vice president. Absent any other appealing offers, it hadn't taken much to convince her to tell her story.

One of the requirements of her joint custody agreement with Marcus was that she'd seek regular medical attention from a psychiatrist, attend weekly counseling sessions, and be compliant with her new prescriptions. The drugs hadn't had an immediate or dramatic impact, but she was feeling steadier day by day.

Marcus had landed a job at a personal security firm in the city.

He'd rented a small apartment on Second Avenue and 58th Street, and he traveled to Katonah on weekends to spend time with Kendall. Twice a month, Tara took Kendall to the city to spend the weekend with Marcus.

Tara called out "ten more minutes" to Kendall and went into the kitchen to start working on dinner. She turned on the news and stood watching footage from earlier in the day of the president landing in San Francisco with Harry and Penelope. She thought she saw Dale walk down the stairs of Air Force One along with the deputy chief of staff and the other White House aides who'd made the trip. Tara pulled lettuce, cucumber, and a bag of carrots out of the fridge for a salad. As she took olive oil and balsamic vinegar out of the cupboard to make dressing, she thought about how quickly the drama surrounding her departure had waned. The very same twenty-four-hour news culture that had accelerated her demise had also made it possible for her to have a future. By the time Tara's memoir was to be released the following year, the investigation that had nearly ended Charlotte's presidency would be all but forgotten. Tara was pulled back to the present by the sound of Kendall and her classmate bounding through the door.

"Can Tamara stay for dinner?"

"Fine with me, girls, but only if your mom approves. Why don't you call from the family room?"

Kendall picked up the cordless phone and ran into the other room.

Dale

From the senior staff hold, she could barely make out the house, but Dale remembered every inch of it. Charlotte wouldn't know that Peter had purchased the beach house for her, and Peter probably had no clue that Dale had traveled to Northern California that weekend with the president. Dale pulled out her BlackBerry to send Craig an e-mail, but she remembered from that day almost a year earlier that BlackBerry coverage was dismal. She tossed her BlackBerry into her bag and walked out of the staff trailer for some air. The trailer housed a mini command center that the White House had set up so that the senior White House staff could work from the president's weekend trip to Stinson Beach. As Dale walked toward the water, she inhaled deeply and tilted her head back. The dense curtain of fog that hung over the coast stretched for as far as she could see.

A little further down the beach, Dale could make out the president's deputy chief of staff and an economic policy advisor huddled under an umbrella. Umbrellas were useless in the fog. The dampness came from all directions. Dale forced herself not to look back up at the house. She was mostly over Peter. As opposed to the all-consuming emptiness she'd felt when they first separated, the pain was more of a dull ache these days. Craig had given her the best advice of all by suggesting she stop trying to get over Peter and simply get used to the idea of living without him. At Craig's insistence, she'd even been on a couple of dates, but most of her time was spent studying for her new job. As the newly minted White House press secretary, Dale had years of on-camera skills to lean on, but she lacked her predecessors' institutional knowledge about the West Wing. She'd developed an intuitive ability to predict the president's reaction to most inquiries, but Dale's relationship with the president was based more on professional respect than friendship or camaraderie. With Craig as the president's newly appointed chief of staff, she knew she'd have all the access she'd need to do a good job, and a purely professional relationship suited Dale fine. In fact, it was all she could handle in the wake of Charlotte and Peter's public announcement of their reconciliation.

On the day of Charlotte's testimony in front of the House Judiciary Committee, they'd gone public with their rekindled romance in a way that surprised the president's supporters and her detractors alike. When the doors to the committee room opened that day, the first image of the president was one of her with her head bent in what looked like prayer and Peter holding her hand. She'd looked slightly surprised, but everyone assumed that an advance person had forgotten to warn her that the doors were opening and that every camera in the world was pointed at her. It was a rare display of emotion from the president—a moment that looked like it was meant to be private. Analysts thought it had helped engender sympathy from the public. Some even credited the moment with helping to halt the impeachment proceedings.

Dale wandered over to the empty motorcade that had ferried them from the airport to the beach. She leaned into one of the vans and asked the volunteer assigned to it if he'd take her into town for a coffee. He gladly accepted the assignment. She looked out the window during the short ride into town and smiled to herself at the organic farms and yoga retreats that dotted the road. This particular stretch of Northern California was a different universe. Dale ordered a cappuccino and walked outside to check her voice mail while she waited for them to dig up whole milk from the back. She had thirteen new messages. Most of the calls were from reporters traveling with them for the weekend, but Michael Robbins had left three messages. She dialed his number. He picked up on the first ring.

"Congrats on the new gig."

"Thanks."

"Listen, sorry to be a buzz-kill, but I've got something that I need to talk to you about rather urgently."

"What is it? I'm out here until Tuesday."

"I'd rather not discuss it over the phone."

"I can't airlift myself out of here. Can we talk next week?"

She could hear him inhaling a cigarette.

"Dale, Melanie didn't do a deal."

She sighed. Michael was obsessed with clearing Melanie's name.

"The president didn't say she did. Last time I checked, she's still the secretary of defense."

"But everyone thinks she was the source for the grand jury and the House Judiciary Committee," Michael said.

"What do you want me to do about that?"

"You're the goddamned press secretary now. You speak for the president, and I'm pretty sure she'd be interested in knowing who the leaker really was, especially if it means that her close friend and confidante, Melanie, was innocent."

Dale sighed impatiently. Michael was going to drive her crazy.

"I'm still unclear on what you want me to do."

"Just talk it through with me, Dale. According to some very senior law enforcement and congressional sources, the original source is someone who is still working at the White House. And it has to be someone very senior. Maybe it's someone who's done very well at the expense of Melanie and Ralph's demise?"

"It wasn't me."

"Easy. I know it wasn't you."

He cleared his throat.

"Dale, are you and Craig Thompson close?"

"Yes, why?"

"Did you confide in him over the summer about the vice president?"

"That's none of your business."

"Did you share all of your deep, dark secrets with each other?"

"You're a fucking asshole, Michael."

"Is it possible that he set you up, Dale?"

Now she was furious.

"Michael, I don't know what kind of relationship you had with Melanie, but it's not going to be my job to run down all your stupid shit. You're out of your goddamned mind."

"Listen to me, Dale. Think about it. He had the material. He has the relationship with the Speaker. He developed the relationship with the president once it became clear to her that she needed to work with the Speaker. And he had a perfect scapegoat in Melanie. It's a perfect crime."

"You don't know what you're talking about. I'm hanging up now."

"No?"

"No."

"Dale, let me ask you one question: Did you and Craig ever talk before Tara's meltdown on national television?"

"What does that have to do with anything?"

"Let me guess: He confided in you about his secret relationship with the Speaker's chief of staff? Am I on the right track here, Dale? Cough once if any of this sounds familiar and twice if you thought you were the only one he tried to enlist in his grand scheme."

"What are you talking about? How do you know about Langston?"

"I used to cover Capitol Hill for the *Post* before I left to do investigative reporting at the *Dispatch*. He gave me loads of scoop in return for keeping his relationship with Langston a secret. It was an arrangement that worked well for all parties. A classic win-win."

Dale was seething now.

"You're the reason so many people are disgusted by D.C."

"Easy, Dale. I'm the reason your guy got the chief of staff job. Don't you think that I could have broken the dramatic news about his decade-long affair with the married chief of staff to the Speaker in the midst of the impeachment proceeding if I'd wanted to indiscriminately ruin people's lives? I don't give a shit who is fucking who in this town. But I do feel a professional obligation to report on how an innocent and loyal public servant like Melanie Kingston gets totally rat fucked and no one, not even the president, does anything to find out if she's even guilty of the sabotage people think she committed. That, Dale, *is* my job. And, more important, it is now your professional obligation to help uncover the truth about your place of employment. In case you are unaware of the history of the White House podium, those who have lied from there have died in there."

Dale felt like her head was going to explode. *How could Michael know these things? Her mind flashed to her first meeting with Craig in the OEOB. He'd been standing outside her office while she argued with Michael. Surely that was just a coincidence. Maybe Michael was the one who was setting Craig up? Or blackmailing him?*

"Dale, just think about it. Didn't it seem curious to you that he knew exactly how to bring the president to the brink of impeachment and then was able to single-handedly avert disaster by working out a deal with the Speaker? A deal, by the way, that results in his longtime lover joining him on the White House staff that he now runs. Did anyone make out better than Craig in all this?"

"You're insane." But it *was* true that Craig had emerged as the most powerful person in Washington.

"Dale, one more thing. Who introduced you to Jim Moffet?"

She was silent.

"Jim was in Melanie and Brian's wedding. He's one of their best friends. She put you in his hands because she was worried that whoever was doing the leaking would take you down, too. She thought you'd be collateral damage and she protected you. Did you ever wonder why someone like Jim Moffet agreed to represent you? And I'm guessing you haven't received any legal bills, either."

"Why would Melanie protect me?"

"I have no idea, Dale. That's just how she is."

"This is all crazy. You're crazy."

Dale hung up and shoved her shaking hands into her pockets. What Michael was saying was impossible. Craig was her best friend. He wouldn't have used her and the president like that. It wasn't true. It couldn't be true.

Charlotte

Charlotte couldn't help but smile when she hung up the phone with Craig. He'd only been her chief of staff for a few weeks, but already she felt she was in better hands than she'd been at any point during Ralph's tenure. The Speaker seemed comfortable with him, too. Craig understood the business of compromise better than Melanie and Ralph combined, and he saw Charlotte for who she was, not who he wanted her to be.

She could only hope that Craig's tenure would end better than those of her two previous chiefs of staff. Ralph had nearly been indicted for perjury, which didn't surprise Charlotte. But Melanie's betrayal had blindsided her. Craig had it on good authority that Melanie struck a deal for immunity and provided the special counsel with firsthand accounts of Charlotte's concerns about Tara. It was never reported because no one could confirm it, but most people assumed that only Melanie could have known things as sensitive and detailed. After her disbelief wore off, Charlotte wasn't angry. It wasn't Melanie's fault, really—it was hers. Prolonged proximity to the flawed people who become president would make anyone disenchanted. Craig suggested that she ask for Melanie's resignation at DOD but Charlotte thought it best to wait and see.

The beach house was something Peter had wanted to show her for a while, and now that things were starting to settle down, Charlotte had agreed to start spending more time on the West Coast. The kids had gone straight to Brooke and Mark's house in Atherton, so she and Peter had the house to themselves for the night. They all planned to meet up the next day at Stanford University for a tour.

Charlotte walked around the house's big open spaces again. The dogs were sleeping in a cinnamon-colored heap in the center of the bed. Peter was standing in the kitchen gazing out at the ocean below. He had a faraway look on his face, and Charlotte wondered if he was thinking about Dale. She didn't ask if he and Dale had used the beach house, but she thought it looked like a place Dale would like. Peter's relationship with Dale had never had anything to do with her. Charlotte had always understood why he had been drawn to Dale. Peter needed to be needed as fiercely as Charlotte needed to be independent. When she'd stopped relying on him, he'd found someone else. It would not happen again. The truth was that she did need him. More important, she wanted him by her side, and while she couldn't get back the years when she thought she'd been too busy and self-sufficient for her marriage, she could certainly organize her life so that Peter was at the center of it.

The twins were trying to take their parents' reunion in stride, but she could tell they were struggling to understand why their parents couldn't have figured out how to be together when they needed them to be together. Penny was swinging between dramatic moments of open hostility and studied indifference. Charlotte wasn't sure whether to coddle her during those periods or ignore her. It wasn't so surprising. Penny was the one who'd taken on the role of Peter's protector for all the years they were apart, and, at some level, Charlotte knew she was afraid of being displaced. Charlotte's regrets about not being a hands-on parent were overwhelming, but she didn't indulge them often. In some ways, Peter had been the one who'd truly "had it all." He still ran one of the most successful sports agencies in the country and he'd been the central parent in the twins' lives. Charlotte turned her thoughts to the envelope Melanie had dropped off before leaving town for a vacation with Brian. Charlotte had handed Melanie Roger's letter on the day she'd asked her to serve as her secretary of defense a year earlier. Charlotte had wanted it back for almost as long as she'd been without it. She reached into the brown envelope and pulled it out. She liked reading Roger's messy handwriting. She'd tried so hard to be strong in the places that his death had made her feel broken. Many of her convictions—about good and bad, right versus wrong, and just versus unjust—had died with Roger. She'd always been po-litically moderate, but since his death, she'd become distrustful and dismissive of anyone who presented a decision to her as black and white. The Oval Office was not a place for such distilled discussions.

Charlotte thought the public was beginning to appreciate that re-ality, and she wanted to find a way to add some texture to the debates that had confounded Washington for years. Surprisingly, even to her, she had the public support to do it. The public had not strayed too far in terms of its approval of her job performance or of her personally during the special counsel investigation and impeachment proceed-ings. She credited the fact that she didn't try to make the situation look any better than it was. Most people have to deal with messy situ-ations in their lives all the time. The voters can handle messy. She'd learned to speak openly about her mistakes and her regrets. For the time being, the public was willing to accept that she'd misjudged Tara. They were also cheered by news of her reconciliation with Peter. She didn't care about popularity for popularity's sake, but she realized that having the public behind her gave her leverage with Congress and around the world. With nearly three years left in her second term, she wanted to tackle big things.

She was more excited than she could afford to let on about the new vice president. It wasn't the sort of coalition she would have envisioned, but having one of the most progressive Democrats in the country as her vice president would be groundbreaking. It had taken a presidential appearance before the House Judiciary Committee, a risk no other U.S. president had ever taken, and a majority vote of the House and Senate. The congressional vote was the easy part since the Democrats controlled both chambers. Maureen McCoughlin had been sworn in as the new vice president of the United States of America the day after Charlotte's visit to the Hill.

Charlotte unfolded Roger's letter and held it against her chest. It was the closest she could get to him now. She held it out and read the faded words she'd memorized the first time she'd read them.

"My darling, I'm sorry to go out on such a grim note. God knows, we've both seen worse, but I promise you that when the shock wears off, you'll understand. (If I'm wrong, we can have one of our famous fights in the afterlife, if, by the grace of God, my bunk is anywhere within shouting distance to yours.)

In my entire life, I've never had a more gratifying experience than serving as your counselor. I didn't realize the extent to which your faith in me had become my entire purpose. I'm sorry for that because I know you'll be inclined to make this about you and feel guilty. Please don't, Char. This is not about you in any of the bad ways you'll undoubtedly presume it is. I have the audacity to ask one more thing of you, my dear friend. If in any place in your heart you can forgive me, it would require a doubling in size of any normal human heart. Please let that oversized heart serve you in noble and generous ways. Seek out more joy, Char. You deserve it. One more thing—look out for Mel. She's not as tough as she seems, and she idolizes you. With love to you always, R"

Charlotte folded the letter and put it back in its envelope.

When she looked up, Peter was watching her.

She smiled at him.

"It's really beautiful here."

"I'm glad you like it. How about taking the dogs down to the beach before dinner? Think the guys would mind?" Peter asked.

"Let me give Cliff a heads-up. I want you to read something first though."

She handed him the letter from Roger and stepped out the front door. Cliff rushed to the door and held an umbrella over her head.

"That umbrella won't help," she teased.

"I've noticed. What is this?"

"It's Stinson Beach fog."

He dropped the umbrella and nodded.

"Cliff, is it too much of a bother for you guys if we walk the dogs on the beach?"

"No ma'am, of course not. Let us know when you're ready to brave the elements."

She thanked him and ducked back inside to put on a jacket and round up the dogs. Braving the elements was exactly what she'd spent the last year doing. She pulled on a North Face fleece and stuffed three leashes and a handful of liver treats for the dogs into her pocket.

Peter walked into the front hall and put his arms around her.

"Thank you for sharing that with me."

She took a deep breath. As much as she did not want to know about Peter's life with Dale, she'd come to realize that she couldn't walk in Dale's shadow anymore.

"I want to ask you about something," she said.

"Anything."

"I want to hear about you and Dale."

She noticed his brow furrow a bit and he seemed to focus all of his attention on the dogs for a moment.

"What's there to say?" he asked.

"You loved her. And she loved you. For reasons you've never shared, you guys are over and now you and I are together. I love that we're here again. But I'm scared that one of us will pull away again if that entire period of your life—the entire three years you guys were together—hangs between us as forbidden and unspoken territory."

He walked toward the windows and looked out at the Pacific Ocean below.

"Just think about it," Charlotte urged.

After another minute, he walked back to where Charlotte was standing at the door and took her hand.

"You ready?" he asked.

"To walk?"

He smiled.

"I know you're ready for that. Your pockets are bulging with treats and dog toys."

She smiled.

"I'm ready for the other things, too," she promised.

He took her hand and they walked down to the beach with the three dogs racing ahead. Charlotte looked toward the staff office and wondered if she should tell Peter that Dale had traveled to California with her. She was her press secretary now. Dale would be traveling everywhere with her. Charlotte shuddered at the thought that she may have placed Dale too close to the people and things she held dear. *What was I thinking?*

"You okay?" Peter asked.

"Yes. I'm just not used to the dampness," she lied.

"I'll take the fog over an East Coast winter."

"Or a D.C. summer. God they are so awful."

"Remember when we lived here and we used to say to each other about once a week, 'Why would anyone live anywhere else?'" he asked.

"Yes! We would watch the tornados in the Midwest and the blizzards in New England and we'd laugh about keeping California a secret," she remembered.

"Do you think you could live here again, Char? Could you make California home again?"

"Yes, of course."

"Because this is home to me. And it's important to me that we could live here again, together, when your term is done."

"I would love it, Peter," she said.

She chided herself for worrying minutes before that Dale could pose a threat, and smiled at the thought of starting over again with Peter in California. She'd just allowed her mind to wander to the life they'd build together when she looked up and noticed a group of young men and women in wet suits fighting with the local police. The Secret Service must have closed the beach while they walked. The reality of her life came crashing down on her. She called the dogs back from the surf and pulled the leashes out of her pocket.

"What's wrong?" Peter asked.

"I hate to ruin the beach for everyone."

"Charlotte, you're allowed to take a walk every now and then, and if it means that the locals have to take an afternoon off from surfing, so be it."

She looked back at the surfers and tried to push her guilt aside.

"You're right." She waved at the surfers and laughed when a couple of them flipped her off.

"I think we're going to have a lot of fun here," she said. She turned to throw a ball for the dogs. Peter smiled and followed her farther down the beach.

Acknowledgments

Thank you to the readers of *Eighteen Acres* for wanting to know what happens next. It was a thrill to meet so many of you this year. You motivated and inspired me.

I relied more heavily on my three-legged stool this year than last. To my agent, Sloan Harris, thank you for putting this project on your back and carrying it at times. To my editor, Emily Bestler, thank you for your brilliant insights and gentle touch. This story never would have inhabited the page without you. And to my husband, Mark, thank-you for loving and supporting me even as my deadlines neared.

Henley Old does the most detailed and precise research in the world. Wendy Button and Ashley Devenish provided feedback at all the critical junctures. Thank you Henley, Wendy, and Ashley for reading more drafts than anyone should have to.

To Michelle Humphrey, Kristyn Keene, and John DeLaney at ICM, thank you for your kindness and generosity. To Paul Olsewski, Lisa Sciambra, and Mellony Torres at Atria Books, I love every second that I get to spend working with you. Thank you for your zeal. To Jeanne Lee, Hilary Tisman, and Katie Moran at Atria Books, you make it all look so easy, but now I know better. And to Kate Cetrulo at Emily Bestler Books, manuscripts would never turn into books if not for you.

To Judith Curr and Carolyn Reidy, thank you for taking another chance on me.

A special thanks to Joe and Natalie Comartin, Mark and Annie McKinnon, Matt and Liz Clark, Steve and Angela Schmidt, Ken Mehlman, Matt and Mercy Schlapp, Geoff and Ann Morrell, Dana Bash and John King, Michael Glantz, Barbara Fedida, Terry and Marci Nelson, Katie Couric, and Pat and Milt Wallace.

And to Courtney, Ashley, Zack, and mom, I love you. Dad, you better read this one.